A New York Yankee

on Stinking Creek

Hummingbird Hill Press

Jacksboro, TN

Copyright 2019

ISBN: 9780578491158

ISBN: 9780578497082

Dedication

To Shann Teague and Regina White
who shared their world
on
Stinking Creek with me.

A New York Yankee on Stinking Creek

Carol McClain

Acknowledgments

God created an exquisite world that man named East Tennessee. I, first and foremost, thank Him for the infinite variety and beauty of our planet.

This area hosts a lovely hamlet with an awful name: Stinking Creek. I couldn't have navigated this community without the help of Shann Teague and Regina White. With love and pride, these two showed me around the land they loved and explained the history of this beautiful segment of Tennessee.

In Shann's honor, and in deference to his request, my hero has been christened Shann. The resemblance ends there. The character remains a work of fiction.

Author and friend, Brooke Cox, schooled me in East Tennessee vernacular. Her expressions would make a 'possum giggle.

Sam Venable's book *How to Tawlk and Rite Good* is a hysterical peek at hill-speak.

This novel wouldn't be as good as it is without my critique group. June Foster and Joy Massenburge gave invaluable help and insights to make the story shine.

I'd also like to thank Lynette Eason. Her brainstorming class at Blue Ridge Mountains Christian Writers Conference really knows how to add the right details to make the story pop.

Always, my husband, Neil, supports my endeavors with prayer and encouragement. He is a creator of cigar box guitars. His work is a masterpiece. Who would have thought a simple item like a cigar box or a "tuba for" could be transformed into works of art, and sound like fine instruments.

My family and friends always encourage and support, especially my mother Vera. All that is good in me I learned from her.

My daughter, Sarah, also advocates for me.

ACFW Knoxville and the Authors Guild of Tennessee also work hard to promote me and our fellow authors.

All these people make me feel like a rock star as they brag about my novels.

Chapter One

L ike a bomb, Kiara's world detonated and dumped her back in time to a stinking cabin on Stinking Creek. It might as well have been an explosion rather than a long cab ride that rattled her brain like mortar fire—or a ride on the A train.

Kiara's eyes strained through the darkness, illuminated only from the taxi's headlights. A log cabin looking like it was chinked with mud rose before her. *Bryce, why did you call this place a haven?*

"The *far's* one-hundred-twenty." The cabbie's gravelly voice jarred her. "We'll skip the cents seein' as I ain't gonna fuss with change at midnight."

Kiara twisted the ring on her left index finger. *One-twenty? I thought Manhattan cabbies gouged.*

The driver jumped out of the taxi, popped the trunk, and grabbed her luggage. He plopped her bags on the front porch. The simple wooden structure stood no more than a foot off the ground. The rough planks disappeared into the gloom around the far side of the cabin.

"The far don't include the tip." The driver grinned. His face, lit by the taxi's headlights looked like a kid holding a flashlight to his face to scare his friends around a campfire. Creepy.

She fished through her handbag and pulled out her wallet. Hopefully, the local taxis would be cheaper. A chirruping filled the air interspersed with a loud croaking. Manhattan was noisy, but this?

"What's making the racket?" She waved her hand—the one grasping the fare.

The cabbie slanted his head and listened. "What? Them insects?"

"They're bugs?" Visions of cockroaches scurrying across her floor in her Manhattan condo scuttled through her imagination. She wouldn't survive these hills.

"They're katydids. 'Bout ready to die off for the season. The loud croakin'—them's tree frogs."

Katydids? Frogs living in trees? Kiara shuddered and handed the cabbie a hundred-dollar bill and a fifty. "Keep the change." She turned

1

her eyes back to the cabin, and her heart wrung out more misery. "Thank you."

She fumbled for her key—the one Bryce had made a year ago when they bought this place. The key, splashed in different colors like a Kandinsky painting created while on LSD, swirled in a wild mix of pink and turquoise and yellow creating an abstract design. She had laughed out loud when he presented it to her as though he were giving her the keys to Windsor Castle.

"The cabin's in your name alone, my cherry-haired leprechaun." He bent and kissed the whorls of hair she'd just begun training into dreadlocks. "Amanda won't be able to lay her hands on it." His eyes had danced with joy. "When we marry, we'll have a retreat like Yaddo. A place for all artists—writers and photographers and sculptors—"

"Don't forget painters," she said.

"Of course, painters." Bryce had pulled her into his arms and held her close. "Tennessee will get to know the world's greatest abstract artist. We're in this together. For the long haul."

He lied.

Three weeks ago, he died.

The crunch of the cab's tires faded leaving only the chirruping of the katydids and frogs to torment her. Can any good thing come out of Stinking Creek?

She took one step up onto the porch.

"Ah!" She danced off it, dropped her bags and flailed her arms. Spider webs tangled in her face, wove into her dreadlocks. She spat the fibers from her mouth. As she choked, Kiara felt a fat, pregnant spider, or worse, its silk-wrapped fly, slide down her gullet. She spit. Spit some more like a truck driver gorging on chew.

She unwrapped the narrow scarf binding up her dreads, scrubbed her hair with her hands to make sure Ms. Arachne didn't take up residence there.

Shivering in the cold evening, she draped the cloth over her face in case another web tangled in the path to the door. No other creepy crawler would slide where only food should reside.

Kiara sank onto the porch's one step. What else lurked in the dark? What else lived in the shack Bryce thought was such a great deal? Possums? Venomous snakes? Kiara shivered and squinted as she surveyed her yard. Nothing pierced the midnight, new moon blackness.

Beyond the bridge to her property and across the road, one light shone on her neighbors' house. Aside from that, just inky black and the scent of a skunk—hopefully far away—surrounded her.

She needed light.

Kiara dug in her purse and flipped on her cell phone's flashlight app. She stood and faced her … what? Her destiny? Not if she could help it. Tomorrow, she'd call a realtor and put this retreat on the market. With its sale, she'd head back to Manhattan. Friends promised they'd let her know when something affordable came up.

Right.

Affordable in New York City? Her art sold well, but only Bryce's wealth enabled her to live there. She could find something in Jamaica or Astoria.

Brooklyn had priced her out a long time ago.

After surveying the porch, she took a hesitant step forward, inserted her key, and the door swung forward. Bryce said he'd left the utilities running.

She ran her hand along the wall and found a light switch. The cabin lit up.

No. Her hand clutched her chest. If the outside was pitiful, the inside was wretched.

Bryce, how did you envision this cabin as a place someone wanted to visit?

At least it was furnished. She wouldn't be sitting on the floor until her few pieces of furniture arrived on Wednesday. Against the wall to her right sat a sheet-draped couch. She yanked off the covering. The worn, brown plaid upholstery sent up whiffs of dust as she slumped onto it. Under the other sheets, she knew she'd find like-minded furniture.

The living room—thankfully plastered or drywalled and not exposed logs—opened to a kitchen. Aside from a small alcove housing the fridge and a washer and dryer, the main floor was one large open-concept room. A farm sink sat under a window facing the road the cab had rumbled down before it clattered across her bridge. A curtain screened whatever plumbing or rodent traps sat under the sink.

Cracked maple doors hung loosely on the cupboards. One baker's rack held pots and pans.

Was this the whole of the downstairs? There'd better be a bathroom. No way would she resort to an outhouse.

A stairwell with no railing rose against the back wall. Empty bookshelves made use of the space beneath.

Bile churned in Kiara's throat. She looked at the key she still grasped. *Bryce, you paid four-hundred thousand dollars for this dump and one hundred acres out in the boondocks?* The board of health better not come snooping around.

She tossed the key onto the coffee table, a 1960s reject with turned legs on ball feet, then stood.

Lifting her ankle-length peasant skirt so she wouldn't step on it with her Nike army boots, Kiara climbed the stairs, trailing her free hand along the far wall. Funny, the treads were wide and long, no chance of falling, but even a flimsy railing would assure she wasn't going to tumble to the wide, pine-planked flooring below.

The stairs opened to a loft. A flimsy rail fenced off this area from the downstairs, though it didn't reassure her that she wouldn't tumble to the room below.

A double-sized brass bed and a mattress she wouldn't donate to a homeless drunk on the Bowery sat against one wall. Across from the foot of the bed, a small dresser hugged the wall. Ragged curtains perched over a single-hung window—one of those guillotine types. Once opened, if you didn't wedge a stick in it, the sash would crash on your neck and decapitate you.

Experience taught her well. Single-hung windows—bad.

Sweat tickled her neck. Too hot.

Kiara unlocked the window and lifted. It didn't budge.

No problem. Her body would not touch that stained mattress.

Back downstairs, she found the bathroom across from the stairwell's landing. It sported a beautiful claw-foot tub with a hand shower. The kitchen sink and this tub were the two saving graces of the cabin. She twisted the water in the bathroom's nondescript sink with chipped enamel. Water sputtered and sprayed.

Bryce, her breath came fast in her chest, *you better have turned on the—*

The water ran rusty. Then it cleared.

She'd drink tea and coffee which she'd boil to make it safe for drinking. A laugh gurgled once more. *Going to think positive.* Her hair had become rusty colored, the fiery red of her youth faded with her advancing years. Maybe the red Stinking Creek water would turn it rosy again.

There, Universe. I can be positive. Pride straightened her shoulders and lifted her head. Nothing conquered Kiara.

From the linen closet, she pulled out sheets and sniffed. Whiffs of fabric softener clung to them, and the stiffness in her shoulders melted a mite. She hugged them to her. *Clean linens, at least.*

In the living room, she shook out a sheet, draped it over the couch, and laid another on top. She'd found no pillow, so she covered a couch cushion with a top sheet. She hoped to sleep.

Not with the house so unbearably warm. The door had no screen. If she left it open, the katydids and tree frogs would dance in here.

On the wall by the stairwell, she'd seen a thermostat. After punching a few buttons, machinery whirled to life. Cool air filtered in.

Water, air conditioning, and a locked door.

She'd survive the night.

Or better, if Karma was kind, she'd join Bryce in his reincarnated life.

4

Kiara tossed on the couch, then the silence bolted her awake.

The bugs outside had stopped their singing.

She held her breath, hoping to hear something. Anything. How could a world be so quiet? How did someone live in this void?

She picked up her phone to turn on her playlist for background noise. Something Zen by Namaste Pranayama to soothe her, but the battery had drained.

Her heart torqued, and the tears welled. She bolted to her feet. "No," she whispered to the empty cabin. Sorrow mangled her like a rag mop squeezed through a wringer.

After fumbling through her carry-on, Kiara found Bryce's favorite sweater. White cashmere, so soft, so full of his life. She held it to her nose and breathed in his scent. Woodsy-citrusy. With it clutched it to her chest, she lay back down.

I'll never sleep again. She squeezed her eyes shut and gripped the sweater tighter. Inhaled deeply.

A raucous noise popped open her eyes. Her heart sped. Birds, louder than the aviary in the Central Park Zoo, tweeted and screeched in the gloom.

Weren't those creatures supposed to be harmonious? The sirens on the streets outside her New York condo made less noise.

She rolled over and faced the back of the couch—the sweater pressed to her chest—and flopped the cushion over her head.

A rooster crowed.

Dogs barked.

Light seeped through the windows.

Might as well see if she had coffee or tea and charge her phone. She slipped the sweater over her tank top and padded to the kitchen.

If Bryce envisioned an artist retreat here, she'd make it so. She'd use her solitude to create, then return to New York the instant the cabin sold. Sooner if something affordable came on the market.

A retreat didn't last forever.

~~

The roosters crowed. Delia Mae McGuffrey rolled over and kissed her husband.

"Lia," Beau mumbled, "how can you be so perky afore light?" He pulled the covers over his head. "Give me another hour."

"Call you when breakfast's ready." Lia slipped on her work skirt and a long-sleeved cotton blouse. After winding her hair in a loose bun at the nape of her neck, she hurried down to the kitchen.

The best time of day—still cool and peaceful before the human world woke. The boys wouldn't budge before noon if not for hunting or sports. Macie and Dixon, Shann's twins, would spring to life like a whirligig if they heard her, but if she were quiet, she could sit on the porch and pray and watch the sun inch its way over the East Tennessee hills.

She sat in her rocker and closed her eyes. Used to be she'd wish Beau would wake with her. Now? She loved these early morning moments. They were her only time to be totally alone with God. The soft stench of a skunk wafted on the morning air. Pleasant smell from a distance and when not on Youtee, her bluetick hound. In the distance, her parents' rooster crowed again trying to wake his harem.

She lifted her tea, breathed in the tang of tannin and honey, then sipped.

A light across the way blinked on.

She shook her head. Those Yankees finally visited. Some people had more money than they knew what to do with—buying the old Oliver place for a price no sane person would ever consider. Then, they never came down to visit. Let the grass grow up to milkweed and goldenrod and wisteria. At least kudzu hadn't taken hold there.

By the grace of God, they wouldn't stay long.

Chapter Two

Kiara rummaged through the cabinets and found a box of tea. As the kettle boiled, she plugged in her phone. Once it had a little juice, she'd type in her shopping list.

A long one.

After five minutes, the kettle whistled. She poured a cup of water and picked up the box of tea.

A ragged-edged hole had been gnawed in the bottom.

Yuck.

Rodents.

Mouse scat littered the bottom of the box. Luckily, the bags were sealed. Could she drink it?

She shoved the tea away.

From the top shelf, she pulled down a package of crackers. The box held the same calling cards from Mickey and Minnie. Hunger drove her to the fridge. It contained only an opened bottle of wine. She uncapped it and sipped. Spit. It had become vinegar.

Her stomach rumbled then churned. She tapped her phone. Only ten percent charged, and the bars showed no signal.

Gray light filled the windows. She stepped out onto the porch and shivered. The cold pierced her more than up north. She wrapped her arms around herself and fingered the sweater's soft wool. Her muscles warmed under the silky cashmere.

She took a few steps into the yard.

Stopped short.

In front of her stood the bridge to her property. It crossed a ravine into her yard—the only access from the road to her cabin. Last night, the cab had rattled over it in the dark—but if the cabbie had seen the wooden monstrosity with one slat pulled away from the trusses, he'd never have driven across.

A wooden railing edged the miscreation. She stepped closer. Shook the rail. Nothing moved.

She tiptoed onto the edge of the span.

Below her, a creek—was it the stinking one?—dribbled. Not much of a stream. Rocks lay strewn along the bottom like a baby giant threw a hissy fit and flung her boulders away.

Mist rose from the bed and forced the trees to play hide and seek. Beyond the field next to the house across the road, mountains rose. Above them, the sunrise painted the clouds.

She saw the scene in oil colors, envisioned faces shifting with the vapors. If only she had her paints.

Wait.

She had a phone. Useless for calls, but the camera would work.

Inside, nabbing the partially charged cell, Kiara took it to her doorstep. Playing with filters, she distorted the world before her until she saw a new painting—a fairy morphing in the clouds, conjuring light from the brook to awaken the mountains. Morning of the first day. An infinity of time stretching before it, waiting for the world to evolve.

Fifteen minutes passed, and the light chased the magic from the countryside. Full sun now splayed over the wooded yard.

Once more hidden in her cabin, Kiara dressed in her Fair Trade embroidered tunic. She wriggled her legs into her torn jeans—a steal from the end-of-summer sale at Nordstrom. Her feet in Birkenstocks and her hand holding her fully charged phone, Kiara headed toward the barn out back where Bryce said the studio would be. Climbing uphill—or into the barn's loft—might snatch a bar or two from a cell tower somewhere in Appalachia. Enough signal to call a cab.

She walked uphill. Up some more. *Am I living in the Himalayas?*

The trees gave way to a large meadow. A path wide enough for a tractor led up through fields of wildflowers—Queen Anne's lace, yarrow, and black-eyed Susans—pretty fields like a Monet painting. It curved up some more to the barn and faded off into the meadows beyond. At its crest—about a billion feet above sea level—sat a cantilevered barn. Its weathered boards seemed solid. No gaps opened between them—unlike her kitchen cabinets. A large barn quilt in blues and greens and splotches of yellow hung above the door centered on the barn's long side.

She swiped her phone. Still no bars.

The lower level of the barn looked typical. The dark space held room for vehicles and whatever people used to maintain a hundred acres. Sunlight streamed through a few windows, but still, the area remained murky.

Upstairs though.

Magic owned this room. Large windows opened over the cantilevered north side, bathing it in diffused light. High, plain walls would hold her canvases. Nothing but a plank floor and a line of counters on the south edge gave her lots of room to work. It held a slop sink and a bathroom in better shape than the cabin's—tiny, furnished with cheap fixtures, but they were new. With a mini fridge and hot plate, she'd live here rather than her cabin.

Perfect.

She glanced at her phone.

Not so perfect.

~~

Visitors from Ohio lingered after the service at Sheep Loop Church. Lia prayed with a few women who answered Beau's altar call. You had to be dead already not to heed her husband's pleas for salvation. At least once a year, prompted by his sermons, Lia hit the altar herself to reaffirm her standing with God.

"No, honey," Lia said as she rubbed the penitent woman's shoulders. "Grace is all you need. God's unmerited blessing means you don't have to do a thing but repent." Her heart kicked up a beat, and she inhaled. "His grace is sufficient."

The woman's sniffling stopped. She smiled and inhaled deeply. "Thank you, Delia Mae."

"Friends call me Lia."

"I feel clean, Lia."

"Answering an altar call always cleanses you."

As the woman waddled down the aisle, Lia sat on the altar steps and watched the last of the congregants leave. Silence settled. Sunlight painted the carpet with the red and blues from the stained-glass windows. Beautiful as a Thomas Kinkade painting.

"Ready, honey?" Beau stepped toward her. "Remember, Shann's coming home today. Promised him your barbequed chicken."

She smiled up at her husband. Still so handsome at forty-five. Salt-and-pepper hair, full lips and eyes the color of the Cumberland Mountains before the morning fog cleared. His square, dimpled chin grew cuter every year. Beau was fit, too. As strong as the day she married him. "Think Shann will come to prayer meeting tonight?"

He gave a small smile—as though Beau forced it. "Let's pray about it." He took her hands in his. "Lawd God Almighty." His voice started in a whisper but built strength like a train engine gaining speed. "Please bring my brother Shann, one who knew You in his youth, who You said would never leave You if he gave his heart and soul to You ..."

His prayer would last five minutes.

She should show him Matthew 6:7—let your words be few. She quit breathing as she listened for him to take a breath.

Beau sucked in air. People in town affectionately called him a "suck-air" preacher from his habit of not breathing as prayer built

9

intensity. When life demanded he inhale, he sucked air like a Hoover vacuum.

She breathed too, as he wound down. She was too ashamed to say how much his preaching style embarrassed her. Right now, she wanted him to finish so she could begin the traditional Sunday barbeque, then clean up before they headed back to church.

~~

After locking her door, Kiara slipped the key into her tunic's pocket and headed to the neighbors'.

Someone had to be home across the street seeing as two ATVs and a MINI Cooper sat in the driveway. She locked her cabin and headed out to ask if she could use their phone.

The bridge stopped her. She studied the boards for several minutes. Nothing seemed rotted. She glanced at the neat house across the road. Glanced at her shabby cabin.

She stepped onto the boards. To be safe, she walked where they attached to the trusses. Nothing wobbled or creaked. She placed her next step in front of the first like a high-wire artist. The structure held. With a third step, she breathed. By the fourth, she stopped counting steps and walked across like a normal human being.

Not so bad. She turned and studied the structure she'd conquered. With a grin, Kiara gave the bridge a curt nod.

She crossed the road.

Kiara unlatched the gate in the wooden fence lined with chicken wire that surrounded a neat yard. A porch wrapped around her neighbors' stone house nestled in a little hollow. To the back of the structure sat a shed, a swing set and trampoline. Children lived here.

They better not be brats. They probably were demanding urchins. All kids were.

The driveway abutted the side door, so Kiara knocked there. No one answered. She rapped a bit harder. This time, a huge dog with floppy ears bounded around the corner of the house and loped toward her. It howled like a subway screeching its brakes.

Her hand clenched over her pounding heart.

Fortunately, the dog ceased baying, but it sniffed the hand still dangling at her side. She jerked it up. The dog snuffled her legs. She brushed it away. He licked her ankles. Its tongue tickled.

Then the hound bolted through the gate she'd left open.

"No!" Kiara jogged after the dog, but it disappeared into the brush beyond the yard.

Could she race through the fields in her Birkenstocks? Spiders and cougars and snakes—and what else?—lurked in those weeds. The katydids—where did they roost?

Still, she let her neighbor's dog loose.

She bounded up to the porch and pounded on the door. No one answered. Nobody was home.

But the dog.

If she didn't go after him, he'd be lost. She scanned the vast emptiness of the meadows before her and the trees rising in the distance. Would the pooch come home on his own? What if a car hit him?

"Hey, boy," she hollered as she jogged along the road after the mutt. Hopefully, she wouldn't have to dash into the fields. From the weeds waving in the distance, it appeared the hound headed deeper into the wilderness. Having no other choice if she were to retrieve her neighbors' dog, Kiara slogged through the countryside. "Here, boy. Come home."

She lost sight of the hound.

And her direction.

She turned. Rotated some more. Then once again. Off to her right, well-spaced trees grew in a line. Had to mark the road.

Trudging toward the contour of trees, the gravel roadway appeared. A ditch furrowed the side of the narrow lane. She hopped over it and landed squarely in the road.

Across the street, the land dropped off and fell into a creek like the one she crossed at her house.

If a car came careening down this street, could she jump out of the way? Where were the sides of the road? Why didn't the town put in shoulders for pedestrians? It's not like they didn't have space.

After heading uphill for ten minutes and passing only one well-tended yellow trailer with a large garden and plenty of outbuildings, she turned around. Kiara trudged downhill until her cabin came into view.

Back in her house, she scrounged up paper from her sketch pad so she could leave a note for her neighbors. She couldn't afford to make enemies before she'd been here twenty-four hours.

Sorry. I came to see if I could use your phone and inadvertently ...

Would these people know what inadvertent meant? She didn't want to sound pretentious and insult them. She crumpled the paper and started afresh.

I came by to ask to use your phone and accidentally let your dog out. I tried to find it, but he dashed through the field behind your house. Please let me know when he's safely home −. My cabin's across the road.

Kiara.

11

After locking her door and tucking the key into her pocket, Kiara trudged back to her neighbors'. She slipped the note between the screen and doorjamb.

Back at the gate, Kiara rubbed her arm. Her fingers grazed a speck. She nipped the fleck.

No.

A tick!

A tick crawled over her. She screamed. Dancing across the road in a panic she brushed her arms. Lyme disease, Rocky Mountain spotted fever, what else? Paralysis? Encephalitis? Bubonic plague?

She pulled off her tunic and shook it, then glanced for traffic on her road. Probably, no one traveled this backwater except moonshine addicts. Too early for them to rise from their hangovers.

On her porch, she stripped naked and shook every item of clothing. No way, no how would she bring bugs into her home. Especially ticks.

Or spiders.

Or a dung beetle. Or whatever sick insects lived here.

Down the road, still out of sight, a car rumbled.

No!

Her heart sunk into her stomach. Her knees buckled.

She twisted her doorknob.

Locked.

Across the bridge lay her bright, pink tunic with the house key hid in its pocket. Here she stood hiding nothing with a car rumbling closer.

Kiara sprinted empty-handed—or should she say empty-clothed— to the back of her shack. She leaned against the house. The breezes blew over her birthday suit.

The car rumbled closer.

Not my neighbors. Please, please, please. She looked down at herself. Not a way to make a good first impression.

If the fates were kind, if her chakras aligned, the car would pick up speed and disappear in a cloud of dust.

The sound slowed.

She crept to the edge of the house and poked her head around the corner. Kiara peered between the notched logs.

The car braked. It hesitated on the road before her house.

It pulled into her driveway.

She tensed. Forgot to breathe.

Don't stop here. Where could she run? Turning her head, she searched for windows. The back housed the stairwell and offered only a solid log wall.

Gravel crunched.

Silence followed. *Have they stopped? Are they getting out?*

12

Tires sounded again and the motor noise receded.

She dared to peek again.

The car had disappeared.

She breathed.

Kiara scurried over the bridge and nabbed her tunic and slipped it on. It fell halfway down her thighs, offering some decency. She rummaged through the pockets for the key.

Found nothing.

Where could it have gone? She scanned the driveway. Inches from the slope to the stream, highlighted in its psychedelic colors, she found her key.

Back in the house, she shoved every scrap of clothing into the washer, clambered into Bryce's sweater and a pair of yoga pants, and collapsed onto the sofa.

Her eyes watered.

Her nose ran.

She wouldn't cry. Never again. Feeling sorry for yourself did nothing.

~~

"You left the gate open, Lia." Beau pulled the van up to the house.

"No, I didn't. You saw me latch it."

"Yeah, Daddy," Paul called from the middle seats. "I saw her."

"Then you didn't latch it tight."

"Yes, I did."

He raised his brows and eyed the fence.

Lia knew the look and swallowed her comeback. Youtee, would be exploring the woods.

The van's side door slid open, and before Paul and Chris could climb down, Macie and Dixon scrambled over them and raced toward the house.

"Last one in's a rotten egg," Dixon called.

"First one's gotta eat it."

Lia wished it was Macie who retorted, but the remark came from her firstborn firebrand, Christopher. You'd think an eighteen-year-old wouldn't act like a preschooler.

Youtee would return. Always did. Too often with a coon or squirrel.

For now, she had to start lunch if they were going to eat before prayer meeting.

13

Chapter Three

Reams of toilet paper lay on the wide pine slats of the floor beside the sofa where Kiara lay. Sobs heaved her chest. She flopped a hand over her head. How long had it been since she cried herself to sleep?

Not even after Bryce's wife, Amanda, denied her attendance at his wake, and her heart had shattered into too many pieces to count.

She scooped up the debris strewn at her feet. *Where's the trash?* She'd seen no garbage bin in the kitchen.

In the bathroom?

She crawled to her feet and trudged into the tiny room.

Nope.

She stood in front of the chipped sink with toilet tissue fisted in her hands. No plastic bags. No place to put garbage. How could her life have come to this? She didn't even own a trash can?

With too much tissue to flush, Kiara opened the cabinet under the sink and shoved the litter inside.

Someone knocked. *Maybe the neighbor found her dog.*

Kiara scurried to the door and opened it a crack, wishing she had a chain lock or peephole. Who knew who lurked out in this wilderness? She'd seen *Deliverance*.

A frumpy woman in a long skirt and white shirt buttoned to her neck stood on the porch. Kiara guessed her to be a little older than Bryce. Perhaps her graying brown hair tied up like a character in *Little House on the Prairie* aged her. The neighbor lifted a pie plate covered with aluminum foil. Whiffs of something grilled filtered through the door.

Kiara's stomach rumbled and she clutched it. People would've heard her belly's cry on a LaGuardia Airport runway.

"I'm Delia Mae McGuffrey from across the way." The woman waved her hand toward the street. "I was wondering if you'd like a little barbeque."

Kiara swung the door open. Should she take food from strangers? She gnawed the inside of her lip. The lady at the door was her neighbor. Neighbors were kind. Most of the time.

Kiara's stomach growled again and settled her uncertainty about the food. "Thank you." She took the plate, the heat of the food warming her hands. "Won't you come and sit for a bit?" With her free hand, she motioned her neighbor in. "You'll have to excuse this place. My ..." *What do I call him?* "My fiancé didn't have a ... well, he passed away and ..."

"I'm so sorry, honey." Delia Mae stepped forward as though to hug her.

Kiara stepped aside. "Please sit." She placed the foil-wrapped plate on the coffee table. The smell of something barbequed—chicken?—made her mouth water.

"I can't stay." Delia Mae fussed with her bun on her nape. Her eyes focused on Kiara's head.

Kiara patted her dreads. "I'm a mess right now. Just woke up." She pointed to the sofa. "Please stay a moment."

The neighbor sank onto the couch. "I can't visit long seeing as my husband's antsy to get to prayer meeting. My brother-in-law's home from touring with his band, and we've got to—" Delia Mae's head jerked forward, and she peered at Kiara. "I swan, girl, have you been crying?"

"Me?" Kiara swiped her eyes. "No. I took a nap." Tears she'd believed she'd cried out threatened once more. She had to change the subject. "By the way, did your dog come back?" She sank onto the couch next to her neighbor.

"My dog?"

"He ran off. I was hoping to use your phone—"

"*You* let him out?"

Kiara cringed. "I left you a note. Didn't you read it?" *Could this hillbilly read?*

"I didn't find a note."

"I left one."

"Never got it. Beau's about to have a dying duck fit over Youtee running off."

"Had I known you had a dog, I would've closed the gate." Kiara's lower lip trembled. *No crying. Not in front of this hick.* She leaned against the couch back.

Her neighbor looked lost in thought, then a small smile played on her lips. "Youtee'll come home. Always does." Her hand patted Kiara's. "Ain't no reason to cry over running hounds."

"U-T?" Kiara lifted her head.

"Spelled Y-O-U-T-E-E. My boy Chris thought it was a funny play on his team's name and the college he's fixin' to get into—or perhaps I should say the football team he wants to join." Delia Mae shook her head. "You can come over and use the phone now if you'd like."

"Do you have the number of an Uber or the local cab service?"

"Cab? We ain't got cab service on the Creek."

"How far's the local grocery store?"

15

"Sugar Creek Diner's about five miles up toward the mouth of the Creek. They're closed on Sunday and only carry milk and bread and such. It's a diner, mostly. The nearest grocer's got to be pert near twenty-five miles. Either Jellico—"

"Jellico?" Kiara chuckle. "Like the cat?"

"The what?"

"The play *Cats* based on T. S. Eliot's poems." Obviously, this woman wouldn't have heard of the play—let alone Eliot.

Delia Mae glanced away then grinned. "Okay. I remember the brouhaha about the play. Macie, my niece, loves those poems. It's Jellico—not Jellicle." She settled back. "Anyway, it's quite a piece away. LaFollette's not any closer."

"So, I can't walk?" Kiara's voice caught. She bit her lip. Didn't want this woman's pity—just a little help.

"Not unless you're in a lot better shape than me." She patted her stomach, as though any fat lurked on Delia Mae's thin frame. "Even though you're lots fitter than me, and you're younger, I can't see you lugging pokes full of groceries back twenty miles."

"Pokes?" *Am I going to need a translator?*

"Sacks—plastic bags. I forgot. You're from ...?"

"Manhattan."

Her neighbor's smile faded.

"I need a vehicle then?"

"I'd say so." Delia Mae nodded.

"Do you know where I can buy a good used one? I've got some savings—but ..."

"My brother owns a car lot in Jellico."

"You said Jellico's twenty-five miles away."

"It being Labor Day weekend and all, I don't need to teach. I don't care to take you."

Kiara glared. She stood. "Thought you Southern Christians prided yourself on kindness."

"What?"

She lifted the plate of food from the coffee table. "You can take your food with you."

"Whoa." Delia Mae put her hand out and stood. "Why're you angry?"

"I didn't ask you to take me anywhere. Then you said you didn't want to—?

"I never said I wouldn't. Said I would."

"You said, 'I don't care to take you.'"

Delia Mae dipped her head again, and her eyebrows rose. "I did."

"Doesn't that mean you won't?"

16

Delia Mae chuckled. "Something got lost in translation from Dixie to Yankee. Like I said, I'd be proud to take you. We Christians *are* kind. It'd have to be in the morning because I promised the twins we'd go to the zoo. Let's leave about eight-thirty." Delia Mae eyed the door. "I've got to get ready. Beau, my husband, needs to arrive at church an hour early, or he's late. As a pastor, he claims it's his duty. Would you like to come?"

Kiara shook her head and struggled not to grimace.

"I would come back and pick you up later. An hour early is rough on anyone."

"No thank you." Kiara waved her hand. "I don't believe in the god stuff." *Zip your lip, Kiara.* She heard her good friend Imani Green chide her. *You better learn to shut your mouth. You'll get in less trouble if you're civil.*

Delia Mae's shoulders stiffened.

Kiara shivered in the air conditioning.

"Okay then." Delia Mae's voice sounded clipped. "I'll be by 'bout eight-thirty." She stepped toward the door.

"Thank you. I could use a friend."

"We can try. But seeing as you're an atheist and a Yankee and think we Southerners are a bunch of hicks—"

"I never—"

"We ain't going to be best buddies." Her neighbor stopped at the door. "We'll make sure you settle in well. It's the way *Christians* behave." Again, the smile Delia Mae gave contradicted the harshness of her tone. The door clicked behind her.

The smell of the barbecue churned Kiara's stomach. She would trash it.

Hunger begged her to eat.

It made one forget her principles.

Chapter Four

The next morning, the crunch of tires had Kiara scurrying for her purse.

Outside, a MINI Cooper pulled up her driveway. Kiara stepped to the passenger side as a curly-headed girl came running up the road.

"Aunt Lia. Wait." Her little legs pounded across the bridge.

Delia Mae climbed out of the car and fisted her hands on her hips. "Macie, what're you doing?"

"Wait for me."

"You're not going shopping with us."

"You promised we'd go to the zoo."

Delia Mae scooped up the child into her arms. "I told your pa we'd go when I got back from Jellico. I've got to help our neighbor. Say howdy to Miss Kiara." Delia Mae glanced at Kiara. "I never got your last name."

"I'm Kiara."

"I know. You told me yesterday."

She blinked. Of course, the yokels never heard of her. "People call me Kiara."

"Then say howdy to *Miss* Kiara," Delia Mae said.

The moppet ducked her head into her aunt's shoulder. "Howdy." Delia Mae's body muffled the child's greeting.

"What else do you say to our neighbor?"

"Pleased to meet you, ma'am. I'm Macie." She lifted her head from Delia Mae's shoulder and pointed at Kiara's. "What d'you do to your hair?"

Kiara rubbed her head.

"Macie." A flush colored Delia Mae's face. "Don't be rude."

"It's pretty. You look like a Muppet."

A Muppet?

"I'm going to call you Miss Muppet."

"Hush." Delia Mae placed her palm lightly over the child's mouth. "Where're Dixon and your father?"

"Him and Dixon are coming down on the Mule."

Mule? Where am I living? Kiara craned her neck, expecting the lanky animal to amble down the lane with a rube like Ichabod Crane perched

18

on its back. In the distance, an odd vehicle kicked up a cloud of dirt. Her mouth dropped open with the realization that a Mule wasn't an animal.

"What's wrong?" Delia Mae asked.

Kiara struggled not to grin. She shook her head. No reason to let this bumpkin see *her* ignorance.

"We're supposed to go to the zoo." Macie pouted.

"We're going later when Chris finishes football practice. He's coming with us."

"Chris'll go?" She clapped then squirmed out of Delia Mae's arms. "Here comes Daddy." She hightailed it toward the bridge. Stopping midway, Macie leaned against the rails and pointed down the road. "See."

"Macie." Kiara stepped toward the little girl. "Careful. The rail—"

"What's wrong?" Delia Mae asked again.

"The bridge isn't safe."

Delia Mae laughed. "Bless your heart. The Olivers kept it in good repair. It'll hold an 18-wheeler."

We'll see.

A motorized vehicle—a cross between a pickup and an ATV—rambled closer.

Delia Mae waved.

The weird truck carrying a man with a beard ZZ Top would envy stopped on the bridge.

"Daddy." Macie raced around the short-bed vehicle and climbed into the back. The strange thing shambled over the bridge.

A tall, lean hillbilly hopped out. A flat top cap covered his short hair. Dazzling blue eyes twinkled. The overgrown Santa-beard hid his neck.

A young boy with a mop of hair as wild as the girl's clambered down followed by his sister.

"Aunt Lia, Daddy let me drive." The boy jigged around his aunt.

"That's not wise, Shann." Delia Mae wagged a finger at him. Her mouth grimaced like she was biting back a grin.

"Lia," the bearded man drew Delia Mae into a hug. "Think you're going to leave me without a goodbye?"

"Breakfast is on the stove."

"Biscuits and gravy?"

"And chocolate chip pancakes," little Macie chirped.

"Did the hound ever make it home?" Shann asked.

"Yep."

"With a critter in its maw?"

"Thankfully, no," Delia Mae said. "I'd rather Chris catch the coons with his rifle."

Kiara stiffened. *Guns?*

19

"Who's your pretty neighbor?" He reached out a hand. "I'm Shann McGuffrey. Just stuck with Lia 'cause my big brother married her. He couldn't get no one else."

Kiara's jaw dropped.

"Don't mind my brother-in-law. He's got a sense of humor that would shame Rodney Dangerfield."

"Ah, I get no respect." Shann's laughter came from his belly and made the birds smile. "You are?"

"Miss Muffet," Macie hollered. "I call her Miss Muffet 'cause her hair looks like one."

"What's a Muffet?" he asked.

"You know, Daddy. Like in the movies."

"Muppet?"

"That's what I said. Miss Muffet."

Shann tilted his head and raised his eyebrows at Delia Mae.

Delia Mae winced, and her face flushed again.

"She says I look like a Muppet," Kiara said. "She's mixing metaphors—or cartoon characters." She offered her hand. "Everyone but your daughter calls me Kiara."

"Kiara what?" Shann asked.

"Just Kiara. I use one name."

"Then how do you get mail and a driver's license."

"The government makes me use Rafferty."

"Yep. The government forces us to do lots of things we don't agree with. Right, Sis?"

"Now's not the time for politics." Her eyes widened. "Did you know Kiara's from New York City?"

Did her voice hold a warning? Was something wrong with being from the City?

"You told us ten times last night—New York City, Manhattan, the Big Apple—what else? The Yankee from Yankee Stadium?"

"I never!" Delia Mae swatted him. "Ignore Shann."

"These are my kids." He nodded toward his daughter. "Miss Macie will talk your ear off once her shyness disappears." He looked around the yard. "Lia, where's Dixon?"

"There." Macie pointed down the ditch to the stream. "He's catching frogs."

"The boy exploring the ravine is Dixon. If he stands still for a minute, you better take his temperature."

"We've got to go." Delia Mae kissed Shann's cheek. "I should be back around noon. Love you."

"You too. 'Specially as you made me biscuits and gravy." He opened the car door for his sister-in-law. "Is Beau home?"

She climbed into the car. "Beau's gone to UT to visit Fleeta Jean. She finally had her hip replaced." Her voice turned pensive as though her mood shifted. "He says he'll meet us at the zoo."

"Nice meeting you." Kiara opened the passenger door.

Shann swept his hat off ruffling the curls his kids had inherited and bowed. "The pleasure's all mine."

Was it wrong to feel the warmth spreading through her at Shann's smile? Bryce passed ... well it'd only been a month since she lost him. Still, Kiara's eyes stayed trained on Shann. "You're very gallant."

"No, he's not." Delia Mae put the car into reverse. "He's Shann McGuffrey. The spoiled baby of a family that should've been named McGruffy." Her voice held no humor and something erased the twinkle in Delia Mae's eyes.

By the time she'd made her U-turn and faced the bridge, Shann and his twins had driven across the road.

"You have a nice family, Lia."

"Delia Mae. I prefer to keep Lia to family."

~~

With Paul off to the hospital with his father and Chris at football practice, Shann relished the quiet in his sister-in-law's kitchen. He could pretend he owned this place—just him and his kids.

Dixon snagged a biscuit from the platter on the granite countertop.

Shann snatched it back. "Go wash your hands. You, too, Macie."

The twins dashed into the hall bathroom. Water sloshed in the sink as they squabbled about who washed first.

Dixon bounded back into the room.

"Do y'all ever walk?" Shann asked. "Where's your sister?"

"Mopping the floor. She splashed water all over."

"Did not," Macie shrieked from the bathroom.

"Not Aunt Lia's guest towel?" Shann glanced toward the hall as he split the biscuits and placed them on the plates he'd put on place mats.

Dixon hiked a shoulder then settled into his chair.

"Daddy," Macie scurried into the room. "I drawed you a picture." She shoved a crayon drawing of three people standing by a house they dwarfed. A tiny angel hung in the clouds. "See. There's Mommy watching us." She looked at her plate and pouted. "I want pancakes." She shoved her dish of biscuits aside.

Shann scraped the biscuits and gravy onto his plate and grabbed two pancakes from the warming tray on the stove. He slipped the dish on the table and doctored the flapjacks as he studied the drawing. "This is a pretty piece of art, Macie. Nice paper." Shann flipped it over.

On the back of the drawing, in a beautiful calligraphy, he found Kiara's apology for letting the dog loose and an appeal to let her know as soon as it came home.

"Where'd you find the paper, Macie?"

"It was lying on the ground when we got home from church yesterday."

Seems my brother spit fire over nothing once more. Shann smiled. When Beau got home, he'd have fun teasing him about judging people. Give him a dose of his own sermons.

Chapter Five

Silence settled inside the car, and Kiara twisted the watch on her right hand. The cool metal soothed and made her forget how unwanted she was. After crying herself to sleep yesterday afternoon, Kiara didn't think she could hurt any more. She needed a friend, but *Delia Mae's* snarky insistence on using her full name made it clear she wouldn't be one.

The lines around *Delia Mae's* mouth hardened. If this tension didn't break, Kiara would explode, and her tears of the night before would seem like a sniffle. "So how long have you and Beau been married?"

"Going on twenty-five." Delia Mae offered nothing else.

This was going to be a long morning.

"Bryce and I were together for five."

"What happened?" At last Delia Mae opened a hole for conversation.

"Heart attack. It was sudden. One moment we were chatting at our favorite bistro. The next moment ..." Kiara stared out the window but didn't see the scenery. Instead, she saw Bryce stiffen, then collapse like a jellyfish. The waiter yelled for someone to call 9-1-1 as Bryce's face turned an awful gray. A diner began CPR. Every person in the restaurant crowded around as though vying for a spot at a Smashboy Lemons concert.

What'd she do? Stood like a Southern belle with her corsets laced too tight.

"I'm sorry. How long ago?"

"Three weeks."

"Why did you come down here so soon?"

Gall churned. Kiara inhaled. She needed to choose her words. "His wife and kids descended like hordes of bargain hunters at a fire sale at Neiman Marcus. Gobbled up everything we worked for. Like they had any right—"

Delia Mae jammed her brakes, fortunately at a stop sign. "His wife? He was still married? Didn't you say you were together five years?" Her chin rose and her eyes narrowed. Worse, her voice, which had been indifferent until now, rose in volume, took on a hard edge.

"They weren't together."

"Marriage ..." She shifted the car into neutral. "Marriage is forever."

Fire churned inside Kiara and burned her empty stomach. Silence for the last fifteen minutes and now this? She ground her teeth. *Say nothing, Kiara.* "How dare you judge me?" Like a volcano, her pain spewed. "Who are you? We've known each other a few hours. You haven't spoken to me since you began driving, and now you turn self-righteous?"

"Kiara, I have to say this—"

"Say nothing." Kiara's voice became shrill. She waved a finger in Delia Mae's face. "You know zilch about our life. Or the affair his wife, Amanda, had. You don't—"

Delia Mae reached out a hand and grasped Kiara's. "He never divorced her. You were wrong, Kiara."

Kiara heaved Delia Mae's hand away and yanked the door handle. She turned one last time. "This is my business. Not yours, you pious—" The words she'd ordinarily spew stuck in her throat. She slammed the door and stomped back the way they'd come. Shame at wanting to curse out this witch made her choke on her obscenities.

Why am I ashamed? She's the one with no right to ... Ten feet from the vehicle she faced it again and yelled. "Attitudes like yours make me hate Christians. You think you're holier than anyone."

Her stomach roiled, reminding her during the past twenty-four hours she'd only eaten the little bit of chicken and overcooked green beans Delia Mae had given her. Pivoting, she stamped down the road, but considered crawling back into the car.

No. She squared her shoulders and clomped toward home. She'd rather starve to death than be beholden to—

"Wait." The tinny sound of a slamming car door preceded the scuffling of gravel. "I'm sorry. You're right. I'm shaming God and proving your point. I have no right to judge. Please, get back in, and let me make things right."

Nausea swelled and Kiara grasped her stomach. Her home held only mouse scat. An hour or two with this hoity-toity fool and she'd never have to see her again.

~~

24

Lia swallowed back the words she wanted to tell Kiara. Who was she to censure? Beau condemned enough ... no. Wouldn't revisit the argument.

Seat belts clicked. Kiara focused ahead of her as Lia shifted her car into drive. Silence weighted the vehicle and suffocated Lia's soul. She heard Beau nag. *Our congregation ... your duty ... submission clothes a woman in beauty.*

Stop it, Lia. How could she escape the morning's fight with Beau? *Scripture. Think the Lord's Word, not your own. Think about things that are lovely, and of good report ... think on these things.* Which commandment should she heed—submission to her husband or reaching out to the lost? Something in this woman—so young, too young to have been a paramour for five years—screamed for mercy, for love.

"This road leads to Rarity Mountain." Speaking would silence her conscience.

Kiara didn't answer.

Lia had to make her talk. Needed to get her mind off her flailing marriage. She bit her lip. Shook her head. *Kiara needs me.* Lia coughed to clear her dry and tight throat. "Back there," she waved her hand in the direction they'd come, "is Stinking Creek." She peeked at her passenger who stared out the window.

Seconds ticked by like hours. How could time move so slowly. "Our town hasn't always been called Stinking Creek, though."

"Why'd they want to change the name to Stinking Creek?" Kiara's voice lost its edge, wafted like a breeze.

Lia leaned back in the driver's seat and loosened her grip on the steering wheel. She inhaled and dropped one hand to her lap. "Used to be called Sugar Creek."

"I like Sugar Creek better. So why change it?"

"Back in 1789 or so, it got cold enough to freeze your nose hairs. Hundreds of animals died down in the canebrake on Hickory Creek— that's the name of the river running through town. Come spring—well, Sugar Creek didn't smell like honey."

"It freezes down here?"

"It does. In 1789, snows began in October. That year the cold froze everything. Don't snow much here." Lia glanced at Kiara. "Even with a skift of snow, expect to be holed up a week. Ain't no one going anywhere."

"Don't they plow the roads?"

"Some, but down in the hollers or up in the mountains, driving becomes dangerous."

"You yell when it snows?"

Lia squinted and her mouth parted. "Ain't said a word 'bout yelling."

"You said holler."

She grinned. "It's like the road we live on—a small valley. Unlike our road, hollers have no way out. Norris Lake, where my mamaw lived before they filled it up, was nothing but hollers."

"What's a mamaw?"

"My mother's mother."

"I thought you guys spoke English."

Lia stiffened then glanced at her passenger.

A smile played over Kiara's lips.

A joke. She's teasing. Lia rotated her shoulders. Hope settled her nerves, and a more comfortable silence fell.

Then Lia's phone rang. Shann's name flashed on the car's call screen. She connected the call. "What's wrong already?"

"Always the optimist, sis."

"The only time you call is to speak to the twins, who ain't with me. You do remember you have them?"

Shann laughed.

How was he related to Beau?

"I found the note the pretty little Yankee left."

"I'm listening, Shann." Kiara glanced toward the radio. Her voice sounded light, but nothing sparkled in her eyes. Aside from looking at the radio, Kiara hadn't moved.

"Oops. Bluetooth?" Shann asked.

"We're in the car. What'd you expect?" Lia said.

"Sorry for the compliment, Kiara. You Yanks are a weird crew—not wanting to hear praise."

Lia's neighbor smiled—a pretty little grin. Kiara's smile came easily—within minutes of their arguments, or after crying herself to sleep, her good nature resurrected. Strong opinions, but swift forgiveness. Kiara *could* be the friend she'd begged God for seeing as He never gave her a daughter.

Wait. She's an atheist.

"... found it on the ground and figured it was scrap."

Lia shook her head. Lost half of what Shann had said.

"Seems Macie liked the paper Kiara wrote her note on—oh, beautiful calligraphy."

"You know calligraphy?"

"Shur 'nuf. We yokels got us a mite o' ejucation."

Kiara chuckled, but it seemed to Lia, her neighbor shrunk in her seat, and her face flushed—almost as red as her hair.

"Macie made me a picture on the back of the note. Sorry."

"Sorry she made you a picture?" Lia asked.

"Oh, sweet Lia—how does Beau put up with you?"

"I'm glad you found the message," Lia said. "We're almost to ..."

~~

Kiara stopped listening to the chitchat. What she needed was food. Something to settle her stomach.

"So how do you make a living?" Delia Mae asked.

Kiara startled. Lost in her hunger, she'd been unaware of the silence. "Sorry. I thought you still chatted with Shann. I'm an artist."

"What kind?"

"Painter."

"I love Thomas Kinkade."

Kiara's stomach flipped.

"Is your style like his?" Delia Mae asked.

"No. More like Helen Frankenthaler."

Delia Mae tilted her head. "Never heard of her."

"She's quite famous. One of the greatest female artists. I'm a cross between her and Georgia O'Keeffe with a hint of Mary Cassatt. I like portraits."

"Like Norman Rockwell?"

Kiara licked her lips. This woman knew nothing about art. Meaningful art. "Not in the least."

"Are you hungry? Any food left in your cabin had to be inedible." Delia Mae said.

"I'm sorry. I never thanked you for dinner."

"Did you like it?"

Kiara nodded.

A generic gas station came into view a few yards from the entrance ramp to I-75. "I can pull in here, and you can pick up a quick bite."

"I could stand a bagel or a muffin and tea."

Delia Mae pulled up to the store. "I'll wait here if you don't mind."

In the store, Kiara wandered the aisles and picked up an egg biscuit from the warming bin. The only tea available had to be brewed from the lukewarm water in the pot on the top of the BUNN Coffee Maker. "Excuse me."

The bored clerk fooled with his phone behind the counter.

"Do you carry chai latte?"

"What?" For the first time since she entered the store, he looked up.

"Chai. Spiced tea."

"We got tea—hot or cold. You want something extra," he pointed to a bin of lemons, "thar's them."

Didn't seem she was earning points with the rubes down here. Her choices? Convenience store coffee or Tetley?

It didn't matter, anyway. In a few hours, she'd have transportation, freedom, independence. The South had cell service, so she could contact

27

a realtor and be out of Hicksville and back in New York City before she used her full tank of gas.

For now? She needed a double dose of caffeine. It would settle her stomach and boost her mood. She filled a large cup of coffee from the BUNN hot plate, dumped in a packet of sugar and two tubs of creamer, and paid.

Back in the car, Delia Mae chatted on her phone.

Kiara snapped her seat belt and sipped her burnt coffee. She should've used an extra packet of sugar. She took another sip and unwrapped her egg sandwich.

"I told you. Not me—Macie ..." Delia Mae's voice pled with whoever she spoke with on the phone.

Kiara's stomach churned. Was it from the food? It couldn't be from the moving car, seeing as they'd stopped here for at least fifteen minutes. Had to be hunger. She forced another bite and a sip of coffee.

"You will? Oh, Beau, thank you." Delia Mae straightened. "Call when you get there." After disconnecting, she strapped her seat belt and started the engine. "Beau can make it to the zoo." She grinned and pulled out of the parking lot.

"I'm glad."

"He's been ministering to a congregant who had hip surgery. Fleeta Jean's doing well today. Roy, her husband, is staying on at the hospital, so he doesn't need help at home. Beau's job's so demanding." Delia Mae chatted too fast.

With a sharp turn, they pulled onto the entrance ramp of the highway.

Kiara's stomach lurched "Pull over, please." If she didn't get out of the car fast ... She needed the car to stop.

"We're on the ramp—" Her neighbor glanced Kiara's way and jerked the car onto the grass.

Kiara scrambled out of the vehicle. She stumbled a few steps to the taller weeds. The few bites of her sandwich and the sips of coffee became dry heaves. Pain stabbed her stomach, strangled her esophagus, and squeezed her chest. *Oh, to just die.*

Warm hands took hold of her shoulder and brushed back a dread that had escaped from the elastic band holding Kiara's hair off her face.

"Are you okay?" Delia Mae's voice soothed.

Kiara straightened. Her face flushed again, like when Shann teased her with his hillbilly dialect. She became exposed. Vulnerable. "Guess the greasy food and curvy roads don't agree with me."

Delia Mae looked behind her as though studying something. "We'd only been driving a minute or two since the store. How long have you been queasy?"

"Since ..." Kiara lifted a shoulder. "A couple of days. Since Br—" She wouldn't think of him. "I need to eat. I'm feeling good now." She stepped toward the car.

"Here." Delia Mae handed Kiara gum after they climbed into the car.

Delia Mae eased onto I-75. She chewed her lips as though thinking about something.

"What's on your mind?"

Delia Mae glanced out the side window then peeked at Kiara before staring at the road again. "Shann's kids are quite taken with you. Did you and Bryce ever consider having any?"

"Goodness. No."

Delia Mae glanced her way.

"He had a vasectomy a year ago."

Delia Mae blinked as though she couldn't believe what she heard. "Why?"

Kiara shrugged. "Kids are demanding. They mess with your stuff. We had our careers ahead of us. Bryce already had two teenagers ..." She sighed. "Well, I never even liked playing with the baby dolls my grandma loved giving me."

"Children are God's gift to women."

Kiara stared out the window and rolled her eyes. "Not a gift I'm interested in."

"I love children. I have two but wanted more. Can't wait until my boys make me a mamaw. Want a girl to dress up." She glanced at Kiara. "Been raising Shann's twins since they were one month old after the Lord took Shann's wife, Abby."

"Not a nice deity."

"How can you say that?"

"He killed Shann's wife and left newborns?" The urge to smack her head against the side window overwhelmed Kiara. When would she learn to shut her trap?

"He didn't kill Abby. A man robbing a store, an illegal immigrant shot her."

Oh no. She's one of those bigots on top of being a god freak.

"Abby was a cop. Got shot."

Kiara clamped her teeth around the gum as though it would glue her lips shut. Bryce's voice echoed in her head, warning her about her uncensored mouth. She heard his sweet baritone, saw his dancing brown eyes and wagging finger. Always, Bryce could quench her anger.

They rode on in silence—Delia Mae clutching the steering wheel once more. At long last they pulled into the lot of Junior's Used Cars.

"Hey, baby sis." The man, clad in a dress shirt and tie approached. He resembled Delia Mae a little with his shock of graying brown hair

29

and blue eyes. The man was prim like her too. Despite the humidity that would soak through a tank top, he wore a sport coat. Buttoned. He pecked Delia Mae on the cheek.

"Kiara, my brother—Cletus Emmett Jones, Junior."

"With my moniker, everyone calls me Junior. My daddy don't even use the Cletus part of our name. Can I help you find a ve-hick-cle?"

His pronunciation of the ve-hick-cle made Kiara grin. *A hick truck, indeed.* "Do you mind if I browse?"

"Take yer time. Inventory's down a bit, but I guarantee our ve-hick-cles."

Junior ushered Delia Mae into the dealership while Kiara roamed the lot holding little cars with no trunk space and almost new pickups.

How long would she be stuck in Stinking Creek? If marooned here for a while, she'd need a truck—something to carry her oversized canvases.

She studied the price tag on a bright red, four-door pickup and jolted. *Thirty-thousand dollars for a used truck?* She wandered to a boring white one with a dented fender. *Twenty?* When did used trucks become so pricey?

She thumbed her phone and checked her bank account. Thirty-three-thousand dollars. Enough to live on for a while, but she needed a down payment on a loft in the City or a couple of month's rent while she found a job in New York. Income from her art sales would supplement her income, not support her.

Like a fool—and believing Bryce and she had a lifetime together—she'd turned down the teaching job at The Cooper Union two weeks before he died.

No. Not died.

He passed away. Bryce wasn't dead. Couldn't be.

She inhaled and blinked.

"Junior says the Chevy's the best deal here." Delia Mae turned toward the red pickup.

Kiara startled at her unexpected appearance and sighed. "Not in my budget."

"He does financing."

"No job at the moment."

Delia Mae's mouth arced as though she understood. "If you need a truck, the Silverado's the one Junior would recommend. This white one has one-hundred-thousand miles. The last owner used it rough." Delia Mae sounded kind, like a mother comforting a child.

Or what Kiara imagined a caring mother should sound like.

"I should've called my brother before we left, but my argu—" She paused a moment. "I guess I should've taken you to LaFollette."

Kiara sought Delia Mae's eyes and tried to smile. Had it registered on her lips? She doubted it. "What am I going to do?"

"LaFollette's got a lot of car dealerships, but Junior would've given you the best deal on a reliable car. With Junior, you'd have an honest transaction and a reliable vehicle."

"You said LaFollette's in the other direction. How am I going to get there?"

"I can't go tomorrow. My boys and the twins pick up their schooling again, and I'm their teacher." Delia Mae held up her hands. Her eyes screamed at Kiara to not lecture her about schooling. Her voice, though, remained soft and her tone neutral. "Then we have *Bible* study, and the Mission Board meets. Wednesday, I can take you."

"The movers come Wednesday."

"Then Thursday. I'll get the kids through the lessons and make Shann take over. We do our art and music on Thursday. They don't need me."

Kiara shivered. She waited for the argument ignorant people made about how unimportant art is.

"We'll buy you a truck then go to Walmart for whatever you need."

Kiara nodded. "There's a grocery store here, right?"

"Save-A-Lot. And it's in Kentucky." She sounded excited about it being in the next state north.

"I don't need you driving to—"

"It's two licks of a hound's tongue down the road."

Kiara laughed.

"What do you find so silly?"

"Two of Youtee's licks?"

"You got a real pretty smile. It shows your true nature."

Kiara's face heated. At the rate she was flushing today, Delia Mae would want to take her to the ER and to check her fever.

"With the store being in Kentucky, you pay no tax on the groceries."

"Tennessee taxes food?"

Delia Mae nodded.

"It shouldn't. What about poor people? They have to eat."

"They've got EBT. Can buy all the food they want at our expense."

"New York wouldn't dream of taxing—"

"You ain't in New York anymore." Delia Mae pivoted and tramped toward Junior's office.

"Sorry," she called after Delia Mae. When she didn't turn, Kiara loped after her and touched her arm. "I didn't mean to offend you."

"Bless your heart. There's a lot you've got to learn." She yanked open her car door. "If you don't care, I'll drop you off and come back and visit with my brother. What's your cell number?" Delia Mae whipped out her phone.

31

As Kiara rattled off her number, Delia Mae tapped it in.

She's pretty quick with the cell. The thought shocked Kiara. *How did these hicks figure things out?*

Her phone dinged.

"You've got my number now. Text me when you're done. Now hop in, and I'll take you to Kentucky."

Chapter Six

Kiara wandered the aisles like a child let loose in FAO Schwarz. Bins of fruits and vegetables. Aisles of coffee and tea. Every cereal known to man—all in one place.

Back home they had to hit several small grocers to find what they wanted. Gristedes, their mega-market, would fit into this store's produce section. In the last year, she and Bryce had taken to ordering food through Chef Nanny—all they had to do was pop the delivered fare into the oven, and voilà. Home-cooked food.

Save-A-Lot offered low prices, too.

Her cart overflowed.

At the checkout, she texted Delia Mae.

While she waited, she googled the names of realtors and made her call. Friday, a realtor from *An American Dream Realty* would come and list her cabin For Internet and a landline, she called Comcast, but they couldn't come out to Stinking Creek until Monday. However, with a truck, she'd be able to find phone service with a short drive down the road.

And Google Maps would tell her how to find things.

With her chores accomplished, Kira peered down the quiet road.

No MINI Cooper wove its way down the tiny street lined with dilapidated shops and a small park that looked like it used to be a railroad depot.

Kiara leaned against her cart and waited. She'd check on apartments. Her best friend, Gina King, promised she'd keep an eye out. Maybe something came up in the twenty-four hours she'd been down here. Given the hour, Gina would be at her shop in East Harlem. She dialed its number.

"Threads. How can I help you?" Her BFF sounded like always—crisp and in control.

"Gina, it's Kiara. Sorry it took so long to call. No signal and—"

"Kiara? So good to hear from you. Hold on a minute."

Muzak played over the phone. Threads, Gina's textile boutique, had to be busy—it being Labor Day and the hordes descending for one last shopping hurrah before fall set in.

33

Kiara tapped her foot as the music played. Gina was worth waiting for. She'd find the humor in Kiara rubbing shoulders with religious nuts.

The Muzak stopped and the standard recording played. "Thank you for waiting, your call is important to us."

After the third repeat, Kiara hung up.

~~

"Lia, it ain't my place to meddle, but you're my baby sister and —"

"Then don't." Lia wagged a finger in her brother's face and grinned.

"If you don't want to hear, why are you smirking like them monkeys you're fixing to visit?"

Lia swatted him and tried to bite back her smile.

"Seriously, Beau's gotten more ..." He inhaled and studied the ceiling as though he could find the term he wanted written there.

"It's not Beau. It's me. Scripture says wives should be in subjection to their husbands. I can't argue with the Lord."

"It also says, husbands should 'give honour unto the wife—'"

"'As unto the weaker vessel.' I need to listen to Beau. He's the head—"

"Lia—"

Her phone chirped. Grateful for the interruption, Lia checked it. "It's my neighbor. I need to pick her up."

"You ain't got to be all things to all people."

"It's my testimony, Junior. 'Be ye holy; for I am holy.'" She stood and handed him her empty Coke can. "Thanks for the sody dope." She kissed his cheek and scurried out.

Kiara proved herself useful. If only she'd text every time Junior got on her case.

~~

Once more back home.

No. Not home. I don't belong here.

Back at the retreat, the silence pulsed in Kiara's ear. She could hear her blood flow with each heartbeat. Loneliness.

If I sit here doing nothing, I'm going to start taming the arachnids or talk to the katydids.

She took a deep breath. Yuck. Dust stunk up the air. What else hung in this atmosphere? The house had been shut up for a year.

Wednesday what little she owned would make their home here when the movers arrived. They'd need a clean space.

34

Upstairs, she tore down the ragged curtains and tossed them over the railing. Dust motes floated in their wake. She wrinkled her nose at the smell. "Dance, dust. Gambol for me."

She clicked on her phone, scrolled to her playlist and plugged the earphones into her ears. Kiara bopped and swayed. She controlled her life—not Amanda. Not her exile. Not her isolation.

The mattress stained with years of use would prove problematic. She'd wrestled with ten-foot canvases since she was a puny thirteen-year-old in her father's pint-sized cottage in Portland. She always won.

Always. In everything.

A stinky—literally—stained mattress didn't stand a chance. She hoisted it. Inch by inch she wobbled it to the stairs and let it topple over the railing. Its crash was music rivaling the Nuclear Gizmos who wailed through her earbuds.

She brushed her hands. *I'm Kiara. Nothing is too difficult for me.*

She boogied back to the bed.

The box springs—stiff and, thus, easier to scrape across the floor—followed the top mattress to the living room below.

Dirt clung to the sweat coating her neck and face and hair. It cleansed her.

Gone was her sorrow.

Her guilt.

Her loneliness.

Several hours passed. Dust and must and rust were busted. The pine aroma of her detergent prevailed. She scrubbed.

Washed Bryce's wife out of her mind.

Scoured the bereavement out of her bones.

Burnished her freedom.

Beneath the clean, she found contentment, but peace eluded her. The dirt was gone.

But so was Bryce.

~~

Sweat trickled down Lia's neck. She swiped it away with a tissue.

"Aunt Lia, look!" Dixon raced into the zoo's splash park.

"Your shoes. Take your shoes off." Lia called to Shann. "Stop him."

"Come on, Macie." Shann ripped off his daughter's sneakers and his work boots and tossed them at his sister's feet.

"Macie doesn't need to—"

Their delighted squeals overpowered Lia's protest.

Father and daughter joined Dixon in the splash park.

Shann placed his thumb over a hole on the water rings and diverted the spray. It squirted Lia standing on the edges of the water pad. "Come on, Lia. Have some fun. Remember, 'a merry heart maketh a cheerful countenance.'" Without waiting for her response, he nabbed his son, spun him upside down and held him over the spray.

Dixon shrieked, delight evident in his high-pitched tone and his grin. They wriggled and wrestled.

"You're going to get soaked, and we just got—" Lia threw up her hands. The zoo's body dryers would zap most of the wet. Another set of sneakers plopped at her feet. Scooping up the sopping shoes, Lia headed for a nearby bench in the shade. "Guess I'll watch and be the sober one."

She eased down onto the seat and checked her phone.

No call from Beau. *Running late. Fleeta Jean means more to him than his family.* She sniffed back the tears. Had to adjust her attitude.

She'd use this time to pray. Closing her eyes, she bowed her head. *Lord, forgive my stubbornness toward my husband. Help me be the wife you want me to be.*

She lifted her head and checked the cell grasped in her hand. Even though it hadn't vibrated, she hoped Beau had messaged her.

Nothing.

She pictured her young neighbor. Although grief etched her eyes and sin clouded her life, something sparkled in her when she talked about Bryce. Had she ever been so in love with Beau?

Of course, she had. Before the boys came and their focus and their lives shifted from attending to each other to child-rearing. Before Abby died one month after the twins were born, and she became their surrogate mother.

Yelps and squawks echoed from the water feature. Other kids frolicked under fake flowers raining streams of water. Their laughter told her it felt as good as it looked. Lia stood. Then she sat again. It wasn't proper for a woman of her age to run like a child. She'd be soaked through. 1 Peter 1:13 admonished her to be sober-minded. Heat prickled her skin and sweat trickled. Oh, to be young ... like Shann.

Kiara.

Even when youth clothed her, in the early years of her marriage, Chris consumed her life. Then Paul. When Sheep Loop Church hired Beau, duties preoccupied—bake sales, mission board, women's Bible studies, home visits, and church dinners.

Had she been happy then?

In her twenties, she believed she was. She sang hymns all the time. Scripture readings lasted hours. She'd kept about a billion journals filled with all she'd learned. Then at forty, something switched. What?

Her phone shook in her hand. A warning signal blared like a tornado notice or an A-bomb attack—her ringtone for Beau. She smiled. If he ever heard the ring she'd chosen for him, he'd have a conniption that would shake his father in the grave, bless Sterling's heart.

"Hello," she answered.

"Paul dropped me off. Where are you?"

"At the water feature. I'll meet you."

At the elephant enclosure, a few yards before the water pad, she spied Beau and picked up her pace until the heat stopped her. She gasped for breath. Instead of racing to her husband, she stepped under the misters lining the pachyderm exhibit.

Beau caught up and pecked her cheek. "Why're you under this water? It'll take the curl out of your hair." He pushed back a strand. "Besides, elephants stink."

She patted her hair and pulled away from his touch. "The humidity's taken out whatever body this mop had. I'll fix it later. Come on." She took his hand. "Let's go find the kids."

"We can't stay long. I need—"

"You just got here."

"We have to meet with—"

"Mondays are your days off." She faced him and crossed her arms. "Also, it's Labor Day. Relax. Have some fun with—"

"Luke 9:58 said the Lord had no place to lay his head. If Jesus couldn't rest, how do you expect us to slack—"

She pivoted and strode back toward the kids. *Don't pick and choose your Scriptures, Sterling Beau McGuffrey. If God, the Father of all creation, took a day off, you can, too.*

Besides, he had no right making plans for *her* life.

But he was her husband.

Why was she born female?

She stood at the edge of the splash park. *Where are Shann and the kids?*

Near the far side, under a water dome, Macie and Dixon shrieked as Shann held onto their hands. If only they'd bathe as willingly.

"Lia, step back, you're going to get wet."

She glared at Beau who strode toward her.

She kicked off her shoes and scurried toward the kids. Nabbing Macie, she carried her to the water dump. Her timing impeccable.

Macie squirmed and squawked, but she flailed for show alone.

A bucket of water tipped over them. Lia's shirt—white and cotton—became translucent. It clung to her.

She didn't care.

The adults at the splash park watched their young 'uns. Not her.

Beau stood with arms crossed. He shook his head.

"Come on, Beau. Have some fun, and make a joyful noise unto the Lord. Let's play like when we first married."

His silence greeted her. He sat on a bench in the sun—far from any cooling spray.

Crossing her arms, feeling exposed like those Hooters girls in a wet T-shirt contest, Lia slogged off the water pad and fished through her soggy purse still looped over her shoulder for dollars to insert into the body dryer.

"Want to join me?" She winked at Beau.

His expression didn't change. He might as well have been the relief of Robert E. Lee carved into Stone Mountain.

Why couldn't Beau see their family needed him more than his congregation? Couldn't he have fun outside of church services?

Chapter Seven

After an hour of meandering up Sheep Loop Road on Tuesday afternoon, Kiara turned around. She never made it to the Rarity Mountain turn. Never found cell service. After lunch she'd explore the other way—the direction the cab had come.

She dragged herself into her cabin. Her legs ached, and her back begged to sit.

Tomorrow, her supplies would be delivered. Oils. Turps. Colors on vast canvases. They'd take her out of Stinking Creek. They'd save her.

How often had she begged Bryce and the art world for more downtime? Fewer hours—days—promoting her work, attending openings, soliciting galleries, and more time for painting? Well, she had it now.

Kiara filled the water kettle and turned on the burner.

She didn't want the time to paint. She wanted people. Friends. Gina could've called. Without cell service and no home phone, she had no way of knowing. Kiara palmed her phone as though a message could float through a dead zone.

Dead.

Bryce.

Her heart.

She shook her head to stop this train of thought.

She also needed to hear from her second-best buddy, Imani. Her inspiration for her dreadlocks. The second side to her black and white cookie, she and Imani joked. They were twins—Imani the negative to Kiara's positive—opposite sides of the same person.

Her stomach grumbled.

At the refrigerator, she slipped in a puddle of water. Scanning the room, Kiara found no sign of a leak. She probably spilled water filling the kettle.

Although, the teapot and the sink sat across the alcove delineating her kitchen from the rest of the cabin. She opened the refrigerator and pushed the milk aside to find a yogurt.

Wait. Why was the milk warm?

She unscrewed the top and sniffed. Sour? It tasted fine last night. Dumb hicks didn't sell fresh food. She shoved the milk back in the fridge. No sense wasting it. She could bake it into muffins or pancakes. She picked up the yogurt. Warm, too.

She touched the tofu. The sliced melon. All room temperature.

After yanking open the freezer, Kiara found the source of the water on the floor. Global warming had hit her freezer.

Ice cubes floated in cool water in their bin. Chicken lay thawing on the shelves.

She wiggled the fridge away from the wall. The plug sat snuggly in the socket. A tripped breaker? Where was her fuse box?

Within a minute, she found it in the bathroom. Whoever had owned this place before Bryce gifted it to her had labeled every breaker. The one for the fridge didn't look tripped. Kiara flipped it off anyway and reset it.

No refrigerator hummed.

Were the breakers labeled correctly? She flipped each one off, then back on. The appliances clicked off, then hummed to life again. Lights flashed. No refrigerator joined the chorus of happy electrical appliances.

The day after stocking the fridge chock full of food she couldn't afford to lose, the stupid thing conked out.

She'd be bothering Delia Mae in the middle of the school day. Like homeschoolers actually worked. Her stepmother's kids never did. Jillian proved homeschool aficionados were arrogant dupes.

She headed to Delia Mae's. No need to lock her door. Only the McGuffreys and one lost car had bothered to ramble down her road. The wooden bridge across her paltry stream clacked beneath her shoes. Not even the board curling up from its nail at the far side bothered her any longer.

Better not get used to it here.

At the McGuffreys' fence, Kiara scanned the yard. Youtee remained out of sight.

With care, Kiara latched the gate behind her and tramped up to the door and knocked. "Delia Mae? Sorry to bother—"

"Come on in." Delia Mae, in a long skirt again and her hair impeccably fixed in a bun at the nape of her noggin, smiled and swung open the door. "Would you like to join my mother and me for a cup of coffee? She brought over a pear cobbler."

Kiara smiled at the woman seated at the table. *Her mother?*

With hair white as goose down and lines carved in her face, the woman had to be in her nineties, far too old to be Delia Mae's mother. She sat in a captain's chair at a long, maple table in the center of the room.

"I'd love to visit, but I've got another issue. Do you know the number of a reliable appliance repairman?"

"Rusty Ford is who we use."

"I need a good truck, not a rusty one." Kiara winked with her joke.

Delia Mae blinked several times as though she'd gotten dust in her eyes. Her lips quirked.

"Could I use your landline to call him? My refrigerator's not working. All the stuff you helped me lug in yesterday will rot."

Delia Mae laughed.

"What? You find my predicament funny?"

"Bless your heart. You're not catching a break." Delia Mae flipped through her cell phone. "I just realized Rusty's name sounded like a junk car. You get used to things being the way they are. Then you don't see the humor in 'em." She handed over her cell.

A signal just across the road?

"I keep my contacts in my phone. The house one's there." She pointed to a cordless phone on the beautiful granite countertop—brown with reddish swirls and flecks of mica twinkling under amber pendant lights.

Kiara took her neighbor's cell. "I'm sorry for interrupting your school day." She scanned the room. No kids worked. Did they do any schoolwork or simply idle away their day pretending?

"No problem. It's two and the kids are finishing up in the family room."

Of course, they probably worked out of workbooks like her stepmom, Jillian, inflicted on her and her own kids. Kiara woke the sleeping cell and punched the number from Delia Mae's contacts into the house phone. As the repairman's number rang, she surveyed the kitchen. Spotless stainless steel appliances glistened in the spacious, modern room. Maple cabinets matched the long, farmhouse table. Not a speck of dirt showed anywhere, not even on the off-white tile floor. Delia Mae's kitchen rivaled her old one in Manhattan.

Made her home across the road look like the hillbilly's.

A voice recorder clicked on and asked Kiara to leave a message and callback number.

Call back? Who knew? "Delia Mae, what's your landline number?"

Her neighbor rattled it off, and Kiara repeated it into the phone, gave the details of her problem, and hung up.

"Rusty'll return your call." Delia Mae chuckled. "What's his real name?" She leaned toward her mother. "Do you know Rusty's given name?"

"Hit's Rufus," the older woman said. "Rufus Little-Ford. His mama got 'er name in hit."

"Who hit Rufus?" Kiara scratched her head.

41

"No one." Lia's brows knit together as though puzzled, but she said no more.

"Do you have a cooler and ice?"

"I'd stash your food in our refrigerator, but you'd have a major problem. If you could fit another thing in it, Chris or Paul would gobble it down like deer in your roses or bunnies in your vegetable garden. Let me call Shann. Have a seat." Delia Mae picked up the landline. "Ma, this is my new neighbor, Kiara. She's a painter from New York."

"Howdy, I'm Queenie."

"Glad to meet you." She scooted into a chair next to the older woman.

"Whet jew done to yer hair?" Queenie leaned forward and squinted.

Kiara tugged at the locks.

"Ma, mind your manners." Delia Mae mouthed "I'm sorry" to Kiara then stepped out of the room.

"Whar jew live?"

Kiara hesitated. Then the meaning of whar dawned on her. "Across the road."

"I live up the holler just past the pastor in the yaller trailer." She pointed behind her. "What jew thank of Stanking Crick sufur?"

Kiara blinked. Wished she'd had a translator. Why did a Jew have to thank a person for sulfur?

"Hey, Mamaw." A young man in his late teens bustled into the room and kissed Queenie on the top of her curls. "Howdy." He offered Kiara a hand. "I'm Paul."

He called down the hallway where Delia Mae had disappeared. "Ma, me and Chris are done with English. I'm gonna take Chris to practice." He didn't wait for an answer but scuttled out of the kitchen.

Just finished English and speaks like that? Homeschoolers. Kiara finally found *real* education once she left home at sixteen and went to college.

Another teen hauling a large duffle bag over his shoulder jogged into the kitchen. "Howdy. I'm Chris." He swung open the refrigerator door, unscrewed a gallon of milk and took a swig. "Late. See ya." He, too, pecked Queenie on the head and ran off.

What kind of manners do these —

Queenie interrupted Kiara's musings. "Thet boy Chris is 'as choked with shoe dust. All 'is borned days been an active care-akter."

Was that English?

"So ,what does jew paint? Inside houses or outside?"

Kiara blinked. Paint she understood. "Neither, I'm an artist."

Delia Mae returned to the kitchen. "Shann's got room in his refrigerator and is going to take your food."

Kiara stood. "I better go."

"No, sit. He'll take care of it. Did you lock the door?"

She shook her head. "No. I've got nothing to rob."

"Hungry?"

Her mouth watered.

"I made plenty of chicken salad, and the garden's producing maters. It's near done for the growing season, but we have a few left. For dessert, Ma made the best pear cobbler. Just picked the pears last week." Delia Mae fussed at the counter by the fridge. "They don't make appliances like they used to. The government's free trade deals have ruined our industries."

"Dadgum govmint got no call to nose 'bout our business," Queenie said.

"Ma, watch your mouth." Delia Mae kept her back to Kiara, but her voice sounded light. Like her mother amused her.

Kiara could picture her smile.

"Regulatin' everything," Queenie continued. "By grab, they'd a tuck are terlet tissue if we'd let 'em."

"Ma. Manners."

"Don't you think regulations are necessary?" Kiara asked. "Keeps industry in check and the environment clean — like solar —"

Delia Mae turned from the counter and sliced a finger across her throat. Her face looked like she'd witnessed a Dean Koontz murder.

Her warning came too late.

"My Cletus got himself fared from the coal mines when the know-all govmint closed 'em. All the rules didn't keep him from catchin' black lung. Them govmint and big business fellers are all et up with stupid."

"Here you go." Delia Mae slid a sandwich in front of Kiara along with a glass of milk. "Ma, you want another bowl of cobbler?"

"Jest a dob."

"Coffee?"

Queenie smiled up at her daughter and lifted her cup. "You kin frashen hit a mite."

Food and company. Here two days, and already Kiara's appreciation of the two rose. She picked up a half of the sandwich. Onions and celery scented the chicken salad and her mouth watered.

"Ain't jew gone thank the Lawd?"

Kiara opened her mouth.

Delia Mae arched an eyebrow, frowned, and mouthed the words "My mother." She shrugged.

Kiara bowed her head and waited. *How long do people pray?*

Her stomach grumbled. *What a hypocrite I am. Who am I praying to?* She closed her eyes and recalled a yoga meditation. She'd take a moment and align her chakras.

"You a good'un. That was a right proper prayer, but you better et thet samich 'for it goes bad." Queenie dumped coffee into a saucer and blew. She slurped the brew from the dish then clinked it back on the table. "My birthday's this Saturday." Queenie grinned like a child.

"Happy birthday."

"I don't look my age folks say."

As she chewed, Kiara studied Queenie. *Probably ninety and not a hundred.*

"How old you think I am?" Queenie grinned and preened. At the moment, she acted more seven than seventy-seven.

How to answer? Kiara took another bite of her sandwich. Took her time chewing to stall. Queenie was Delia Mae's mother, and her neighbor was about forty-five. Add twenty years, at least. *No way she's sixty-five.*

"Come on. Give yer best guess." Queenie's shoulders hugged her neck. She sipped more coffee from the saucer.

"Umm, seventy-five?" The number sounded safe. But Bryce's folks were in their seventies and looked about fifty years younger than Queenie.

"Pert close. Turnin' eighty."

Struggling to keep from choking, Kiara coughed. Time hadn't been kind to Queenie.

"Yep. We're havin' a party Saturday."

Seeing as Kiara understood about every third word Queenie said, she let her ramble.

"Well? What'd jew say?"

Kiara realized Queenie had been asking her a question.

"I'm sorry. I was distracted."

"We be startin' 'bout noon. Jew kin come any time after thet. All my kids'll be here. Delia Mae and Junior and Cornie—"

The door clanged behind Shann. "Unless you want to be homeless, I'd suggest you turn off your burner."

Kiara jolted to her feet.

Shann raised a hand. "It's off now. Teapot's welded to the rings until they cool. You'll need a new one. Teapot, that is. The burner will be fine. Lia here's done it a billion times when schoolwork bogs her down."

"Do not." Although she scowled, humor laced Delia Mae's voice. "You're a brat, and Beau should disown you."

He pecked Queenie's cheek and squeezed her shoulders. "Hey, Aunt Q."

She swatted his hand, but her face glowed with pleasure. "Shann here'll be thar. We'll have plenty of vittles." Queenie winked at Shann, then smiled at Kiara. "You two'll git to know each other better. With his beard," she nodded at Shann, "and yer hair, y'all a match made in heaven." She giggled like a schoolgirl.

44

Kiara sank back down and bent her head. She tucked a dread behind her ear. With her hair down, perhaps she could hide behind the mop.

"Your food's all at my place. Seeing as Lia feeds us most of the time and I've just gotten back from tour, my refrigerator's half empty. I'll show you where it is when you're done here."

"Tour? What do you do?"

"Daddy." Macie, clad in dungarees matching her father's, came running with a notebook and pencil clutched in her hand.

Shann scooped up his daughter and kissed her cheek. "Done with your schooling?" He tickled her, and she squealed.

"Yep. See." She held up the notebook.

"You know the *whole* alphabet?" He pulled out a chair across from Kiara and settled Macie on his lap.

She nodded.

"Do you know how to make the letters when they're mixed up and not in order?"

"Yes, Daddy." The little moppet rolled her eyes.

"Give me a capital S."

Macie laid her notebook on the table and pages crinkled as she found a clean page. With her left hand she curled an S.

"Now an h."

She complied.

"An a. An n."

"I know. One more n." Macie gnawed her lip and added a second n then straightened. She squared her shoulders and lifted her head. "That's your name. I gots a surprise." She doubled over and everyone watched as though observing a virtuoso work. Her right arm hid what she wrote. With the book clutched to her chest, she sat up and grinned. She flipped her notebook around and held it in the air. "A-b-i-g-a-i-l. That's Mommy. I practiced a lot."

Shann rubbed his sternum. His smile faded.

"Daddy, I wanna—"

He stood, slipping Macie to her feet. "Go play with Dixon."

"I wanna show Kiara my portraits."

"Portraits?" The twinkle returned to his eyes as he gazed down at his daughter. "Who taught you them highfalutin' words?"

"Aunt Lia." Macie stood by his side. "You knowed that."

"Not Aunt Lia. She taught you nothing." He scooped Macie in his arms and tipped her upside down. "Tell me who taught you, or I'll never put you down again, and the tickle monster will get you."

"No." Macie squealed and wriggled at the word tickle. "Aunt Lia teached me. Honest."

Shann put her down, and she ran off.

45

"This could take a while." Shann settled back into his chair. "Judging by my nephew's grammar and my daughter's, my sis-in-law ain't good 'nuff at ejucation." He winked at Delia Mae.

Everyone laughed.

Kiara settled back in the chair, resigned. A childish art show was a small price to pay for their help.

Macie scampered back in with a fist full of pictures. Instead of clambering onto her father's lap or her aunt's or Queenie's, she climbed onto Kiara's.

Kiara stiffened. The urge to shove the child off overwhelmed her as the Macie's boney rump wiggled into a comfortable position.

"See." She shoved a crayon drawing inches from Kiara's nose. "This is Aunt Lia and Uncle Beau." Her little fingers bopped Kiara's face.

Kiara took the drawing and laid it on the table. She leaned in, her arms curling around Macie as Kiara studied the immature drawing. Amazing. Unlike most five-year-olds, these portraits showed sophistication. Delia Mae's bun sat primly on the back of her head—a little saucer with stray lines like the wisps always escaping. Her eyes, blue and upturned, rimmed with lashes, sat in the correct proportion halfway down her face.

The man standing on the other edge of the paper had to be Beau. Kiara hadn't met the elusive preacher, yet. This man wore a suit and tie. Curly, gray hair sprouted atop his noggin. Macie had drawn his eyes in narrow curves as though they were angry slits. A small circle sat at the bottom of his square chin.

"What's this?" Kiara asked.

"His dimple." Macie screwed her index finger into her chin. "God said, 'I done a good job' and chucked his chin."

Kiara laughed. "You're too much, Macie." She straightened the drawing. "This is good." Kiara's bowed her head to better study the work. Her cheek nestled against Macie's head. The child's curls tickled, and Macie nuzzled in closer. Snuggling a kid didn't feel odd, for once.

"They just got home from church. That's why Uncle Beau's wearing a suit." Macie pulled a picture cluttered with people from her pile. "This is Mommy." She pointed to a figure in the upper left—an outline. "This is me and Dixon." She rubbed her index finger over the two small individuals—the same height and shape, one with long curls, the other short.

"Who are these two people?" Kiara pointed to a couple holding hands. One was a woman with crimson hair in funny ponytails and large brown eyes dominating most of the face. The man had a beard that would've made Rutherford B. Hayes's look tame. She breathed in sharply.

"That's you and Daddy. Mommy," again she indicated the vague outline in the top left corner, "says it's okay if you become my new mommy. She doesn't like Jorie because—"

Shann jumped to his feet nearly toppling the chair. "I ought to show you where your food is."

"Daddy—"

"Run along." Shann grasped Macie's shoulders. "Go play with Dixon. Keep him out of trouble." He gave her a slight thrust toward the family room.

Kiara stood. "Thank you for feeding me again."

"My pleasure," Delia Mae said.

"It was nice meeting you." Kiara nodded toward Queenie.

"Shann's Jorie's a good 'un. Real purty and sweet. You'll meet her Saturday," Queenie said.

"Ready." Shann coughed and shuffled his feet.

"Remember my party. We be havin' a bobacue. Lots of food."

"I wouldn't want to intrude."

"Ain't tekking no for an answer."

"Then I'll be there." Being with someone beat being alone.

Chapter Eight

His family had no business bringing up Jorie. Shann's face heated beneath his beard as he held the kitchen door for Kiara.

Of course, they did. He and Jorie had been seeing each other off and on for almost a year. His brother hoped she'd bring him back into the fold.

When Abby was alive, she never liked Jorie. Abby said she needed dynamite to blast a word or two out of the pretty, little china doll.

Still, Jorie's smile always warmed him. It was so genuine. Her face made him think of a heart with her broad forehead with its widow's peak, and her cute, tiny chin.

And could she cook. All someone had to say was, 'Jorie's bringing a cake or a casserole or a salad,' and his mouth would water like Norris Dam at flood time.

Was food enough reason to marry?

"Wait for me." Macie jumped off the trampoline and bumped into Kiara as they walked to the Mule. Macie climbed into the driver's seat. "Can I drive?"

He lifted her out. "No. In the back."

"You let Dixon drive the other day."

He needed to warn Kiara about his daughter's clinginess. "No, honey, I need—"

"Daddy. Wait." Dixon zipped from behind the garden shed with Youtee on his heels. "I'm coming, too."

"Did you hear Macie mention your name?" He turned toward Kiara. "Can never escape these twins. No matter where they are, they come running home with me." He grinned at the twins. "I don't have kids. Abby birthed homing pigeons."

Dixon flapped his arms. "Coo, coo." He climbed into the bed of the Mule and pecked Macie with his nose.

Not once. Or twice. Like a woodpecker.

"Daddy, Dixon's bothering me."

"Stop." Shann started the Mule. "Sorry, Kiara. When I'm home ... " He sighed then grinned. "Heaven descends when I'm home."

Kiara smiled, but her eyes didn't meet his. "They want their daddy."

Youtee leaped up after Dixon and Macie, and Shann lifted the mutt while the kids hauled him up by his collar. The three looked like an illustration from "Rub-A-Dub-Dub" three McGuffreys in a tub. Shann had to reach out and touch them. He ran his hand over Macie's hair, and she curled into his palm.

Dixon swatted him away.

Youtee nudged his own head under Shann's fingers as though making up for Dixon.

"They're a crew." Shann's eyes stayed trained on the kids.

"They are," Kiara answered from the front seat.

Shann shifted into gear, and the Mule lumbered down the lane.

Within minutes he pulled into his driveway. The unpainted board and batten house made a small footprint on the edge of the McGuffrey acreage. Not much, but his. Abby would've hated it. Their place in Knoxville was small, about a thousand square feet, but spacious compared to this. Her cop salary covered the mortgage. His gave a few luxuries.

Without her? His cabin was snug and cold.

What did Kiara think of it? He glanced her way.

Macie grabbed her hand and was dragging her toward the house.

He lengthened his stride to catch up to his crew.

Dixon swung open the cabin door, and he and Youtee bounded into the kitchen.

Macie still clung to Kiara's hand like cat fluff stuck on Velcro.

"Let go of our guest before you cut off her circulation."

She dropped her hand.

"Run off and play with your brother."

She pouted for a minute, then jumped on the couch where Dixon and Youtee lolled.

"Outside." Shann pointed to the open door.

"Daddy." Macie whined.

"Come on, Macie. Last one to the pond's gotta drink the water." Dixon dashed out.

Macie flew after him.

"Wait!" Shann ran after the twins. "No one drinks from the pond. You'll end up with the epizootics."

"The what?" Kiara sounded startled.

"An old mountain saying. It's any weird disease." The three rascals were out of sight. "Lia gets mad at me when I use the term."

"Why?"

"Mountain folk also use it to describe an STD."

She nodded and glanced in the direction the kids scooted. "Aren't you afraid the hound will run away?"

"Not with the kids. You think Macie clings? Youtee's a burr when they've got him." He yanked open the door to the refrigerator behind where they stood in the kitchen. "Here's the icebox. As you can see, most of it's yours."

The cabin closed in on him. The smell of Kiara—incense-like, but faint—filled the gap between them. She'd glanced at him, but never sustained eye contact. What color were her eyes?

According to his daughter's picture, brown.

Macie was always dead on with her portraits. There weren't refrigerators enough in the world to hold all her drawings.

"Thank you." Her gaze slid his way, but she averted her eyes before he saw them.

Why was he drawn to her? After Abby, he couldn't give his heart to anyone. He thought he loved Jorie. At least, his brother hoped he'd love her—faithful in Sheep Loop Church, fervent in faith. Pretty. Employed. Stable—mentally and financially.

It'd been five years since Abby died. Why'd he still expect to see her walk through the door or feel the weight of her next to him in bed? Could almost smell her.

Ivory soap and pine. Fresh. Crisp. Clean.

At the moment, all he smelled was incense.

He coughed. "Like I said, the place is small. The loft over the living area is Dixon's domain." He pointed up the ladder at the end of the couch. Its rungs crawled up to an alcove over the sofa. "We have two bedrooms." He pointed toward the opposite wall. "Bathroom's in the master."

"It is snug." Kiara twisted the diamond on her left hand.

It twisted Shann's gut. Focusing on her action, he forgot to listen.

"Shann?" Kiara waved a hand in front of his face.

He shook his head. "Sorry. I got distracted."

"I said, your home reminds me of Manhattan apartments. Makes us creative with our space." She crossed her arms and leaned against the sink.

"After I lost Abby, didn't need much room. The kids spend their free time with Lia. I work in my shop."

"What do you do?"

"My band recreates the musical traditions of the area. Washbasin Gentry, our name, plays original tunes, mountain music with a cross of country and blues."

"What's mountain music?"

"We use tools at hand like washboards, oil drums, a bass made from a crutch, and my guitars. Our out-of-state tours run from Easter until Labor Day. Off season, we hit only Tennessee and closer states. In between, I make cigar box guitars."

Finally, Kiara looked at him.

Macie hadn't gotten her eyes quite right. Flecks of gold and green dotted the brown. They made him think of agates.

"What are cigar box guitars?

Shann didn't answer. Staring into her eyes for a fleeting moment made him forget he stood in his kitchen.

"Shann?"

Kiara's rich voice brought him back into his kitchen, aware of the close walls and incense. Her proximity made his breathing hard and thinking harder. "Come to my workshop. I'll show you."

~~

Shann's cubicle of a house made Kiara grateful for her own stinking cabin on Stanking Crik, as Delia Mae's mother called the hamlet, but his shop rivaled her barn. It smelled of fresh-sawn wood and of varnish. Odd musical instruments vied for space with the scent.

"These are lap guitars." Shann held up an instrument made from one piece of lumber. "Made from a "tuba for" as the hill folk called this hunk of wood." He sat with the two-by-four, then strummed. It sounded like a steel guitar or Dobro, but more primitive. The Grandma Moses of the music world.

Other lap guitars painted orange or turquoise or gray and strung with guitar wire hung on pegs. They almost paneled one section of a wall.

Adjacent to the lap guitars, shelves lined with boxes filled a small bay. She took one down and ran her hand across the label on the black lacquered box. A gold rimmed, gray label with a Renaissance-style group of people ran across the front. "Beautiful. I didn't know they made such pretty boxes for cigars, of all things." Kiara looked up at Shann. "How do you make them into guitars?"

He ran through the construction in detail—told of sawing holes, planing wood, varnishing. "To finish the pieces, I use whatever hardware I can scrounge—screws, hinges, even old deer bone from Chris and Paul's hunts."

She wrinkled her nose. "I hate hunting."

"Won't escape it. Coon and squirrel season now. Chris is nuts about any hunting. Paul goes along with it, more to be with big bro. Deer season starts in about a month."

"Hate guns more."

"They'll grow on you. It's a way of life down here."

"Won't be here long." Kiara picked up a guitar and strummed. "What's it tuned to?"

"G."

She strummed the guitar, bridging several chords.

"You know how to play?"

She lifted a shoulder. "I play the basics on a few stringed instruments—cello and upright bass. Those instruments obsess my mother and her boyfriend and their son. When I ..." She bent over the guitar and fingered a few chords.

"When you what?"

Kiara handed him the guitar. "Play something for me."

He plucked out a melody—one she'd never heard— then sang. His tenor was melodious and mountain, a folksy blend of blues and Southern gospel.

She studied his fingers as they flew across the strings, picking like Yo-Yo Ma lost in a pizzicato. "I never heard that song before."

"It's one of —"

"Daddy! Daddy!" Macie's screams made her jump.

Was there a horrid accident?

Shann laid the guitar on his bench and dashed from the studio. "What happened now?"

"Dixon fell in the pond."

"I told you —" His flight cut off his words.

Kiara stood frozen in the studio. Her hand fluttered to her stomach. *Here come the epizootics.*

~~

Shann pointed to the flatbed of his vehicle.

"I didn't drowned. Just slipped." Dixon stuck out his bottom lip and stomped up into the Mule.

"Should've thought of that before you disobeyed me," Shann said.

Youtee leaped into the back and shook, spraying all of them with pond water.

"I tolded him," Macie scolded as she sat next to him.

Dixon shoved her away with his shoulder and yanked off his wet sneakers.

Macie lectured. "Honor thy father and thy mother: that thy days may be long upon the land." She'd perfected her 1611 King James English. If only their twenty-first century English was as good.

Shann's brother had done his work well.

"Your days are going to be short, Dixon," Shann called over his shoulder. "If you don't kill yourself, your father might."

"How do you manage touring and creating with the kids? They're a handful."

Shann grinned. Couldn't help it. His kids—even spending half their lives with Lia—were his. And Abby's. As wild as her. Free-spirited like him. "A handful of blessings and an overflowing bucket of joy."

Kiara stared at him. Her mouth moved as though she wanted to say something. She was an odd-looking creature with her dreadlocks, mini-skirt and sneakers. She wore a long-sleeved shirt over a Nuclear Gizmos tee. On anyone else it would look careless. On her? Mountain and modern like a hillbilly tune.

He stroked his beard and remembered Jorie. After a year together, she was probably hoping for a ring. Every time he thought about proposing, his spirit sagged.

In everything, Jorie showed kindness and grace, but she went to Beau's church. Could he convince her to go somewhere else? Doubtful, seeing as her mother and her mother's family had gone there for as long as her family existed. Attended before Beau took over.

She had beautiful blonde hair, but wore it in the most unflattering style like Lia used to before she decided pinning it up made her more— what? More prim. His sister-in-law was becoming more rigid as the years went on. He never noticed until he started touring. Long months away made the changes more obvious.

They bounced over the bridge to Kiara's cabin.

She touched his hand.

Warmth zinged. He had to remember. This woman was an atheist. He didn't go to church himself, but atheism?

Not for him.

"Thanks for saving my food. I owe the McGuffreys big time." She climbed out of the ATV.

"Remember to turn off your burner. My cabin's a mite small for—"

No. He bit his tongue. Not going to hint about living with someone outside of marriage. Had to find a church before he backslid.

Her laughter answered for her. "A fire would be a good thing for this dump." She hitched a thumb toward her cabin. "I'd move into the barn. Might need to move anyway while I wait for the property to sell."

"Sell?" Why'd his stomach drop? He didn't know her from Adam's off ox. She could be a lunatic and given the way she dressed and forgetting to turn off her burner ...

Macie leaped out of the Mule. "I'm gonna visit." She flung her little arms around Kiara.

Kiara absently rubbed Macie's back. "Yep. The realtor's coming Friday. Manhattan's calling me."

"I didn't think you had a phone?" He winked and tried to make a joke of it even though he found nothing funny in her leaving. Or his daughter's clinginess. "Climb back in, Macie. I got work to do at home, and Dixon needs dry shoes." He scanned the yard for his son. "Where'd your brother go?"

"He's down at the stream. He likes frogs," Kiara said.

"Dixon."

"Minute, Daddy."

"Macie, back in." Shann nodded at the seat Kiara vacated. "Let's go, Dixon, or you're walking home." Again, he glanced at Kiara. Tree shadows dappled her skin, painted her in watercolors. Made her like the abstracts Lia said she fancied.

"See you." Kiara stepped toward the cabin.

Shann started the truck and rumbled it over the bridge.

"Daddy, wait." A barefooted Dixon scrambled up the bank closest to the road. Whatever hadn't been soaked before was wet now.

How did Lia manage these critters?

Chapter Nine

L ife moved seamlessly for Kiara. At last.

Or at least the movers did on Wednesday. Rusty Ford had to order a refrigerator part. Said he'd be back Friday, so Shann would have to house Kiara's food for another two days.

It didn't take the movers long as they hauled only Kiara's personal effects and art supplies. All Bryce's wife left her. Two hours after they'd gone, Kiara found her oils and stood in the barn, dabbed with paint, and surrounded by turpentine fumes. The six-foot canvas *Manhattan Seraph* leaned against her studio wall. She stepped back and studied her creation. The painting needed a heavy-handed dose of pigment. It yelled at her, "Give me one happy swath of unadulterated pink. I'll show you hope."

Kiara picked up her tube of rose madder and squeezed a healthy dollop onto her pallet.

"Miss Muffet, I couldn't find you."

Macie's breathless voice shoved Kiara back to Stinking Creek. "Shouldn't you be in school?"

"It's after dinner. Daddy said I could play outside."

This wasn't outside. "Does he know you're here?"

She nodded but ducked her head. "Can I watch you paint? I ain't never seed a real artist."

Kiara glanced at her watch, the one Bryce gave her for their first anniversary. The one Gina envied and bought for herself. "I'm almost done."

"You paint fast."

"Fast? What do you mean?"

Her little finger pointed at the canvas. "You covered everything."

Kiara grinned. Had she ever been so innocent? "No, honey, I don't paint fast. I started this before my boy ... before Bryce died." *Died. No. Passed. Remember, Kiara.* "Been working on it for weeks."

"You just got here."

The naïve statement made Kiara smile down at Macie. "Started it long before I moved here."

Macie dragged the extra stool closer to Kiara and climbed up on it.

55

"Make yourself at home." Kiara cringed. *Shouldn't use sarcasm on a kid.*

Macie leaned forward, taking Kiara at her word.

"I do have to work. Why don't—"

"I'll be *real* quiet." Macie placed her index finger over her lips.

"Okay. Not a word though."

Macie whispered. "I'll be quieter than, than ..." She looked around the room.

Turning back to her canvas, Kiara swirled her brush into the rosy paint. *Manhattan Seraph* made its demand. She would deliver, but only a slice—on the top left, sweeping over Manhattan.

"Than the birds chirping," Macie shouted.

Kiara jumped. Good thing she wasn't holding a brush to the canvas. "What?" She glared at the imp. *Kids. Who invented them?* "You said you'd be quiet."

"I just thought how quiet I'd be."

"Not a word. Promise?"

The child nodded so vigorously, Kiara feared she'd fall off the stool.

Kiara took her three-inch brush and with a twist against the canvas, dabs of pink blended with the still wet green and amber. A face appeared in the strokes. Kiara had pictured this emotion. This symbolism.

"Hey."

Macie's little voice jerked Kiara out of her painting and into the studio.

"You use the same hand as me."

Kiara studied her fingers curled around her brush. She lifted her hand. "This one?"

Macie nodded with her eyes wide and a tiny smile.

"Artists tend to be lefties." Kiara picked up her one-inch brush and swept it through the green, painted whorls around the ribbon of rose. She allowed the quiet color to tone down the vivid hue.

"Dixon says I'm backward." Her voice sounded small, almost sad. "Aunt Lia says I'm a mirror twin."

Kiara studied the girl. In the tone of her voice, Kiara heard Jillian call her contrary. Her stepmother would point to her own kids and ask why Kiara couldn't be like them. Her biological mother forced Kiara to play the cello right-handed. In the child's lament, Kiara heard her mom's pride when her brother, Chester, proved to be a virtuoso—better even than his father.

"Don't be sad. Lefties are creative. They think out of the right side of the brain and—"

"I knowed about the right and wrong side of the brain. When we use the wrong side, we got to go to the altar and confess."

Kiara studied the child, then her meaning dawned on her. Laughter gurgled. "No, Macie. Not like that." How did one explain to a child? "There are two parts to our brain. One side is artistic, the other rational."

"What's rational?"

"It thinks about math and science." She gnawed her lip. "Like Dixon loving frogs—"

"And spiders and snakes."

Kiara crunched her shoulders and shook her head. "Right-brained people think about art and music. We create."

"Hey look. There's a face." Macie jumped off the stool and pointed toward the rose madder. She squinted. "It looks like me."

Kiara stepped back. Didn't see the child in the face she'd strove to create.

"See." Macie stretched on tiptoes. "There's curly brown hair and measle eyes."

"Measle?"

She pointed at her eyes.

Kiara leaned in. "You mean hazel."

"Yep. See the green and brown and gold. Them's measle."

Kiara didn't bother to correct her again.

"How d'you get your hair like that?" Macie asked.

"I took the brush"—Kiara picked up a clean one from the container holding her array of brushes—"and flicked my wrist."

"No. Not on the painting." Macie stared at Kiara's head. "*Your* hair." She studied Kiara in the way children do. Boldly. Unafraid. Like they saw through you.

Another reason she never wanted a kid.

"My dreadlocks?"

Macie nodded, and her *measle* eyes danced.

You have to make lots of little ponytails and tease them."

"Tease? Like Dixon?"

"No. Not joking. It's a style of combing like this." Kiara picked up a lock of Macie's hair. With her fingers, she back-brushed the strand. "You make a little rat's nest of it."

"Dixon would like teased hair. He likes rats. Can I feel your dreadlocks?"

Kiara ducked her head. The child was gentle—her fingers warm on Kiara's scalp causing a shiver to run down her spine.

"I like them. Why d'you make them?"

"My hair was so curly, and my good friend Imani had lots of braids. They're extensions but look good on her because she's black. On me—"

"I'm gonna make ponytails, too."

Maybe conversation wasn't needed with five-year-olds.

"You're pretty."

57

"Thank you. It's time you run home. I need to clean up here."

"I want to learn how to paint like you."

"You need to study it. In school."

"Aunt Lia has us do boring things like coloring or reading books with pictures in it." She looked down.

Kiara opened her mouth to speak.

"Will you teach me to paint?"

"Sure." She'd promise anything to make Macie leave.

"Like you." Macie leaped off the stool and hit the ground with a thud. "I want to paint like that." She threw her arms over her head as though indicating the size of the work she wanted. "I want a painting bigger than me."

A grin gurgled and struggled to show itself. Kiara held it back and forced her features to look stern. "I will if you go home and let me finish."

"I want to do a *big* picture." Macie stretched out her hands. "Bigger than the room."

"We'll start small."

"Promise?" Macie turned up her measle eyes and begged.

"I promise."

The child skipped out of the room. Kiara's focus lingered on the path Macie'd taken, as though fairy dust lined its way.

In her absence, darkness weighted the loft.

~~

Early the next morning, Macie bounded into Lia's kitchen.

"Law, child, what d'you do to your hair?"

Little ponytails of varying sizes stuck out all over Macie's head. Some teased into a Möbius tangle. "I'm gonna make dreadfuls."

"Dreadfuls?" Lia squinted at the pixie.

"Does your father know about your new hairdo?"

"I'm gonna 'prise him when he comes to take us to Knoxville. We're going to the art museum today."

"You won't have dreadlocks by then."

"I got them now. Course they don't look like Miss Muffet's."

"It's Miss Kiara."

"No." Macie stuck out her bottom lip. "She likes me to call her Miss Muffet."

Lia nodded. *I doubt it.* "Come here. Let me fix them."

"No!" Macie dashed to the far side of the kitchen. "Don't touch me."

"Now why can't your aunt touch you?" Beau walked into the kitchen and kissed Lia's cheek.

She hustled to the coffeepot and poured him a cup.

"I want my hair in dreadfuls. She'll ruin it."

While Macie whined to Uncle Beau, Lia doctored the coffee with two teaspoons of sugar and half-and-half. "Here you go." She handed it to Beau, then wiped down the counter with a clean cloth.

The cup clinked against the counter. Warm hands encircled her waist, and Beau drew her to him and kissed her neck.

"Eww. Gross." Of course, Dixon chose that moment to enter.

Lia leaned back against her husband as his arms soothed her.

"I'm sorry. I haven't been the husband I should've been. You need a man to love you as Christ loved the church and gave Himself for it."

Lia turned in his arms and palmed his face. She ran her finger along his jaw and let it linger on the dimple. "I love you, too."

"God graced me with the best woman ever created." Beau picked up his coffee and sat at the table. "You taking the Yankee to LaFollette?"

"After morning classes." She sat in the chair closest to Beau and took his hand. Perhaps she could prod more compliments from him.

"Invite her to your ma's party."

"Ma already has."

His smile warmed the kitchen. He lifted her hand to his lips.

His kiss, soft on the tips of her fingers, melted her spine. Reminded her of their courtship when nothing in the world mattered more to him than her. *He loves me, still.* When Beau released her hand, she closed her eyes and tried to feel the touch — the tenderness.

"Your ma does love birthdays. Should make 'em national holidays. Has she got her tiara?"

Lia opened her eyes and nodded. "She's already worn her feathered boa. Ma took down her box of birthday treasures a month ago."

Beau leaned back in the captain's chair. "I love Queenie. What a character."

His eyes took on the look Lia adored. They sparkled with love and softness like the Sterling Beau McGuffrey she fell in love with.

Macie and Dixon tiptoed toward the door.

Their exaggerated steps reminded Lia of schooling. "You think I don't see you?" She picked up two storybooks. "Here. Read the story. I'll be in shortly."

The kids scowled, but they took the books."

After they headed to the den, she turned back to Beau.

He sipped his coffee. "This afternoon, ask our Yankee neighbor to Ma's party again. Who knows, perhaps, surrounding her with godly people will turn her from her sin."

Lia's stomach flipped. *Maybe she'll notice the love of God. She ain't a commodity.* "I'll ask her." She stood. "Do you want grits with your eggs?"

"No need to ask, honey. With the way you cook, even your grits could win a cooking contest." Beau picked up the newspaper.

Lia busied herself dishing up Beau's meal, but her mind circled back to her neighbor. Despite her strong opinions, something in Kiara moved Lia. Something begged to be seen—not as a soul to be saved, but as a human. Someone worth time and energy and love because she existed. Because God made her. Even if she didn't realize God existed, He never doubted Kiara's reality.

He made her in His own image.

He wanted her loved just because.

But why did He have to use her to love Kiara? Lia had enough to do.

Chapter Ten

Kiara toyed with her cell as Delia Mae drove her through Stinking Creek. She grinned at the bars appearing at the top of her phone.

They had service here. She looked up. Quiet country dotted with trailers and run-down homes streamed past the car. An itch to call Gina pulled Kiara, but she didn't want to break the peaceful mood filling the MINI Cooper. Kiara almost imagined her and Delia Mae as friends with no need to talk, comfortable in each other's presence.

"There's Sugar Creek Diner, the restaurant I've told you about." Delia Mae pointed to a café perched by the river. Cars filled the parking spaces bordering the road.

"Is Stinking Creek the river behind it?"

Delia Mae nodded. "Its proper name is Hickory Creek, but no one thinks of it as Hickory. We're Stinking Creek, now."

Again, silence filled the car.

No one lived in this little town. She'd never been in an area without a gazillion people. Singapore, Portland, Manhattan. Even her grandma who lived in the country of Northern California lived with more humans.

Sugar Creek Diner was the only business in this empty village.

They passed a cement block building, now boarded up. A lopsided For Sale sign hung on what used to be the front door.

"That was the town's only bar," Delia Mae said, her voice gentle. "Closed up years ago, praise God. He closed that den of iniquity."

Kiara rolled her eyes. *Here we go.* She should shut her trap. The words flitted through her mind when she blurted, "A little wine doesn't make you bad."

"The Good Book says the works of the flesh are envyings, murders, and drunkenness.'" She pierced Kiara with a glance. "'They which do such things shall not inherit the kingdom of God,' Galatians 5. The *Bible* tells us the heart of man is desperately wicked."

"That's why I hate your *Bible*."

Horror radiated from Delia Mae's eyes which couldn't stretch much bigger. If her brows rose a centimeter more, they'd be in her hairline.

Kiara saw her neighbor making the sign of the cross in her mind as though to ward off a vampire or demon. "My best friend, Gina, loved my watch." She lifted her wrist. "She was envious. So how could a god throw her in hell and let her burn because—?"

"You've misinterpreted. Envying leads to other things. You become discontent with what you have. The dissatisfaction leads to adultery or thievery or another wrong. Because the heart of man is evil, he becomes worse left to his own devices."

"You're wrong. People are good."

"No, they're not. Think of the mass shootings, the drug addiction, adultery—"

"Because Bryce and I loved each other, you're saying I'm evil? How can you?" She inhaled a slow, deliberate breath, shifted toward Delia Mae and clenched her fist. She wanted to smash her neighbor in the face. *Why? She wasn't guilty of adultery. Bryce's marriage ...*

She thought back to when she met him out at the Hamptons. Amanda and his kids frolicked on the beach while he flirted with her and Gina. Suddenly, her stomach ached as though guilt stuffed it. *No. Amanda had been sleeping around back then. His flirting didn't count.*

But Bryce and Amanda were married. They were still married when he died.

Shut up, Kiara. If you hang out with the McGuffreys much longer you will turn into a cult-following religious nut dressed in robes, drinking Kool-Aid, and believing you're descended from aliens.

Delia Mae had stopped talking.

Kiara hadn't heard the end of her conversation. Maybe that was better. Christians were so judgmental. The afternoon had been pleasant so far. She didn't need to squabble with her self-righteous neighbor. Come Monday, with a house phone and Internet, she'd have full access to Imani and Gina. "Sorry. Don't mean to bicker." *Liar.*

"Me, neither." Delia Mae patted Kiara's hand resting on the console. "It's not the Southern way."

"Are you saying ... ?" *Bite your tongue.*

"You believe I'm judging you." Delia Mae's voice was soft. "Yes, you're right. I am. It's wrong."

Kiara sat back and crossed her arms. *Gotcha.*

"Since I met you, God's been showing me how critical I've become. My ma raised me to love others and to accept them. I lost the skill as I aged. Can you forgive me?"

This was interesting to hear. A Christian admitting she was wrong?

"Aren't you guilty of the same sin?" Delia Mae asked.

"You're judging me again."

"No, I'm not." Delia Mae's voice held no hostility. "I'm trying to understand. You've lumped me with your concept of Christians before you knew me. I'm mouthy. Believe me, Beau reminds me." Her warm

62

smile softened her features. "I've done nothing to you but help. Still you accuse me."

Nothing in Delia Mae's voice condemned. She spoke factually. Yet, without reason, Kiara gritted her teeth. Her chest burned. *Say nothing. Say* —" Me?" Kiara pointed at herself. "I don't judge."

She stole a peek at her neighbor and glanced away.

Delia Mae's brows rose a fraction, but her face remained passive. "We all measure ourselves against others. When we find someone's character weak, we justify ourselves. It ain't right. Like I've said before, one sin ain't better than another."

"I'd say murder was worse than, oh, say shoplifting." *Remember, Kiara, shut your trap. A religious freak is driving.*

"Sin separates us from God. Isaiah 59:2 says —"

"Not everyone believes in the *Bible* or God."

Delia Mae shook her head. "Then think of sin as something that hurts us or another human."

"What about — ?" She bit her lip. Better than biting the hand that fed her — or drove her as the case may be.

Anger churned again, more intense as Kiara tried to control it. Why? Delia Mae didn't say anything offensive, but Kiara's defensiveness rose. She judged Delia Mae worse than any Christian did her. At least to her face.

"All sin is hurtful. Either to us, or another, or to God."

"I want people to be happy. To live up to their full potential. We shouldn't be forced to live according to another's dictates. The Muslims think like you. Do you want to walk around in a burqa? I don't." Kiara ducked her head to hide her grin. The way her neighbor dressed was not far removed from Islamic dress. Or a nun's.

Delia Mae smiled. It took ten years off of her features. If she styled herself into the twenty-first century, she'd be beautiful. She had an exotic, Meryl Streep sort of look hidden behind the graying bun and ill-fitting skirts.

"I want the same thing for mankind," Delia Mae said. "That's why I live my faith."

Kiara nodded — a little too much like a bobblehead. "And why I don't live your faith."

Delia Mae scowled, then her face relaxed, and she smiled her pretty grin. "We're two halves of a black and white cookie. We're coming from opposite angles for the same goal."

Kiara pictured her need for Imani. Delia Mae could never take Imani's place, but Kiara needed to look at her neighbor through the lens she used for everyone *but* Christians.

That was a thought. Everyone in her world was right *except* Christians. Why? She respected Muslims, Hindus, and Scientologists.

Never Jesus-believers. Was her liberalism as biased as the conservative view?

Weird thought. If she hung out with Mrs. McG much longer, she'd be rolling down church aisles in religious ecstasy.

"I'm not trying to convert you. Just want you to settle in and be as happy as me."

If religion made Delia Mae happy and created a pleasant life and harmed no one, then it was good for her. The tension that had built since passing the blue, abandoned bar evaporated and the peace of the drive swaddled Kiara again.

They turned down a narrow, tree-lined highway. A Confederate flag hung on the porch of one ramshackle house.

Kiara scowled and shook her head.

"What's wrong?" Delia Mae asked.

"How can people hang Confederate flags from their homes? Don't they know the slavery it represents?"

"It's culture," Delia Mae said. "It's important."

"But can they see how the South abused humans, like my close friend, Imani's, ancestors?"

"It's true. Slavery is wrong. By that measure, all people should buy Fair Trade clothes or those made in America because the cheap overseas factories disguise contemporary slavery."

"Still, the Civil War represented treason. We can't honor—"

"Wait a minute." Delia Mae's voice hardened. She glanced at Kiara with tight lips and slitted eyes. "I know your argument, but consider this. We cannot judge the past by today's standards."

"But—"

Delia Mae held up her hand to silence Kiara. "Take something acceptable today like abortion."

"It's our reproductive right."

"So you believe. Hear me out." She inhaled. "Suppose a woman has an abortion today. In twenty years it becomes illegal, maybe even a capital offense. Do we charge her with a crime? Throw her in jail?" She peered at Kiara then turned forward again. "We can't discount all the good she did in her life because she believed something society no longer accepts."

Kiara studied Delia Mae who looked straight ahead. Her face held no anger. More than her calm, the truth of her analogy unsettled Kiara. She leaned back against the car seat and studied the countryside.

The road curved, and they drove under a railroad trestle. The rest of the ride to LaFollette remained quiet.

They pulled into a Ford dealership perched on a hill by a busy four-lane clotted with fast-food restaurants.

"Here we are." Delia Mae turned off the MINI Cooper. "Oh, and when you have a chance, can you put Macie's hair into them little rats' nests?" She pointed at Kiara's hair. "They might as well look artistic. Heaven knows, I ain't gonna convince her to leave her hair respectable."

~~

Lia left her pretty neighbor to the paperwork at the dealership. Finally, she was done with the eccentric woman.

She frowned. *Do I want to be rid of her?* She shook her head to purge the odd thought.

Lia doubted Kiara would stay away. Every time she turned around, the Yank begged for help. Kind of like Betina and Rosalyn, her closest friends.

Her neighbor was different though. All the church ladies demanded Lia's time like she owed them. They assumed they paid her to be their servant, not Beau. Kiara's need was palpable. She asked for what Lia could give—an icebox, a ride, or a phone number. She didn't hear complaints about her husband's sermons or how to better decorate the church or a hospital stay she'd missed because her own mother had fallen and sprained her ankle.

Kiara disagreed with Lia's faith but didn't hide behind hypocrisy. Something refreshing existed in their relationship.

Honesty.

How often had she told her sons she could accept anything from them but a lie? Openness sometimes cut like stinging nettles, but you always knew what you were up against.

Plus, the sting always faded.

At any rate, Kiara didn't know any better.

What about her past? The comments the girl made about her childhood and her parents spoke of hurt. Rejection.

She wouldn't disregard Kiara, too.

The child was so lost.

Outspoken and ornery, but lost.

None of the scenery heading back to Stinking Creek registered as her thoughts nagged her.

Lia, wife of mine, you'd catch more sinners with honey.

Lia, her mama would always say, *if only you were less like us Joneses.*

How many times had people told her even a fool was considered wise when she held her peace? Why couldn't she shut up? Why'd she always blab the first thought popping into her prefrontal cortex?

Who was the worst sinner? Kiara or her?

Chapter Eleven

Kiara stared out her kitchen window like a kid waiting for the gates at Disney to open. Five o'clock Friday and the realtor's black Mercury pulled in front of the house. She could smell liberty from this bucolic hell. Freedom smelled like the fumes of subway trains mixed with oil and grease and a plethora of humans. It tasted like Schlacter's Deli and everything bagels and lox or New York pizza oozing cheese. It looked like this middle-aged woman, adjusting her dark blazer and straight skirt.

The car door gave a metallic clunk and heels clicked on the porch.

Kiara swung her door wide.

"Hi. I'm Maggie McLemon from An American Dream Realty." She held out her hand. "Sorry I'm late."

"I'm Kiara." A laugh bubbled up as she stuck out her hand to shake.

"What's so funny?" The realtor's firm grip helped Kiara refocus and regain her composure.

She shook her head. It didn't seem wise to tell this woman who had her life in her hands the name McLemon did not inspire confidence in the sale of her home.

"I had a showing. It resulted in a bidding war on a ranch house up in Jellico. The place isn't worth much more than a hundred grand and already it's at one-fifty. The market's been hot. Can't keep the inventory up."

"I'm glad to add to it. The cabin isn't much, but the barn's wonderful. It comes with a hundred acres."

Maggie surveyed the downstairs.

It took thirty seconds if Kiara timed it right.

"You need a railing installed." She indicated the stairway. "It won't pass inspection without it."

"But Bryce bought it."

Maggie already had climbed halfway to the loft. She faced Kiara who stood at the base of the stairs. "Did he have an inspection?"

Kiara shrugged. Who knew Bryce's thinking when he bought this dump?

"Not a lot up here. How many acres did you say?" Maggie called over the railing.

"One hundred."

She shook the flimsy rail cordoning off the upstairs' bedroom. "This needs to be reinforced. It's a hazard." She descended, her heels once more making smart little clicks on the stairs. "You'll also need to put up curtains and paint the loft." Maggie peeked into the bathroom.

"I love the tub," Kiara said. "I think it's original." An antique had to count for something.

Her realtor only tilted her head. She didn't have much of an opinion about her home. Not that Kiara regarded it as a great gift.

Except, it came with Bryce's love. She thumbed her ring as loss threatened her again.

"It is a good feature." McLemon made little noises as she surveyed the bathroom then headed for the kitchen. "Uh-oh."

Uh-ohs weren't good. "What's wrong?"

"You've got termites." Maggie kicked a rotted board on the threshold to the side porch.

"I'll buy spray." Kiara whipped out her phone to type herself a note.

Maggie shook her head. "You will need an exterminator and a handyman to repair this. No one will touch a place with termite issues

"How much will it cost?"

"Depends on the damage." She scanned the cabin. "How big's this place?" She swiveled her head scanning the house. "Can't be much more than a thousand square feet, can it?"

Again, Kiara shrugged. Her trapezius muscles were getting a good workout this evening.

"Termite control runs a thousand for a place this size. The eradication will add to it. I can't tell what the repairs will cost. A contractor will have to tear things out, see what's going on." She gnawed on the pencil she held for notetaking.

"I've got to sell this place and get out of here."

"That's what I'm here for." McLemon flashed a smile, then picked at the door's side jamb. "I've got a declarations page. You'll have to mention you had termites and had a termiticide solution installed. Again, it won't pass inspection unless you these critters are exterminated." Maggie pulled the wood off. An ant-like creature scurried.

Every nerve in Kiara's body jumped. Breaths came rapidly. In cockroach infested Manhattan, they never had insect issues. Of course, in Deliveranceville creepy-crawlies would infest. "Do you have any names I can ... I need ..." Kiara sank onto the couch. "Who do I call?"

"I've got information." She sat across from Kiara and pulled papers from her briefcase. "So, what are you hoping to sell this for?"

"We paid four-hundred-thousand a year ago, so I thought—"

Maggie shook her head.

Kiara plunged on. "We've got a gorgeous barn."

The head shake continued.

"Wait until you see—"

"I'll take photos, but even in top condition, this place, and it being in the middle of a crossroads to nowhere, is only worth one-fifty or two hundred."

"You haven't seen the barn."

"No one will pay four-hundred grand because the land contains a nice cowshed."

Bryce did.

"Plus, you have to make these repairs."

For the next hour, Maggie took photos while Kiara filled out paperwork. Business cards for inspectors and pest control and handymen littered the coffee table along with the yellow copies of the contract as Kiara walked Maggie to her car. Dark descended by the time the Mercury drove off.

Bryce.

Kiara needed him.

Back in the house, she slipped on her flannel pajama bottoms and pulled Bryce's white sweater over her head. She breathed. Citrus and strong arms surrounded her. The softness of cashmere caressed her.

She flipped through the business cards. An exterminator. She counted the cost. A handyman, how much? Paint? Curtains?

If she didn't receive a check from a sale soon, she'd need a job. Her agent once suggested making cards and T-shirts from prints of her work. She'd laughed at her then. Secure in Bryce's influence, Kiara fired her a week later. Bryce's connection had her art all across Manhattan and other cities.

Living here? She'd have to find galleries on her own.

She snorted. *How far have the mighty fallen?*

If art didn't support her, what could she do? Work the registers at Walmart? Minimum wage wouldn't keep her in coffee or oil paints.

Hunger drove her to the kitchen. The door between the end of the counter and the washer and dryer grabbed her attention. Bugs. A million bugs crawled in there. She closed her eyes and saw the termite mounds from the documentaries she'd watched. Never saw a mound around her house. Where'd they live?

She opened her eyes. They lived here. In her doorway.

She scurried like one of those flying ant-beasts back to the couch. Wrapping her arms around herself, hugging Bryce to her, she threw herself onto the sofa.

Her back itched. She swatted a termite.

Her stomach growled.

She swatted a bug off her arm. Scratched her leg.

Nothing's there. It's all in your head.

A termite crawled in her hair.

She pulled her feet under her and tried not to itch. The more she strove to find reason and sanity, the more she knew swarms of insects crawled up her legs and arms and hair.

This house—spiders, termites, mice and what else? She was getting out of here. When she picked up her truck yesterday, she'd stopped at Walmart and bought an inexpensive microwave and a mini-fridge and stored them in her studio. She'd sleep there until Bug-Man rid this hovel of termites.

Kiara stacked her folded blanket and pillow and threw toiletries into an overnight bag. Tomorrow the furniture store would bring her mattress. She'd ask Shann to move her bed frame to the barn, and she'd live where she should have gone in the first place.

Kiara lugged her sleeping supplies up Mount Everest to the barn.

Huffing at the doors, she remembered, she now had a truck. Trucks could drive up gravel paths and maneuver potholes. Hers had yesterday. What a dummy she was. For the rest of her junk, she'd use her truck.

Under the floor-to-ceiling windows, she scanned for critters, then made her bed. If she had to sleep on the floor, she'd at least see the stars or the fields and forests beyond the glass.

Now for food. She opened the fridge. A few bottles of Perrier and Diet Pepsi populated the shelves. Bubbly water wouldn't fill her stomach. Back in her kitchen, she had cans of soup. Cheese and crackers. Fruit. She'd restocked her fridge with her Save-A-Lot food once Rusty finished the repairs. The cabin had sustenance.

She'd planned to snack in her barn. Not live.

By now, pitch saturated the outside world. No moon rose, but she knew the path. She strode down the hill. Mentally, she re-tallied what she'd already poured into this place, a dump worth two-hundred K. Her truck cost ten thousand. The junk at Walmart, a supposedly cheap store, ran almost five hundred. A mattress without bedbugs? Now she'd have to shell out more than a thousand.

A rock rose up, nabbed her foot, and twisted it. Before she could blink, she'd landed on her rump.

"No!" Her mouth opened wide with her scream. She gulped sulfur. The stench in her face made her want to claw her eyes out. How could this reek burn?

She swiped her face and smeared her hands with an oily substance. Kiara rubbed them along the cashmere sweater.

In the darkness, a white streak wobbled away.

Spiders. Termites. And now — skunk.

Chapter Twelve

Once more Kiara stripped on her front porch. Her eyes wouldn't open all the way with the fetid skunk-spray burning them.

Oh, to crawl into the tub and wash away the burn.

She kicked aside the last of her garments. No way would she bring her putrid clothes into the hovel. Ms. McLemon would order her to hire an aromatherapist to cleanse the slum.

Kiara filled her tub with scalding water. Once in it, she scrubbed. Rinsed. Sniffed.

No patchouli from her artisan goat's milk soap wafted up. If anything, the stench intensified. Her eyes watered still. Scooping fresh water from the faucet, she bathed her eyes, working hard not to blink as warm water ran over them.

She licked her lips like a rabid animal.

Rabies?

New York City didn't harbor skunks. Animal control got rid of them because they carried rabies.

Could she catch it from skunk spray?

Edgar Allan Poe died of rabies.

She was going to lose her mind. Write awful short stories more frightful than Stephen King or Dean Koontz.

With a frenzy, she scrubbed again, but all she smelled was skunk. Did the water strengthen the odor? She examined her arms and legs. With no open wounds for germs to penetrate, would the soap kill the infection?

Handmade soap from all-natural ingredients bought in the boutique off Washington Square Park had no antibacterial elements.

Weren't rabies viral though? Her antibacterial lotion wouldn't threaten a virus.

If only she'd owned the antiseptic, germ-annihilating soap her stepmother favored.

Delia Mae would know about rabies.

At least, she'd know how to eliminate skunk reek. She'd know where Kiara could get shots. Weren't they injected into your stomach? She clutched her abdomen and felt foot-long needles jab her.

Out of the tub, she gave a cursory rub with a towel. Sniffed it. Cringed. This miasma had multiplied in the water. She had rubbed her skin red, burned it with water one degree below rocket fuel, and still, it stunk worse than sulfur.

She struggled to jiggle into her underwear. Having not thoroughly dried herself, the clothes tangled. Her leg caught in her yoga pants. The t-shirt wouldn't shimmy down.

At last, clothed in apparel not exposed to the stench, she stepped onto her porch. "Whew." Her head whipped back, and she held her nose as her eyes watered again. She slipped her feet into her Birkenstocks. How would she remove the stink from them? You couldn't wash shoes.

Would she still be able to smell this odor when rabies smote her? Who'd care for her when she lost her mind?

She jogged across the road. Banged on her neighbor's door. Remembered the fence. What if she let Youtee escape again?

Lights clicked on upstairs while she dashed to the gate and latched it. By the time she returned to the house, the kitchen light flipped on. The door creaked open.

Delia Mae stood in the light. Her hair, hung in long waves and framed her like an angel—a merciful angel. She stepped back. Put a finger under her nose. "Someone had an encounter of the polecat kind."

"What do I do? Washing made it—"

"Worse?" She nodded. "Wait on the porch." The door clicked behind her.

Kiara paced. She wanted a drink of water, something to remove the taste from her mouth. Wait. Did she have hydrophobia? One of her English classes said Poe—

No. She wasn't afraid of H$_2$O, just thirsty.

The door opened. Delia Mae stepped out with a bulging plastic bag. She clicked on a flashlight. "Do you have a washer and dryer?"

Kiara nodded.

"Good. We don't have to use mine. Beau'd pitch a fit if I brought this stank into the house. Let's go get you smelling as sweet as a baby's tush."

"Do I need rabies' shots?"

Delia Mae quit walking. "Rabies?" She laughed. Its mirth warmed the chilly night. "Law, girl, where that idea come from?" They resumed their trek across the road.

"Skunks carry the disease."

"Did this polecat bite you?"

"No."

"Then all you have to worry about is stinking worse than the creek."

By now they stepped onto Kiara's porch.

72

Delia Mae jerked back. "You got it good. What a bouquet."

"I left my clothes out here.

"Good thing." After shaking her head, she followed Kiara into the house and unloaded a two large brown bottles of hydrogen peroxide, a box of baking soda, a bottle of dish soap, and a green bottle of lemon juice. "Got mixing bowls and cups?"

Kiara gathered supplies from the kitchen.

Delia Mae measured and mixed then handed the liquid to Kiara. "Go bathe." She picked up the bottle of lemon juice. "Not part of the formula, but once you've washed and rinsed the solution off, pour some of this over your hair. Scrub and rinse. It won't eliminate the stink, but you'll be able to be within ten feet of another human within a year."

Kiara's hand clamped over her thumping heart.

"I'm teasing, girl." She gave Kiara a playful shove toward the bathroom. "Only six months."

Delia Mae's humor, like a popping bubble, raised the leaden weight in Kiara's core. Relief dizzied her.

"While you fumigate, I'll wash your clothes."

"Thanks." Kiara stepped toward the bath while Delia Mae walked toward the porch. "Wait."

Her neighbor stepped back into the house, leaving the door ajar.

"The white sweater. It's Bryce's. It ..."

Delia Mae's soft smile returned, and she tightened the belt to her robe. The action accentuated a trim, lovely figure.

"You know, you're a beautiful woman."

Delia Mae stepped back. Her lips parted as though to speak.

"Why don't you highlight your beauty? You've got a ton of years before you hit the old fogy era."

"The *Bible* says a woman's beauty shouldn't be outward adorning, like braiding hair or lots of jewelry."

Kiara chewed her lip. "Don't wear too much gold, then." *Clothes in the right size would do.*

She stepped toward the bathroom then stopped. "Please, put on apparel, no matter what your Bible says."

Delia Mae chuckled and waved Kiara off. "Go and bathe before I die from the vapors."

Kiara's jaw dropped. "You can—?"

"Joking," Delia Mae bent over the pile of fetid clothing. She straightened once more, holding the white sweater. "While you cleanse yourself, I'll toss all but this into the washer. I'll hand wash the sweater. It's nice wool."

"It's cashmere."

"I figured. It may not turn out as soft as it is now, but it'll be wearable. Go scrub before I catch the epizootics from smelling—"

73

Kiara's laughter chased the last of her tension. "Now, Delia Mae, you said this funk wouldn't make me sick."

She waved her hand and feigned slapping Kiara. "Go wash before you prove me a liar."

~~

Kiara sniffed. Skunk reek still hung in the cabin, but it had faded. Delia Mae had returned home and left behind the warm scent of drying cashmere from the sanitized sweater. The dryer clunked. With each tumble, fabric softener wafted through the kitchen.

By the termites.

After the skunk debacle, winged ants no longer terrorized her.

She rummaged for the frayed blanket and sheets in the bottom of the linen closet, the worn bedding she'd planned on using for drop cloths. Kiara spread them over the couch. She couldn't step outdoors at night again to retrieve her good bedding from the barn. One run-in with Pepé Le Pew was one more than she cared to experience.

She lay down.

So grateful had she been to her angel-neighbor, she agreed to go to Queenie's birthday party tomorrow.

They'd have food. Having forgotten to eat, her stomach recoiled.

She could handle an hour or two of the McGuffreys

Shann would be there.

She smiled, and her body relaxed.

Chapter Thirteen

L ia slipped off her robe and snuggled next to Beau.

"What time's it?" Beau grumbled like a train rumbling as it faded into the distance.

"About midnight."

He shifted. "What'd our neighbor ...?" He sniffed. His body stiffened against her, and he pulled back. "Had a run-in with a polecat?"

She murmured and nuzzled into him.

His body softened as he ran his hands through her hair. "Love your hair at night when it's all down and flowing." He burrowed into it. "God knew what He was saying when he called it a woman's glory."

"Sometimes I'd love to shear it, dye it into purple spikes."

He chuckled. "That's the second reason God gives for divorce. Adultery and baldness." Beau pulled her tighter and rested his cheek at the top of her head. His arms relaxed and soon soft snores wafted.

Lia closed her eyes. She curled against him and replayed Kiara's compliments. Sometimes looking godly seemed more frumpy than necessary. Cornie got away with highlights and shoulder-length hair. Of course, her sister fixed hair for a living. Cornie couldn't let herself go.

Let herself go? What does this say about me?

Beau shifted to his other side.

When'd she become so dowdy? As a teen, she loved fashion and tried to imitate her sister. Throughout the years, her ideals shifted. Half the women at her husband's church dressed like her. The other half, more contemporary. Beau never nagged any of them but Cornie.

Sleep tugged at her tired body, and she drifted off.

She jumped out of a birthday cake wearing a suit of armor. Her hair, covered with icing, hit Ma who'd been busy blowing out candles.

She bolted upright. Her eyes widened and her heart pounded.

Beau snored on.

Mom's birthday is tomorrow.

What did she need to do?

Cake?

Done.

Deviled eggs?

Yep.

Lia lay back down. Cole slaw ... corn pone ...

~~

Lia watched morning drift in with the fog. She rocked on the porch, sipped her tea and prayed. Across the road, lights popped on.

"Like clockwork, Lord," she whispered. "My neighbor keeps the same schedule I do." She rocked more and studied the cabin as morning light illuminated it. *What torments Kiara? Why am I drawn to the woman? We've got nothing in common.*

The roar of an ATV in the distance grew louder. Within minutes, its lights shone into her driveway.

Lia sipped her tea. Chris must've been hunting.

"Any luck?" she called when the front gate clicked open.

Youtee bounded onto the porch and nudged her hand, sloshing lukewarm tea.

"Mom." Chris leaned over and kissed her head. He settled on the edge of the steps and let his long legs dangle. If he grew another inch, they'd hit the ground—no need for steps. He leaned his back against her legs.

Lia played with his hair, praising God Chris didn't pull away and complain about her babying. Next year, he'd be gone to UT. Half her boys off in the world. *Lord, I hope I did a good 'nuff job raising them.*

She sipped the tea. "How'd hunting go?"

"Got two coons." He straightened. "At the last minute, me and ... " he paused and found the yard in front of him interesting. "I nabbed a passel of squirrels. Left 'em on the ATV. Figured you didn't want dead critters interfering with your prayer time."

"Nope. Nor sons."

"Right." Chris laughed easily. "I'll dress 'em out, and we can eat the squirrels at the barbecue. Mamaw loves her some fresh rodent."

"Who d'you hunt with?"

Chris looked away.

"I know that look. Are you still hanging out with Bobby James?"

Chris gave a slow nod.

"You know—"

"Ma." Chris held up his hand. "Bobby's been my best friend since we were five."

"He's on the wrong path. I hate to see him drag you down."

"I know I'm not the spiritual guru like Paul, but I've been praying for Bobby. How's he going to change his ways if every godly man avoids him?"

Lia lifted her cup to her lips to cover her smile. *Man.* She looked at

76

her boy, now more man than child. Lifting her head, she watched the shadows move in Kiara's window. "Be not deceived, evil communications corrupt good manners."

"Ma, Scripture also says, 'And how shall they believe in Him of whom they have not heard?' Daddy always says someone's got to be a light."

Again, Lia's eyes sought her neighbor, but nothing moved beyond the windows. "You said you intercede for him?"

"I have."

"I guess you can't pray and not be moved to reach out."

"That's what Daddy always says." Chris stood. "I'm gonna dress out my kill before the vultures find 'em." He kissed her head once more.

"Do you have a home game today?"

He nodded. "I'll be back by party time. Can't disappoint Mamaw." He stepped off the porch. "I'll leave you to pray for our neighbor. Don't become an atheist hanging with her."

"I'd never—"

"I ain't gonna be a druggie hanging with Bobby." At the gate he called over his shoulder. "By the way, Bobby, Larry, and R.D. are coming to the party."

Chris unlatched the gate. "Let's go, Youtee." The hound loped off after him.

She closed her eyes. Her heart quivered, and a shiver ran down her spine. *Pray for Kiara.* The thought was almost audible.

~~

Kiara studied the rotting side door while her tea boiled.

The kettle whistled. She poured the water and looked out the front window. An all-terrain vehicle pulled up to Delia Mae's house. She squinted. In the light of the four-wheeler, Delia Mae rocked on the porch. An early morning person, too.

Kiara swirled honey into the tea without taking her gaze off her neighbor. Whoever rode the ATV joined Delia Mae.

Loneliness stirred her stomach. She wanted to take her tea and sit with them.

About as likely as a bunny cuddling up with a rattlesnake.

Once she had phone and Internet, the ache would leave, and she wouldn't need Delia Mae.

Despite her neighbor's judgmental and opinionated attitude, Kiara liked her. Perhaps she found her doppelgänger. Dixon was Macie's mirror-twin. Maybe Delia Mae was hers?

For now, paint called. She'd finished *Manhattan Seraph,* and true to Macie's comments, the angel did resemble Shann's little sprite. She started her new one, *Stinking Morning*, created from her first photos from the Creek. The painting captured her move down here—dark and foreboding. Nothing like the mood of *Seraph*.

Once she finished, she'd paint the twins—kind of a Sir Thomas Lawrence's *The Calmady Children* with a Frankenthaler twist?

She needed a picture. She couldn't fathom either of the duo sitting long enough for her to capture their likeness on canvas.

To paint would mean treading up Mount Kilimanjaro to her barn. The road took her through skunk territory. Did she dare brave it? Light brightened the cabin. Perhaps Odie Cologne hid during the daylight like vampires and bats.

The skunk smell hung in the cabin but no longer burned her eyes. It became almost pleasant.

She picked up the white sweater stretched out on the counter and held it to her nose. The wet wool reeked—animal smelling, like sheep—not that she made a habit of sniffing sheep.

She didn't smell Bryce.

She clutched the pullover to her. Damp seeped through her T-shirt.

Bryce was gone.

She had to move on.

Once more she lifted the sweater and breathed in. She almost snorted. No trace of his scent remained.

Maybe she could buy his cologne?

She plopped onto the couch still clutching her piece of Bryce. Like Walmart would carry an Acqua di Parma scent at two-hundred bucks a bottle.

No sense crying over wet wool. She tossed the pullover aside. Today she'd move on.

No more moping. She lived on Stinking Creek. The new mattresses would be delivered between eight and ten this morning, and she'd move off this couch.

No wonder the Olivers didn't take the sofa when they ditched the Creek. The springs were ready to pop through like jack-in-the-boxes. Every evening she expected one of them to give way and eject her into the stratosphere like a fighter pilot.

At Queenie's birthday party, she'd snap photos of the twins, devise a happy painting and start her life over.

Life on the crik wouldn't last forever. Painting would make it pass fast.

~~

At eight a.m., a young guy dressed in jeans and a bright orange

Tennessee Volunteers T-shirt stood at her door. "Where do you want the mattresses?"

"Upstairs."

He returned to his truck.

I want it in this cabin and not the barn?

Kiara didn't know her own mind. Until this moment, she assumed she'd live out yonder past the medder—as Queenie called it. The cabin now seemed the right place.

I hope I'm not getting used to this place.

Ten minutes later, the mattresses settled, and the delivery confirmation signed, Kiara was free to roam. She climbed into her truck determined to work on *Stinking Morning*.

Instead of heading to her barn, her truck took her by Shann's cabin. A mile farther, she passed a small white church on the corner of Sheep Loop Road and Stinking Creek Road.

She needed a friend.

Somewhere in the stankin' crik lurked cell service. She'd find it.

Or get lost trying.

The road through the hamlet looked familiar, so Kiara had to be going toward the diner and thus to the land of cell towers. Fumbling through her phone, she searched her contacts. The truck swerved and cut far too close to the drainage ditch. She needed to write a letter to her senator or congressman or alderman, whatever an alderperson was, and convince the town to install shoulders. A person could kill herself texting and driving on roads without shoulders.

Then again, she could read the truck's manual and activate the Bluetooth.

Back on the road, Kiara tossed her phone onto the passenger's seat. A mile or so down the road, if she drove in the correct direction, Sugar Creek Diner should appear. She'd buy a coffee and a pastry and chat with Gina.

Within a minute or two, the eatery came into view. Cars and trucks packed the parking area. It appeared many people knew about this diner. Where'd they come from? Did they live like hobbits beneath the tree roots? She didn't remember seeing enough homes to house all these customers.

She edged her truck into the last space at the end of the lot, grabbed her phone, and hit Gina's number. It rang once, then disconnected.

Kiara studied the two signal bars of her phone. Must've been a bad connection. She dialed again. It rang once. Rang some more. Voice mail would click on with the next ring.

"Hello, Kiara."

Kiara knew this voice, and it wasn't Gina's. "Hey, Art. Guess I have too much time on my hands. I wanted to chat with Gina before the store opened."

"She's already there."

Bits of puzzle pieces shifted in Kiara's mind. A quick disconnect, a phone call nearly hitting voice mail, but the final key? Gina didn't take her phone to work.

Seeing as Gina King glued the contraption to her hand, and the phone grew out of her paw like her fingernails, her best buddy didn't want to speak to her!

"Sorry to bother you, Art. Gina couldn't talk last Monday. I hoped we'd talk today."

"Sorry you missed her." Art's voice sounded less stressed. His words mellowed. His voice became as smooth as Greek yogurt. In short, he sounded like Arthur King. "Can't talk now. I'm in the middle of one of my accounts."

"Tell Gina I'm doing fine. I'll have a house phone on Monday. I'll text her my number when I'm out and have a signal."

"She'd love a text." Art's voice emphasized the last word.

She'd love a text rather than a call? Not the Gina I know.

Kiara disconnected and climbed out of the truck. In the restaurant, she sat near a back window in a booth painted a happy red. Hordes crowded the other tables in the cozy dining room. Sugar Creek Diner sported red gingham curtains and repurposed antiques giving it a homey feel.

A low murmur of happy voices filled the restaurant. Everyone sat with a friend. She settled alone with her phone. *To be in New York.* Homesickness tempted her to pity her life.

Instead, Kiara flipped through her cell. Imani had texted four times. The same basic message, "Call me."

"Got news. Call."

"Miss you."

"Call."

Imani. With it being a little after eight, maybe ...

"What can I get you?" The waitress asked.

"Coffee. Do you have Danish?" *Did they know what a Danish was?*

"No Danish."

"A muffin?"

She shook her head. "Sorry."

"What do you recommend?"

"The biscuits."

"I'll take them with the coffee."

Unlike Queenie and Delia Mae's brother, Junior, Kiara understood every word the waitress said. Kiara lifted her phone and hit Imani's number.

On the first ring Imani picked up. "Key, I'm so glad you called, but I have to be—" She called to her boyfriend. "I'll be there in a second, Lance."

"I was afraid it was too early—"

"No. Perfect timing." Imani laughed. "Oh, girl, when you hear the news. You sitting down?"

"At a diner in Stanking Crik."

"Where? I thought—"

"It's a joke. The way these hicks talk. It's good to hear English again. Why should I be sitting?"

The waitress slid a coffee and a plate of biscuits swimming in white gravy.

Kiara's stomach churned. She looked toward the waitress, but another family caught her attention.

"Lance and I are getting married."

"Really?" Kiara straightened on the bench. "When? I need to make reservations."

"Can't. Doin' it right now."

"Now?"

"Not this minute of course, but you caught us—"

Kiara couldn't hear through the static. The phone disconnected.

Imani would call back.

Kiara, too hungry to care about a dropped call, cut into the biscuits and lifted a forkful to her mouth. The creamy gravy moistened the fluffy biscuits. Flavor exploded on her tongue.

Not bad. Maybe she could like Southern fare. She sipped her coffee. Oh my.

She sipped more of the first good brew since she moved.

Her phone rang.

"Sorry, Key. We were in the elevator. Lance's hailing a cab now. We're off to get married. Right this minute." Imani squealed.

"Sorry. You've called the wrong number. The person I hoped to speak with was my suave, reserved friend, not this happy child."

Merry laughter greeted her. "Ain't down for suave. I'm going to be a wife, and I've never been happier."

"Why the rush?"

"Last Sunday ... You're still sitting, right?"

"No, I'm dancing at a club."

"Lance and I converted. We're Christians."

"You're what?" The gravy-soaked biscuits stuck in Kiara's throat. "You?"

Had the end of the world come?

"Have aliens abducted you?"

Again, Imani's chuckle told Kiara their standard joke still amused her. "The cab pulled over."

81

Indistinct voices sounded through the phone.

"I have to be quick. We learned living together was wrong. Once we understood the truth, we made our decision. The pastor's going to marry us in Central Park. At the Ladies Pavilion. It was available at nine. Can you believe it?"

No. Married? A Christian?

"I'll call you after I'm Mrs. Greaves. Here's something else you won't believe—not only will we marry, I'll take his name."

"Excuse me. Where's my friend?"

Imani's laughter told Kiara her friend understood the joke.

"I won't have cell service later. I'll call on Monday when my house phone's installed."

"Key, I so want to talk. Can you imagine? Me? A bride. I'm even wearing white. Remember the lace dress Gina created?"

At the mention of Gina's name, shards of shattered glass sliced Kiara's heart. *Life went on without me.*

She gulped and steadied her voice. "You paid a fortune for it." Kiara saw the knee-length ivory lace against Imani's milk-chocolate skin. It made her glow, even without wedded bliss on the horizon.

"Never wore it, it was so expensive. Now, I know why I bought it. Why I saved it. It's my wedding dress." Imani's voice became muffled as though she were covering the mouthpiece. "Honey, I'm going to go. Call Monday."

Kiara disconnected.

Married. She eyed her ring.

Imani laughed when Kiara accepted Bryce's proposal.

"How bourgeois. How mainstream," Imani had said.

What shocked Kiara more? Imani's quick marriage or her conversion?

Chapter Fourteen

At two, Kiara left the barn and headed back to her empty cabin. Across the road, cars and trucks crowded the McGuffreys' driveway. They lined the side of the road, their tires straddling the drainage ditch. Smoke rose from grills and cheerful voices wafted from the McGuffrey yard.

So many happy family members. Who knew such a thing existed?

In her kitchen, she rummaged for lunch. Kiara pulled out yogurt and luncheon meat and bread. As she slapped boring cold cuts on dry bread, she stared out the window. Happy throngs ate juicy hamburgers at Queenie's party.

She couldn't crash a party of strangers. Even if she was invited.

She slid the plate onto her coffee table, but she didn't sit.

Laughing with neighbors beat solitude. She *could go.* Queenie had invited her. As did Delia Mae. How awkward would it be?

If she went, she'd imagine herself celebrating Imani and Lance's marriage. She'd attend their wedding by proxy.

After a quick shower, she fished her fashionably torn jeans from the clean clothes sitting in the dryer. She sucked in her gut and wiggled the zipper up. It had been fighting her during the last week or so, but after last night's stint in the dryer, they shrunk ten sizes. She wished she'd bought the full-length mirror she'd eyed in Walmart. She craned her neck to view her legs and hips. Hopefully, the pants would resume their shape and let her breathe.

She slipped on her favorite tank top, but this, too, strained across her torso. She flexed her biceps and stuck out her chest. *Hulk Rafferty at your service.*

Gotta cut down on the chow or eat only rabbit food.

Stripping off the uncomfortable clothes, she wriggled into a pair of leggings and a tunic. She slipped on her Fair-Trade Aztec socks and tied on her army boots. Was it too warm for all of this? If so, she didn't have far to travel to find a cooler outfit.

With an inhale, she stepped onto her porch and eyed her neighbor's yard. Hesitant steps carried her across the bridge. She paused, one last time, next to her brand new An American Dream Realty sign posted the night before.

Kiara crossed the road. Her breathing came hard. *Why the nerves?*

So many strangers.

"Hey, come on in." A young man about Delia Mae's sons' ages waved her through the gate.

Once in the yard, Queenie stood and wagged her hand. "Where jew bean? Party's gone on fer hours.

Kiara didn't try to hide her grin.

Queenie wore a tiara. A florescent pink feather boa draped across her shoulders, and a sash proclaiming her a birthday girl hung beauty-pageant style across her chest. Queenie's smile accentuated every crease on her face. Her eyes shone like a child meeting Minnie Mouse. Such innocence.

She and Gina and Imani mocked the naïveté when they'd seen it in Manhattan. However, here, on Delia Mae's mom, it looked like royalty. Made Kiara want to be more like her neighbors.

"Why ya lookin' like a mule at a new gate? Ain't you seed a party afore? Come. Jine me." Queenie searched the crowd and signaled someone like a monarch summoning her court. "Chris, fix are naybar a mess o' vittles." She sat and patted the orange canvas chair with a monogrammed T next her.

"Anything in particular you want?" the young man asked.

Kiara glanced at the buffet table and back at Chris. "Anything. I'm hungry enough it all appeals."

He hurried off.

Kiara turned to Queenie. "Congratulations."

"Jist a moment." Queenie held up a finger. She leaned toward another woman who spoke to her.

Chris returned and handed Kiara a paper plate.

"Here you go." He'd heaped it with corn bread, baked beans and barbecued chicken.

"G'won and et it 'fore it gits cold," Queenie said.

Kiara dug into the food with the plastic fork, then remembered Queenie expected her to pray. She bowed her head. The wonderful smell wafted up. Corn bread. Schlacter's Deli made it sweet and gooey—more cake than bread. This one had no butter, but if it was anything like Schlacter's, she could manage.

She lifted her head. "Happy birthday, Queenie."

The woman beamed and preened. She sat taller in her chair and lifted her chin. "I lived a good life." She reached up to another woman who bent to give the birthday girl a hug.

Kiara smiled and picked up the corn bread. She could almost taste it before she took a bite. She studied Queenie. "You've got to be good people. Everyone here looks so happy to celebrate with you."

"God blessed me rale good." She leaned toward Kiara. "Quit waving thet bread. Eat hit. Lia makes good pone."

Kiara bit.

Queenie watched as though waiting for the delighted visage of a woman biting into pâté de foie gras. Or at least, a cannoli from Patty's Cakes. "Delicious ain't hit?"

Kiara couldn't answer. The corn bread crumbled down her throat. She choked and tried to muffle her coughing. She eyed Queenie.

Did the older woman notice?

Kiara waved her hand in front of her face.

"Hit go down the wrong pipe?" Queenie asked.

Kiara gasped and struggled not to spray Queenie with the dry, bland and crumbled bread. She wanted to spit, but no one would appreciate being sprayed with sawdust masquerading as corn bread.

Liquid. She needed something wet to wash it down. Chris had brought her nothing to drink. She gulped, and a fragment of the unexpectedly dry corn bread inched down her gullet.

"My Lia knows how to cook."

Kiara cleared her throat, or tried to. She settled for nodding. She'd eaten enough of Delia Mae's cooking to know the woman could find her way around a kitchen. Obviously, she forgot to put sugar in this.

And shortening.

And whatever else made bread stick together.

Her cheeks heated and her face had to be turning as red as her hair. Kiara coughed and covered her mouth with a napkin. As discretely as she could, she spit out the corn bread and crumbled the wadded paper in her fist.

"Somethin' wrong?" Queenie's wide eyes looked worried.

"Not like," she coughed. "New York's corn bread."

"We knowed how to bake hit here."

With another swallow, another molecule of the bread cleared her throat. The baked beans looked moist, perhaps they would serve as water. She lifted a forkful.

The wet and sweet beans slid down, washing away the crumbly bread. Once certain she wouldn't choke to death, Kiara stood. "I need something to drink."

"No. Set." Queenie gave her sovereign wave once more, and a younger, shorter version of Chris darted to her side.

"Yes, Mamaw?"

"Paul, git are naybar some sweet tea."

"I can get it," Kiara said.

"I'll do you," Paul said.

Kiara leaned back, her mouth agape. Hopefully all vestige of the bread had been swallowed, and no one could see it lingering in her fly-catching trap. She lost something translating Paul's comment. A preacher's son wouldn't be lewd, would he?

He'd dashed off, and no one blinked. Like Delia Mae's 'I don't care to' uttered when they first met, 'I'll do you' couldn't mean the same thing as in Manhattan where people spoke real English.

She nibbled at the food on the plate on her lap. Aside from the bread, it was typical McGuffrey. Tasty.

Paul returned with a red SOLO cup brimming with ice and tea. She reached up to take it, and her paper plate slipped off her lap. It landed upside down on the ground.

She leaped to her feet. "I'm so sorry."

Queenie flipped her hand as though swatting away a fly. "No use cryin' over spilt milk. We got us plenty o' cows a'crying to be milked, and they cry enuff tares fer all o'us."

Kiara blinked. Why were cows crying? What tore for all of us?

She stooped and scraped wet beans coated with pebbles and grass bits onto the plate. The bread, to her surprise, held together. She plopped it on top. The barbecued meat had to have been magnetized—stones, clay and insects clung to it. Grease and barbecue sauce coated her fingers.

"Better git to the kitchen, an' warsh yer hands." Queenie nodded toward the house.

On the porch, Kiara dumped the food into a trash bin. Guests crowded the yard, sitting in little clusters. She hadn't seen the dog. Maybe Youtee was leading another city slicker on a romp through the woods.

She scanned the yard for Youtee.

Off, behind the trampoline behind the house, a boy—she thought it was Chris—bucked Dixon on his back like a wild bronco. Youtee darted back and forth licking Chris's face. Their laughter carried through the chatter in the yard. Chris bumped Dixon off. Both of them fell to the ground. They held their stomachs and laughed.

At the house, she let herself into the kitchen, and wriggled her fingers in front of Delia Mae. "Mind if I clean up? Got food all over."

Delia Mae nodded to the sink. "Betina," she spoke to the woman who was adding mayonnaise to a potato salad. "I put plenty in the taters already. There's more than enough mayo."

"They was a mite dry." At the rate Betina scooped the mayo, they'd all need heart stents before the party ended.

"Where's the lady's room?" Another woman dashed into the kitchen.

Delia Mae pointed down the hall.

Kiara let the kitchen water run as she pumped soap onto her hands. "Sorry. I dropped my plate."

"We got plenty more food," Delia Mae said.

"I'll put this on the table." Betina lifted the bowl of potato salad swimming in white and pushed open the screen with her hips. The door clunked behind her.

"I can't guarantee the quality of the taters. Once Betina gets to working the kitchen, all sense disappears." Delia Mae handed Kiara a towel as she shut off the water. "You smell pretty good this morning. No polecat rank. Did the sweater turn out okay?"

"Doesn't smell like skunk."

"That's a good thing."

She leaned against the sink. "Doesn't smell like Bryce, either."

Delia Mae arched her brow.

"It had been a comfort." Kiara twisted her ring. "I could wear it and almost think Bryce was in the room with me."

Delia Mae took Kiara's fingers in hers. "I understand. Smell evokes powerful emotions. When you're lonely," she lifted Kiara's hand, "look at the sparkle. Think of the gleam in his eyes. Recall the shimmer of his proposal."

Kiara nodded and offered a thin smile. "It's okay. His scent was a vapor—make believe. It's time to move on."

"You do need to grieve."

Kiara nodded.

Another lady, about Delia Mae's age burst into the kitchen. She hurried to the cabinets. Her short, spiked hair stuck out behind her as though blown in the wind. "Need more tea." She dug through the cabinets as if she owned the kitchen. The lady pulled out a cardboard container of iced tea. She shoveled heaping scoops into a plastic jug.

"Rosalyn, not so much," Delia Mae reached to stop her.

"No. The last batch was too bland." She grabbed the sugar and added it to the sweet mix. "This'll be good."

Kiara and Delia Mae waited in silence as Rosalyn added water and ice.

No sooner had she dashed out of the kitchen then Beau popped his head in. "You coming out, Lia? We need a hostess." The door slammed behind him.

Kiara looked at her neighbor. "Was he your husband?"

Delia Mae nodded.

"He's a handsome man." Kiara drilled her finger to the bottom of her chin. "I recognized him by the dimple from Macie's portrait."

"I love the dimple." Delia Mae didn't sound like a woman in love. Her voice sounded resigned. Tired.

87

Kiara studied Delia Mae. She didn't want to leave, but no words of comfort came to mind. "I've been rude."

"How so?"

"I never thanked you for yesterday. Your help eased a dreadful day."

"You've got the place on the market, I see. Didn't notice the sign at midnight."

Kiara nodded. "By the time An American Dream Realty left, it was darker than ... Hades." *Why did I need to change my words? Getting conservative in my old age.* She searched Delia Mae's face.

Sympathy still shone in her eyes.

She had so much to do, and still, she listens to me. "Then it turns out I've got termites and repairs, not from the bugs alone, but banisters and painting. I guess Bryce hadn't checked everything out before he bought the place. I'm not sure how I can fix it enough to sell and have a down payment for an apartment."

"Shann's a good hand with wood."

"I've already intruded on your lives enough."

"Ma," a teen called through the open window. "Mamaw wants to know when we're having the cake."

"Soon." Delia Mae leaned against the counter and inhaled a long, slow breath.

"Are you sure I can't help you do something?"

Delia Mae straightened and shook her head. "No. They can all wait." Her eyes sought Kiara's. "Shann doesn't mind helping. He works for a lot of people. Are finances going to be a problem?"

Kiara shrugged. "My art sells well, but it's been a while since I received a check. Know anyone hiring?"

"Could you teach?"

"I'd rather not, but it would beat starving. Or getting an EBT card."

"Monday, you can hit the school boards and put in an application."

"Monday I'll be sitting around waiting for the phone people to come."

"Then Tuesday. Until then, let me pray with you."

With me? Kiara studied her feet. For whatever reason, she couldn't meet Mrs. McG's eyes. Prayer wouldn't hurt. If any god existed, she wanted him or her to help. Doing things on her own wasn't working. Perhaps the prayer would align the universe in her favor. She smiled. *This lady's turning me agnostic.*

Delia Mae took Kiara's hands in hers.

Kiara trembled at her touch but didn't pull away.

"Lord, You know what Kiara needs for work, support, and finances. We put her into Your hands and trust You as the Father of all, the God

Who created us, Who loves us, and supplies all our needs. Having made the universe, You've never stinted us. Thank You. "

The words warmed Kiara with comfort—a rarity since Bryce died.

No.

If she honestly assessed her life, comfort had evaded her long before then.

Kiara never experienced this peace—at least not since her grandmother died twenty years ago. "Thank you, Delia Mae."

Delia Mae pulled her into a hug. "Now, head on out there and get yourself some grub unadulterated by our red clay." She released her.

~~

Lia picked up the cake in its carrier and placed it on the table. She rubbed her pounding head and stepped down the hall. In the bathroom, she grabbed the bottle of Advil and shook out two.

"Aunt Lia." Dixon swung open the bathroom door.

"Dixon, knock. What if I was—?"

"Look what I found." He held out cupped hands and opened them. A winged insect like a green tree leaf fluttered to the floor.

Lia jumped back. She should've expected a critter to escape from his cupped fists.

"Wait." She plopped the pills into her mouth, filled a cup with water, and sipped.

"What is it?" Dixon asked.

Lia bent over and scooped the critter up. It wriggled its long antennae and tickled her palms. "A katydid."

"Ain't they supposed to be in trees?"

"They're going to die now that fall's coming."

"Gross."

Lia handed the katydid back to Dixon. She cupped her hands over his. "Be gentle, but take it outside."

He scooted into the kitchen nearly knocking one of Chris's friends on the way.

"Mrs. McG? Any other tea. The stuff on the table's almost rock candy."

She'd had enough. "The box is there." She pointed to the cardboard carton of tea Rosalyn left on the counter. "Be a dear. Make some." She headed upstairs to her bedroom. The cake could wait. The whole party could wait. If she tried any harder, she'd scream at the next person needing her attention.

Closing the blinds, she lay down. Every nerve jangled. Arteries pulsed in her temples. Her head thrummed like the bass playing from car radios.

89

No sleep. Too many demands. God was growing her and stretching her character. He was letting patience have her perfect work, so she'd be perfect and entire.

Lord, help me to be holy as You are. Let me be as flawless as You. The Lord had patience. What was wrong with her?

Lord, help me to love with forbearance and with all lowliness and meekness.

Why couldn't she be what she was supposed to be? If she tried any harder ...?

She had to. If God asked her, she could.

Chapter Fifteen

Kiara headed to the buffet line. When she picked up her plate, her gaze grazed the tool shed. Two teenaged boys stood behind it. A dark-haired boy cupped a cigarette in his hand. He took a puff and handed it off to his buddy who stood with his back to Kiara.

She knew the posture.

How dare they get high at Delia Mae's? Good neighbors deserved respect and not a drug bust.

Kiara strode toward them. "Excuse me."

The original smoker jerked his head. The other took another toke, dropped the joint, then ground the butt under the sole of his boot. He was about the height of Delia Mae's boys with hair short on the sides, a small poof on top like theirs.

He better not be one of the McGuffreys. "You have nerve. How can you smoke dope here?" She crossed her arms. "These are good, religious people and deserve respect."

"We're not smoking weed," the boy facing her said. "Don't jump to conclusions."

She made a show of sniffing the sweet-scented air. "I suppose this aroma comes from tobacco?"

"Homegrown." His strong grin mocked. Brown eyes squinted as they dared her to contradict him. "You Yanks ain't never smelled home-grown 'backer."

The boy with his back to her laughed as he scuffed his foot over the extinguished joint.

Kiara grabbed his shoulder. "You. Look at me."

He met her eyes. He had a long face and a beard. His eyes squinted in mockery. Not a clean-shaven McGuffrey.

She'd never seen these two before. Her shoulders softened, and her breath came easier. "I'd suggest you ditch the dope or leave. If I catch you again ..."

They shifted their eyes and bowed their heads.

Kiara squared her shoulders with pride. She could be as good and righteous as Delia Mae.

"Hey, Bobby." Chris strode to where the three stood. "Howdy, Miss Kiara."

Her shoulders sagged again. She didn't cow these hoodlums. Chris did.

"See you met one of my best buds." Chris tilted his head. "This here's Bobby." He nodded toward the boy who'd faced Kiara. "We've been friends since—"

"We were five," Bobby said.

He turned to the bearded boy. "I haven't met you yet."

"Leo Marsh."

"Good to meet you. Y'all want to ride?" Chris asked. "Cake's not coming out for a while. Not sure where Ma got to."

"Sounds good," Bobby said.

"Yeah," Leo agreed.

"Tell Ma I'll be back before too long." The three strode off together.

Bobby squinted at Kiara. Every line of his face hardened. The arch of his brow and coldness of his eyes cursed her. As though to punctuate his attitude, he spit on the ground.

Kiara shuddered. She didn't like these boys. *Why is Chris friends with them? Is he like them?*

The ATVs roared to life, and Kiara returned to the buffet table. Here she bypassed the corn bread and scooped baked beans onto her plate. The squeal of kids jumping on the trampoline serenaded her. Innocence sounded so much happier than cynicism. She studied the gleeful, jumping children. When she shot their photos, she had to nab the purity and joy leaping before her.

"Someone's lost in dreamland." Shann nudged her.

"Do they ever tire out?"

Shann studied the direction Kiara looked. "When they do, no one wants to be near them. They become changelings."

"Dad." Dixon leaped from the trampoline and raced toward them. "Come jump with me." He grabbed his father's hand and yanked.

"I'll catch you later," Shann said as Dixon jerked him forward. He trotted off to join the kids. Before climbing up onto the trampoline, he turned.

Kiara caught his look. *Innocence lives in adults.* She waved, but shyness overtook her, like a middle schooler and her first crush.

Turning back to the buffet, Kiara searched for something other than beans. Most of the meat was gone, but one plate still held plenty. She took a few pieces of barbequed something. She'd find out what it was when she ate. Bypassing Betina's liquid potato salad, Kiara poured a glass of fresh iced tea.

A man she thought was Junior now sat in her orange chair near Queenie. An older fellow pulled up another seat. He held Queenie's hand, and his eyes focused on her, the adoration obvious. A small smile played at his lips. His eyes danced. He leaned in toward her as though too much space separated them. The man had to be Cletus Emmett Jones, Sr.—or Emmett, as people called him. Why did these Southerners have first names if they used the middle ones?

Had Bryce loved her like Emmett did Queenie? She hoped so.

Toward the back of the house, two women occupied a picnic table. Kiara headed toward it. "Mind if I join you?"

"Not at all." A middle-aged woman cleared away clutter from a spot next to her. Sunlight daubed her shoulder-length dark blonde hair, its layers highlighted with a golden blonde. The strands danced in the light breeze. "I'm Lia's sister Cornie McGuffrey." She held up a hand to the other woman as though to stop comments. "Cornie beats Cornelia, my given name. Queenie's my ma."

Delia Mae's sister? Not only did she style her hair, Cornie wore makeup and a trendy sundress. It had sleeves and a high neckline, but looked beautiful. The blue of the dress highlighted the gray of Cornie's eyes. In them, Kiara saw Delia Mae. Her sister even wore jewelry—a simple necklace and dangling earrings.

"I'm Kiara." She placed her plate on the cleared spot and clambered over the bench to sit. She speared a piece of meat. *Chicken?* She nibbled. *No. A mite greasy.*

"If you're Delia Mae's sister, why do you have the same last name?" She bit again. *Must be duck.*

"Married Beau's brother, Jimmy. By day, he's an elder at Sheep Loop Church. By night, shift manager at Thermador."

Kiara widened her eyes. "You don't—" How could she say she didn't look like a frump and be polite? "Don't look like Delia Mae."

She found it hard to imagine this pretty woman as Delia Mae's sister and, from her linguistic skills, Queenie's daughter.

"Nope. She's the religious one in the family. Takes everything to the extreme. Always has, even as a child. When we played house or school, no one wanted to let her be the mother or teacher. She expected more from us than the real adults. In college, if she earned an A-minus ... "

College? Okay. Guess I assumed wrong about her education.

Cornie continued. "As the years have gone by, Lia becomes more and more pious, like she's trying to earn her way into heaven."

The woman sitting across from Cornie chuckled. "Like anyone can."

Cornie nodded at the woman who'd spoken. "This here's our cousin on Jimmy's side. Samantha who used to be pure McGuffrey before she ditched us, married Junior. She got all women's lib on us and hyphenated her name. Samantha McGuffrey-Jones."

"I couldn't desert my clan," Samantha said. "I wanted to start our own town—McGuffreyville. Cornie voted it down."

Kiara put her fork down while the women laughed at their banter. This intermarrying sounded ... She closed her gaping jaw.

"Sounds inbred, don't it?" Cornie laughed like Delia Mae—just a bit lighter, more carefree. "Got to seem strange to a Northerner who's heard all those *Duck Dynasty* stories. We're a small community. Not much to pick from." She nodded at Samantha. "Why else'd anyone marry Sammy."

They laughed good naturedly.

"You're brave," Samantha said.

"Why?" Kiara picked up a bone and nibbled. Fingers worked better than the plastic utensils.

"Didn't think Northerners ate squirrel." Samantha nodded at the bone in Kiara's hand.

Kiara quit chewing. Her mouth went dry. She struggled to swallow and took a sip of the crystalized sweet tea. Grimaced.

"Your face says you're shocked," Cornie said.

Kiara licked her lips. "Yes and no." She swallowed and shoved the cup away. "Someone got carried away with the sugar."

"Had to be Rosalyn. The sugar queen would melt in the fog." Again Cornie laughed.

"I think she's made of sucrose," Samantha said.

"I ate squirrel?" Kiara looked at her plate. Only bones remained of her meat. "I thought I ate duck."

"Ain't duck hunting season. Chris shot them this morning. Good thing Lia won't let him cook up coon," Cornie said. "Them things is et up with germs, as my mama says."

Should I stick my finger down my throat? Kiara waited for her stomach to protest. It didn't.

Cornie half rose. "We should go see if Lia needs anything." She waved to a young woman. "Hey, Jorie, come here." She looked down at Kiara. "Jorie's about your age. You haven't met her yet, have you?"

Kiara shook her head but her stomach tightened. She didn't want to meet Jorie.

Chapter Sixteen

The young woman, with hair the color of corn, walked toward Kiara's group. Its poof with mall bangs reminded Kiara of the pictures she'd seen of her mom as a teen. Had she styled her curly hair with a Weedwhacker or blown-dried with a leaf blower?

"Kiara, this is Shann's girl, Jorie." Cornie picked up the last of the paper waste on the table. "Samantha and I will catch you later. We have to irritate Lia with our help." The two women headed toward the house.

"Hello." Jorie's face reddened. "Don't listen to them about Shann and me. We're more friends than sweethearts." She scanned the yard as though searching for him. "It's everyone's wishful thinking."

Kiara's abdominals relaxed. *Not his girlfriend.*

"Shann says you're an artist?" Her voice was a rich alto like waterfalls over mossy rocks. Soft and soothing.

"Yes."

Jorie climbed over the bench and sat across from Kiara.

Kiara waited, expecting more from the woman. The silence hung like lowering clouds over them. She had to speak and fill the space with something. "I'm fortunate because I can make my living with it." *Sort of. With Bryce's help.* "Though I need to find galleries down here."

A few more seconds crawled by. *Seconds? Perhaps a millennium.*

"What do you paint?" Jorie asked.

"Abstract." *My answer's going to dead-end the conversation.*

"Do you paint like any particular artist?"

Kiara arched a brow. Jorie had answered without a deadly pause. "Have you ever heard of Helen Frankenthaler?"

"I'm not familiar with her. Is she like de Kooning or Hofmann?"

"You know those artists?"

She nodded.

Kiara tapped her foot and looked around for Macie. Maybe Dixon found a tree frog. Would Cornie and Samantha come back? Anyone who could carry this conversation. "Did you study art?"

Jorie nodded. "I majored in fine art at ETU. After two years, I switched to a dual major in math and accounting."

"What's ETU?" *Had to be a GED program or something.*

"East Tennessee University."

Kiara held back a sigh. *Give me something to talk about, please.* "Math and art are a strange juxtaposition." Kiara paused.

Jorie didn't fill in the silence.

Did this girl know the word juxtapose? "They're a strange mix. All the artists I know have hideous skills with numbers. Can't wrap their right brains around it."

Jorie smiled. Her full upper lip formed a deep curve. If her mouth wasn't so wide, her lips would be heart shaped. Like her face. A little makeup and a hairstyle, she'd be gorgeous.

A lesson on conversation would enhance her personality. It reminded Kiara of wet wool.

"The only artists I know who are good with numbers are graphic artists like M.C. Escher." If Kiara moved the conversation toward the mathematical elements, it would encourage Ms. Harpo Marx to talk. "Are you familiar with him?"

Jorie's brow crinkled. "Isn't he the artist who drew his hand drawing a hand?"

"You know a lot about art."

Jorie smiled.

Kiara waited for a reply.

Only the wind whistled through the trees

Kiara glanced toward the house. Perhaps she could help wash dishes. Working took less effort than trying to make this woman to talk.

Perhaps she could go home.

Jorie toyed with Kiara's rejected cup of tea.

"Pure sugar," Kiara said more to break the silence than to criticize.

"Has to be Miss Rosalyn's brew."

"Would put me in a diabetic coma if I drank it." Kiara paused, waited for a reaction from Jorie. "Why did you change majors?"

"By a boring set of circumstances. You wouldn't be interested."

Kiara thought Jorie would move into her explanation, but silence settled over them again.

I wouldn't have asked if wasn't interested. Kiara would move the conversation along if it killed Jorie. "Ever since I was a little kid, I wanted to paint. My mother said I came out of the womb with my digits coated with finger paints." She wriggled her fingers as though still covered.

Oops. Bits of paint clung to them. Kiara folded her hands in her lap.

"I was only good enough to teach it," Jorie said. "Teaching terrified me. I'm not much of a talker."

"No." Kiara winked.

Jorie laughed—a sound as rich and soothing as her speaking voice. "Math gave me more employment options." She tilted the cup and frowned at the crystalizing tea.

96

Silence clawed, again. It scratched against Kiara's psyche. Seeing as she'd never interact with this silent lady after today, she could afford to be rude and prod into her personal life. "Like what?" Kiara studied the grass struggling to pop up in the graveled driveway.

"I'd hoped to marry a pastor and keep our church's books." Jorie leaned toward Kiara.

Perhaps she *would* talk.

"I never guessed I'd end up with H&R Block. Turns out I love numbers more than children."

"Me, too," Kiara said. "Kids aren't my thing."

Jorie smiled.

Kiara tapped her fingers on the table. After a few seconds, she moved to stand.

"My minister, who needs a treasurer wife, hasn't shown up yet." Again, Jorie flashed her smile, one that would melt Antarctica.

Kiara sat once more.

"Hey, Miss Muffet." Macie came running.

Never had Kiara been happier to see a kid. Macie would fill in the long spaces in the conversation.

"Muffet?" Jorie asked.

Kiara pulled at her dreadlocks. "Macie thinks I look like a Muppet. Only she mixes them up with Little Miss Muffet."

The child tugged Kiara's hand. "Come jump with us."

"I'd love to." She turned to Jorie. "Join us."

"I couldn't. My dress. It'd be unseemly to jump."

Kiara stood. She tilted her head and squinted to feign evil eyes at Jorie. "The dress is long. It's loose. You're going if I am."

Jorie shook her head.

"Daddy's jumping." Macie tugged Kiara's free arm harder.

"Okay. Guess a few jumps wouldn't hurt." With a shy grin, Jorie walked with them toward the gleeful leapers.

"Daddy, our turn." Macie didn't need the trampoline. She bounced as though the ground tossed her.

"Afternoon, ladies." Shann hurtled into the air then plopped with a few bounces onto the springy surface, pulling Dixon with him. "Let's give the women space." Shann held Dixon's hand and steadied him as the child dismounted.

"You're quitting?" Jorie lifted her large eyes toward Shann.

This girl's got it bad. Kiara looked from Jorie to Shann. He didn't return her adoration. Kiara'd seen the reaction with Gina toward Bryce before her friend met her husband Art.

"Need a lift?" Shann offered his hand to Kiara.

"No, I'm good. You can help Jorie. In a dress, it's difficult." Kiara climbed onto the trampoline.

"Here you go." Shann held Jorie's waist and hoisted her.

While watching the two, Kiara could imagine his large hands encircle her own waist. Their imagined pressure warmed her, and her belly burned. *No. Not thinking sex. Never with Shann.* Still, lust pounded in her chest.

Bryce. I need to focus on Bryce. She couldn't weasel her way into Shann's life with Bryce gone a month.

With Jorie loving him.

Shann lifted Macie up. The two tottered to Kiara.

"Ready?" Shann asked.

Glee shivered up from Kiara's stomach. How long had it been since she let loose?

"Set. Go." Macie squealed and pummeled her legs against the trampoline.

The three ladies jumped. Gained height.

Jorie's shoulders and back remained rigid for the first few leaps.

"Go, girls," Shann cheered. "Touch Heaven for me."

Almost like a rag doll, Jorie's joints loosened, as though Shann told her she could have fun.

Within minutes the three of them squealed. Macie attempted a split in the air. Jorie's hand grasped her chest, and she laughed. Kiara pumped her arms to gain height.

Freedom.

Had Kiara ever been so happy? So free?

"Wow, Macie. You never jump so high with me," Shann called.

As though Shann's words poked a hole in the helium buoying her, Macie collapsed on the trampoline's surface. She splayed like a marionette whose strings had been cut.

Jorie and Kiara fell—Jorie next to Macie, Kiara halfway on top.

"Don't suffocate my daughter," Shann called. "She's got chores to do, yet."

As her laughter subsided, Kiara rolled off the child.

Giggles stole Kiara's air and made breathing difficult. At last the three girls lay still on their backs while clouds tinged blue floated above them beyond the limbs of the nearby tree.

Macie sat up. "Can y'all do a flip?"

"Not me." Jorie scooted to a seating position. "Staying on my feet as I jumped is as far as my skill goes."

Kiara sat up. "I used to be able to." She reached into her pocket and pulled out her phone. "Hold this for me." She handed it to Macie and chucked her chin. "I brought it to snap pictures of you and your brother."

Shann reached toward his daughter. Grabbing her by her arms, he helped Macie off.

Macie held onto the sides of the trampoline, her eyes wide. "Why do you want pictures of me?"

"'Cause it's my turn to paint your portrait."

The child clapped and jumped. "Daddy, she's going to paint me."

Shann ran his hand over her head. "As long as it's a portrait and not your body."

Macie pouted.

Jorie's mouth gaped.

"Silly, Daddy. You don't paint *on* people."

While the trio chattered nearby, Kiara balanced herself on the center of the trampoline. She jumped. Aimed for the stratosphere until she floated in the air. Kiara tilted her head. The limbs from the giant, leafy tree arced over her. She aimed to reach them and pluck a leaf for Macie.

"Yeah, Miss Muffet."

"Go, Kiara. Go."

"Be careful. Don't hurt yourself."

When she was little, she wanted to walk on clouds. They looked so fluffy. She told her mom she'd use them for her bed. With each thrust of her legs, Kiara aimed to stroll with the angels. The cheers became indistinct as Kiara strove to flop on top of a big, ol' cumulus.

To keep her equilibrium while she flipped, Kiara needed to spot. She found Shann and focused on him.

His eyes, startling blue at any height, locked on her.

With a cloud-reaching leap, she extended her arms, tucked her legs, and rotated. The world spun like new love.

Lasted seconds—about as long as love.

Kiara didn't stick her landing and flopped on her back onto the trampoline. The clouds swirled over her. Tree branches twirled. Although Kiara lay still, and the trampoline quieted, her stomach jumped. Nausea swelled. Maybe the squirrel she'd eaten by mistake was what it sounded like—disgusting—and not what it tasted like, pretty darn good.

How'd she grow too old to play? Would she turn into her mother?

Twenty-five wasn't old, though. She was young enough to avoid being Mom.

"You okay?" Shann leaned over and held out his free hand.

Macie clutched his other one.

Jorie stood behind the duo.

Kiara struggled to sit up. "I've become a doddering old lady. Get me my walker."

"If you're old, I'm ancient," Jorie said.

"Never." Shann shook off his daughter's hand and offered both to Kiara.

Who did he speak to? Her or Jorie? Kiara scooted across the trampoline and let Shann help her down. His strong hands grasped her waist.

His grip didn't feel like she'd imagined when he lifted Jorie onto the trampoline.

It was better. Warm. Secure. Doted on.

Had Bryce ever made her feel this?

Her foot caught on a rock as she hit the ground. She fell into Shann's chest and had a clear view of his amazing eyes.

His long beard tickled like cashmere. It smelled of grills and barbecue and offered a nest for her to settle in, at the least, to nestle against.

She stiffened, then pulled away. "Thank you, my knight."

His smile made her want to cling to him.

She had to remember Jorie. The McGuffreys liked her. Shann belonged to her.

Chapter Seventeen

Lia climbed out of bed. Her headache had settled. Her head pulsed beneath her tightly wound bun. She undid the elastic holding it up and shook her hair out. Relief replaced the tension.

Squeals echoed with the springs of the trampoline. She pushed the curtain aside. While she massaged her head, she watched Kiara, Jorie, and Macie jump and laugh.

Jorie jumping?

She never expected quiet, shy Jorie to let loose. She was becoming more and more rigid in her faith.

No, not her faith. In her works. Her dress, her hair and her attitude followed rules so closely that Jorie would suffocate if she didn't find her liberty in Christ.

Have I been making a disciple?

She shivered as she watched the youth frolic. Oh, to play, to cut loose and soar. Her stomach soured. Had she ever been so carefree?

Could I return to those days?

Would Beau love me again?

Everyone climbed off the trampoline except for Kiara, who kept jumping.

Higher with each thrust.

It looked like she could fly, like nothing mattered—not death or termites or skunks.

Shann studied her. He never glanced at Jorie standing by his side, so close they touched.

Shann and Kiara?

No, Lord. Her brother-in-law had become so distant from the things of God. Loving an atheist would damn him forever.

Kiara jumped higher, somersaulted and landed on her back.

No one hurried to Kiara, so she didn't hurt herself.

Laughter, muffled by distance, filled the bedroom.

Shann held out his hand and scooped Kiara up like in the Christian romances she hid under her mattress.

Kiara fell into Shann's arms.

Not good.

"Lia?" Beau called up the stairs. "Everyone wants cake."

"Be right there."

With her hair down, the headache had fled. Lia ran a brush through it. Winding the locks to the side, she fastened them with combs she found in her toiletry drawer. She picked up a hand mirror and brushed a strand over her shoulder.

I look twenty years younger. She smiled.

In the kitchen, Lia took the cover off the cake carrier and lit the candles. Then with straightened shoulders and a smile, she butted the screen door open with her hips. She forced cheer and volume into her voice as though nothing marred Ma's birthday. "Let's all sing to the greatest mother God ever placed on the earth."

Lia placed the cake on the buffet table. Pa helped Ma to her feet and led her to the center of attention.

Ma's smile broadened.

Lia hadn't seen her mother frown all day. The simple joy of another birthday delighted her.

Had she ever enjoyed life like her mother? Had she ever experienced her mother's childlike faith and satisfaction?

Beau's baritone rang out. "Let's all sing."

As one, people sang, "Happy Birthday."

~~

"What's wrong?" Kiara asked Jorie as they stood by the trampoline.

Jorie's eyes were wide and as calm as the blue September sky. Judging by the lilt of her head, she focused on Shann and Macie as they hurried hand-in-hand to surround Queenie and sing.

"Come. Sit with me while my stomach settles."

Jorie followed.

Back at the vacated picnic table, Kiara edged next to Jorie. "You like him, don't you?" Kiara didn't need to clarify who Jorie liked.

Jorie studied her fingers clasped on top of the table.

"You don't have to say anything. It's clear in your eyes."

Jorie's eyes widened and seemed sad. "He used to like me." Her shoulder hitched. "Or so everyone said. Lately?" She paused. "I gave him my heart and lost his interest."

What can I say to comfort?

During their silence, critters scurried through the bushes. Birds twittered.

Kiara took a deep breath. "My fiancé died a month ago."

Kiara scrunched her eyes closed. Although she never controlled her tongue, she shouldn't be blabbing about her personal life to this woman. Jorie would use it against her. People always did.

"I'm so sorry." Jorie's eyes widened. She took Kiara's hand.

"I remember when Bryce and I met. It was my twentieth birthday. I'd just graduated college."

"At twenty?"

"Had to get out of my home. Enrolled in college early and worked to graduate as soon as possible. The quicker I did, the less it cost me." Still babbling, Kiara offered a slight smile. "That's not my point. At the beginning of June, my friend Gina and I headed out to the Hamptons. It was too cold for swimming, but not sunbathing. I saw Bryce walking on the beach. Believe me, he was hot."

"Even in the cool temperatures?" Jorie's innocent eyes narrowed. She opened her mouth as though to speak, then closed it.

Kiara blinked. Then Jorie's meaning dawned on her, and she bit back her laughter. "Hot, as in sexy. Lush hair, narrow hips. You know what I mean?"

A blush reddened Jorie's face.

"Gina and I both wanted him. He was a good deal older than us—twenty-years more than me—but his body. Every proton and neutron in me wanted him. Gina craved him, too."

Jorie fidgeted and looked away.

"I had to do something, so he'd notice me and not Gina. I tightened my bathing wrap. You know, hint at what's here," she ran her hand over her shape, "without being brazen."

"I couldn't be immodest." Jorie half stood, then plopped back onto the bench. "I'm sorry. I didn't mean to insult you."

"You didn't offend me. Modesty attracts men. I knew how to entice without ... well, without ... " *How do I say this?* "My story's not about me." Kiara pinched in an inch of Jorie's oversized dress. "Take your dress in a little. Make it fit."

"But—"

"No. Look." Kiara pointed. "See, Beau?"

Beau handed out the cake Delia Mae sliced. His T-shirt strained against his pectorals. Strong legs clad in shorts strode with determination and vigor.

"He's an attractive man. The way his clothes fit, he knows it. His T-shirt defines his chest. He's wearing shorts. Does he look obscene?"

"No."

"How about Cornie?" She pointed to Delia Mae's pretty sister who handed out cake to the crowd across the yard. "She goes to your church and is—"

"She's a hairdresser."

"According to Delia Mae's theology, what's right and wrong isn't subjective. If Cornie or Beau can look contemporary and sexy and be holy, why can't you?"

"The *Bible* says—"

"Does it say one thing for you and another for Beau?"

"He's a man."

"So?"

"It's different for men than for women."

"The reason I avoid religion."

Jorie's hand clasped her chest as though she had a heart attack. "How can you say that?"

"I'm an atheist." She inhaled. "Don't try to convert me." Even Kiara heard the sharpness of her tone. She softened it. "Sorry about my anger, but don't argue with me. I'm trying to learn how to respect our differences. I'm figuring out how to talk about opposing views without insult. One of the benefits of living near Delia Mae."

"She's never held back." Jorie's hand covered her mouth. "Sorry."

"No. She gives as good as I do, but she's the opposite of me in philosophy. I want to respect that, not accept it."

"It's not a philosophy."

"My point is Cornie's a woman—or doing a good impersonation."

Jorie's eyes widened. Her breath hitched.

"I'm joking. I'm aware she's female." Kiara touched Jorie's hand. "What's true is always true. It's not circumstantial. Like you can't be both dead and alive or tall and short. Truth is truth. Right?

Jorie nodded.

"So why is it okay for Cornie to be hip and current and not you?"

"Because ... " Jorie squirmed off the bench. "I'll be right back." She hurried off.

Truth is not circumstantial? Where'd that come from?

"Want cake?" Samantha held a couple of plates in front of Kiara. "Turns out we ditched you prematurely." She slid a plate on the table. "Never found Lia."

"Can we have two? Jorie will be back in a minute."

The woman plopped the second plate onto the table. "The coffee's on the porch."

It sounded good. Kiara's stomach had settled, so she headed to the coffee urn and filled a Styrofoam cup and doctored it. She'd pour Jorie a cup, but didn't know how to fix it.

Back at the table, she sat. Butterflies fluttered in her gut. Kiara ran her hands over her stomach. The food didn't make her queasy when she ate. All the jumping must've unsettled her.

Jorie returned. "Here's what the *Bible* admonishes women." She flipped open a book and ran her hand over the print. "'Whose adorning let it not be that outward adorning of plaiting—"

"Delia Mae told me this before."

"Wait." Jorie scanned the book. "Here. This is the important part. A woman's beauty should be 'the hidden man of the heart ... even the ornament of a meek and quiet spirit, which is in the sight of God of great price.'" She sat back as though she'd said it all.

"I didn't read anything about never wearing clothes in your size."

Jorie's head jerked as though Kiara slapped her.

She wasn't as thick-skinned as Delia Mae. "Look," Kiara said. "Doesn't the next part of this passage say you should be a good person and revel in your nice personality? I don't see anything about not wearing nice clothes or fixing your hair stylishly."

"We need to be modest." Jorie flipped through her *Bible*.

"Wait." Kiara put her hand over Jorie's. "Half my friends are all about fashion and designers and who they know. Obviously, I'm part of the second half of my buddies." She picked at her tunic. "My fashion divas don't care about their character as long as they look good."

Delia Mae called to the crowd from the buffet table. "Sorry, y'all. I forgot to bring out the ice cream. We can't eat cake without it." She headed to the house.

"Delia Mae looks tired." Kiara stood. "Want to go help her out?"

"Of course." Again, Jorie looked soft, fragile, and not of this world. She held an ethereal beauty.

Kiara couldn't explain it. The woman could stand a lesson — or ten — in conversation, but she owned an inner light. It pulled Kiara to it.

The women bumped into Delia Mae as she stepped back onto the porch.

"Do you need help?" Kiara asked.

"I'm good." Delia Mae's tired, down-turned eyes told Kiara that her neighbor lied. "Help yourself to ice cream." She lifted the three cartons balanced in her hands.

"I can help serve." Jorie took a carton and grabbed a scoop. She wandered into the crowd.

Kiara patted her stomach. "And I couldn't fit another morsel. Going to head home after I snap a few pictures of the twins. I want to paint their portraits."

"Macie'd love it." Delia Mae took a step while Kiara fished in her pockets for her phone. Delia Mae stopped. "Do you think you could give Macie art lessons? She's not too young, is she? We'd pay you."

"I'd enjoy giving her lessons."

Where'd my phone go? "I've got to find Shann. I think he's holding my cell for me."

Kiara found Shann and Jorie talking back at the picnic table. At least, Shann talked.

The forgotten chocolate ice cream puddled in the carton on the table.

"Do you have my phone?"

"You gave it to Macie."

No.

"But I, your knight, had the good sense to take it from her before she lost it." He half rose and smiled up at her while his hand dug into the back of his jeans. "Kept it warm for you."

"Where are the twins? I want to paint them."

"They get dirty enough without having paint—"

She swatted him.

He caught her hand and laughed. "Gotcha." He held on. His smile faded. His eyes became hooded.

If she had to paint his eyes, she'd make them smoky.

Jorie shifted. Her hands caught her attention, and she fidgeted with her fingers.

Kiara looked back to Shann. His eyes ...

She'd seen the same look in Bryce's the day he met her and Gina. She gulped. "I'll leave you and Jorie alone."

Kiara pulled her hand away. *Find the kids. Snap a shot. Go home. Now.*

Chapter Eighteen

Darkness descended and chased the last of the McGuffrey partiers away. The silence in Kiara's cabin settled over her like a suffocating gag. Life in the South would kill her soon if she didn't get out of here.

The roar of an ATV drew her to the window. She peered out and wished to see something—anything to break the solitude. She yawned. It was nearing nine p.m., but her eyes begged for sleep. Maybe Kiara was the one who was forty-five like Bryce or her neighbor and not the spry twenty-five-year-old.

How'd Delia Mae manage everything she did?

Kiara had only seen her at the party twice. First in the kitchen when everyone wanted to doctor her wonderful food and make it awful. Then near the end, Delia Mae showed up when she brought out cake and ice cream.

If being a Christian woman meant being a slave, Kiara would pass.

Her brand-new mattress called from the loft. "Come. Sleep. You've never laid yourself upon me. I'm lonely."

Kiara had some nerve making it wait so long.

She eased her tired body onto the virgin mattress set. Her bed hadn't lied to her. The edges seemed to curl around her and cradle her. The fragrance of the clean sheets lulled her. She closed her eyes.

It had been a lovely day. Delia Mae had a sweet family. Queenie was a stitch.

Butterflies flitted up her stomach.

Kiara ran her hand over it.

They pattered back down.

Little bumps patted her.

Not just on the inside, but against her hand. She bolted up and pressed hands against her belly.

No. It can't be.

She hyperventilated as the knowledge hammered into her soul with each breath.

I can't be pregnant. No.

What a nightmare.

Last September, the day before Bryce proposed, he had a vasectomy.

Vasectomies prevented pregnancies.

She pressed hard. Felt nothing.

Finally, Kiara slipped down on the bed and pulled the covers up. It had to be close to her time of the month.

How long had it been? Stress would cause her to miss a cycle.

She counted. Bolted upright again. *Four months?*

No, no, no, no. She had no time for kids.

She squeezed her eyes shut and saw Macie dogging her everywhere. Dixon? How would she keep track of a little boy wandering the woods? Keep him from being bitten by poisonous snakes or falling out of trees?

No. No woods grew in Manhattan where she would head. Then she saw the streets outside of Gina's boutique in East Harlem. The traffic and crowds down on Delancey. The deep dark of Central Park at nightfall. New York streets posed more risk than these woods.

Kiara hated the dirty little creatures that always had sticky hands and filthy faces and projectile vomiting. Kids took everything important away. They demanded every second of your life. Couldn't be left alone so you could work. Brought insects into the house or fell in ponds. They cost a lot, and she had no money.

Worse. The brats divided finite love and left you destitute. Like her half-brother, Chester. Or her dad's new kids.

What would she do if she were pregnant?

After climbing out of bed, Kiara paced her bedroom. Made it to the window, pivoted, sat on the bed, then stood again. She walked downstairs and put the teakettle on. She wandered the perimeter of her living space while water heated.

The kettle whistled. Its high-pitched screech acted like the proverbial light bulb over her head. It shrilled, "Dummmmb."

How stupid I am. Her heart stilled, and she poured the boiling water over the tea bag. *I don't need to have a kid. My life. My body. My reproductive rights.*

She blew air out of her lungs and doctored her chamomile with honey.

Upstairs, she crawled under the covers once more. Kiara sipped her tea and leaned her head against the brass headboard. She closed her eyes to savor the warmth of her brew and the relief her reproductive rights brought.

Wait.

Kiara threw off the blanket and stood. She strode two whole steps to the window. Outside the tarry pitch of Stinking Creek allowed her to see nothing.

Where would she find a doctor who'd remove this fetus?

Delia Mae wouldn't tell her. She probably marched outside of Planned Parenthood and denied women their rights.

Although, if Mrs. McG didn't know my plans? She could tell Delia Mae the pregnancy was a false alarm. Lies improved life.

How far along was she? At what stage of a pregnancy did Tennessee cease performing abortions?

She counted months again. Came up with four once more.

She laid her head against the cool window. *Couldn't be.*

Still, she'd felt the ... she fished for the word. Baby came to mind.

Why'd her brain freeze up? She couldn't call this thing a baby.

No. Stress caused women to skip their cycles. Vasectomies were foolproof. They failed rarely. A whole year passed since Bryce had it.

She was mistaken. Not pregnant.

Again, her breathing slowed. Her blood pressure settled. Back at the bed, she picked up her cup of chamomile. The brew was cold, so she headed to the kitchen to dump it.

At the sink, she studied her termites. Kiara closed her eyes and listened. The house creaked and settled. Were those sounds the noise of the bugs chewing up her stinking cabin?

Not pregnant.

Her clothes were getting tight. Yes, she was pregnant.

No, not possible.

Wait.

Walmart never closed.

She jogged up the stairs like an Olympian and threw on yoga pants and Bryce's sweater. Kiara climbed into her Ford and drove in the direction she believed Jacksboro lay. Hopefully, she could find her way.

~~

"Lia," Beau called from his study. "Chris got home. Deal with your son."

Lia tightened her robe and stepped into the hallway. "I was hitting the shower."

Beau stepped to the bottom of the stairs and called up to her. "I've got to finish the sermon. The Lawd gave me a new one. Was going switch from Ephesians 2: 8-9 to James 1:4-8. God showed me the church's true function is to produce godly character. It's His factory on earth." He took a few steps up. "Our character produces good conduct."

Lia rolled her eyes. Of course, Beau would skip the passages on grace and turn, once more, to the book of James. Work. Work some more.

She shut out his monologue. She'd listen tomorrow. Maybe.

Silence focused her on Beau again. "It's only nine. Why do I need to talk to Chris?"

"He and his no-good friend, Bobby, and another reprobate took off this afternoon before the cake came out. Bobby James and his friend — what's his name? Leo Marsh, I think. Bobby and Leo ain't never up to no good."

"I'm tired. I'll do it tomorrow."

"Remember Proverbs 6. God's holy word cautions us against laziness."

"Beau, did you see all I did today?"

Beau said nothing.

"I thought so. If you'd paid attention, you wouldn't club me with Scripture."

"I know you went upstairs and took a nap when our guests were waiting for the cake."

"I ..." Her protests faded with a sigh. It didn't matter. Beau would hear her speak but wouldn't listen. Anything she said would filter through his interpretation.

"I'm the breadwinner in this family." His voice rose and drew her attention back to his words. "The church pays me good money —"

"The church doesn't pay me. And it shorted last week's paycheck."

"This isn't about church. It's about raising up our children."

Lia knew the lecture. She took a step down the stairs.

"I've got to be obedient to God and give the word the Almighty gave." He glared up at Lia.

She paused on the stairwell. Her eyes stared at the accusatory finger.

"You understand Christopher better than me. I'll deal with Paul." He pivoted. The door to his study slammed.

Lia sighed and trudged down the stairs to the kitchen. Chris stood at the table digging into the remains of the cake. She glanced down the hallway as though Beau watched.

"Hey, Ma," Chris spoke around a wad of cake shoved in his mouth. "Good stuff. Sorry I missed it."

"Use a plate and a fork." She grabbed them from their cabinets. "Here. Make believe you're civilized." She sat at the table.

Chris plopped a large slice on the plate. He licked the icing off his fingers.

"Where d'you go?"

"Me and Bobby and Leo rode out toward Rarity. Got us turned around." He pulled a jug of milk from the refrigerator.

"Daddy and I worried." Lia bit down. *Forgive the lie, Lord. I don't have the energy.* She hadn't even known he was gone.

Chris unscrewed the gallon of milk and took a gulp.

"Use a glass. You think you're a hillbilly?"

Chris fumbled in a cabinet next to the refrigerator.

"What'd y'all do? Have I met this Leo fellow?"

"He came to the party with Bobby. He's older than us—has a beard. I don't know if you met him. Leo lives in Tazewell. The three of us explored the mountains—tried out a new trail."

She studied him.

"Don't fret none, Ma. Nobody did drugs or drank."

"Are your words condemning you?"

"Ma." He clunked the glass on the table. "Trust me. We rode. Got lost. Came home." He poured a glass of milk and plunked the plastic jug on the table. Picking up his plate of cake and balancing the milk glass, Chris stormed out of the kitchen.

"Chris, the milk?"

He walked into the den.

She stepped out on the porch, then sat in her rocker and closed her eyes. With the rumble of Kiara's truck, she opened them.

Where was she going at this hour? Going to learn, ain't nothing happening on the Creek when it the dark falls.

~~

An hour and a half later, sitting on her closed toilet seat in her teeny bathroom, Kiara took out her phone and timed the e.p.t. stick. Instructions said to wait two minutes. Still, she peeked at it. Nothing changed. Leaving it on the bathroom sink, she paced out of the room, crossed her living room, and walked the perimeter of the kitchen. She counted the whole time. *One-thousand-sixty, one-thousand-sixty-one ...*

Her phone buzzed in her hand.

She darted into the bathroom. Picked up the stick. Looked.

Closed her eyes.

Breathed.

A dark blue line. Unequivocal.

Oh, Bryce, what did you do to me?

Chapter Nineteen

Kiara studied her painting. The boring Sunday afternoon inched along second by incremental, ugly second. Nothing changed on the canvas. *Stinking Morning* proved her a prophet. Nothing good came from Stinking Creek.

How would she find a doctor to rid her of this baby?

She slammed her brush down. *Fetus. Not a hard term to remember, Rafferty.*

Wrapping her arms around herself, she stroked Bryce's sweater. In its softness, his arms caressed her. The wool became his chin in the mornings before he shaved when it scratched and tickled. She picked at the neck's edge and held it to her nose. The skunk had destroyed its scent, so now she wore it to protect her clothing from oil and turpentine and pigments. Wrapped in cashmere, she'd remember their love—its richness and tenderness. In the soft material, she touched his skin. In the warmth of wool, she'd hold him.

Firecrackers popped behind the barn.

She mixed up viridian green pigment. Swirled it with the cobalt blue. Hit the alizarin crimson.

What'd I do?

She looked from her palette to the brush.

Yep. She'd made mud from her paint. Kiara had created a hue so ugly, even this canvas didn't deserve it. She swirled the brush in the turps. The paint debris had settled to the bottom of her can while she moped. With the swish of her brush, the dross churned. The turpentine turned as putrid as the color she'd mixed.

She dropped the brush into the jar and picked up a new one.

The firecrackers burst again.

She dabbed the palette.

Wait.

Not firecrackers. Guns.

On her property.

Who in their right mind would trespass and shoot firearms?

Stomping to the far end of the studio, she opened the north-facing window, leaned out and surveyed the woods beyond her fields. Pops stuttered once more. Definitely guns.

She slammed her hands on the sill. *Stupid rubes.*

An ATV roared to life in the distance. Within a minute, it zipped along *her* driveway and passed *her* barn.

"Hey," she hollered. "This is private property." She let loose a string of words. Shame heated her face. Even Gina wouldn't use the language she spewed.

Not to mention Imani—who, even before her brainwashed conversion—didn't know the expletives existed.

The vehicle vanished around her cabin. The sounds faded a few seconds later. Had to be the McGuffreys.

She tossed the brush onto the palette. The idiot religious freaks would be gun fanatics. Unthinking hicks.

I'm not going to let this go. What if those kids killed someone?

If she'd been walking in her woods, not that she'd be brave enough to trek through the forest.

Mrs. McG was going to get a piece of her mind. Or ...

With her back now pressed to the wall, she sunk to the floor and doubled over. Kiara held her head in her hand. Instead of a piece of her mind, perhaps Delia Mae could find Kiara a little peace.

~~

"Get ready for service, Christopher," Lia called. "Daddy's fuming, so nuke the dinner and eat fast." She handed him a plate.

He shoved it into the appliance.

The microwave dinged as someone thumped at her door.

Lia inhaled and held her breath. Only one person wouldn't realize that at 4:50 on a Sunday afternoon, she'd be racing to get the family back to church so Beau could be an hour early.

She opened the door partway as Youtee leaped and barked, hoping to lick the trespasser to death or snitch a dog biscuit from her. As she suspected, her neighbor stood on the porch. "Yes, Kiara? I'm late."

"Your kids are hunting on my property."

A good afternoon and howdy-do to you, too. Lia tilted her head up and struggled to keep her self-satisfied grin at bay. *Didn't speak my snark out loud.*

"Are you going to do something about it?" Kiara crossed her arms. Her scowl deepened.

"Are you sure it was my boys?" Lia's arm held onto the house door as though it would keep Kiara out. It shielded her home from the interloper. Lia shoved the hound back and called into the house. "Paul,

113

come get the dog." She turned back to the Yank. Lia didn't invite Kiara in. Her neighbor could talk through the screen for all she cared.

"I saw whoever rode the ATV—and the engine's still hot—drive down my driveway. It's parked right there." Kiara pointed at the field behind her. "Guns are an evil."

"Stop. You have no call to shout at me."

"I'm not shouting." She jabbed her index finger at Lia. "Guns kill."

"My boys are trained. They took gun safety classes."

"Don't tell me about how good they are. They're on my property shooting who knows what?"

"Okay, okay." Lia threw up her hands. She knew the argument liberal New Yorkers made against guns. They overlooked the fact her boys had background checks. They'd been hunting since they were seven and eight. Who knew if Kiara or her neighbors in Manhattan had a criminal history? No one there got drug tested or had their private lives checked out. Liberals forgot Second Amendment rights and the tyrannical government our colonists escaped. Those Yankees took all their ideas and shoved them down everyone else's craw. "If it'll make you happy, I'll talk to Chris and Paul."

"Happy? It's common courtesy." Kiara's tone sounded resigned. She walked away.

Her posture stopped Lia from closing the door. The slope of the young woman's shoulders and the heaviness of her step said something heavy weighted her. Guns didn't make her overreact. *What's wrong with you?* Lia flung the door wide and stepped onto the porch. "Kiara."

The New Yorker kept walking across the yard as though she hadn't heard.

"Something's wrong. Beyond the guns and my boys riding on your land."

With head ducked and shoulders slumped, Kiara edged away.

Lia crossed her arms as she watched. *What do you want from me, Lord?*

Her heart wrenched. She opened her mouth to speak. Shut it again.

Her neighbor turned to latch the gate. She was like the Muppet Macie called her. This puppet had no hand inside her.

"Give me a moment," Lia called. "I'll be over. You need to talk."

Kiara crossed the road with slow, leaden steps.

Beau'd be tied up like a bow if Lia didn't make it to church on time, but they had more than an hour before prayer meeting started. What good was worship if the widows and orphans weren't cared for? Beau'd skipped that portion from the Book of James this morning when he pontificated on works and character. From what her neighbor had told her about her life, Kiara was as good as a widow and orphan. She needed a mama to love her.

She hollered down the hall. "I'll meet y'all at service. I'll take my car. The boys are going with you."

"Lia."

"Ma."

"Hey."

The hound bayed.

Kiara already had crossed her bridge.

Lia jogged after her.

Her neighbor swiped at her face as though wiping away tears.

"Wait."

Kiara paused.

"Can we talk?"

"I've got to work on my painting."

"We can talk while you work."

Kiara hitched a shoulder. "Suit yourself."

The women plodded the rest of the way up the hill.

In the barn, Kiara flipped on a light, and they climbed a steep staircase. Wide, weathered planks covered the walls of the narrow stairwell. Nothing adorned them. A bare light bulb hung from the ceiling.

Then Lia stepped into the loft.

Wow.

Kiara hadn't lied about the old barn being the more livable space. Open and airy. In full daylight, sunlight would saturate this room. Lia'd rather live here than in the dingy cabin Kiara called home. "Beautiful space. The Olivers never brought us up here."

Her neighbor said nothing. She stopped by a table loaded with paints and brushes and palette knives. The piney scent of turpentine told of the hours Kiara'd spent creating here.

Lia sniffed oil, like the linseed she used on her cabinets.

Kiara scraped a stool near the small worktable holding more brushes than Hobby Lobby.

Lia looked up. The sight before her made her stumble backward. The most awful painting she'd ever seen leaned against the wall. Gray swatches and green whorls coated the canvas. How big was it? Taller than Lia. "I thought you said you were an artist?"

Kiara jerked her head in Lia's direction. Her narrowed eyes and tight mouth said Lia'd overstepped her bounds.

Still, the monstrosity rising before her chased away all sense. Her tongue shifted into autopilot. "What in tarnation is that?" Lia scrunched her mouth.

Shut up. You came here to comfort. This ain't gonna do it.

"It's my latest work." Kiara's quiet voice sounded resigned.

She made no retort?

"Not coming out the way I envisioned it." Kiara sank onto the stool as though the last of life deflated.

I hope my sarcasm didn't sound as bad as I thought? "I'd say. It's uglier than a cow's nose."

Lia slapped her hand over her mouth. *You're gonna make sure she understands she's insulted. What a fool I am.*

"What do you mean?" Kiara faced Lia once more. Her reddened eyes glared. Then her face softened. She picked up a brush, slipped it through paint which looked more like sludge and held it up in front of her face. Kiara examined it as though she *couldn't* figure out what she'd done. "You are honest." One side of her mouth tilted up. "I think Phineas G. Bloom can paint better than I can."

"What's a Phineas G. Bloom?"

"Only the worst abstract artist in the world." She snickered—a snort far out of proportion to any humor spoken in the last fifteen minutes.

Lia stared at the behemoth rising before her. "With painting all those dull colors, how can you think Thomas Kinkade is awful?"

Kiara fisted her hips, but her eyes sparkled. "Is my work so awful?"

Remember, be tactful.

"Be honest. How else would I ever be able to trust you?" Once more, she focused on her foul painting.

Lia waved her arm toward it. "When you splash paint like my boys at a paintball tournament. It's ugly."

Probably too blunt."

Kiara stood and glared at Lia once more. "I'll tell you what's ugly." She pointed at Lia's head. "Your flying saucer."

"Flying saucer?"

Kiara wound a bunch of her dreads into a tight, little ball.

Lia grabbed her bun. "This?"

She couldn't tell her she was right. My hair is from outer space. Strange, though, the freedom to insult, to speak her mind liberated her. "You wear dreadful dreadlocks, and you think clean hair is ugly?" She faked a pout, jutting out her lower lip.

"I washed my hair yesterday." Kiara stuck her tongue out at Lia and gave a sassy wag of her hips. "Your corn bread is as dry as the Sahara." Kiara smiled a sad, little grin. Her eyes lost a fraction more of the sorrow weighting them.

"What? My corn pone?" Lia slumped her shoulders.

"I went too far?" Kiara's lips quivered and her nose reddened.

"It's okay. We're both mouthy."

"It feels good to be honest." She sighed. "In New York, everyone raved about anything I did. Art critics proclaimed my work contained symbolism I'd never intended. Everyone wanted to be a part of my world." She looked at her painting. "Considering how everyone dropped me when Bryce died, they wanted his world. Not mine."

Lia reached out and laid a hand on Kiara's wrist. *What do I say, Lord?*

Her touch seemed to empty Kiara of her bones—and of the last of her strength. She fell into Lia's arms. "I'm sorry."

Lia stood rigid. What had happened?

The child clung. Her body heaved.

Lia looped her arms around the desolate woman who sobbed. Lia stroked her hair and rubbed her back. Prayers bubbled inside, but she couldn't find the words to utter them. God had to intercede for her.

Kiara's crying soaked Lia's shoulder, and after several minutes quieted into little hiccups and deep breaths heaving her chest.

Kiara straightened and swiped her eyes. She grabbed a paper towel and blew her nose. "You probably forgot to add sugar."

"What?"

"The corn bread. It was so grainy and bland. I'd say you forgot to add sugar."

"You don't add sugar to pone."

"Without it, it's inedible." Kiara sniffed, and the tears brimmed her eyes once more as though another downpour would follow.

"No use crying over spoiled pone."

"I believe you were saving the sugar for Rosalyn?" Kiara gave a snort of a laugh. Her eyes glistened. Renegade tears clung to her lashes.

Lia pulled Kiara close once more. "Shh, child." She ran her hand over her head.

Kiara's hair was clean, indeed. The child hadn't lied.

~~

"You were right." The weight inside her lightened, and Kiara shifted away from Delia Mae.

"I'm glad someone's discovered I'm right about something. Want to fill me in on what I got correct?"

Kiara climbed back onto the stool. She studied her fingers studded with muddy paint and picked at her nails.

Delia Mae dragged the second stool next to her.

"Why aren't you offended with all the awful stuff I threw at you?"

"It hurts." Delia Mae offered a shrug. Something in her posture made Kiara think Delia Mae carried a heavy secret, too. "Sometimes I'm unsympathetic and critical, myself. Too harsh-tongued."

"It smarts when I'm on the receiving end," Kiara said.

"We're kindred spirits—from polar worlds."

"Through the looking glass?"

117

"Or into Narnia via a wardrobe. You're a good woman, Kiara."

"You like me?" She studied Delia Mae, looking for a truthful answer. Hoping she'd hear what she needed. "How can you?"

"You're honest."

"You should be screeching at me." Kiara found her hands fascinating again. If she looked at them and not Delia Mae, she could talk.

"Yelling would inflame the situation. When there's no wood—the fire goes out."

Kiara glanced at her. "Huh?"

"Scripture."

"Oh. Adding fuel to the fire." Kiara nodded. "Got it." She rubbed her hands against her legs. "Guess you're turning me religious. I can figure out your jargon."

"Tell me what's going on?"

"I'm at your place 24-7 begging for help. You see I'm hurting and follow even though I made your life miserable. I hurl insults. Call you self-righteous. Insult your faith. Still, you sit. You try to understand me."

Delia Mae touched Kiara's hand.

Warmth seeped into her bloodstream.

"Look at me," Delia Mae said.

She couldn't.

Delia Mae waited.

Kiara peeked up.

Delia Mae sat on the second stool with her hands, once more, clasped in her lap. She looked at Kiara like she'd always imagined the real mothers looked at their offspring. Not like an inconvenient reminder of past mistakes. With love?

Was it love showing in her gray eyes?

"I've got a problem." In her own ears, Kiara's voice sounded as quiet as the chirping birds as Macie said.

"I can help."

She inhaled and wished it possible. "I don't see how."

"At least, I can pray."

"You'll judge me."

"No, I won't."

Kiara inhaled. Every time she needed someone, the universe dropped Delia Mae in her path. This woman was her serendipity.

Seconds passed.

Kiara peeped at her neighbor. Peace surrounded her like an aura. Kiara would paint Delia Mae's atmosphere blue, not a florescent cerulean, more ultramarine—a calm and serene pigment.

Her kind eyes stayed trained on her.

Then Kiara knew. Delia Mae *could* be trusted.

118

"I'm pregnant." Kiara's lips trembled. Cold spread through her body, and it shook. Her teeth chattered. "Delia Mae, what ... "

She couldn't finish.

Delia Mae grabbed her in her arms once more.

How'd she get to me so fast?

She rocked Kiara like a mama. Delia Mae palmed her hair. "Shh, baby. God's in control. Like the lilies or the sparrows, God'll take care of you."

God?

Sobs stilled. *Could Delia Mae's deity help her? Change her world?*

When Kiara was little, she believed in Santa. Christmas had always been enchanting. The magic disappeared when Santa proved a fiction.

God, if you're real? Kiara sighed. *Let me believe.*

~~

"I'll make you a cup of tea. We'll talk." Lia released Kiara and looked around the studio for a clock. "Do you know what time it is?"

Kiara looked at her wrist and ran a finger over the traditional watch face. No digital for this modern child? "Almost six."

Six? Well, Beau will be hog-tied. Too bad." Do you have herbal tea at the house? You should avoid caffeine."

Kiara shook her head in long slow movements.

"What?" Lia suspected what her neighbor thought, but it wouldn't happen. Not while Lia breathed.

"I told you. You'll judge me."

"Let's go to your cabin where we can sit on something other than a stool. My back's too decrepit for backless seats. It's getting so, one of these days, I will bring my own pew cushion with me to church like the biddies do."

"Pew cushions?"

Lia waved the question away. "I'll make us tea. We'll talk."

In silence, they descended the studio's steps. Mute, they walked to the cabin. Knowing the problem, this silence didn't haunt Lia as her trek up to the barn an hour earlier had.

Kiara sank onto her sofa while Lia searched the cabinets. It didn't take long to find the chamomile, boil water, and pour two cups. Honey sat on the countertop. She stirred half a teaspoon into each cup.

"Here. It'll help you feel better." Lia handed Kiara a cup and settled next to her on the couch.

They sipped a little of the hot, flowery tea. Steam warmed Lia's face. The sweetness and the steam soothed like a dip in a hot tub.

"This is perfect." Kiara took a second sip. "I'm glad Rosalyn didn't make the tea."

"You like to save a dob of honey for the bees?"

She smiled as she nodded. "Not a fan of licking the sugar bowl." Kiara clinked the cup onto the coffee table but didn't lean back on the sofa.

"Any idea when you're due?"

Kiara shook her head.

"How far along?"

"I think I'm four months. I can feel the ..." She took a long breath and shifted so she faced Lia. "It's moving, so I think at least four months. Do you ..." She swallowed. "Know a doctor?"

Lia nodded. "I'll send over the number." She leaned forward and placed her teacup next to Kiara's. "From your concern about my judging, I'm assuming you want to terminate?"

Tension flowed out of Kiara. She straightened. Her eyes brightened and looked like a child believing her birthday wishes had come true.

"You know I'm going to talk you out of it."

"You won't." She shook her head. "I can't have a child. I don't like them."

"You don't? You put on a good act. I see life and joy course through you when you interact with my niece."

"Well, Macie grows on you."

"Do you think this one won't?"

"I've seen what children do. When my grandma died, I had to go live with my mother in Singapore. She didn't want me. Chester, my brother, was five by then. With him meeting all her expectations, my mother had no need for me, and I took up precious space in their minuscule apartment. She sent me to live with Dad and Jillian in Portland. I swear." Kiara's eyes widened. "Sorry. Didn't mean to swear."

"I swan, child," Lia placed all the irony she could into the word swan, "You never hear me utter a foul word."

Kiara shook her head. "I don't. So, don't judge—"

"I swan is Southern for I swear. How many times have you heard me utter it?"

"Fifty billion?"

"Fifty-billion-twenty-one. You need a little help with your counting."

The two women chuckled and leaned back on the couch.

"Go on," Lia said. "What about Jillian?"

"I believe she kept a calendar counting the days until I left for college." Kiara made check marks in the air.

"Your mom and dad have nothing to do with you being a good mother."

"I can't support myself. I have a moderate health insurance policy Bryce got for me, but it runs out in December. How can I afford a

120

pregnancy, let alone raise a child?"

"You can give it up for adoption."

Kiara's mouth dropped. Her eyes widened and her hand covered her chest.

If Lia didn't know better, the child looked all righteous indignation.

"I could never give away a baby of mine. I know what it's like to be tossed aside."

Lia raised her eyebrows. "You can kill it, but not give it away?"

"I wouldn't be killing. I ..." Kiara trembled. She crumbled back on the sofa. "I don't know."

"Remember when you had the skunk run-in."

"Can you breathe?" Kiara gave an exaggerated sniff. "The rank likes to hang around."

Lia picked at Kiara's white sweater. "Why did cleaning Bryce's sweater bother you?"

"It smelled like him. Why do you ask?"

"What greater comfort would it be to have, not Bryce's scent, but a piece of him?"

"I can't afford it."

"Whether the child lives with you or somewhere else, there'd be a piece of you and Bryce, a unique creation only the two of you could've crafted. Bryce and your love would exist forever."

"I can't do it by myself."

Lia pulled Kiara to her. She snuggled the Yankee under her arm and pointed toward her home. "There, a few yards away, is a family who will help you."

"Do you promise?"

Lia nodded.

"Without judgment?" Although Kiara's body stayed stiff, her voice sounded hopeful.

"Who am I to criticize? With the same measure I mete it out, it will be measured unto me."

"Whatever that means." The child relaxed.

For approximately ten seconds.

Kiara sat upright. "You know as soon as this place sells, I'm off to Manhattan. What do I do then?"

"Do you have friends in New York?"

Kiara nodded.

"True friends help. Let tomorrow worry about itself."

"I have enough to worry about today." Kiara snuggled back in.

Lia bit back her smile, and she eyed the young woman in her arms. *There's hope for you, Kiara. Quoting Scripture without being taught it.*

~~

Is this what a mother's supposed to feel like?

Being wrapped in Delia Mae's arms wasn't weird. Every muscle in Kiara's body softened. Cocooned this way, love seeped into every pore. This moment poured every dream Kiara had into the core of her being.

Bryce. Kiara looked toward her belly and rubbed it like every pregnant lady she'd ever seen. *Could she love this ... baby?*

Delia Mae's breathing comforted Kiara. Little did her neighbor know how important she'd become. Something in this woman strengthened her.

Delia Mae stirred. "What time is it?"

Kiara glanced at her watch and sat upright. "Half past seven. How'd it get so late?"

"I swan." Delia Mae smiled, and Kiara joined her.

Kiara slapped her neighbor's hand playfully. "Cussing again. Bad girl."

"I missed Beau's prayer meeting." She settled back. "After this morning's sermon, I'll get a recap of tonight's—for my character's strengthening."

"If church is so—"

"That's a pretty watch." Delia Mae took Kiara's wrist. "Not many young'uns like the analog watches."

"Bryce gave it to me when we moved in together. He called it his heart monitor. Every time I looked at it and saw the second hand move, I'd see his heart beating for me. It'd remind me we'd be together as long as his heart pumped." Again, the urge to pat her belly tempted Kiara. She needed to comfort, or be comforted by this fetus.

Or baby.

How could she have considered aborting this piece of Bryce?

Delia Mae stood. "I need to go home. Prep things for everyone's return."

Kiara half rose.

"Don't get up." Delia Mae leaned over and kissed the top of her head. "I meant every word I said. You've got a home across the way."

Kiara watched her neighbor leave. Wished she had a modicum of her strength.

~~

Delia Mae finished the last of the dinner cleanup when the van pulled into the driveway.

Chris skulked into the house and gave a furtive glance at his mother.

122

She arched her brow understanding their almost telepathic signals. "That bad?"

He nodded and slipped away.

The door swung open and Paul stepped in. "Tonight was not a night Uncle Shann would've wanted to be at prayer meeting." He trailed after his brother.

Lia steeled herself with a deep breath.

Beau entered.

She wiped her hands on a towel and stepped over to her husband to kiss him.

He turned his head.

She swiped his cheek.

"Sorry I didn't make it to church." Her spirits rose with her news. "Kiara seems to be opening up to God and—"

"You are *never* to talk to that neighbor again. She's a bad influence."

Hot magma churned in Lia's stomach.

Beau strode up the stairs to their room.

Right, husband. I know who I need to listen to. It's not you.

Lia stepped outside. The cool air was icy against her hands, still damp from the dishes. The last hint of color faded to the twilight's gray—a muddy hue like Kiara's paint.

God had given her direction, and she'd be obedient.

It'd been a long time since she defied Beau. He'd be seeing the Delia Mae Jones he'd courted twenty-five years ago.

A woman could only serve one master.

Chapter Twenty

Kiara waved the Comcast guy goodbye. He'd arrived on time, and two hours later, she was connected to the world.

Who will be my inaugural call?

Gina?

Hearing her sarcasm wouldn't suit the situation. She'd been here a little more than a week, and already the thought of Gina's cynicism made her feel like she'd swigged apple cider vinegar. If she stayed in Stinking Creek much longer, she'd turn into a real-life Sesame Street character in love with the world. Maybe start singing Beethoven's *Ode to Joy*.

Imani?

No. She had enough Christianity with Mrs. McG.

Kiara stood in her kitchen and gripped the phone and eyed the slip of paper Delia Mae had sent over this morning. At her door, termites gleefully devoured her house. At last, she could call the creepy-creature eradicators.

She picked up the slip of paper and dialed. While pacing the floor, she wrapped an arm around her waist. Why did this phone call excite her? Why did she call his office before the pest control guy?

"Dr. Hussey's."

She'd read the name on the paper, but hearing it spoken made her laugh. Such an outrageous moniker. "I need an appointment. I'm pregnant."

"Have you been here before?"

"No. My neighbor, Delia Mae McGuffrey said you were taking new patients."

"One moment." Background noises from the doctor's office filled the receiver.

Who'd think I'd be this thrilled?

"We had a cancelation. She can see you Friday at one."

She? Not a he? Guess I'm still viewing the world through its bias. "Perfect." She hung up, tapped the information into her calendar, then called the pest person.

Now with the afternoon free and her chores complete—done by herself without any outside help, she'd paint.

Back in the barn, *Stinking Morning* laughed at her. Gray and brown and olive pigment marred the canvas. This painting held no hope.

She'd prove to Delia Mae she could paint better than Thomas Kinkade or Norman Rockwell or Edvard Munch.

She'd make Delia Mae abandon her love for schmaltz.

Her heart soared like it did on the trampoline. She was going to have Bryce's baby. She'd hold him every time she held his daughter. Or his son.

She picked up a 24x36 inch canvas—small for her repertoire—and with a pencil and a composite of the photos on her phone, she sketched a portrait of the twins.

What would Shann think?

Would he like her baby?

She looked up. *Dumb girl.*

She meant would he like the portrait of his twins?

If she and Shann had babies, what would they look like? She saw the thick, wild hair all ratted up like Bob Marley's. They'd sport facial hair to their toes. What was the TV show she'd watched on reruns at Grandma's—some monster spoof with a character who was nothing but hair? Cousin Itt?

"Miss Kiara, Miss Muffet." A duet sang her name as little feet clumped up the stairs.

Thank heavens for interruptions. If she kept to her current thoughts she'd imagine herself living with Shann and spending the rest of her life in Podunk. She flipped the canvas over. "What are you guys doing out of school?"

"Uh, duh."

Macie punched Dixon's arm. "Be polite."

He shoved her.

Kiara needed to rethink this baby thing. She patted her stomach and smiled. *It is Bryce's.*

"We don't go to school forever," Dixon said. His sister's remonstrance did nothing to allay his wisecracking. "I want to show you something cool," Dixon said.

"It's gross," Macie chirped. "What d'you draw?" She stood on tiptoes and peered at the upside-down canvas on the table behind Kiara.

Kiara stepped more squarely in front of it. She winked. "It's a secret."

"What?" They both tried to climb around Kiara and grab the canvas.

"It's a portrait of you two. You can't look until it's done."

Macie clapped her hands and bounced on little feet.

Dixon rolled his eyes. "You gotta come see."

"See what?" Kiara asked.

The kids each grabbed an arm and tugged. They let go as they scrabbled down the stairs and ran ahead of her toward the woods behind the barn. About fifty feet from Kiara, they stopped. Macie backed away.

Dixon picked up a stick. He poked at another branch lying across the road.

"No! Don't stab it." Macie shrieked.

Kiara took several steps closer.

"He's still eating it." Dixon's voice contained a mixture of grossness and excitement.

Kiara peered around the kids. A scream froze in her throat.

A black snake stretched across the roadway. In his mouth, opened wider than the Midtown Tunnel, the hind end of a rabbit protruded. A large lump gorged the snake's throat.

Did snakes have throats?

Kiara squealed and yanked the twins back. She danced them several steps down the grass-covered driveway. "Get your uncle. Call your father. Someone has to kill it."

"Naw. It belongs out here," Dixon said.

"Is it poisonous?" Kiara asked.

"It's a timber rattler." Dixon broke loose and poked the snake with the stick again.

"I thought rattlesnakes were a lighter color and had a ... " What would the word be? "A snakeskin pattern to it."

"Not all of them. Daddy says black timbers are rarer. We're special 'cause we gots lots of 'em." Dixon jabbed at the rattler again.

Kiara snatched the branch away. "Don't be stupid. Stabbing a snake is dangerous. Even *I* know rattlers can kill you." She leaned in. Sure enough, this creature had a snake-like pattern to it.

"It ain't nothing to be afeared of with a rabbit in its mouth," Dixon said.

Kiara hugged Macie to her, gripping the stick in case Dixon's prediction proved wrong and the reptile coiled to strike. Still, something pulled her closer.

No, no, no. Didn't snakes hypnotize you? She had enough sense to keep the kids behind her.

The snake did nothing but make the bunny disappear at an infinitesimally slow rate.

"How do you know it's a rattler? I don't hear any shaking?"

"There." Dixon pointed to its tale. He counted. "Seven rattles. This fellow's been around a while."

"Let's go." Kiara shivered.

"Rattlers don't bite much. Watch out for copperheads." Dixon stepped toward the snake. "They' s mean and loves to pizen y'all."

Kiara wrenched him back. "Those snakes have enough 'pizen,' as you say, to kill you guys. We're going home."

They walked back to the cabin. Rather, she and Macie did. Kiara clutched the child's hand as her eyes scanned the path. The wildflowers blew.

She jumped. *Wind.*

Dixon chased a toad into the weeds.

"Get back here," she yelled.

Like a scolded dog, he scuffled back to her.

Fifty steps later another snake appeared. "Watch out. There." She grabbed Dixon by the shoulder and pointed at a snake lying in the roadway.

"It's a stick." Dixon's voice sounded old, like a cranky parent tired of explaining the same thing again and again to a child who refused to listen.

The kids chattered. Kiara thought they talked about snake habitat and mouse food and which snake would kill you fastest. She heard snippets. Spiders, skunks, bats, termites—and, now, snakes.

A twig snapped.

She jumped and scratched her head. In her dreads, she felt serpents. Kiara yanked her hand away. She needed to rid herself of her Medusa dreads.

At the back door to her house, she shooed the kids off to Delia Mae's. Braving termites, which would be gone tomorrow, she stepped inside.

For the first time since she'd locked herself out of her home and left herself naked on her porch, she twisted every lock into place.

Leaning against the last locked door, she shivered.

Chapter Twenty-One

Kiara's stars aligned. The morning fog danced as she watched from a safe distance—she hoped—as the pest guy drilled holes ten feet apart into the ground around the perimeter of her cabin. While he hammered termite bait stations into the holes, the man explained how they worked.

The killing procedure didn't matter to her as long as the termites died. Now.

Footsteps clumped behind her. "How bad's the damage?" The voice traveled on a scent of varnish and fresh wood. Could only belong to one person.

"He hasn't said yet," she said.

Shann stepped over to the pest control guy. They talked in low tones, then walked to her kitchen door. They squatted and chatted, pointed and gestured.

With Shann in control, she stepped into her cabin. Murmuring voices from outside made her brave. She could face the buggers. "Say goodbye, my little friends. Arrivederci." She poked her finger at the termite-ridden door. "Time to die."

After an hour of trap setting and poison spraying, Bug-Man promised to return and make sure none survived. She wrote out her check and watched him drive off with her fifteen-hundred bucks.

Shann plopped a canvas toolbox on the counter. "Repairs shouldn't be too bad. We caught them in time. The damage is in one beam under the porch and in the door. You're lucky. They just started their foraging feast."

Lucky? Not me.

Shann rummaged through his toolkit. "The hard part will be tearing out the damaged section and salvaging the rest. Especially with the porch being a foot off the ground. Can't crawl under it to inspect."

"No foundation damage?"

"Not any we saw. Once we've torn it out and fixed everything and put it back together, you won't be able to see the patch on the porch from a galloping horse."

"Translate, please."

Shann grinned. "You won't be able to tell the old porch from the new."

She rolled her eyes.

"I've got trim in my shop, and Beau has a jack. The materials will run you a grand, according to my guestimate." He snapped the tape measure in his hand.

"What about labor?" Kiara asked.

"Included." He stepped onto the porch.

Kiara followed.

"Hold this." He handed her the end of the metal tape measure.

"Why?"

"Can't measure without help." He ran it across the porch and jotted notes on a pad.

"What're you doing?"

"Measuring."

"I can see the tape."

"Can't buy materials if we don't know what we need. Let's head inside and check out your railing problems." He tucked his pencil in his beard.

Like a gosling, Kiara followed Shann into the house.

"How d'you know I needed new balustrades?"

"Balustrades. Ain't said nothing about whatever them things are."

"The handrails."

He arched a brow. "To answer your question, you've met Lia. Beau's wife tries real hard, but if it ain't gossip, she tells it." He tossed her the tape measure once more. "Hold it." Shann ran the tape up the stairs, wrote more on his notepad, then tucked the pencil back into his beard.

She let go of the measuring tape, and it rattled and snapped as it rewound into its canister.

Shann shook the upstairs railing. "This won't take much to reinforce."

His boots made happy, clopping sounds as he bounded down the stairs and rejoined her in the living room. "Want to take a ride?

"Where to?

"Lowe's."

"Why?"

Shann stuck out his hand. "Either you come with me or hand over your credit card." He stepped closer.

She swallowed hard. Underneath the scent of varnish, he smelled of outdoors and fresh air.

"Well?"

"I need to find a handyman."

Shann held out his arms. "You've got him." He inched closer. "If

129

you want him." His voice lowered. His eyes softened. Or hungered.

She could see smudges of their blue. The black of the pupils clouded the brilliance of his irises. Bryce's eyes were brown. Ordinary brown, but sultry. Not beautiful and innocent like Shann's.

Shann's lips parted, moving the whiskers. The pencil wiggled.

The motion of his lips and the comical motion of the pencil broke her trance. She needed to push him away but longed to have him close. *What would his arms feel like?*

No. She couldn't be untrue to Bryce.

She tugged the pencil out of his beard. "Lose something?"

He swiped it from her hands but didn't smile.

Her heart heaved. Kiara wiped her sweaty palms against her thighs. She closed her eyes and warmth grew as he closed the space between them.

She popped her eyes open. Her back stiffened.

Bryce. She couldn't cheat on him.

Jorie. She loved Shann.

With two hands pressed against his chest, she pushed him lightly and stepped away. Had to let her body cool down.

~~

Despite his disappointment with the thwarted kiss, Shann enjoyed watching Kiara squirm.

He looked at his notes and allowed his hormones to settle. Once the heat left his face, he sought her eyes. "Here's my price."

Kiara fiddled with a purse. "Go on. I'm listening." She pulled out her checkbook and scribbled.

So like Abby in this. All business. Clipped. Efficient.

"I'll give you a check for the supplies. Anything left over can be a down payment for your work." With the *zip* of paper, she handed off a check.

Shann latched his hands behind his back and shook his head. "That won't cover it." He eyed the paper. Even her check matched her personality. Waves of blue and green and amber swirled through it. Her handwriting, as beautiful as the note she left when she'd let Youtee loose.

"How much more?" Her thin eyebrows rose. She flipped open the checkbook once more.

"You can pay for supplies, but I don't want money for the work."

"I won't be beholden." Her voice took an edge.

This woman had moxie. In that way, too, she was like Abby. Knew her mind. Would work to get her way.

"You won't. I've got a gig at the Bijou Theater in Knoxville a week from Saturday."

"Okay."

"The kids want to go. I can't perform and leave them running wild. The Bijou frowns on kids wandering onstage or outside on a whim."

"They'd let snakes or toads loose or crawl on your lap in the middle of a ballad."

"Exactly." He stepped closer, close enough to smell her soap, the incense scent he associated with her. Patchouli, he thought it was. He looked into her amber-flecked eyes fastened on him. Her teeth were so white they made snow look yellow. He breathed her in. "I need someone to watch them and make the world think I've raised civilized children."

"I'd be happy to help. Babysitting hardly compensates."

"We have to eat afterward."

"Okay." She nodded.

Could he feel her heart beat or was the thumping coming from his chest? The artery on the side of her neck danced. If he kissed it, would the throbbing stop? Did he dare step in closer?

"Couldn't Jorie do—?"

"No." He slipped his hands onto her shoulders, and she didn't pull away. "Jorie would interpret the night as a date." He tugged her closer, gave a slight pressure on her shoulders.

Her body stiffened, but she tilted her head. Her eyes half closed.

His lips sought hers.

She softened. Slid her hands around his shoulders.

She didn't kiss like Abby.

He pulled Kiara close, and she was all liquid in his arms. Yielding, soft and warm.

With a thrust that could send a rocket into orbit, Kiara pushed away. "I'm sorry." Her breathy voice told him the kiss thrilled her as much as it did him. "I shouldn't."

"I know. We shouldn't." If they continued, he wouldn't ever want to stop. Never had he wanted anyone more than Abby.

Abby? He didn't feel the tug of loss. In five years, never had he kissed a woman and not found her wanting compared to his wife.

He stepped toward Kiara and longed to kiss her again. He stopped and closed his eyes.

Abby, is it time to move on?

Chapter Twenty-Two

As dark fell the next day, Kiara pulled into her driveway. The whole day shot, but at least one gallery in Gatlinburg took the three pieces she'd toted down there. They told her a guy by the name of Joey Something-or-other lived in her area. This Joey, married to Leslie, dealt in art as an agent or a middleman. The gallery owner didn't remember. Kiara'd have to ask around. Someone up here must know him.

On the porch, sat piles of two-by-fours along with newels, spindles, and bunches of other woody things. The porch smelled like a funeral parlor with the chemicals from pressure treated lumber. Like a funeral home, she'd have to spend a fortune to get rid of the dead "body" aka, her house. Bury it and leave it behind.

It'd been several days since she'd gone to her mailbox. She ambled across the road. Her box stood near the McGuffrey's driveway, beside Delia Mae's, twins nestled on the roadside.

As she wiggled out the jammed in flyers and junk mail and whatever else stuffed the roadside postbox, the McGuffrey's van pulled out of their driveway. It drew up next to Kiara, and the passenger window unfurled.

"Howdy." Beau leaned across the console. "How're you doing?"

"Doing good. Went to Gatlinburg today." She stretched her back. "Long day. Isn't it pretty late for you to be heading out?"

"Jist dropped the family off from midweek service and got a call. Jorie's ma, Barbara, is in the emergency room. They think it's her heart."

"How awful."

He nodded. "She's a young'un, too, pert near fifty. Barbara's the only relative here 'bouts Jorie's got left. Say a prayer."

Pray?

Beau scrolled up the window.

Before it shut, Kiara asked. "How's Jorie doing?"

The window rolled down once more. "Scared."

"Is Shann with her?"

"No. Need to run." The window rolled upward, and Beau drove off, his van kicking up dust as it pulled away.

Lights clicked on upstairs at the McGuffreys.

In the dimming light, Kiara flipped through the circulars and crossed back to her house. Junk, junk, rubbish and trash. Amid the potpourri of detritus, she found the electric bill and an envelope from Different Strokes Gallery.

In the cabin, she tossed the refuse into the trash, flopped the electric bill on the counter, and plopped on the couch.

She held the letter from the New York gallery to her lips as though discerning what it contained. The smell of paper enticed her to open it, but she wanted to delay the pleasure. A notice from them could mean one thing. The gallery had four of her pieces. With a thousand of her dollars transformed into lumber and sitting on her porch, this letter, she hoped, contained dividends from a sale.

With a rip to the envelope, a check fell into her lap. Kiara smiled at the appropriateness of the action. A literal windfall.

She looked at the check and her jaw dropped. She straightened. Five K.

She leaned back, closed her mouth, and dreamed. The check didn't recoup the money she'd spent for the truck. Still, every penny she shelled out on this dump had been returned to her.

Straightening, she picked up the letter and read:

Kiara, at closing time on Saturday, the Smithfields, you remember them, don't you? They owned the Hampton beach house Bryce loved? Anyway, the Smithfields discovered your canvas True Love. *They bought it on the spot.*

She wrapped her arms around herself, closed her eyes and savored the words she'd read. The sale came in on Saturday. At closing time. That would've been around five.

Wait.

Saturday at five, she'd been at Queenie's party. Delia Mae had prayed for her about her finances then. Now a sale.

Was there a connection?

She'd read once where people who were prayed for in hospitals without knowing about it, got better more frequently than those who weren't prayed for.

Perhaps Mrs. McG's prayer unleashed a cosmic force?

Or a wonderful fluke.

She had to take off these clothes. They grew tighter with every breath. After changing into her flannel PJs and Bryce's sweater, Kiara hit the bathroom to wash up. She piled toothpaste onto her brush and scrubbed the coffee residue from her mouth.

She leaned over to spit.

A stick under her tub? How'd—?

A scream tore from her gut. The rabbit-eating black rattler had found its way into her bathroom. It wriggled under the claw-foot tub. Dropping her toothbrush in the sink, she jerked out of the room and slammed the door.

But ...

An inch of space stood between the door's edge and the floor. If the snake got out?

She nabbed the cushions off her couch and wedged them against the door. Could the serpent slither under them?

After grabbing an iron skillet, Kiara plopped it on top of the cushions with all the firmness her muscles could muster. No snake would find a millimeter to squirm through. At the kitchen sink, she rinsed her mouth.

With being pregnant, her one bathroom had become the most important room in her household. Could she run up to the barn every time nature called? Or the baby kicked?

How would she get the snake out of here?

She picked up her new landline. What was Shann's phone number? *Who knew?*

Delia Mae's?

She only had the cell number. Useless out here.

Terror crawled up her spine. She twisted her engagement ring and tried to think of some way to get rid of a rattler rattling around her bathroom.

Dread pushed her out her front door, and she tore across her bridge. Kiara stepped on a stone and doubled over. She hadn't thought to put on her Birks. She looked back at her snake-infested den. The cabin door stood open and gave all the creatures of the night the chance to enter and party in her living room.

She glanced at Delia Mae's. Shoes would wait.

She scurried across the road.

Snakes? Did they slither down the street in the dark? She curled her toes and wished for wings.

Safely on the McGuffrey porch, Kiara pounded on the door.

~~

Lia stepped out of the shower. Wrapped in her robe, she towel dried her hair. From downstairs came a wild banging. Considering the timing, it could only be one person.

"Paul?" She called down the stairs.

No answer.

"Chris?"

Still nothing.

134

With Beau guaranteed to be out for several hours, the boys had snuck out their *Call of Duty* video game. She'd left the two battling each other in the den. Let them believe she was as oblivious as she hoped everyone was with her romance novels.

With heavy steps, she walked to the door. "Hi Kiara," Delia Mae said before the door had fully opened. "What's wrong?"

"A rattler. In my bathroom."

"A rattler?" She stepped back as if Kiara held the snake in front of her. "Are you sure?"

"Yes." Her voice rasped. Her head nodded as though a ligament had come unhinged, and she couldn't hold it steady.

"How do you know it's a rattler?"

"Dixon showed me a black one eating a bunny."

Lia arched her brow. She would *not* send her boys after a rattler. "Let me call Shann. Come in."

Kiara stood in the doorway. Her hand clutched her shirt. "I'm sorry. This is a bad time."

Lia punched Shann's number into her phone. "Step in and close the door before all the crickets and moths invite themselves in." She listened as the phone rang. "It's never a bad time." She threw Kiara a small smile. "What makes you think it is?"

"Have you looked at yourself?"

Lia's fingers ran through her wet, tangled mop. *Yep, bad time.* "Shann?" Her brother-in-law answered and gave her no time to worry about her appearance. "Do you still have your snake trap and gloves?

"Ain't getting rid of them living in my open-air retreat," he said. "Those critters like my abode."

"Seems a timber snake got into Kiara's house."

"A rattler? Unlikely. Does she have it contained?"

"She says it's in her bathroom. She peered at Kiara who stood beside the screened door. "Did you close your bathroom door?"

Kiara nodded

Lia relayed the information to Shann.

"Can you send one of your boys down and watch the twins? They're both asleep."

"Absolutely." Lia covered the mouthpiece and yelled down the hall. "Chris? Paul?"

"Yeah, Ma," Chris hollered back.

"Can one of y'all watch your cousins while Uncle Shann rescues Kiara?"

"No prob."

"Chris'll be there."

Shann promised to head to Kiara's as soon as he found the trap, and she hung up.

"Do you want a cup of tea?" *Lord, please make her say no.*

"I've caught you at a bad time. I'll meet Shann."

"You sure?"

"The snake's barricaded behind a shut door. Think I'll be okay."

"Hey, Miss Kiara," Chris dashed into the kitchen. "Cornered yourself a snake?" He slipped on sneakers without bothering to untie them.

"In my bathroom."

"I reckon if it don't slip into the heating duct, Uncle Shann'll get it." The screen door bounced closed after him.

Lia could swan her neighbor turned three shades of white.

~~

The heating duct? Kiara hopped-scuttled across the street, cursing herself for being barefoot and pregnant in Hoo-doo-ville.

She slowed on the bridge hoping to avoid splinters, then dashed onto her porch.

Light spilled into the dark yard from her open kitchen door. Where was Shann?

As though he heard her, the Mule clattered down the road and over the bridge.

"Your knight has arrived on his trusty steed, m'lady." Shann hopped out of the vehicle."

His reassuring voice stilled her night terrors.

Shann stepped into the beams of the kitchen lights.

Her jaw dropped. She laughed.

"What?"

"Your beard." She squinted at his whiskers tied up in four or five unevenly gathered ponytails. Elastic bands in pink and yellow, and one small scrunchie adorned the brown hair. "What have you done?"

He fingered the hair. "Fashionable, heh?" Macie's creation and your fault." He fumbled in the back of the ATV and pulled out a wire trap, a thick pair of gloves, and a hooked stick something like DMV workers used to pick up trash.

He strode to her, his legs clad in knee-high boots. "Hold these." He handed the trap and grabber to Kiara and slipped on welders' gloves. "Like my armor? When I wrangle rattlers, I like full protection. Gauntlet. He held up his arms. "Greaves." He lifted a leg and nodded at the boot, then indicated the garbage-grabber in her hand. "My sword."

He bowed. "Let us proceed." He crooked his arm and offered it to her.

Kiara slipped her hand into his bent arm. "Aren't you mixing metaphors, Mr. Knight?"

"How so?"

"You are a suited knight riding his trusty *mule* to rescue a damsel in distress, but you walk me into the house like a Southern gentleman off to a cotillion."

"What should I do, scoop you up onto my charger and ride into your castle? I think the vehicle would do more damage than a snake."

With their laughter, the remnants of Kiara's terror vanished.

"I perceive you've locked Mr. Sizzzzzle in the bathroom?"

"Not only are you Sir Galahad, but Sherlock Holmes." Kiara shut the door and faced Shann, her hand still linked onto his arm. She fingered a lock of his beard. "How am I to blame for Macie's creation?"

"A few days ago, Macie tangled her hair in little ponytails in an attempt to make 'dreadfuls' and look like you." He ran his finger over Kiara's hand still resting on his arm.

She pulled away.

Did he look disappointed?

"I'm sure you noticed. We had to have Cornie cut her hair to get the tangle out. She pitched a fit that would've made a mule proud. I told her she had to wait until she turned seven to wear dreadlocks."

"That still doesn't explain your beard."

"Practice." Macie practices every night, so she never has to have Cornie cut her mop again. 'A woman's glory is her hair,' she quotes to me. Lia's influence has some negative consequences." He grinned. "Shall we wrangle Mr. Mephistopheles?"

Shann handed Kiara the skillet from the top of the barricade. "Planning on frying him up? I know a recipe."

She grimaced but said nothing as she placed the skillet back on the baker's rack.

Shann shoved away the cushions and opened the door.

"See him?" Kiara crowded his shoulder and peered around him.

"Nope." Shann looked behind the open door.

"Where could he go?"

"Not too many places in this tight space. Perhaps under the tub." He bent from the waist and peered under the bathtub. "I'm not putting my face on the ground. If it's a rattlesnake, I don't want my visage within striking distance."

"He couldn't have gotten into the register, could he?" Kiara struggled to not shiver, but her body betrayed her. She trembled.

Shann looked around. He tapped the rectangular grate by the door with his toe. "Heat and air would work better if it was open." He flipped the little lever open, then closed it. "So, I'd say, no."

Kiara screamed. She pointed. In the far corner behind the tub, the black serpent wiggled.

"That?" Shann's laugh came from deep inside. "It ain't no rattler, m'lady. What you've got here is a good ol' black snake. The critters are keepers."

"I'm *not* keeping a snake."

He chuckled and held out his hand. "Give me the grabber."

Kiara slapped it into his palm like a surgical nurse handing off a scalpel.

Shann kneeled. He prodded under the tub.

The snake slithered forward. Fast.

Kiara danced out of the bathroom, dashed to the couch, and climbed onto it. She tucked her legs under her, but never took her focus from the bathroom door.

A stick clattered on the linoleum. Shann emerged with the black thing held behind its neck. "Easier to pick him up than use the stick."

The critter slithered and curled around his arm.

Kiara's shriek could've woken the twins down the road.

Holding the snake in front of him, Shann stepped outside. When he strode back into the house, he was snakeless.

~~

Shann joined Kiara on the couch. "Feel better?"

She gave a shy shrug and looked down. "Embarrassed about my terror. Is Tennessee full of awful creatures?"

"Define awful?"

"Singing tree bugs and toads and skunks and spiders and bats and snakes."

"You left out scorpions."

"No!"

"We have two types. One's native, one's not. They leave you alone. You have more to fear from a yellow jacket. Our scorpions' stings are not as bad as a bee's."

She sat with her back straight. It looked like every muscle in her body had become a spindle.

Shann looped his arm around her. "Ain't nothing to be afeared of. Those critters are harmless."

His words didn't comfort. She sat stiff under his arm.

"Are they like those huge southwestern scorpions with the curly tails?" She held her hands out about a foot apart.

"Nope." Shann took her hands and closed them so they sat six inches apart. "About so."

"No." Kiara yanked her hands away and covered her mouth.

He spread his fingers an inch apart. "This big. Harmless."

She shivered and pulled into him as though looking for warmth.

Shann wished Stinking Creek had another varmint he could scare

138

her with to make her burrow closer. He gentled his hand over her head and coaxed it onto his shoulder.

Chapter Twenty-Three

Kiara walked on rainbows as she left the doctor's office in Jellico. Songs bubbled up and offered to carry her far over the sparkly arcs.

This baby would turn her into a girly girl—all glittery and lustrous. It would make her the clichéd pregnant woman—glowing under the aura of love.

She stopped to look at her sonogram printout one last time. Her baby didn't like having its picture taken. Every time the paddle neared it—no, she couldn't call this child an *it*, and never again would she refer to it as a fetus.

What pronouns could she use? He? Yep. A little Bryce. Or a baby Key?

As the sonogram wand hovered over him, she moved away.

She/he had a mind of his/her own.

Who would've thought?

She struggled to bite back her grin. The little thing inside her looked like a baby. It looked human.

Sort of.

It had a big head, fat belly, and spindly limbs. A real live kid swam around inside of her. She had to wait another month to find out if it was a boy or girl scuba diving in her gut.

She had to wait until February to meet her own lil' munchkin.

What'd she want? If she had a boy, she'd name him Bryce Birch Rafferty.

A girl? Leah Grace was a pretty name. She'd have to use her neighbor's name somewhere. It—the baby—wouldn't be born if not for her.

She stuffed the picture into her purse and nixed the name Grace. She *hated* it.

Wait until Imani and Gina learned she was expecting.

She pried her phone from her back pocket as she resumed her walk to the vehicle. Then she tucked it back into her pants' pocket.

At the moment, she needed to savor the idea of the baby by herself. To wonder at the awesomeness of the universe. Two teeny, tiny cells defied the odds and made a baby. Gave her Bryce back.

She climbed into her Ford and drove toward I-75. Pictures of baby Rafferty swam in her head. She hardly saw the road.

Fifteen minutes later, Kiara exited the highway and headed down Lowes Branch Road. It wouldn't be long before she lost cell service, so she called Gina.

"Hey, Kiara." Gina answered on the first ring. "You caught me at the end of my lunch."

A voice sounded in the background.

"I'm sorry. Fridays are nuts. I've got to handle this. Call me later?" Gina disconnected before Kiara could answer.

Kiara asked the Bluetooth to dial Imani as they started down the mountain. The phone made dialing noises but wouldn't connect. Having delayed too long, she lost the signal.

Ten minutes later she turned into her driveway. The jumble of wood on her porch had been rearranged.

She checked the kitchen porch. New wood stood out in stark relief against the old. Shann had exaggerated his skill. Even on a space shuttle —let alone a galloping horse—she would see the difference in the repair and the old decking. Stepping onto the porch, she walked and tested the wood. She rocked on her feet. Nothing tried to give way and send her hurtling six inches to the ground below. She jumped a few times. Stayed upright and standing on wood.

Shann did a wonderful job.

She stepped down, knelt on the rocky soil and peered under the decking. Darkness stared back. Judging from the quickness of the repairs, the fix didn't entail too much just as Shann promised.

Kiara stepped through her bug-free kitchen door. After brewing a steaming cup of honey-doused pomegranate tea, she sat on her couch and pulled out her phone. Tapping the photos, she scrolled through them until she found her favorite shot of Bryce. She held it an inch away from her belly.

"Look, Baby. Here's your daddy." She ran her finger over the picture. "Bryce, wherever you are, can you see? You have a son. Or a daughter. Thankfully not both."

She'd leave twins to Shann. One kid was one more than she could raise to be a well-adjusted human.

She ran her hand across her stomach tightening the cloth covering it.

She continued talking to Bryce's picture. "See how fat I am. Going to get bigger."

Talking to the cell didn't satisfy.

She needed a friend. It was time to chat with Imani. They both had surprises to explain.

If Bryce couldn't share in the joy of her pregnancy, and Gina once more had no time for her, she'd talk to the newly minted Christian about her newly created baby. Her heart swelled with longing for Imani and Lance Greaves. For Gina and Art King. For Manhattan and its galleries and parties and sheer exhilaration of living. How much longer would she be condemned to live in this hole in the wall?

She dialed the number. Someone knocked at her front door. She disconnected. "Come in."

Shann stepped into her life.

No.

She wanted no one to interfere with her time with Bryce or her New York City world.

~~

"Are you ready, Lia?" Cornie swiveled her salon chair around so Lia faced the mirror. Her sister removed the pins and graying hair fell around Lia's shoulders and half-way down her back. Cornie ran her fingers through it. "I've wanted to do this for twenty years."

"Twenty years? It hasn't been bad for two decades."

Cornie hummed as she fussed. Her bracelet jingled like wind chimes.

"I've cut my hair."

"A self-serve trim is not a haircut." Cornie still looked in the mirror as she fluffed her sister's hair. "So what do you want done?"

"Keep it long. I want to ditch my flying saucer." Lia clamped her lips and her heart sped up. The thought of defying Beau scared her.

And liberating.

She inhaled.

"I'd always envied your mane when we were kids," Cornie said.

"Yeah. I remember you cutting your doll's hair off and pinning it under your own."

"Ma had a fit." Cornie tilted her head as she pulled on locks of Lia's hair."

"Because you fixed it at school and went the whole day with your "extensions" poking out of your head in weird patches."

The women chuckled.

"You'd look good with hair my length," Cornie ran her hand beside her chin.

"Beau'd have a fit."

"If only your hair keeps him happy, then your marriage failed. Jimmy likes mine, and he's as rigid as his brother."

Lia shook her head.

"Does your headshake mean you don't think Jimmy's as legalistic

142

as your husband, or does it mean no to the short cut?"

"Both. If a woman's glory—"

"Jimmy's of the McGuffrey lineage. Follows their faith. Beau couldn't object. If he does, give him a piece of your mind. You're not shy about sharing it with everyone else."

Again, Lia shook her head, like a tremor rather than a simple no.

"I'll cut to here," she touched Lia's shoulder.

"No."

"Okay here." Cornie took a strand and pulled it several inches below the shoulder. "Then, to make me happy and make it look like I did something, I'll layer the sides. This way, you can wear it up." She swept the back into a sloppy, handheld ponytail. "It'll be cool on the muggy days, and the sides will frame your face." Cornie dropped the hair.

Lia studied herself in the mirror. With her graying hair loose, she looked frumpier than she had with it tied up in knots. "Okay."

"How about highlights—"

"Absolutely not."

"The appointment after yours canceled. It was my last one for the day, so I can spend as much time as you need. I won't do anything drastic. Just a little green."

Lia's jaw dropped. Her hand clutched her chest.

"Joking." Again Cornie fluffed Lia's hair. "I'll use your natural color. It'll make you look your age."

"I'm not sure."

"Look at Dolly Parton, and no, I'm not going to make you look like her." She leaned over her sister. "You don't have a prayer of looking like that seventy-year-old babe."

Mirth overtook the terror of the beautician's chair.

"She's a good, Christian woman. Raised and donated tons of money to the Gatlinburg fire victims several years ago. Gives schoolkids books. Her Dollywood shows always include glory to the Lord. If she can look hot, you can, too."

Lia's mood lightened a little more. Cornie looked like her, or so everyone said, but her sister seemed alive. Vivid. No one ever doubted Cornie's faith. She nodded. "Let's do it."

Two hours later, the moment of truth arrived. Lia pulled her car into the driveway. She pulled down the car's visor and fluffed her hair in the mirror. She looked young. *Dare I think it? I'm pretty.*

She stepped into the empty yard. No Youtee bounded to her begging for pats. Inside, the kitchen had been cleaned of everything except the aroma of fried catfish and okra. The crew had been fed— probably by Chris who loved cooking as much as football.

"Beau?"

Voices murmured in the den. After tossing her purse aside, she stepped into the room and stopped. In the playroom, eased back in his recliner, Beau sat with Macie on one knee, Dixon on the other. Propped among them was *The Rhyming Bible*.

Dixon had lifted his shirt and, even in sleep, fingered his belly button. Both kids slept.

Despite the dozing urchins, Beau recited the poem from John, chapter four "Give me some water, please, precious daughter. The sun's shining down and my friends are in town."

She must've moved or made a noise.

He looked up. His eyes, sleepy before, opened wide. They danced. "Hello, pretty woman. I perceiveth thou hast been with Cornie."

She pulled her hair. "You noticed?"

Obviously.

"Aside from you stepping into our den shorn of your gray hair, Jimmy warned me. Turn around." He swiveled his head to indicate she should turn.

She pivoted.

"I like it. I'd like it better if'n you help me with these tykes. Right now, my arm's sounder asleep than them."

"Why do you have the kids?" Lia lifted Macie. The child squirmed, but soon nestled back against Lia.

Beau stood, shifting Dixon whose only movement came from Beau as he hoisted the dead weight. "Shann's gone over to work on the railings at Kiara's."

Beau followed her into the room the twins used when Shann traveled. They laid the children down, one on each twin bed. Neither child twitched.

"Where are Paul and Chris?" She pulled the comforter up to Macie's chin.

"Hunting or riding. Took the hound, so I'd say hoping for coon."

She turned around to find her husband right behind her. She slipped her arms around Beau and pulled his head to her and pressed her lips against his. A thrill shuddered down her spine, and she leaned in close.

His body pulled her tighter. He ran his hands down her back. His breath came heavy.

Beau didn't see her haircut as a defiant act? Why'd she worry?

Here was the man she married. The Sterling Beau McGuffrey she adored.

~~

144

Shann's hammer pounded on the stairway as Kiara drained the pasta. She poured hot RAGÚ over the noodles, dumped them into a large bowl, and placed it on the coffee table next to the two dishes of salad. "Dinner's ready."

Shann looked down from the landing. "Perfect timing." He gave one more whack of the hammer. "This railing will hold a swinging gorilla—or Dixon when he climbs it." He tossed the hammer into the toolbox and left it in the loft. He joined Kiara at the coffee table. "Looks good."

"It's basic stuff. RAGÚ and boiled noodles."

"That's fine by me. I'm a simple man. Let's pray." He took Kiara's hand and said a grace lasting no more than thirty seconds.

"So you're as religious as Delia Mae?" Kiara cut her spaghetti.

"What are you doing?" Shann pointed his fork at her.

"Eating."

"No one cuts spaghetti."

"I do."

"This is how you eat it." He twirled a forkful of pasta and stuck it in his mouth. Then Shann sucked the strands. They slurped as they slid into his mouth. Sauce splattered his face and whiskers.

Kiara put her fork and knife down. She looked as though he'd eaten the snake from her bathroom.

He laughed and wiped the mess off his face and beard. With his index finger, he reached over and lifted Kiara's chin. "Close your mouth." He winked. "That would be Dixon's interpretation of sketti eating. It would start a competition between the kids on who would be the grossest."

"You'd win."

Shann took a smaller mouthful, and not a drop of sauce hit his beard. "I do need to trim or shave. Grooming this thing takes time away from guitar building." He sipped water. "Did you know Arvol Hogg ordered one of my electric guitars? Arvol, the greatest country artist since—"

"I think you're avoiding my question. Why don't you go to your brother's church? Delia Mae says you believe the same stuff as they do."

"The stuff, as you call it, isn't a myth, like you believe."

"Then why don't you go?"

"The McGuffreys come from a long line of preachers, probably stretching back to King James himself—which is why they read the sanctified version of the 1611 KJV."

"KJV?"

"King James Version of the *Bible.*"

Kiara nodded.

"With every generation, the straight and narrow has become straighter and narrower. Not being a tightrope artist, I couldn't abide the McGuffrey theology and left my brother's church."

"Abide?"

"Yep, ma'am. We hillbillies shore kin tawlk rite."

She swatted the air and grinned. "If you believe, like you say, why don't you go somewhere else?"

"Why is an atheist so concerned about my salvation?" He shook Parmesan cheese on his pasta and his salad.

"Are all Christians as hard-nosed as Beau?"

He shook his head, chewed the salad, and swallowed. "When I tour, I go to service with the guys. I believe the *Bible*."

"Why?"

"Do I go to service or believe?"

"Both," Kiara said.

"I believe because it's true."

"How can you say it's true? It tells all those mythological stories about a big flood and the Tower of Babel and some guy making wine out of water." She put her fork down. "Water to wine sounds like a good party trick, though."

"Not a party trick." He sipped his water.

Her eyes stayed focused on him.

He owed her an honest answer. Still, honest could get complicated. "I believe because I've seen prayer answered like when Beau gave me a piece of his land, and Lia offered to care for my kids after Abby died."

She opened her mouth to speak.

He held up his hand to silence her. "I believe because I've seen changes in people when they've given their lives to Christ. Because of the peace I find reading Scripture. When I look at the universe at night, and the stars shine overhead like Christmas lights, it's the only thing that makes sense. It explains my existence."

"Evolution does, too."

He nodded. "It does."

Her eyes widened.

"Belief in God or belief in evolution both take faith. My conviction is confirmed in everything I do."

"So you don't have to go to church and do penance and pay for masses, or whatever, to be a believer?"

He smiled. "First, I don't have to do anything. Becoming a Christian is an act of grace."

Her head snapped to attention as though he called her name.

"Something wrong?"

"No." She shook her head. "Go on."

146

"You don't have to do anything except acknowledge you're a sinner and desire to turn away from all wrongdoing. Once you accept Jesus, your desires change, and you want to follow God's ways. It happens naturally. Perhaps I should say, supernaturally."

Shann leaned forward. Something propelled him to explain his belief as though Kiara could give him answers to his questions. "Going to church helps Christians maintain the correct spiritual direction. Kind of like following a blueprint to build a house or frets on a guitar neck. It guides us. Helps us even as we help others."

"If you don't like your brother's church, find a new one? I've been in town for two weeks. It doesn't take a genius to see if you spit anywhere in Tennessee, you hit another church."

He said nothing and couldn't meet her eyes. Kiara spoke the truth. Leave it to God to use an atheist to convict him.

"I love yoga."

He raised his brows and looked at her again. This was a rather abrupt change of subject.

"My last yoga instructor got weird. He started all this Eastern Mysticism. I hated it."

"You should. Mystical stuff—"

"I switched studios. The one I went to before Bryce died ... " She swallowed hard. "The new one helped us stretch, reinforced our mindfulness and brought the release of tension I wanted. Same discipline. Different flavor. Couldn't a different church do the same for you?"

Shann picked up his dishes. "Let me help you clean up."

They stood shoulder to shoulder at the sink. The thought of leaving Kiara tonight laid heavy on Shann. Her shoulder warmed him. He hated when she stepped away to stash a dried pan. How could he prolong this moment?

God, if you want me here, make a way.

"Would you like to watch a movie or something?" Kiara asked.

"You don't have a TV."

"I have a computer and a subscription to Amazon Prime. We could find a show we both like."

"Sure." Would Kiara understand this was another reason he believed in God? He always opened the path He wanted you to travel. Sometimes, it was the route you wanted for yourself.

When the last of the kitchen had been cleaned, Kiara dimmed the lights, and he followed her into the living room.

With her computer open and the laptop warming their legs, they settled inches apart. They scrolled through movies.

"This looks good." Shann pointed. "It has romance and fighting and fantasy."

"It had good reviews." Kiara clicked the icon, and the movie buffered. She snuggled closer as they waited for the opening scene.

Not allowing God's answer to his unspoken prayer be wasted, Shann shifted nearer.

She moved in.

He laid his arm on the back of the sofa.

She leaned in.

Opening credits rolled. He let his hand slip off the couch.

She didn't move.

He dropped his arm.

Kiara relaxed under it.

His mind roamed as the film showed two lovers and the electricity sparking between them. He looked down at Kiara whose head now rested on his shoulder. *Little Miss Atheist, convincing me to go to church?* He half smiled. *Do you know you're going to be a believer sooner than we can imagine?*

A car chase roared on the computer. He refocused. Then the romance developed once more. He yawned. His mind wandered back to Kiara's exhortation about yoga studios and church.

Band members mentioned an awesome church a few miles away in Duff. Sunday he'd check it out.

Action scenes resumed. Apparently, they did to Kiara what the romance scenes did to him. Her head grew heavy on his shoulder. Her body relaxed into his. Soon she breathed in soft, regular intervals.

A romance scene played once more.

His own eyes closed. He should go.

Kiara's weight and her scent enticed him to stay a minute more.

~~

A cramp started in Shann's fingers in the arm wrapped around Kiara. He wriggled his hand, but the spasm worked its way up into his biceps. Every muscle wanted to wind itself into a coil tighter than a rattler ready to strike. He gritted his teeth and unwound himself from Kiara.

Little stings and prickles worked over his hand. Shann stood and shook his arm like a housewife shaking dust from the rug. The circulation seeped back through his veins at the speed of a possum.

Kiara stirred. Her head lolled on the couch back.

He laid her down and lifted her legs to the sofa. Grabbing the afghan, he tucked it around her.

The dark outside looked lighter. It had to be nearing dawn. He'd left Beau with the kids—not a good move. His brother would lecture him tomorrow — or that would be today — about his duty as a father and the raising of his twins. He glanced at the couch.

Kiara slept. She looked so vulnerable. This woman had so much zest and life in her. Even Dixon begged to hang out with her. He saw her flipping on the trampoline. Watched her laugh and cry and yell. Listened to her love for Bryce.

In those ways, Kiara didn't match Abby who kept life controlled. Abigail felt life deeply but contained it. His perfect, beautiful Abby.

He shoved his hands into his pockets. Feeling refreshed despite the awkward sleep through the movie, Shann stepped onto the porch. He breathed in the fresh air. Beautiful start to a wonderful life. The morning fog drifted in the cool, dark air. Across the road, lights flicked on.

Lia kept it dark when she got up. She savored the solitude. Beau had to be stirring.

Shann climbed into the Mule and headed home. He'd brew a cup of joe, and once Lia had prayer time, he'd go and apologize for not picking up the twins last night.

A van rumbled by when he stepped on his porch. He started coffee. His phone's handset showed he had a voice mail. While the coffee dripped, he called up his message.

It's Beau. Sorry to call so early, thought you'd want to know. Jorie's mom died. I'm heading out in a few minutes.

Shann blinked his shock.

His heart torqued. Poor Jorie. Her mother was all she had left. They shared a closeness he always envied. With Barbara, Jorie opened up. Talked with abandon. Mrs. T brought out her daughter's beauty and enhanced Jorie's virtue.

What would she do now?

He dialed Beau, and Lia answered.

"Is Beau there?"

"He left two minutes ago."

"Are they at LaFollette Medical?"

"Yes."

"Do you mind watching the kids?"

After pouring coffee into his travel mug, Shann climbed into his truck. He'd lost Abby too soon. Both of his parents had lived in heaven for a dozen or so years. He'd been the surprise baby born ten years after Jimmy, so Shann grew up like an only child.

His experiences taught him what Jorie must feel.

Chapter Twenty-Four

Daylight opened Kiara's eyes. She stretched on the couch. For the first time in this dump, the morning sounds serenaded her rather than sounding like a car alarm.

She'd dreamt Shann had been here all night. So real.

Of course, he would've left at the movie's end to take care of the kids.

Lying under the covers was as delicious as sipping peppermint hot chocolate with a double dose of whipped cream. She pulled the blanket over her head and closed her eyes. *Just a minute more.*

Thirty seconds later, she climbed off the sofa. Her stomach twisted. The grumble told her she'd lollygagged too long. She plopped bread into the toaster and watched daylight paint Delia Mae's house.

Lighting in New York was never this ethereal.

The morning sun daubed Stinking Creek in grays and greens and subtlety. Fog danced, and birds sang.

New York was harsh and stark. Still, Manhattan's glamor and its excitement tugged at her. The bustle of people and important careers meant life. It infused energy into her. Because of its zest, her creativity blossomed. Artists and eccentrics and geniuses splattered the City with an invigorating color.

More than its vitality, her friends lived there, and they knew the grief of her loss. They'd shared memories of Bryce.

Her friends would be shocked to learn she was expecting.

Gina would never believe the pregnancy excited Kiara. How they mocked all the Madonna wannabes rubbing bellies and wearing too tight maternity clothes. She and Gina used to slump and plump out their bare stomachs. They'd cup their hands around their phony baby bumps and post the pics on Facebook.

Kiara needed a dose of Gina's sass. Her BFF left for her store around eight on Saturdays, so it wouldn't be too early to call.

As Gina's cell rang, Kiara buttered her toast.

"Good morning. If seven-thirty is ever good." Gina laughed.

"Hey."

"Kiara." Her tone hardened in the one uttered word. "I almost didn't answer with the strange phone number. Thought it was a telemarketer. I should've figured it was you seeing as it came from Tennessee and before anyone human woke up."

"Do you have a moment to chat?"

Gina paused. "I'll have to head to Threads soon, but I haven't heard anything about your new home. Tell me." Her voice resumed its merry lilt. Kiara could picture her pulling her morning java to her, propping her head on her fist, intent on hearing every detail Kiara had to share.

"Well, before that, I have surprising news."

"You're coming back to New York." Gina's comment sounded like a statement of fact.

"Nope. This is better. Bryce and I are going to have a baby."

Silence greeted her.

After an eternity, a noise rattled through the receiver. "I thought he'd," Gina coughed. "Excuse me." Once more, silence filled the line for a beat. Gina sniffed. "Sorry. I'm coming down with a cold. Let me find a tissue." At last, the phone clattered, and Gina spoke again. "Bryce told me he'd gotten himself fixed."

Why would Bryce tell her?

Kiara bit her toast, more to collect her thoughts than from hunger. "Obviously, vasectomies aren't fail-safe. I'm due in February."

"Are you sure it's Bryce's?"

"Gina! From the moment I laid eyes on him, you knew he was the love of my life."

Gina inhaled. The sound echoed over the receiver. "I'm not stupid."

"It's weird. Neither one of us ever wanted kids. Now?" Kiara paced, the phone pressed to her ear and the forgotten toast in her other hand. "Now you and I can enjoy a little bit of Bryce when I move home."

"When are you coming back?"

"As soon as the house sells or you or Imani find an apartment I can afford." She bit into her bread as her hunger resurrected and spoke around the cold mouthful of limp toast. "I had to spend beaucoup bucks exterminating termites. Then I had to put in a handrail on the stairs."

"Those steps scared me."

"Scared you? When did you see them?"

Gina stuttered a few unintelligible words. "I think Bryce showed me pictures."

Kiara breathed again. *Pictures. Of course.*

"Anyway, everything's fixed. It's listed. I hope I'll be in New York before snow flies."

"Yeah. We can hope."

Was she imagining an edge to Gina's voice? The toast hardened in Kiara's stomach like plaster setting up.

"I've got to run. Threads won't run itself." Gina gave a lame sounding snicker. "With you having a home phone, it'll be good to keep in touch."

"Keep your eyes open for apartments."

"I'll do just that." Her voice, again, sounded like she'd say anything to get off the line.

As though underscoring Kiara's feeling, Gina clicked off without a goodbye.

Suddenly wanting a little sweetness with her breakfast, and something to moisten the dry clay she'd been eating, Kiara slathered jam on her second slice. She ran the knife back and forth on the bread, again and again.

How come Bryce never showed me the pictures of this place? I saw nothing of Stinking Creek until the cab dumped me here in the middle of the night.

She slipped the jam back in the fridge. Shut the door. Her hand rested on the handle.

Maybe he wanted to surprise me?

She picked up her plate and headed to the living room. She'd seen Bryce's photos, all of them. Kiara loved watching the life she missed with him when they weren't together. When they'd been apart, she'd flip through his phone. He'd laugh and accuse her of spying. He'd kiss her nose and say he had nothing to hide.

Never did he have a picture of this place. How'd Gina know about the house?

Those sniffles? A cold didn't show itself intermittently. After she found her tissue, she didn't cough or sniffle. Her voice—sarcastic and sassy—held no hoarseness from a cold.

Gina had cried about the news of Kiara's pregnancy.

Kiara'd shed enough tears during the past two months to recognize sorrow.

Gina had been avoiding her phone calls. She didn't sound happy about Kiara coming home.

She chewed but tasted nothing.

When Bryce came down here last year, Gina took off for a trade show.

Then in the pit of her stomach, Kiara knew.

From the start, she and Gina competed for Bryce. Her friend was anxious to hear even the most intimate details of their life. When he died, Kiara thought grief for her devastated Gina.

Bryce cheated on her with her closest friend.

Every nerve in Kiara's body shook. She hurled the last of her toast across the kitchen.

How could she?

Kiara's heart pounded, and she placed her palm over her sternum and pressed, tried to still the racing heartbeat with pressure from her hand.

Bryce and Gina?

No, no, no.

Kiara inhaled to the count of five. Held her breath for another count. Slowly, she exhaled. She needed to be mindful and think this dilemma through.

She twisted her engagement ring. As though she'd never seen it before, she stared at it.

Morning light caught the diamond, and it winked at her. *Aha,* the ring said. *Thought he was faithful.*

He was.

He swore he loved her more than his own life.

Her breathing calmed until she saw Gina's eyes at the last art opening she and Bryce hosted. Never did they linger on Bryce's face. Instead, her gaze flowed over his body. Gina's dress with the plunging V? Bryce loved it. Their friendly hands touched arms and cheeks. They'd glance at each other when they thought no one looked.

Kiara rubbed her eyes, but her ring twisted and the diamond scraped along her face.

She yanked it off.

He cheated.

Bryce and Gina bamboozled her.

Kiara hurled the ring across the room. It clinked somewhere in the kitchen, then skittered across the floor.

The creeps.

She closed her eyes. Yearned to blot out the revelation, but saw Gina standing in the corner of Birch Gallery. Bryce stood too close. Because he didn't move away when Kiara approached, because Bryce draped his arm around Kiara and pulled her close, she believed his faithfulness. His action had chased her suspicion away.

After getting to know Shann and Jorie and Delia Mae, she understood how she deceived herself. In the McGuffrey clan, she saw an honest family — one who loved, who behaved like they loved. Who acted the way they thought. Without deception.

Wrongheaded. Too conservative. But without hypocrisy.

How could she blot out Bryce's betrayal? She absently twisted her finger and remembered she'd hurled the expensive ring across the room.

She thought it had skittered under the baker's rack. If she sold the ring, she could afford an apartment for half a year. She headed into the kitchen.

Tucked next to the fridge sat the bottle of wine she'd opened before she knew she was pregnant. *Wine. A small glass will settle my nerves. Clear my head.*

She poured a half of a goblet of ruby wine and sipped. The ring could stay lost. She wanted nothing of Bryce's.

Kiara paced while she clutched the glass by its smooth bowl.

She ran her sweaty palm over her leggings. It glided over the small swell of her belly. Kiara yanked it away as though burned. She took another swig. She shouldn't drink.

Plunking the glass down, Kiara figured she'd find her yoga mat. With meditation, she'd see that she misconstrued her conversation.

She stepped up one stair. Stepped back down.

She misinterpreted nothing.

Back in the Hamptons five years ago, after her first night with Bryce, Gina didn't talk to her for a week.

Kiara found her half-full glass, slugged the wine and paced again.

When Gina married Art, she confessed how jealous she'd been about Bryce choosing Kiara instead of her. Gina laughed like it'd been a childish thing. They talked about the prowess of their respective men. Even then, newly back from her honeymoon, Gina took too much interest in Bryce.

Kiara finished the goblet of wine.

She poured herself another glass. *Think, Kiara. Think.*

She'd confront Gina and ask her point blank. This way, Kiara would find out she made a wrong assumption. Then she'd crawl around and find her ring before she lost it for good. Gina should be at Threads by now.

Kiara dialed the store.

"Threads, how can I help you?" Gina's voice was all businesslike.

"Were you shleep—um, sleeping—with Bryce?"

"Kiara, are you drunk?"

"Answer me. Did—"

The phone clicked off.

She dialed again. It rang. Rang some more. Voice mail picked up. She had her answer.

Not bothering to pour another glass, Kiara picked up the wine bottle and chugged. *Not good for the ...*

Who cared?

Standing by the sink, she stared out the window at nothing. A minute, two or three sips later, a van pulled into the McGuffrey driveway.

Shann's truck drove in behind it.

Shann. He'd know. He'd calm her down.

She slipped on her Birks and ran onto the porch in time to see him reach up to the passenger side. His strong, wood-calloused fingers wrapped around Jorie's arms. He helped her down.

Jorie fell into his embrace, and like he did to Kiara last night, he ran his large hands over Jorie's head and pulled it to him.

She buried her face in his chest. His beard grazed her hair.

Delia Mae came onto the porch. She held the door open. Beau, Jorie and Shann went in.

She'd been shut out.

Back on the sofa, Kiara drank.

Bryce. The fat rattler had devoured her life.

She picked up her phone and scrolled through pictures while she swigged wine from the bottle. She deleted photo after photo of the snake. Them at the Hamptons — deleted.

Them at her first opening at Birch Gallery — gone.

Bryce on their bed. Cooking breakfast for her.

Delete. Delete.

Gone.

Kiara came to the picture Imani had taken of their engagement. Behind Bryce stood Art, mostly hidden by Bryce's head. Apart from Art, almost as though she wasn't with him, Gina frowned. More than a chance expression phones were notorious for catching, her eyes looked sad and gazed toward Bryce — wide and downcast.

How much more proof do I need?

The stupid fetus moved. It became a tumor sucking the life out of her.

She took another gulp of wine.

She fished the sonogram photos out of her purse. "I don't want you," she hissed at the grainy printouts. Kiara ripped them in half. Halved them again. Tore some more.

Shreds of paper fluttered to her stomach. She rubbed her hands hard against it. "Get out of me."

She drank the last of the wine and hurled the bottle across the room. It shattered against her cabinets.

She had another bottle.

In the kitchen, she tried to open it.

The paper around the top proved problematic.

Grasping the bottle, she staggered to the utensil drawer. Wooziness forced her to take careful steps. She dug out a knife. Inched it under the foil binding the cap shut.

The knife slipped.

She slit her finger. Kiara popped it into her mouth and sucked the blood. The salty copper fueled her desire, like a vampire's foreplay. She needed crimson wine.

Kiara nipped the binding of the wine bottle and unwound it in a long string like an umbilical cord. Tossing it to the floor, she twisted the top. The cap refused to budge.

Shann had left his toolbox. She rummaged through it. Found a pipe wrench. Screwed it onto the cap, twisted it off and tossed the pipe wrench with the cap still attached. She lifted the bottle. "Here's to nothing."

Once more she stared out the window and studied her truck. What was she doing to herself? Why was she sulking in Stinking Creek waiting for someone to fix her woes? Waiting on the realtor, on an apartment, on Shann or Delia Mae or Imani?

She'd find a way out of this mess—a mess she did not create. She sat on the couch. This time Kiara filled a goblet halfway with the red silk, like civilized women did. She swirled it.

Her pregnancy was early enough, she could still terminate. Where would she find a doctor?

In New York, she had a great ob-gyn who'd refer her. Here? This conservative backwater would have waiting periods, consultations and more hoops to jump through than a Southern belle dressing for a ball.

New York.

What an idiot she'd been. She could go home.

Imani had offered her a space on her couch. Once up there, she'd find an apartment and start anew.

Kiara lifted her wineglass and drained it.

She was going home.

She stood. The room spun. "Ooh." She put a hand out looking for something to hold. The twirling stopped. *Stood too quick.*

She climbed the stairs, found her largest suitcase. Lobbed in slacks and dresses and underwear and her flannel pajamas. She picked up the white cashmere and held it to her nose. The smell had been as short-lived as Bryce's faithfulness. She tossed it aside. It landed on the lampshade.

After clomping the overstuffed suitcase down the stairs, she hit the bathroom. There, she threw soap and cream and toothpaste into her toiletry bag. With the bag looped over her shoulder, Kiara retrieved the suitcase and dragged everything outside.

She lowered the Ford's tailgate and hoisted the baggage. The weight stumbled her. *Who made truck beds so high?*

Using her back and bracing her legs, she hove like a drunken longshoreman loading a cargo ship. The suitcase scraped against the metal bed. The slamming tailgate rattled and clanked and chafed her nerves.

She tossed her toiletry bag into the cab.

Climbing into the driver's seat, Kiara started the engine.

Wait.

She jumped out, ran toward her cabin. Kiara didn't lift her feet high enough as she darted onto the porch. Her foot caught and twisted. She fell heavily on the edge and slipped to the ground, rasping her knee against the wood before slamming it into the dirt.

She sat on the floorboards and hugged her knee to her chest. Blood oozed through her torn leggings. Her skin stung like Shann had run a sander over it. Or his bristly beard.

Using the porch's post, she pulled herself up. Clinging to the wood, she waited for the spinning world to settle.

She breathed in. Exhaled. Stiffening her back, raising her chin, and slowing her steps, Kiara walked inside.

On the counter sat her open bottle of wine. She couldn't find the cap. She picked up the bottle by the neck. Her leg still stung, and she bent to examine it.

Can't go with my clothes torn and bloody.

She clunked the bottle back on the counter, then stripped off the leggings. They tangled on her army boots, so she plopped on the floor. After unlacing the boots, she removed the leggings and tossed them. They slapped the side door and splayed on the floor.

Her tunic came halfway down her thighs. Long enough to be a dress. A little short—but fashionable. She shoved her feet into her boots without bothering to lace them. She'd be driving, not walking. Kiara picked up her half-empty bottle and stumbled out of the cabin and to her vehicle. The cabin's front door stood open like a gap-toothed grin mocking her.

Let the skunks and rats have free access to the hole. She was done with it.

Kiara climbed into the running truck. She fumbled with the seat belt, but couldn't snap it. She let the belt slide back into place.

Which way to Manhattan? I-75 went north. It hit Jellico and therefore Kentucky. Seeing as she bought her food in Kentucky, she knew Kentucky was north. She tipped back the bottle. After Kentucky came another state. Missouri? Iowa? Who knew?

She had a GPS. It would figure out how to get to New York.

She shifted into gear and inched the truck over the bridge. Took it nice and slow so she wouldn't fall into the anemic creek below. At the road, she headed right.

Her destiny belonged to her. She'd no longer be a loser sitting nowhere waiting for someone to rescue her from this mess.

She stepped on the gas.

The truck lurched and accelerated. Speed was good.

Except.

The road curved uphill. The truck went straight.

Kiara hit the brake.

The truck picked up speed.

What?

No.

She'd hit the gas. Kiara stomped her foot on the brake this time, but the truck hit gravel and swerved. The tires grabbed the edge of the road by the creek bank. They pulled the Ford. It slammed down the incline, and she bounced the truck headfirst into a tree on the embankment.

Kiara fell forward as airbags deployed and swooshed like a Pillsbury Doughboy on steroids punching her with burning powder. Her head lurched to the side and smacked her window. The glass spidered.

Blood ran down her head and into her eyes. The truck listed toward the creek. Held fast by the tree, it didn't topple.

She clicked off the ignition and leaned against the headrest. Closed her eyes and waited for her heart to quiet. The bottle of wine lay under her feet. Its fruity, alcoholic vapors filled the truck and mocked her.

She blinked, but her eyes clouded. Running her hand across her forehead, she smeared blood down her face and onto her clothes. At least she could see.

Her nose hurt. Her skin burned. Beyond the windshield, the creek flowed.

She shoved the door. As it tilted toward the sky, it didn't want to open. The stupid law of gravity weighted it against the truck's body. Using her elbows and torso, she thrust the door upward and out. It opened enough for her to clamber out. Kiara fell against the bank as the door slammed shut once more.

More blood flowed into her eyes.

Voices sounded above her. "Are you deef, Emmett? The truck's down there. Someone needs air 'sistance."

Kiara inched up toward the road. Every muscle hurt.

Two faces appeared at the top of the embankment.

"Looks like air naybar." Emmett looked down. "Here, tek my hand." He reached out.

Kiara nabbed it.

Emmett pulled Kiara to the roadside. He turned toward Queenie. "Best call Lia, and git me a towel. By the smell of hit, air naybar's drunker than Cooty Brown."

A few dizzy moments later, Queenie ran back with a towel and pressed it against Kiara's head. "You done a number on yerself. This'll hep the bleeding."

Kiara couldn't answer. As she sat in the dirt of the roadway, she took the towel from Queenie and pressed it against her head. She felt okay though. Bruised from the airbags. Every muscle hurt. Drunker than the skunk who attacked her last week, but otherwise, her body wasn't broken. Nothing but her head bled.

She didn't lose the baby. The thought forced a small smile.

"Yer truck's sigoggelin an' the tar's flat. Shann or Beau'll tow it," Emmett said.

Looking at her vehicle, and translating through the haze of alcohol, Kiara figured Emmett was talking about the truck leaning sideways on the bank and its flat tire. She was lucky it didn't flip.

"Oh, my, Kiara." Delia Mae's voice traveled on the sound of running feet. She knelt beside her. "Are you okay?"

Kiara trembled but said nothing. Like every time she tried to fix her universe, things got worse.

"She's drunk and driving." Beau had come with his wife.

Chapter Twenty-Five

Lia lifted the towel from Kiara's forehead. "We need to get her to the hospital. The gash isn't too long, but it's deep enough for stitches. The airbags did a number on her, and we'll have to make sure the baby's okay."

"Ma," Beau said to Queenie. "Call 9-1-1. Have them send an ambulance."

"I can take her," Lia said.

"Then call the sheriff," Beau continued. "This needs to be reported."

"There's no need for the sheriff or an ambulance." Lia studied Kiara.

She looked away.

Lia took Kiara's chin and tilted her head so she could study her eyes. "Look at me."

She didn't move.

Lia shifted and aligned her face with Kiara's. "Where do you hurt?"

Still staring into the distance, Kiara touched her head and groaned.

"She might have a concussion," Lia said.

"Sin has consequences," Beau said. "Drunkenness is an abomination before the Lawd. Let her learn from her mistakes."

"She only hurt herself. If the cops come—"

"The law is a minister to us who do good," Beau said. "Call the cops."

Her parents stepped back. Their shoulders touched, and they clasped hands but said nothing.

"Let's go home." Beau held his hand out to Lia. "She ain't dead nor in imminent danger. She'll live."

"Lia, chile," Pa said. "You kin call the amblance from air phone. You know more 'bout our naybar then us'n. I'm afeerd I won't give the right information."

"I'll give you a cup o' chamomile, Lia. It'll calm yer nerves." Ma looked to Beau. "Thet set all right with you?"

He nodded. "Go call. I got to write my sermon. Barbara's passing put me behind schedule." Beau strode off. He stopped and pivoted. "Ma, keep Lia with you 'til she's calmed down. Okay?"

Queenie smiled and nodded.

They watched as Beau disappeared down the hill behind the curve.

Pa shoved his hand in his pocket and pulled out keys. "Go." He flicked his head. "Tek my ve-hick-le." He nodded toward Kiara. "Make sure she ain't bad-sick."

Lia looked from her father to her mother. "Beau told me—"

"Who'd jew lissen to, a man or God?" her father asked.

"God, of course, but the Lord said—"

"You ought to 'bey God rather than man. It be Scripture," Pa said.

Lia unclasped her fist, but crescents from her nails still marred her palms. She couldn't leave this confused woman bleeding on the street waiting for strangers. God demanded mercy. "Thank you."

"Don't thank us'n. Go," Ma said, "'fore she bloodies up the whole, dadgum road."

"Would you call Shann when he returns from Jorie's, and see if he can haul the truck out of the ditch?" Again she stooped to Kiara's eye level. "Are the keys in your truck?"

She nodded.

Pa tugged Kiara to pull her to her feet.

The Yankee jerked back. "I donna ... umm, don't need help." She stumbled to her feet.

He linked her hand onto his arm and walked with her and Lia to his car. "We be prayin' for ya."

Once more, Kiara jerked back. "God doesn't exist."

Lia glanced at her folks. Her nerves crackled waiting for their response to Kiara's atheism.

Only compassion shone in their eyes.

"Thanks, Kiara needs it," Lia said.

"Pa didn't mean jist her."

Lia fastened the seat belt around Kiara who seemed too stunned or drunk to do much for herself. "What do you mean?"

"Yer Beau. You knowd we love 'im, but he's gettin' ornerier than Youtee with a coon these past years."

Lia stared at her folks.

"Why jew lookin' at us like a mule at a new gate?" Pa said. "You know'd Beau's been off last few years."

"Years?" Lia slammed the car door. "No, Ma. Just a few months. Beau's stressed. Church finances are tight, and we ain't been paid on time for the last few weeks. Chris's down payment for college will be due soon, and last year's finances eliminate him from most of his financial aid."

"We'll help you with that." Pa pointed toward the trailer. "You helped us plenty."

161

"Then, the funeral for Barbara put him behind in his preparations for Sunday."

"He don't have to tek it out on you," Pa said.

"I shouldn't take Kiara." Lia looked down the road for Beau.

"We'd taught ya better," Pa said. "Only one Man you got to lissen to." He pointed toward the sky. "We be prayin'."

~~

Lia's twenty-five-minute drive to LaFollette Medical Center seemed to last an hour. Kiara's silence made her think Jorie talked too much.

After parking in the hospital's lot, Lia ran around her car and opened Kiara's door. "Can I give you a hand?"

She got no answer.

Still, Lia helped Kiara out of her father's little Kia. Her neighbor didn't resist when she took her arm and walked her into the emergency room.

Kiara walked with a steady gate. If it wasn't for the fumes circling her head like gnats, she could pass for a sober patient.

What do I say when they ask me what happened? She shivered. *Lord, I can't lie.*

If she said Kiara'd been driving drunk, they'd ticket her neighbor. Would her license be taken away? If so, how would she get around? What about the baby? She glanced at Kiara's stomach, just a small bump beneath her shirt. Certainly, no one would call her top a dress.

Inside, while the triage nurse questioned Kiara, Lia assessed her neighbor. The short tunic fell a few inches down her thighs. Kiara hadn't laced her army boots, and blood stained everything. Lia wouldn't have to answer any questions. The cause and effect were obvious.

"This way." The triage nurse stood.

"Wait. Kiara didn't tell you. She's pregnant."

The nurse's eyes widened. She sat back down, tapped on her computer. "Any bleeding or cramping?" The nurse looked up at the standing women.

Kiara shook her head.

The triage nurse stood once more and ushered Kiara back into the examination area. "Here, take everything off and slip this on. You're going to need a pelvic exam." She handed her a hospital gown. "The opening's in the back." She turned to Lia. "A doctor will be with your daughter shortly." The nurse closed a curtain across the cubicle.

Lia paced the corridor. *My daughter?*

Like a coating of warm oil, understanding soothed. *Yes. As good as my child.*

She walked to the end of the ER then strode back to the closed

162

curtain. She had to be dressed by now — or undressed, seeing as hospital gowns covered nothing. "Kiara?"

No one answered.

She stepped inside. "You've got to talk to me."

Kiara sat on the exam bed, the sheet pulled up to her waist.

Before Lia could say another word, the curtain rippled apart to admit a doctor. "Good afternoon, I'm Dr. Voiles. So, what happened?" He slipped on neoprene gloves.

Kiara shrugged.

The doctor had to smell the alcohol.

He asked Lia. "What happened to your daughter?"

Kiara's eyes widened, and she bit her lip.

What should she say? My neighbor, not my daughter, drove her truck off the road. Why? She didn't know. Kiara, who she'd never seen take a drink, drove a vehicular winery today. "I wasn't there. She'll have to tell you."

Dr. Voiles fingered around Kiara's gash. "You'll need stitches." He probed her neck. "Headache?"

Kiara nodded.

"Tired?" Dr. Voiles checked her eyes with a light. He had her follow his finger as he moved it from side to side. Again, he spoke to Lia rather than Kiara. "It appears she has a concussion." He spoke to Kiara again. "How many weeks pregnant?"

Kiara said nothing.

"Four months," Lia said.

He looked at Kiara. "Did you lose consciousness?"

Kiara shook her head.

He faced Lia. "We'll skip the CT scans for now, but don't let her go to sleep for at least an hour. Bring her in if she's confused or her condition worsens. We'll do the tests then if need be. Don't let her drink and drive again."

So, Lia didn't have to discuss Kiara's drinking or her accident. She didn't have to lie.

The doctor listened to Kiara's lungs and heart. He pressed her belly. "Doesn't appear to have any internal injuries. Our physician assistant will stitch her up. Dr. Voiles left and silence descended once more.

Minutes ticked by.

What could've triggered this episode?

The PA came in. He, too, inspected the gash. "You have a nice little laceration. I'll numb it up. Three or four stitches will keep it from scarring. Once we've taken care of the bleeding, we'll check on the baby."

He cleansed the wound. Numbed it. Then sewed away on Kiara's head. With a clatter, he dropped the scissors and needle onto the metal

163

tray, the only sound from Kiara's ER space. He turned to Lia who hovered by the curtain. "If you'll excuse us, I'll do an internal."

Lia stepped out. Unable to sit, she patrolled the ER. She counted cubicles, floor tiles, and plastic chairs. She sat. Stood. Paced again.

Fifteen minutes later, the PA admitted Lia. "All looks fine. The baby's kicking away. Heartbeat's good. If the patient bleeds or cramps, bring her back in. We'll finish the discharge papers, and you're good to go." The PA never looked at Kiara once Lia entered the cubicle. For all she knew, he'd forgotten her neighbor sat, still silent, behind him.

With papers in hand, the women headed to the parking lot. Lia checked her watch. Two hours? *How'm I going to explain such a long cup of chamomile tea to Beau?*

In the car, Lia wilted against the driver's seat. Her limbs liquefied. She ran her hands through her hair and closed her eyes. *Had I been that stressed?* She stared through the windshield as cars on the road blurred before her eyes. If her neighbor didn't start talking, Lia would have nothing to do but fret about Beau's anger during their twenty-minute ride home. "Say something. Please."

"I like your haircut."

Lia closed her eyes. A low groan escaped her lips.

"I know what you want from me. What can I say? I got drunk and drove my brand-new truck into the creek. I'm an idiot like my mother always said."

Lia shifted and looked at Kiara who stared straight ahead with her thoughts locked tight inside her concussed mind. "First of all, you're not an idiot."

Kiara's lips twitched.

Was it in disbelief? Self-effacement?

"What I need you to realize is drinking—"

"And driving. I know."

Lia shook her head. "No. Drinking and pregnancy. It's bad for the baby."

"I'm not keeping it."

Exhaustion fled. Muscles knotted once more and threatened to twist like towels caught in a washer's agitator. Lia leaned toward Kiara. "What do you mean by 'not keeping it'?"

"When I get to New York, I'm having an abortion."

"Kiara—"

"Despite what the doctors in there said, you're not my mother. This is my life." Kiara's nose flared. "I need to survive." She didn't yell, but with the harshness of her voice, she might as well be screaming.

"What changed your mind about the pregnancy?"

Kiara opened her mouth and spewed the tale about Gina and Bryce. Shock sealed Lia's lips as her heart skipped beats. *Poor dear.*

Lia listened to the betrayal by Kiara's lover and closest friend, the hatred of Bryce's scorned wife, the rejection by both parents and the loneliness eating Kiara like a worm on a mater bush. *How can one person take so much?*

"That's why I can't do this."

"I understand." And Lia did. Still, this baby would survive. He did nothing wrong. "What about adoption?"

"Why do you care?" Kiara slammed her hand on the dashboard and glared at Lia. Then, like a rag doll, she flopped back against the car seat and rubbed her head. She spoke in a low growl between gritted teeth— from rage or anguish? "My head hurts. I'm sobering up. Worse, I spilled my guts to you. Delia Mae, I'm broken. You and your God can't fix it."

Yes, He can.

Lia played with her keys. She fished for words, for an argument that would keep the human growing inside of Kiara alive. No way would Lia let this baby die. "Why not adoption?"

Kiara stared out the side window. Her voice came soft and sad. "I told you once, my medical insurance runs out in three months. How can I afford a pregnancy?"

"Don't make the baby pay for Bryce's treachery with its life."

"Will you support me?"

"We can't afford it." *Not with the second mortgage we took out last month.* Kiara didn't need to hear her woes.

"Like everyone else, you're all talk, so butt out of my business." Kiara unsnapped the seat belt and opened the door. "If we're not going home, I'm out of here." Leaving the door ajar, Kiara stormed toward the hospital.

Lia jumped out of the car. "Get back in. I'll take you home."

Kiara didn't stop.

Lia scurried after her and grabbed her by the arm. "How are you going to find your way back to Stinking Creek? You couldn't find your way off our road."

Kiara stopped.

"Be reasonable. I'll shut up *if* you get into the car." She pointed at the too-short dress. "Besides, you'll catch a chill."

The stiffness left Kiara's arm. Without a word, she shook off Lia's hand and scuffled to the Kia.

Settled back in the car, the women drove in silence until they reached 25W.

"In many adoptions, the adoptive parents pay," Lia said.

"You said you'd shut your trap."

"Listen to me, please."

Kiara crossed her arms and shifted so she stared out the window. "What choice do I have? I can't hop out of the car when you're going

165

forty-five."

"You can arrange a private adoption. I can help. Our finances are in limbo right now. We can't pay your bills, or else we would. I will help you *if* you opt for adoption."

Kiara said nothing. She leaned back and folded her hands in her lap. She closed her eyes. If Lia didn't know better, she'd think all went well for her friend.

"Hey." Lia playfully tapped her friend's arm.

Kiara jerked her hand away.

"No sleeping. I know of no Prince Charming who can kiss your concussed mind awake."

The playfulness in her voice must've penetrated Kiara's skull. She smiled.

"You're saying your brother-in-law's no prince?"

Lia laughed. "Is there any sister in the world who thinks her brother's a charmer?"

"Not me."

Although no conversation resumed, the tension evaporated by the time Lia dropped Kiara off. Her truck sat in the driveway. It looked like Shann had cut away the airbags. The front fender on the passenger side had crumpled, and the driver's side window had a small web-like break, but the truck looked drivable.

"God was with you, Kiara." Lia ground her teeth waiting for the sharp comeback.

"Thank you for all you do. Someday, I *will* repay you."

Kiara dragged herself into her cabin.

Now she had to drag herself across the road. Face her own enemy.

~~

"I'm home." Lia headed toward Beau's study off the front room. "How's the sermon going?" She bent over and kissed his head.

He swiveled in his chair and glared up at her. "You defied me."

She jolted back as though his words slapped her. "How?"

He rose, stepped toward her and towered over her. "Shann pulled the truck back to her place."

"I'm not responsible for what Shann does."

The tightening of his lips told Lia now was not the time to assert herself.

"Your parents—"

"Since when am I my parents' keeper." She backed into the living room.

"I told you to call the troopers and a tow company." Beau grabbed her arm.

166

Never had Beau manhandled her. Lia stiffened.

He dropped his hand.

"How can we be complicit in the Yankee's sin?"

She picked up an afghan that had slipped off the back of the sofa and shook it.

Beau's arm gripped her shoulder and spun her around. The comforter fell to the floor. "I also told you to call 9-1-1. Instead, you take your parents' car, are gone all day, and abandon your own family for a heathen who couldn't care less."

Lia bent to retrieve the afghan. "Ain't we supposed—?"

"To obey? I'm your husband. It's on me if you get into trouble. I'm responsible for your soul and our church."

"My soul is my responsibility. The church needs to mind its own business." Lia smoothed the afghan over the couch. "It would help if our church paid its pastor on time."

"These are difficult circumstances."

"I know."

"I'm responsible for the eternal salvation—"

"No, you're not." Lia's head spun as anger, more than twenty-five years of suppressed, submissive anger boiled to the surface. "Everyone shall bear their own burdens." She jabbed her finger in his face. "This is my burden. Not yours."

Beau grabbed her hand. "Don't go taking God's Holy Word out of context. The way we live teaches the congregation. If our actions stumble our flock, the sovereign Lawd will hold us accountable. I told you before, and I tell you again, you are *never* to associate with Kiara again."

Lia squinted into his eyes but said nothing.

"Do you hear me?"

"God wants us to have mercy. He came to call the sinners not the righteous to repentance." She straightened and tightened her lips.

"Do not cross me. As a pastor, too much is at stake." Beau stepped back into the office. The door clicked behind him.

Lia studied his door. Five minutes later she stepped into the kitchen.

This room had been her dream when they built the house fifteen years ago. Then it grew into her sanctuary. She cooked for everyone. She taught her boys and Shann's twins. In here, she waited for Beau to come home late at night after comforting a lost soul.

Lately, it'd become a prison. Barbecues, soups, cakes, dinners. Demands for bake sales to eke out another payment on the church's extension or a mission drive. Millions of demands.

It neared five. Everyone would be clamoring for dinner.

Slinging open the refrigerator, Lia pulled out hamburger. She stood with the bloody package in her hand, then shoved it back in. They had

167

leftovers and a microwave. Packaged pizza sat in the big freezer.

Let the world feed itself.

She jogged up the stairs to her bedroom. From under the top mattress, she slipped out her newest June Foster romance. The heroine's guilt about her abortion was destroying all chance of love with the hero. She knew they'd make it but wasn't sure how. The certainty of the romance genre comforted her.

At the moment she hated Beau.

And Paul who was too much like his father.

She knew forgiveness would come.

All she had to do was allow God space to work.

~~

Kiara woke on her couch an hour after she'd gotten home. She wasn't supposed to have gone to sleep.

Unfortunately, she was able to wake up.

Her head pounded as if Shann's nail gun shot spikes through her temporal lobe. It'd been a long time since she'd been hung over. She washed down two Tylenol with a large glass of water. Supposedly, dehydration caused hangovers.

Her suitcase sat next to the refrigerator. After lugging it back upstairs, she folded the clothes she had thrown willy-nilly into the bag and tucked them back into the drawers.

After stashing the suitcase into the closet, Kiara took Bryce's sweater off the lamp. She wadded it into a ball and returned to the kitchen. There, she threw it out. The leggings lying cockeyed—one leg inside out—followed the sweater into the trash. She swept up the shredded sonogram pictures and dumped them.

This monstrosity of a cabin had to sell. It'd been on the market for ten days. The repairs had been made. She called Maggie McLemon.

"An American Dream Realty, Maggie speaking."

"This is Kiara Rafferty out on Sheep Loop Road. All the repairs have been taken care of."

"Fantastic. Thanks for letting me know." The woman sounded too chipper.

"Has there been any interest?"

"I'm sorry."

Kiara hung up. *Rude.* She should call back and apologize, but she couldn't. She'd do it tomorrow. Happy people depressed her right now.

Instead, she trudged up to her studio. If she ever relocated to nowhere again, it'd be in West Texas where a hill never existed even after the big bang boomed.

In flat Manhattan, the civilized had escalators to transport them.

Out here? If her quadriceps ever got big enough to tackle the hills without killing her with a heart attack or asthmatic seizure, they'd be too huge to fit into any pair of pants.

In the studio, Kiara sat before her portrait of the twins. It was now sketched and ready for paint. She mixed her burnt sienna, titanium white, and phthalo blue. She laid down the background. Within minutes, she stepped into the painting and became the pigment. Her soul renewed itself with the softness of the oils as they glided over the canvas and blotted out the emptiness. A new universe transported her out of Stinking Creek.

Two hours later, with the canvas covered with the base coats, Kiara stepped back into the real world and studied the portrait. She absently twisted her ring.

Nothing there.

She examined her empty finger. The one carat, perfect princess cut diamond had flawless chips studding the platinum band. Bryce had bought it at Tiffany's.

If she sold it, she could almost recoup the cost of her truck.

Even repair it so she didn't have to drive around like a hillbilly sloshed on moonshine.

She should go back to the house and sweep and put it away. Somewhere in Knoxville, a jeweler would pay big bucks for the bauble.

She looked back at her portrait. The blond of the twins' hair needed to be laid out. She squeezed out titanium white and burnt umber.

Chapter Twenty-Six

Sheep Loop Church never held so many people. Lia scooted out ahead of the mob comforting Jorie on the loss of her mother. Barbara's internment would take place in the ancient cemetery behind the building. Afterward, everyone in attendance would arrive at her place looking for her to feed them.

"We're coming with you," Paul hurried after his ma and climbed into the front seat.

"Enough of funerals," Chris said. "We're meeting friends up in Jellico."

He climbed into the back seat.

"When'd y'all get to the service? I didn't see you come in."

"We got there just before the casket arrived," Paul said. "Funerals are tough. I don't know how Daddy holds it together when someone as godly as Mrs. Thomas passes."

"Faith." Chris leaned forward and socked Paul in the arm. "You should know the answer to the question, Preacher Boy."

"Hey, Rocket Man." Paul twisted around and play-punched his brother.

"PK punk."

"Fuel brain."

"Enough." Lia ducked her head to hide her grin. Her sons would invent any number of nicknames to insult each other. If she didn't stop it here, they'd devise off-color nicknames.

"If you don't like it, Ma," Paul said, "quit grinning.

In five minutes, they exited the car. She stepped through the side door to an explosion of casseroles and cakes in her kitchen. "Where'd these come from?" This room had been empty before she left this morning aside from the pulled pork simmering in her slow cooker.

"People have been stopping by," Paul said.

"Nonstop," Chris said. "We couldn't get anything done."

"The video games do have a pause button." Lia grinned.

"See if your NASA pals are as righteous as we Christians." Paul slapped Chris's head. "They ain't gonna bring buckets of banana pudding to comfort us mourners." He bounded up the stairs to his room.

"Ow, ow. Mommy, Paulie's being mean." Chris laughed and headed out to the living room. "Wow."

"What's wrong?" Lia peered down the hall.

"The front porch is full of stuff." Chris carried in a cake in one hand, and a fruit salad in the other. He plopped them on the table and flipped the lid off the carrier. "Coconut." He rummaged for a knife and raised it to cut into the white, fluffy cake. "Looks like Miss Betina's."

Lia grabbed his hand. "Not until the mourners arrive."

"Ma, we'll be gone."

She pointed toward the front room. "Bring in the rest of the food then get out of my domain."

Chris left as a soft knock sounded at the kitchen door.

Lia opened it. "Kiara." She glanced behind her. Beau would be finishing the burial. "Would you like to come in?"

Kiara licked her lips and hesitated. "I don't know Jorie well and don't want to intrude. She held up a 9x12 glass pan. "I made taco salad."

Chris returned balancing several casserole pans on top of one another. "Hey, Miss Kiara." He clunked the pans on the table. "Got a plate of cookies and rolls left. Then I'm outta here." He loped out of the kitchen.

"Guess you don't need this." Kiara eyed her casserole.

Lia took it. "Thank you."

Beau's white van carrying Jorie, Shann, and the twins pulled in.

Lia's breath hitched.

"I'll be going." Kiara's words rushed. She stepped away.

Didn't hide my worry, did I, Lord?

Kiara waved toward the van full of family and crossed the road.

Lia laid out a stack of paper plates next to the SOLO cups and plastic utensils.

Beau came up behind her. He whispered in her ear. "I'm gone an hour and you invite *her* in. You see the example she's setting for you? Rebellion is as the sin of witchcraft."

"Beau, I ..."

People crowded into the kitchen.

Lia stepped outside and smiled to those who poured out of cars. She crossed the road and knocked at Kiara's. The door opened. "Come on over. It's an open house. Jorie likes you, and I have way too much food."

Kiara twisted her finger.

"Where's your ring?" Lia took her hand.

"I think it rolled under the baker's rack."

"You think? That was a huge diamond."

"It's in the house unless Mr. Snake had a snack. I'd love to come over. I'll be by in a few."

Lia returned home. Or floated home. Obedience to God liberated her.

Then the civil war raged once more. The other part of her, the Lia she'd become during twenty-five years of marriage, trembled. Her marriage did matter. She had no idea how she'd become so rigid in her faith, so committed to becoming the godly wife she pictured from Proverbs 31. The woman depicted there had to have died from exhaustion by the age of twenty.

The command to be as holy as God was not humanly possible.

But it had to be. God wrote it down in Scripture.

All she ever wanted was to be in the dead center of God's perfect will. Why was the path so narrow? Not even the Flying Wallendas could navigate the tiny lane she'd constructed.

Inside, people chatted and laughed. Shann sat with Jorie. Her shy smile danced on her lips. This was a true church, coming together to support and encourage and love. In Christ, joy could even be found in death.

She kissed the top of Jorie's head as she passed by.

Jorie grabbed her hand. "Thank you, Miss Lia."

Lia patted Jorie's hand then filled a plate with food and found a spot in the den. She hadn't seen Beau since her return from Kiara's. She swallowed hard. Fortunately, Beau would never be cruel to someone in front of his congregation. They all believed him to be invincible and would call him an apostle if they existed in modern days.

Rosalyn and Betina joined her. They chatted and laughed with their memories of Barbara.

Rosalyn sipped the last of her coffee. "Do you have any more?"

"If not, I'll make a pot." Lia stood and wandered into the kitchen for coffee. At the table, Kiara sat across from Beau whose back faced Lia.

Lia's heart quit beating. Where had her defiance fled? Should she say something?

Kiara waved.

Beau turned.

His face looked beatific. "Come here, Lia." He pushed out the chair next to him. "Kiara and I have been talking about sin and salvation."

Lia sat and studied Kiara's face. It was impassive, not as bad as after she tried to drive to Manhattan via the Sheep Loop Creek, but Lia couldn't discern any emotion.

"You know, my wife used to be the most submissive of women. Godliness radiated out of every cell of her body. Lately," he glanced at her and smiled, his eyes remaining cold. "Been more free-spirited. What do you think of that, Kiara?"

The young woman looked at Lia. Her eyes begged for the right answer. Her shoulders lifted.

Lia gave a slight shake of her head. Today wasn't the best day to be rebellious.

Kiara inhaled a deep breath. Her exhale came long and slow. "I believe we need to live as our genetics demand. My whole life, I'd been manipulated like a marionette. I had to act like whoever pulled the strings wanted me to act. The sad part of the whole deal? I never realized I wasn't me." She looked at Lia. "Delia Mae needs to be what the universe wants."

"The universe?" Beau asked.

"We have one life before the big nothingness. Happiness must be grabbed. Excuse me." The chair scraped as Kiara stood. "I need to give my condolences to Jorie. Then I have a portrait at home needing my attention."

Chapter Twenty-Seven

Kiara's phone rang while she sat in the tub prepping for tonight's foray to the Bijou and her first dose of mountain music. She threw her head back and groaned.

The phone remains mute all week. I take a bath, and voilà. Wrapping a towel around herself she scurried to answer it.

"This is Maggie McLemon from An American Dream Realty. I've got a couple who wants to look at your place. They're in my office now. We could be there by four if you don't mind."

"What time is it now?"

"Three."

"They just show up and want to see my place?"

"Sometimes it happens this way. You do want to sell, don't you?"

"No problem. I'll be out of town, but you have the lockbox combination." She hung up. The showing showed up with bad timing, but Kiara couldn't fret about it. If she didn't let strangers see her house, she'd never ditch the hinterland.

Only one way would she prep this place and be ready for Shann and their night at the Bijou—lies and deceit.

For the next half hour rather than primping for her first night out in Dixie, she cleaned. Dirty clothes found themselves in the washer and dryer. Dirty dishes hid in the dishwasher. She ran a dust cloth over every visible inch of the house and wiped down the surface of the sinks.

Lies and deceits, she'd always called this kind of cleaning. Looked good as long as you didn't look too closely. Good thing new home buyers didn't peek under beds or examine dryers.

She hoped.

A few minutes before four, Kiara slipped on an embroidered, one-size-fits-all Indian dress. She fastened the tie behind her. The loose garment felt feminine and pretty. She looked in the mirror. Mint green soothed. It calmed her jittery stomach and brought out the amber of her eyes and hair.

After applying mascara, blush, and lip gloss, she threw a kiss to the mirror. Didn't look too bad for having just been a scullery maid.

Little feet pounded on her porch. No knocking preceded the

running entrance of two moppets.

"Let's go, Miss Kiara." Dixon grabbed one hand.

"Sit in the back with me." Macie grabbed her other.

Kiara stumbled onto the porch, pulled more than guided by the happy twins. She twisted the lock and shut the door.

After three steps to the truck, she remembered her lost ring. Again.

She did have to look for it even if it would never go back on her finger. She wanted to sell it. Hopefully, Bryce paid a million bucks for it.

The watch still lay on the coffee table. Now strangers would inspect her house? What would she do if it disappeared?

She could sue. Kiara grinned imagining the millions she'd gain from pain and suffering. *Please take the watch,* she begged the prospective buyers. *Make me rich.*

With the gazillion dollars she'd extort from Maggie McLemon, she'd be home free—in the literal sense of the phrase. She crossed her fingers.

Shann stood by the truck. "What are you grinning at?"

Kiara bit back her smile and shook her head. "Glad to get out."

He opened the rear door of the truck. "Climb in, kids."

"I want Miss Muffet next to me." Macie tugged at Kiara's hand toward the back seat. "You climb in first."

"No." Shann lifted his daughter. "You guys in the booster seats. Miss Kiara's up front with me." He strapped in Macie.

Kiara walked around the vehicle and attempted to fix Dixon's seat belt.

"I'm not a baby." He grabbed it from her.

"Neither am I." Macie unhooked the belt Shann just fastened. Then couldn't re-hook it.

Fifteen minutes later with everyone tied into place, they drove off.

At last, they pulled into the empty parking lot next to the theater in downtown Knoxville.

The Bijou was a quaint old theater on Gay Street. Outside, it looked like a white stuccoed apartment building. Inside, red velvet chairs, crowded together like seats on an airline, swept down to a small stage painted black. Two balconies rose in the rear of the theater. On either side of the auditorium, overlooking the mezzanine, box seats lined the wall.

Shann stood behind Kiara on stage and bowed his head near her ear.

His beard tickled her neck, but instead of wanting to move away, she snuggled a little closer like a bird in its nest.

"We've reserved those for you." He pointed to the balcony box overlooking stage right.

"Making me your Juliet?"

"Oh yes." His lips brushed her hair, and she trembled. "Except, I ain't killing myself over you."

She looked up into those hypnotic eyes. "Shann, oh Shann, wherefore art thou? Deny your brother and refuse your name, and for that name—"

"I'd take you at your word," he winked. "I'd even give up Lia's barbecue."

Kiara surveyed the empty auditorium and shivered from her dreads to her tootsies. She could envision the crowds coming to hear a good concert. If excitement coursed through her, what must Shann and his band feel?

"If we're going to have a concert, we've got to quit lollygagging and set up." Cool air chilled Kiara as Shann stepped away. He needed to move, or she'd find herself too heated up to work. She stood still, tried to think of something to lure him back to her.

"Are you going to earn your tickets or stand around like a stage-frightened artist?" Shann called from the wings.

For the next hour, Kiara and the kids pulled instruments and chairs into position while the band members connected amplifiers and microphones and did sound checks.

"I never dreamed I'd be a roadie," Kiara told Shann when the echoes of the last sound check dimmed.

He leaned in close. "You're a woman of many talents."

His lips lingered close to her head, almost brushing the bandage hiding her stitches. Tingles zipped up her spine. He stepped away.

Remember, girl, no good comes from these feelings.

As the first concertgoers arrived, Kiara grabbed the kids who had been surprisingly helpful in the setup. They climbed a flight of stairs and took their seats.

The view would be magnificent. Kiara rested her arms on the ledge and surveyed the theater. Sitting here made her feel like royalty. The show performed for her and the children alone. They had the entire box, room for five, so the twins had enough space to squirm or do cartwheels and somersaults.

Or do chin-ups from the balcony.

The theater, no Carnegie Hall or Lincoln Center, rivaled any small venue she'd attended in New York. Knoxville offered a vibrant art community. She'd check it out next week.

No, she wouldn't.

At this moment, contracts were being signed for the cabin. She'd be in Manhattan next week.

"I'm thirsty," Dixon said.

"I want sody dope." Macie echoed her brother.

"Dope?" *What on earth?* "You can have a soda, but no drugs."

"Drugs?" Dixon laughed. "We're too young for drugs. We want Coke."

Kiara winked. "See, drugs."

"Huh?" Dixon looked more perplexed than a college kid taking a final.

"We want soda *pop*." Macie pulled Kiara toward the hallway.

As patrons filled the seats beneath them, Kiara stepped down to the foyer with one small hand in each of hers. At the concession stand, she corralled the twins between her legs and the bar. She ordered sodas and chips for all of them. Back at their booth, the kids chatted and drank and chomped while she perused the program.

The performance offered original tunes written by different band members. Standard country and folk ballads filled out the first half of the show.

After intermission though, Shann's band, "Washbasin Gentry," would play Ravel's Bolero. To hear this played on a washbasin, saw, and a bass made from an old-fashioned wooden crutch would be interesting.

The lights dimmed and a loud applause filled the Bijou. Shann and his crew entered and picked up their odd array of instruments.

Two little bottoms climbed onto Kiara's knees. So much for plenty of room in the box seats.

A lively melody the program called "Tennessee Showdown" filled the theater.

Shann's group carried the three of them to another realm.

~~

Three hours later, they sat in The Tomato Head on Market Square. Remnants of two large pizzas—a cheese and an everything—littered the booth. Macie sat on one side of Kiara. Dixon perched on the other. Shann, still glowing from three encores, sat across from her.

"Kids, give Kiara room. You've been clinging like ticks on a hound since before we left the Creek."

The kids wriggled an inch away. Immediately, like static cling, they nudged up against her again.

"At least you had room in the booth at the Bijou."

Kiara shook her head and pointed toward her lap.

Shann sank back. "Sorry."

"They kept me warm."

"Did you like your first taste of mountain music?"

"Loved it. Especially when Dixon clogged to it."

Shann rolled his eyes. "I've threatened to give him ballet—"

"No. I ain't taking no dance lessons." Dixon crossed his arms and flung himself against the booth back. His pout, if not a prelude to a

177

meltdown, made him look like a sulking bulldog.

The two adults ignored him.

"I can't believe you played Ravel's Bolero with a saw and a crutch. It sounded professional," Kiara said.

Shann's forehead scrunched. "We are professional."

She shook her head. "Formal and professional. It sounded like something my mother's fiancé would play — if he touched anything other than the cello. I could believe your interpretation of the piece. Fireworks exploded when you modulated from C major to E. It made me want to shout."

"Hallelujah?"

"Glory to the universe." She winked.

"I'm amazed you knew the key we played. You do know your music."

"If you lived with my mother a day, you'd be able to teach at Julliard." Kiara picked up her fourth slice of everything pizza. "I'm so hungry, I can't stand it." She bit.

"We are made for each other," Shann said.

Kiara put the slice down. *This declaration isn't good.*

"We love the same pizza. The kids adore you." He reached across the table and took both her hands in one of his. Shann's eyes told Kiara what he wanted to say.

"Hey, guys." Kiara nudged the kids aside more to free her hands than to give herself room. If she could, she'd cover herself in the twins and avoid what was coming next.

"Kiara, I like you. Maybe next week we can have a real dinner."

"This is real." Kiara lifted her pizza slice, bit into it and chewed. "I love Italian," she said around a mouthful.

"Something other than pizza and without distractions."

"I gotta go to the bathroom." Dixon climbed out of the booth.

"Can you wait a minute?" Shann smiled and glanced at Kiara. "See what I mean?"

"No. I drank dope at the theater and two glasses here —"

"Three," Macie interjected.

Dixon danced a little jig, and Shann excused himself.

Kiara had a moment to plan her response.

"Me too," Macie said.

Kiara brought her to the ladies' room. After Macie loitered in the stall singing to herself, she couldn't reach the faucet to wash her hands, so Kiara lifted her. Using her body, she wedged Macie against the sink while she rubbed soap into her hands.

"You're squishing me," Macie complained.

Kiara put her down.

"I can't reach the water."

Kiara picked her up, but Macie needed help rinsing the soap off. Kiara wedged her against the sink once more. Why couldn't bathrooms have little sinks or at least a stool a kid could climb on?

Kids *needed* to wash their hands seeing as they used their little paws to haul themselves up on the toilet and hold themselves in place. Yuck.

Germs. Another reason she wanted no kids.

They finished washing. Macie pounded her hand against the on button of the hand dryer. The air, rather than evaporating the water, rearranged her hair. She squinted against the blowing heat. None of the hot air reached her hands. Again, bathrooms weren't designed for half-pints.

They returned to the table. Macie wiped her still-wet hands against her pants.

Shann stood by the table helping Dixon into his jacket. "All set?" He picked up Macie's sweater. "Let me help—"

"No." Macie swiped it out of his hands. "You help me." She handed it to Kiara.

Shann took Dixon's hand in his. Kiara took Macie's, and they exited.

The lights from stores and bistros illuminated the shopping square as they headed back to the parking lot by the Bijou. They strolled through a small park filled with huge art sculptures and a fountain flowing through it like a river.

"I like Market Square," Kiara said. "It reminds me of a suburban Manhattan with the art and quaint shops and good restaurants."

"Pizza? I wouldn't term it fine cuisine even though The Tomato Head is one of my favorite spots." His hand took hers.

She wanted to pull it away, but his hand warmed and comforted her.

"So would next Friday work for you?"

She swallowed hard. He was picking up his question for a date, but she couldn't, and she didn't know how to let him down.

"I'm pregnant, Shann."

"I have twins."

"What?"

"If you state the obvious, so can I."

"Religion seems important to you guys, but I don't share your faith."

"Beau accuses me of not sharing his either."

They smiled at each other, their shoulders bumping as they walked hand in hand.

"Our differences don't mean we can't enjoy each other's company."

They approached a bench on a plaza leading to Gay Street. She sank onto it and tugged on his hand. "Sit."

He stood in front of her. "Sitting means you're not giving me the

179

answer I need."

"Jorie loves you."

He sat next to her, and the kids raced each other in the lamplight. "Stay away from the water." Shann nodded toward a splash pad near the curb. Lights shone on the fountain spraying from the concrete. It invited youngsters to dance in its jets and get soaked and miserable and make their parents crazy on the long ride home.

"Dad." The tone of both kids' voices told the world they had an idiot for a father.

"We don't have our bathing suits on. We won't go in," said Dixon as if a lack of swimwear would stop a five-year-old.

"I don't love Jorie. I can't help what she feels."

"Nor do you love me."

"True. But I could."

"Jorie believes you could love her."

"I don't understand."

"My closest friend slept with Bryce. They'd probably been involved for the five years I lived with him."

He reached over to pull her into his arms.

She pulled back. "No. I gave myself enough pity last week." She watched the kids. Shann and all the McGuffreys didn't hover over the children, and the kids thrived under their supervision. She didn't remember ever having so much liberty and being accepted because she was herself like these children were. "I know the pain of being cheated on. Jorie needs her chance with you."

"I don't—"

She held up her hand. "At Barbara's funeral, Beau lectured me. Told me I was hell bound. The essence of his lecture stated I had to forget everything I loved and turn from my wanton ways and act like Delia Mae." She sought out Shann's eyes. "Shann, no love will ever allow me to be like Delia Mae. She's a *good* woman. She accepts me as I am. Is more a mother to me than my mother or Jillian. I would've starved to death if not for Delia Mae. I'd have no truck. No chance of an income. I'd have bled to death on Sheep Loop Road from a concussion."

"You would've sobered up before you bled out."

Kiara surveyed the park in front of her. If she didn't look at Shann, she could convince him of what was best for him. "I don't want to be tortured the way Delia Mae is. The rules she follows would kill me. I refuse to follow her mean God who makes life so very, very hard."

"Lia's a good and loving woman, but she lost her way, and only God can set her straight."

"Maybe—"

Shann touched his finger to Kiara's lips to silence her. "We're saved by grace."

180

"I'm an atheist." The picture of the prayer for finances and the subsequent check flitted through her mind. "Although, if I hang out with you much longer, I may convert to agnosticism."

"See." He looped his arm around her. "Kids," he called to the twins who started to pull off their shoes and socks to play in the water fountain. "Put the shoes back on."

"Dad." Both protested but obeyed.

"Also." Kiara breathed in. "The realtor brought a couple to look at my house. I'm moving as soon as I can. If I sell my work or find the art dealer, a guy named Joey Something-or-other," she turned to him. "Do you know Joey?"

He shook his head.

"Anyway, I have enough savings to live for a while up in New York. When the house sells, I'll never be back. Manhattan's my world."

"Your conditions sound insurmountable."

She nodded.

"I do know a God who can conquer the impossible."

"You're incorrigible."

He looked at his hands, his eyes questioned. "No. Not corrugated. Flesh and blood."

She slapped his hands. "Silly boy." As she stood, the actual answer she'd been grappling for became obvious. "I'll make you a deal. You pray to your God. If He makes me stay of my own free will, makes Jorie not love you, and if your deity makes Beau like me, then I'm yours."

He stood and stuck out his hand. "Deal."

She grasped his hand to shake.

He drew her into a hug. "Kids?" He looked around for them.

The twins made gagging noises. "Ugh, Dad. You're hugging a girl."

"Miss Muffet, are you going to be my mommy?"

Kiara jolted away from Shann. Her hand fluttered to her chest as her mouth dropped.

Shann lassoed the kids but didn't bother to correct them.

On the way home, smugness permeated every pore in Kiara's spirit. She set the bar impossibly high. Her cabin would be sold, and she'd return to New York.

But most important, she'd never do to Jorie what Gina did to her.

Chapter Twenty-Eight

Sunday morning, the sale of her cabin obsessed Kiara more than a Kardashian with a mirror. Despite the hour, she called McLemon.

"How'd the showing go?"

"Do you realize it's eight a.m.?"

"If you didn't want me to call, why'd you give me your cell number?" *Shouldn't be so snarky.* "Sorry. I'm antsy about going home."

"I understand. The couple liked the land."

"Did they make an offer?"

"No. They said the place needed too much work."

"I got rid of the bugs, replaced the rails—"

"The bathroom and kitchen are outdated."

"But the barn?"

"No one will pay for a—"

"Thank you." So much for disproving people's stereotypes about New Yorkers' surliness.

Kiara drummed her fingers on the countertop. Shann's goodbye kiss last night, chastely placed on her forehead, haunted her. It shouldn't have felt so good. She shouldn't have wanted his lips on hers or her body pressed to his.

Shaking her head then slipping on her shoes, she schlepped out the door to hit her studio. Within a few steps, she pivoted and picked up her broom and swept. Her ring needed to be stored some place other than her kitchen floor. The buyers didn't steal her watch, so no lawsuit about its theft would net a million and get her out of here. She moved the baker's rack. No ring. Behind the trash and under the curtain hiding the sink's plumbing, no ring hid.

It definitely clinked into the kitchen. She hadn't been so drunk she couldn't remember. Her throwing arm was weak, so it didn't land in the upstairs bedroom. Only bulky appliances could now be the culprits hiding it.

She wriggled out the refrigerator. No dirt nor new Adams and Eves created from the dust of the earth hid there. A few weeks ago, Rusty Ford's fix to the fridge enticed her to clean behind it and beneath it.

The stove?

She wriggled the heavy appliance out from the counter.

Her pride in her cleanliness vanished.

Grease glued globs of dust to the sides of the stove and the counters like fake whiskers. Years of grime from the Oliver family shellacked the floor.

One bright spot glinted.

Unidentifiable foodstuffs gripped her ring in their sticky grasp.

With two fingers, she retrieved it and swiped it against her leggings — the only pants fitting at the moment. Kiara stuffed it in the leggings' back pocket. Retrieving her watch, still on the coffee table, she headed upstairs.

Once in the loft, her phone rang.

She plopped the ring and watch onto the bedside stand. They clinked as they clattered onto the table. She paused long enough to make sure they didn't roll off the stand and scoot under the bed. Almost skipping downstairs, eager for companionship, praying to Shann's deity it'd be him, she nabbed the phone.

"I was composing my lecture for the answering machine. I thought you weren't home."

"Imani!" She was better than Shann. Better than any other Yank from New York. "Or should I say, Mrs. Greaves?"

Imani giggled like a teenager. "I'm still not used to being married. Yesterday was our two-week anniversary."

"So tell me, you were adamant about stodgy churches and the middle-class marriage traditions. What changed your mind?"

"You know we went to Zion Resurrection the week before Bryce died?"

"For your sister Jayla's baptism."

"Yep. Something in the service clicked. I told myself if it affected Lance, I'd go back. When we got home, Lance said, 'Now don't leave me, babe, I've got a confession.' Forgetting my deal with God, I believed Lance was going to tell me he was having an affair. Then he said he wanted to jump and shake with joy during the worship like a Holy Roller. I told him I felt it too—like a weird fluttering above my head. Kiara, I can't explain the sensation. Watching Jayla get dunked made both of us shiver."

"Isn't church boring?"

"No, girl. I wear my fancy hats and we dance in the spirit like a Broadway chorus line. Last week, I joined the praise dance team. Between regular service and dance practice, I've lost five pounds. An added benefit, my legs are looking hot from all the exercise."

Dancing? Kiara couldn't picture Delia Mae jigging in church, let alone when no one watched. "Aren't you supposed to be quiet and follow rules?"

"No. It's the coolest thing." Imani jabbered for about ten minutes. Kiara wished she believed Imani's tale of a real god she could experience. In her friend's stories and her laughter, Kiara forgot about Gina. The fact she sat in Stinking Creek disappeared. For the half hour they chatted, they were sitting together in Café Bean sipping pumpkin spice lattes and eating cheesecake. No time, no space separated them.

"I've been blathering forever," Imani took a breath. "What's new with you?"

Bryce and Gina's treachery, her pregnancy, and the lost direction of her life reappeared. Kiara didn't have the heart to share her sorrow with Imani's joy. "Nothing. Same old. Let me know if you find any affordable apartments."

"You know I've been looking. I thought I found one in Jamaica, but it got nabbed before I knew it was on the market."

"One will show up." Even though Kiara forced positivity into her voice, her heart doubted it. She needed the twins to pray to their Jesus fellow for her.

With hearty farewells, the women hung up.

A heaviness settled over Kiara as she stepped out the kitchen door to head to her studio. Shann's truck pulled into the McGuffreys' yard.

Jorie hopped out and hurried into the house. Shann flipped the back seat to retrieve one of the kids.

Kiara refused to watch more.

She trudged up the mountain to the studio. The portrait of the twins called her, but oils took forever to dry. The paint needed to set up before she layered on the next coat.

Instead, she turned her attention to *Stinking Morning*. Somehow she'd make this monstrosity work.

~~

Shann glanced at Kiara's cabin as he retrieved the twins from the back seat. *You were right, Kiara. A different flavor church satisfied. You'd even like Grace Church.*

A sugar-induced coma knocked out the kids in the back seat. In Sunday school they'd learned how God's spirit filled every life it touched. To illustrate, they baked cinnamon rolls and made sugared tea. In theory, the teachers said a little sugar flavored every morsel of the treats, like God's spirit sweetened our lives.

The lesson his twins had learned was — sugar good. Want more.

Afterward, Macie and Dixon grabbed brownies and Kool-Aid off a refreshment table set up in the foyer. They protested when Shann corralled them and reminded them Aunt Lia needed everyone home for lunch. Nutritious, non-sugared lunch.

Shann carried Macie into the house. He lugged her through the kitchen where Jorie gathered dishes to help Lia set the table, and Beau read the *Knoxville News Sentinel*. After laying his daughter down in her twin bed, he gathered up Dixon.

With both kids conked out, he joined Beau. His brother read and barely offered a nod when Shann scraped the kitchen chair out and sat.

Lia dumped creamed chicken out of the Crock-Pot while Jorie pulled biscuits from the oven.

"Chris? Paul? Dinner." Lia's sweet voice carried on the tang of her Sunday meal.

The teens, who never walked anywhere when food was involved, raced each other into the kitchen.

"Boys," Beau's paper rattled. "Be civilized."

"Sorry, Daddy," Paul said.

They scooted into their regular seats.

"Would you say grace, Beau?" Lia asked.

The six of them joined hands. "Lawd, thank you for this food. This morning you showed us how to walk according to Your word ... " Beau decided to make up for his silence. He recapped his sermon. Rambled on forgetting the Lord's commandment to let his words be few. Perhaps he wanted Shann and Jorie to hear the sermon they missed by going to an unhallowed church quoting Scripture from the New King James — or worse — the NIV.

Shann quit listening.

At last, amens resounded. It was safe to join the conversation once more.

"Jorie?" Lia passed the platter of biscuits. "How did you like Grace?"

"It was good." She blinked heavily. "Without Mama, it was difficult."

"We missed her." Beau passed off the biscuits to Shann. "I thought of your ma when I composed the sermon. I used her favorite passage."

Jorie brightened. "James 2:26?"

"Yep."

Lia passed the chicken, and Beau launched into the entire sermon. So much for escaping his brother's theology.

The boys had the same reaction, even Paul. Shann had never seen two kids eat so fast. With their plates scraped and in the dishwasher, the teens left. Paul to his room. Chris to meet friends.

Macie slipped into the kitchen and onto Shann's lap, rubbing her eyes. Her hot head was sweaty from sleep.

"You didn't call me for dinner." She scratched her head. "I'm hungry."

"Here." Shann scooped chicken over a fluffy, still-warm biscuit.

185

Macie shoved it away. "I hate chicken."

Never had Shann been so glad for a cranky kid. Her fussing shut out his brother. He ran his hand over her head pressed against his chest.

He glanced at Jorie.

Her eyes were glued on Beau as though he held the keys to the kingdom.

The kingdom Shann wanted, lived across the road.

Then he knew.

Last night, Kiara had given him the keys to her world. Make Jorie decide she didn't want him. That one was easy. He knew how to be ornery. Abby reminded him regularly, as did Lia and Beau. However, with Jorie out of the picture, the second stipulation became more difficult. Beau wanted Shann to marry Jorie. If he got rid of her, Beau would blame Kiara. Beau'd like Kiara if Shann dated Jorie. Catch-22.

If he figured out the last item, then his love would be enough to make Kiara stay.

Chapter Twenty-Nine

On Monday, Kiara headed back from Knoxville. She'd found two new galleries. The owners recognized her name and practically salivated at the chance of displaying her work. She explored the Knoxville Art Museum—no Metropolitan Museum of Art, but quaint. Now, if the elusive Stinking Creek art dealer would bump into her, she'd be able to afford to live.

As a bonus, a jeweler paid her six grand for the ring and threw in another five hundred for her watch. She still hadn't cashed the check from Different Strokes Gallery. She needed a local bank to deposit local monies.

Seeing as Tennessee had as many banks as churches, she picked the first one she found as she headed into Jacksboro. With a new account and a deposit made, she drove to Stinking Creek.

Being five o'clock, her stomach screamed. The stupid belly had a mind of its own—a rather insistent one. How could anyone eat as much as she'd been?

The thought of cooking, then eating the goop she made by herself felt too lonely after a day of art-oriented people and the business of Knoxville. Maybe someone at Sugar Creek Diner knew where this Joey dude lived. Then with luck, the cooks might've baked their German chocolate cake today.

Once inside, Kiara ordered the special of the day—pinto beans and greens. She had them hold the corn bread. No reason to take a chance on Southern pone if Delia Mae's was any example.

The waitress took her order as she settled into the red booth closest to the back windows facing the creek. A few minutes later, the waitress returned with Kiara's coffee.

Decaf, unfortunately. Her drunken episode and battered truck told her she had to be good if this kid had any chance.

"Food will be out in a minute," the waitress said.

"By the way?"

The waitress tilted her head and waited for the question.

"Would you know an art dealer named Joey who lives around here?"

"Joey? Nope." She called to the patrons filling the next table. "Any of you know Joey, an art dealer."

People mumbled together.

"You mean Joey and Leslie Shellnut?" one man asked.

Kiara had to hide her snicker. *Shellnut?*

"Yeah, Joey Shellnut," said another customer. "I think Joey and Leslie are in Nashville right now. Her mother's sick or something."

"Do you know how I can find Joey?" Kiara asked.

"They live on old Stinking Creek Road. Big stone house by the second bridge."

That narrows it down. Any house not falling down or a trailer had been made out of stone.

"Why do you want to know?"

"I'm an artist." She saw no reason to give her name. None of these people would've heard of her. "I need to find someone who can get my work into bigger galleries."

"You ever give lessons?"

"I have." Kiara cringed. She pictured the work these yokels produced — stiff one-dimensional paintings like those of Grandma Moses or Henri Rousseau. No one down here would be able to paint.

Although, Macie had talent.

A woman got up from her table with her cell phone in hand. "Here're some of my paintings. Do you do watercolor?"

The diner scooted into the seat across from Kiara and held the phone in front of her face.

Little spiders crawled down Kiara's neck. Tact, Delia Mae had told her time and again, was not Kiara's strength. Delia Mae laughed before Kiara retorted. McG said it took one tactless person to recognize another. Kiara needed to be polite if she was going to frequent the only diner in Stinking Creek.

Kiara took the phone and thumbed through her brain for a diplomatic lie so she wouldn't devastate the woman when she heard the truth about her talent.

On the screen was a lovely watercolor landscape. Not photorealistic, not surreally beautiful, but artistic. It captured the mood of the landscape, peaceful, with a hint of turbulence. *Wow.* "Not bad. Where d'you study?"

"After high school, nowhere. I went on to prelaw and had no time to paint. With my practice, I have to start finding a stress reliever. It's either paint or shoot my husband."

They both laughed. "I've been there — not with a husband, but ... " Kiara studied the picture some more. "You did this with high school art?"

The woman nodded like Macie when the child was asked if she

188

wanted pie.

"Either you had a phenomenal teacher, or you've got a lot of raw talent."

The woman said nothing. She probably couldn't speak seeing as her grin etched her face. She clutched her hands tight on the table.

"I plan on moving, soon, but I can give you lessons while I'm in town."

"Really?"

Was she going to jump like Kiara had on the trampoline?

"How much do you charge?" The woman's mouth grimaced as though anticipating an unimaginable sum.

She couldn't afford lessons from Kiara.

"In Manhattan, individual lessons go for fifty an hour."

By the raised brows and sudden stiffness in her posture, fifty, as expected, was a mite much. "I can manage it. Still, I may have to shoot my husband. My clients have shown me plenty of ways to not get thrown in the hoosegow."

"Shooting the hubs is a bit extreme. If you got several people together for group lessons, you'd bring the cost down—two people for fifty, three for ... " Kiara hitched a shoulder, " ... sixty-five."

The woman smiled. "I've got a few friends interested. Can I have your phone number?"

Kiara scribbled it on a napkin and handed it to the woman.

"Here's my card." She handed a business card to Kiara. "If you find yourself needing a good defense attorney, call Annie Joy at Faircloth, Enfinger, and Grizzle. Unfortunately, I'm the Grizzle in the practice." Annie Joy returned to her table.

"I wish we had a gallery around here." The waitress returned with Kiara's food. "We got us lots of good artists on the Creek."

"My fiancé wanted to turn our place into an artist retreat."

"Wow. That'd be a fabulous addition to the community."

"It'd bring in business."

"Maybe compete with this dive."

The last comment earned the speaker a playful slap on the back of the head from the waitress. "If Sugar Creek Diner's a dump, you're a garbage picker. You're here *every day*."

The laughter and chatter swirled around the cozy diner as Kiara dug into her food. The sooner she ate the greens and beans, the sooner she could eat Sugar Creek Diner's desserts. Nothing beat their sweets and coffee. Even if they had to brew decaf for her.

~~

The next morning, Kiara hit the studio once more. The portrait

189

neared completion. She dabbed on highlights and the roses of the children's cheek bloomed. Their eyes sparkled. The large hands clasping them against whiskers covering denim overalls looked as though they'd stretch out and touch hers.

She stepped back. Her chest swelled as it always did when she nailed a painting. It pulled her in and made her long to paint herself into the family.

The picture combined the illustrious light of John Singer Sargent and the hominess of Mary Cassatt. It captured the essence of Shann's brood. Why'd she ever want to do abstract?

She looked up at *Stinking Morning*. Nothing she did made the painting palatable. Her negative work intensified the misery of being stuck here.

In a day or two, she could varnish the portrait of the twins. When the finish dried, she'd frame it and give it to Lia. Um, Delia Mae.

She'd been in town nearly a month. She owed her life to her neighbor. Kiara wished she'd let her call her Lia.

~~

The following Monday, Lia's boys fled the house as though she'd held them hostage. Shann had already retrieved his brood, and Lia'd have an hour before Beau got back from church.

Then dinner, choir practice, and prep for tomorrow's lessons. She put on the kettle.

A quiet knock rapped her kitchen door.

She opened it. Her spirit skipped even as she double-checked for her husband. The kids might blab about her visitor, but she no longer cared. Kiara didn't deserve rudeness.

"Is this a bad time?" Kiara asked.

"Is something wrong?" Lia eyed a canvas held facing Kiara. "What's this?" Still, she held the door as though her arm could keep her neighbor from barging into her world.

"A thank-you gift."

"For who?"

"You."

"Why?" Lia flung the door wide. *Too bad, Beau. Love thy neighbor. Remember the verse?* She ushered Kiara into the kitchen. "I put tea on. Want some?"

Kiara nodded. "Delia Mae, you've been good to me, even though you hate my art."

"Art?" Lia busied herself with tea bags and honey. "Just not my style."

"I thought this would do double duty. This portrait would thank you for all you've done for me."

"I've done nothing."

"Right." Kiara slipped into a seat at the table. "Second, this will prove to you I can paint."

"Law, Kiara." Lia brought two teacups to the table. "You don't need to prove—" Not another word escaped her mouth.

Before her, Kiara held the most incredible likeness of the twins she'd ever seen. Unlike a photograph, it captured their impish spirit. Their joy and beauty. Curls caught the light. Cheeks glowed. Eyes glistened with the soul of the children. Shann's strong hands clasped their chests and pulled them against his insane beard. Kiara captured in those hands, her brother-in-law's love and protectiveness of his offspring. If he loosened his grip, the kids would spring off the canvas and wreak their havoc.

"I guess you do have talent."

"Gee, thanks." Kiara laid the canvas down.

"I made you ginger peach. Okay?"

Kiara nodded.

Lia sat and eyed the portrait. "Shouldn't this go to Shann? It's his kids."

Kiara stirred a little honey into her tea. "No. Shann has helped me, but not like you."

"I'm being a good neighbor. Anyone would do what I did."

Kiara frowned. Her face looked solemn as though she need to share her soul. "It's beyond neighborly. You're honest. I don't have to guess at your agenda. You want nothing from me ... "

Her tone spoke of pain.

Lia leaned over and laid her hand on Kiara's shoulder. "It's okay. No need to say more."

"I want you to have this painting."

"Thank you."

"Plus, this shows I can paint better than Thomas Kinkade." Kiara winked, and she hid her grin by sipping her tea.

"So this is an 'I'll show her gift'?"

A grin fought the scowl. She nodded.

"You showed me, all right." Lia ran her finger over the paint. In some layers, the pigment rose in thick ridges and added depth to the curls and luster to the fabric. In other areas, it lay smooth as the children's silky skin. "It almost looks like their eyes will blink." She looked up at Kiara. "You've got an amazing gift from God."

"Not god. Genetics."

"Maybe. I can't paint a lick." She smiled. "Nor can I paint a wall or anything. Ain't got the genes for it." She pulled her focus from the painting and looked at Kiara. "It's beautiful."

191

Kiara leaned back in her chair and grinned. "I hope Beau won't be upset with my gift."

"Why would he?"

"He doesn't like me."

"What makes you say that?"

Kiara lifted a brow.

Lia tilted her head and lifted her teacup. "It's something you get used to."

"I don't care to get used to his surly nature."

"This is my husband you're bad-mouthing." The peace of the moment morphed as Lia's heart vised in her chest.

"Why do you stay married to him? He treats you like property, and not property he wants to keep."

"Not always." She studied her neighbor. The lilt of Kiara's brows and tilt of her lips told Lia she wasn't convinced. "He's my husband. I promised I'd stand by him for better or worse."

"Has he always been so cruel?"

"Cruel? My Beau isn't."

"Yes he is." Kiara threw up her hand. "I don't understand. He demands everything from you. During your mom's birthday, he played with the kids, entertained his friends while you slaved."

"It's part of our roles."

"So you're not allowed to have fun."

"I like taking care of people."

"Seems to me he could help you."

The kitchen door clattered.

Kiara stiffened.

Beau glared at her. As though his eyes' lasers zapped her, they zipped Kiara's mouth shut into a thin, tight line.

He glowered at Lia who froze with his stare. Beau walked out of the kitchen with quiet steps.

"I'm sorry. I came over hoping to make things good between us." Kiara stood. "I didn't mean to anger Beau any more than I already had. Delia Mae, I like you. If I could ever —"

Lia held up her hand. "Things have been tough. Finances are tight, and we had to mortgage the house. We're adding on to the church. Barbara died."

Kiara nodded. "Thank you for the tea." She stepped to the door.

"I'm sorry you don't like my husband, but he's my husband. My marriage is important."

Kiara kept her hand on the door. "Then fight for it, Delia Mae. Fight."

~~

Kiara stepped onto the side porch of the McGuffreys' as the Mule rode into the yard.

Shann waved. "We forgot our homework." He turned to the kids. "Go get it. Both of you."

The twins climbed down.

"And check out my portrait of you two." Kiara held open the kitchen door. "I gave it to your aunt."

The kids ran inside.

"Glad I caught you," Shann said.

"Don't get your hopes up about Beau ever liking me. He heard me—"

"Let me walk with you. I have something I need to ask, and I don't care to cause any trouble." He lifted his chin toward the house.

Kiara clamped her teeth together to keep from cursing. Or screaming. Or worse, crying. "Then you have to say it here. I won't be accused of leading you astray, too."

"Kiara!" Shann took her arm and pulled her away from the door.

She wrenched her arm free and stepped back. "Beau's abusing his wife. He makes everyone walk on eggshells. Broken eggs stink!" Her voice rose. "Stink worse than a corpse plant."

"Shh." Shann turned her to him and placed a finger on her lips.

As though he were a magnet, she wanted to cling to him and take comfort in his calm. "How are you related to him?"

The kitchen door knocked her from behind. Macie ran onto the porch.

"Macie," Shann said, "watch it."

"I hate the picture." She crossed her arms. She stuck out her bottom lip so far it could hold a dinner plate.

"Don't be rude," Shann said.

Looking at Macie, Kiara's anger evaporated like rubbing alcohol on a fever. She had to bite back her laugh.

"It's not the way Miss Muffet paints."

"If Miss Kiara painted it, then it *is* her style," Shann said.

Macie shook her head so hard the curls flopped across her face. "I want one like your *big* pictures." She stepped on tippy-toes and held out her hand.

"Hesh, girl. You're impolite," Shann said. "Another word and you'll spend the evening in your room."

"You're already in a huge painting," Kiara said. "In *Manhattan Seraph* you're the angel with the *measle* eyes."

"When you teach me, I wanna paint like you."

Shann took Macie's shoulders, opened the screen door, and propelled her inside. "Go keep an eye on Dixon, please, and let me talk

193

to Miss Kiara."

He waited until the screen door bounced shut. He took Kiara's arm and stepped her off the porch. "Can Macie start lessons on Thursday? If not, we'll change the art day at school."

She crossed her arms to put distance between Shann and her.

"Kiara, I understand." Shann turned her head with gentle fingers. "I've lived with or near Beau for thirty years. Abby found him abrasive, and if you knew Abby—she loved the world. Nothing you do or say will change him. Only God can."

She stepped away.

"Contrary to what you think, I've seen God do the impossible."

"Thursday's are good. If you'll excuse me, I've got work to do."

Chapter Thirty

The changing colors of the autumn leaves were one of two things varying in Kiara's life. Despite her calls to the realtor once a week and lowering the price on the land five-thousand dollars, McLemon brought no one to her cabin.

The second change—art lessons. Every week someone new called looking for classes.

"I'll walk you out," Kiara told Annie Joy Grizzle and her two friends who finished a session. "Annie Joy, if you're as good a lawyer as a publicist, no one would ever go to jail. I've got more people calling based on your recommendations."

"I should sue for commission."

"Then I'll have to charge more."

"I'll skip the commissions." The four women laughed at the banter.

Kiara handed out mixing charts so they could capture the autumn scenes around them.

"Isn't this beautiful?" Annie Joy gazed over the pasture to the mountains in the distance. Tired reds and yellows flecked with dried brown pigment filled out the trees.

Kiara nodded. In its anemic way, the fall colors in Stinking Creek held a beauty, but not like in the north. A little more than a year ago, she and Bryce had vacationed in Stowe, Vermont. October had just begun, and the colors dazzled in their brilliance. Sugar maples turned a bright cadmium yellow or alizarin red. One day, a soft sprinkling of snow added a contrast to the tints.

If Tennessee wanted autumn colors, it needed to head north. The universe knew how to paint a landscape in New England.

In happy chatter, the three women drove off, and Kiara walked toward her house. Dressed in a gauzy shirt and low rise palazzo pants giving lots of room for the baby, Kiara did enjoy the warm, dry October sunshine. By now in New York, she'd be wearing a winter coat to ward off the rain so cold it turned you to ice.

Almost every day down here she wore her Birks without freezing her toes. They hadn't had a frost. Dull leaf colors were a good trade-off.

At her kitchen porch, she watched Lia's home. She should stick with thinking of her as Delia Mae because she'd forget and anger her neighbor by assuming an intimacy Lia didn't want. It'd been a month since they'd talked. She missed her bossy friend. Wished she'd have a problem so Delia Mae would have to spend time with her.

In her kitchen, Kiara slathered mayonnaise on bread and layered on bologna and cheese. She hated bologna, but this baby loved it. She'd been buying it in cargo containers lately.

As she ate at her coffee table, she read the adoption documents from New Beginnings. She'd put off calling the agency for weeks. When she did contact them, the papers came within days. If she didn't send them out soon, she'd be stuck with a kid.

With a sandwich in her right hand and a pen in the left, she filled out her name on the top blank. Easy enough to do. The next slot asked for her address. She paused. Bit into her sandwich. *I guess I'd use this one. The post office will forward it if I move.* She rubbed her belly and put the pen down.

If the agency accepted her application, would she have to stay around here until the baby was born so the parents could pick it up?

Probably not.

She knew women who'd pay for a trip on a space shuttle to Mars to adopt a kid.

She filled in a few more blanks.

The next question asked if the adoptive parents could take part in the delivery.

Yuck. Who wanted strangers looking at her private parts while she cussed Bryce for knocking her up? They could anesthetize her, cut the kid out, and give it away.

She took another bite from her sandwich and mayo squished out on her fingers. Mayo and sweet pickles, two other food items that had grossed her out before the baby, now engrossed her appetite. She licked her fingers and went to write some more. Her saliva didn't remove all the mayo goo.

She pushed away from the coffee table and headed to the kitchen sink. With the water running, she squirted soap into her hands and lathered. A motion outside caught her attention.

Dixon?

He balanced on the railing of her bridge. She tapped at the window.

He looked up suddenly and windmilled his hands.

Not good. She wanted to yell, but Dixon would startle and fall. She darted out the front door.

"Dixon, get down right now." She strode toward him.

He bent his knees preparing to dismount when something disoriented him. With a whirl of his hands, Dixon fell backward into her rocky creek.

"Dixon!" Kiara ran. "No. No. No."

Her legs buckled, but she pummeled them against the ground. The world blurred as she raced.

"Dixon!" The scream tore from her throat. She skidded to the top of the embankment. Her breath stopped while her heart pumped staccato beats against her ribs. Splayed on rocks below lay little Dixon. His legs spread at a cockamamie angle. His closed eyes didn't twitch.

She breathed.

"Delia Mae!" Kiara shrieked. She glanced to her neighbor's home, then down the gulch, and back at her house where her phone was.

After this moment's hesitation, she scooted down the bank and knelt in the water. Fortunately, this stream flowed slower than the goop in a grade-schooler's glue bottle. Ankle deep, it posed no threat of drowning Dixon unless he twisted onto his belly. Not likely in his current state.

How would she get him out of here? If she moved him, she could paralyze him. She fingered his neck for a pulse. Little thumps of life throbbed beneath her fingers. "Dixon," she called. "Dixon, wake up." She scooped water in her hands and poured it over his head hoping the cool water would bring him to.

Not even an eyelash fluttered.

She looked around hoping to find help somewhere, an answer floating in the air telling her what to do. Shann was on his way to a gig in Nashville with Jorie, having promised Jorie a mini-vacation for the weekend.

He needed to be here.

She needed a cell phone in her hand. Plus a signal for it.

"Dixon." Her voice came breathy on her pounding pulse. "Wake up so I can leave you and find help."

Why didn't the McGuffreys watch the kids better? She lifted her head and screamed, "Delia Mae! Beau!"

No one came.

She patted the child's cheek. "Come on, Dixon." She lifted her head and screeched again.

Her throat rasped. She coughed in the strain. She had to leave Dixon alone in the creek if she was going to be able to call the EMS. If she climbed up the hill, would he turn his head into the water and drown? Would he wake up and try to move?

She had no choice.

While Kiara scrabbled up the far embankment, her sandals slipped off. Ignoring rocks digging into her toes, she scrambled across the road. Not bothering to knock, she flung open the McGuffreys' door, dashed to the phone.

"Delia Mae! Beau! Boys!" She picked up the receiver and dialed 9-1-

1.

Delia Mae and Beau skidded into the kitchen at the same time.

"Six-three-two Sheep Loop Road, Stinking Creek."

"What's going on?" Beau asked.

"Dixon fell. In my creek. Go!"

She turned back to the phone to answer emergency service's questions.

~~

"Macie's napping upstairs. Can you watch her?" Panic clogged Lia's throat. It pounded her heart.

Macie, Shann, hospital? Too much. God was giving her far too much to handle.

With the phone still wedged between her shoulder and ear, Kiara's soft hands gripped Lia's shoulders. "Go."

Lia ran. She caught up to Beau as he dashed across the road. In the ditch beside Kiara's bridge, Dixon lay motionless.

She paused. If she descended, would she find out he died? Why wasn't Beau watching him like he was supposed to be doing? No time to blame. She scurried down. Lia slipped and rasped her knee. Pain knifed her, but it dulled the panic.

Finally at Dixon's side, she knelt in the water. It seeped up her skirt and soaked her. She didn't care. Lia cupped his head with her palms, careful not to move him. She studied his face. Long lashes rested on pale cheeks. "Oh, Dixon. Wake up." She leaned over and kissed his forehead, careful not to jar anything.

Beau prayed. "Lawd, bring him to."

Eyelashes fluttered, and Dixon opened his eyes.

Beau smiled. His shoulders relaxed.

Lia gritted her teeth. *Your holiness saved him? I think not. He came to in order to shut you up.*

Her eyes searched Dixon's. "What happened? What were you doing?"

He closed his eyes.

"No, Dixon, no." Lia stared at Beau. "Why weren't you watching him?"

"I thought you were."

"I told you I was heading upstairs to lie down."

"To read the trashy books you hide under the mattress."

Her stomach felt like she swallowed a rock. "Call Shann," she said. "I'll stay with Dixon."

"My brother and Jorie are off to a show in Nashville. Shouldn't we wait and see what happens? Call when we know?"

"What if this was Paul?" Lia knew the son to name. "Wouldn't you want to know immediately? Wouldn't you leave a big revival to stand beside your son?"

Sirens sounded down the road.

Tires crunched above them.

"Down there." Kiara's voice sounded like an angel's.

"My brother. I want Daddy." Macie sobbed in Kiara's arms.

Still in ankle-deep water, Lia stepped aside as a paramedic worked. Beau helped her to the roadway. He stood stiffly by her.

She wanted his arms around her. Stepping an inch closer grimacing at the pain in her knee, she bumped against him praying he'd take the hint.

His arms hung at his side.

Lia looked down the embankment and gnawed her nails and shuffled wet feet. Neck braces and backboards and a zillun other instruments surrounded her nephew.

A warm arm pulled at her shoulders. She leaned in, a feeling a peace. Then Lia stiffened. It wasn't Beau who held her. With Macie's legs around her waist clinging to one side of her, Kiara pulled Lia close to her other side.

Lia glanced at her husband. He stood uselessly on the edge of the road, his lips moving, his eyes trained on the EMS workers.

Lia hated Beau.

Bile flowed through every capillary in her body. Through the fillings in her teeth. Her heart hammered against her ribs in loathing. She hated the man she once believed to be her soul mate.

"I'll keep Macie with me," Kiara said. "You go with Dixon. I'll make sure your boys know the details when they get home. I'll call Shann. Don't worry."

The gurney reached the road, and Lia ran to Dixon's side.

The child, awake with eyes clouded with fear, looked at her. "Where's Daddy?"

"He'll be back. We're calling him as soon as you're in the ambulance."

The EMTs lifted the stretcher into their rig. "Don't worry. We've got this." The paramedic climbed in after the gurney. "His vitals look good." He's in good hands."

"My husband and I will see you in LaFollette."

~~

Kiara stood in the roadway with Macie in her arms. Dust billowed behind the ambulance and MINI Cooper tailing it down the road. She watched until the last of the debris settled. Her arms ached with the weight of the child, and she put her down.

"Let's go inside." She took Macie's hand.

In the kitchen, Kiara poured milk and found a few Oreos, now soggy in their open package. "Let's have a snack." She placed the cookies on the coffee table in front of Macie who stared into the distance. She picked up the remains of her lunch and the adoption papers, plopped them on the kitchen counter and returned to Macie. Kiara sat next to her. "He'll be okay."

Macie looked up to Kiara. "Will you pray for Dixon?"

Pray? She swallowed hard and looked away. "Of course." She'd say anything to calm Macie, but what use would prayers be? She studied Macie once more. Her large eyes stayed trained on Kiara. She didn't think the kid had blinked since she woke up.

"Go on. Pray now." Macie's little voice begged.

At Queenie's party when Kiara bowed her head over lunch, Queenie was convinced she prayed. With Macie's plea, Kiara bent forward and studied the cookies on the table. *Should I move my lips?*

"No." Macie patted her face. "Say them out loud."

She jerked her head up. She opened her mouth. Closed it. Opened it again feeling a mite like a guppy gulping air.

Honesty. It was the only recourse she had.

"Why don't you pray for us?"

Tears pooled in Macie's pretty eyes. "You." She sniveled. "Grown-ups do it better."

Kiara had no choice but to confess. "You'll find this hard to believe, but I've never prayed. I don't know how."

The child's eyes widened. She blinked rapidly. "You *never* prayed? How do you talk to God?"

Why didn't someone tell Kiara how impossible it was to talk to kids? With Shann or Delia Mae, she'd call them idiots and demand they stop meddling in her business. Macie's face told her this request was of paramount importance.

"No one I know ever prayed."

"No one?" Macie's eyes grew larger.

Kiara shrugged. "If you teach me, I'll do it."

The child's smile was the reward Kiara needed. "Fold your hands like this." Macie clasped her hands and held them against her chest.

Kiara mimicked the stance.

"Now bow your head."

She did.

"Say, 'Dear Jesus.'" Macie said nothing more.

Kiara looked at her.

"Go on. Say it."

"Dear, Jesus," Kiara said.

"I love you. You are the God who made us, and we love you." Macie stopped speaking.

"How did you come up with that sentence?"

"It's how we always start our prayers with Daddy."

Kiara repeated the words. The process sent a warmth coursing through her. How nice it would be if an omnipotent deity cared about them. If he or she took care of her needs, what a burden would be lifted.

Without worrying about addressing this fictitious divinity, Kiara repeated each of Macie's words. When the sprite uttered an amen, Kiara asked if she felt better.

Macie bobbed her head and reached for the stale cookie.

Kiara felt better, too. The words had taken fear away, like when Bryce would hold her and kiss her curls and tell her how much he loved her.

Could it be?

~~

Four hours later, Shann raced down the hospital corridor. Jorie followed close behind. His son wasn't in the ICU. Being in a regular room meant he'd recover.

Soon.

He burst through the hospital room door to find his little body tucked into bed.

Dixon didn't move. Didn't shift with the noise Shann made.

Beau and Lia rose from the chairs where they sat vigil.

"He's sleeping." Lia's voice was soft, almost resigned. "He regained consciousness before they got to the hospital. He's tired."

Jorie slipped to the far side of the bed and stood near Beau and Lia. She studied the boy but didn't move to touch him.

"How bad are his injuries?" Shann studied Dixon. He looked at peace—like all would be well.

"He broke his leg." Lia eyed her nephew, her voice solemn. "They already set it with an external fixator. He'll need to use a wheelchair."

He smiled at Lia and Beau. "He'll love it." For the first time since he'd heard the news, the iron stiffening Shann's body softened. "I can see him doing wheelies or trying to jump the bridge like Evel Knievel."

"He better not," Lia said. "The doctor said given his age, the break should heal in six weeks."

"He's got a concussion." Beau moved around the bed and laid his hand on Shann's shoulder while Lia fussed with the covers. "They're monitoring it tonight. The doctor thinks he'll be home tomorrow."

Shann eased down the bed rails and sat next to his son. He ran his hands over Dixon's head.

201

"I'm sorry your mini-vacation was cut short," Lia said to Jorie.

"Mary Lou isn't." Jorie added nothing else, but she grinned like this was the most original joke.

Lia and Beau looked from Jorie to Shann.

"Mary Lou's the other single lady with us at the Nashville venue," Shann said. "She'll have a private room at half the price." He glanced at Jorie who whispered prayers from the other side of the bed.

Lia looked back at Dixon. "I'm sorry we caused —"

"You're good." Shann caught wisps of Jorie's prayers. Her voice, the thing he liked most about her, gave him a vague comfort, but he wanted her to touch his son, not hold herself aloof like she was afraid of him.

That was it. Jorie feared she'd hurt Dixon if she touched him.

Dixon opened his eyes and grinned at his father. His smile, wan and fleeting, warmed Shann like God handed him a down comforter and wrapped it around him.

"How're you doing?"

"My head hurts." He smiled again and pulled the covers off his leg. "Look'it." An external brace held the bones in place. "I got me an erector set on my leg."

"Does it hurt?"

Dixon nodded. "Ouch. It hurts to wiggle my head."

"Then don't move it." Shann pulled up the covers then ruffled his curls. "Go back to sleep."

He didn't need to give the last command. By the time he kissed his son's forehead, Dixon's breath came in slow even puffs.

Now he had to face his brother. "What happened?"

"I believed Lia watched him." Beau's shoulders sagged, and he averted his head.

Here's the man who always brags on the husband's duty to his wife. Shann's heart nearly broke his ribs. He ground his teeth. *Never read where God said to blame the wife at every juncture.*

"She'd told me to watch him. She would be upstairs, but I got lost in my sermon prep." Finally, Beau looked at him. "When I think about my carelessness ..." He inhaled a deep breath, like one gulped after a crying jag. "Apologizing can't make up for my carelessness. This accident rests on me, alone. I can only praise the Lawd Dixon will recover and beg you to forgive me."

So much for fire and fury. With an exhale, all Shann's anger deflated. Judging by his brother's soft voice, his sorrow held regret and pain. He took the blame and spared his wife.

Who was Shann to judge, anyway? A month ago, Dixon fell in the pond on his watch. Two months before that, he needed stitches after jumping off his loft. They all lapsed with the kids.

Abby never would have.

Shann looked toward the ceiling. *Abby, why did you die? I can't do this without you.*

"The doctors say he'll be fine," Lia said. "He'll have no permanent injury. They said he could resume easy activities, but no skydiving from bridges."

Shann chuckled. "Why don't you guys head home? It's dark out. Gotta be late. I'll stay here."

"What happened with your show?" Lia asked.

"Vern Murphy—a gift from God—will make it to Nashville in time to sub for me." He looked up at Jorie. "I'm sorry your vacation came to an early end."

"Don't apologize. This is more important." Jorie looked to Lia and Beau. "Can you take me home?"

"Why don't you stay?" Shann asked.

"It's late. I won't be any help here."

Shann wished for company—solace, a human nearby who understood. He watched Jorie as she gathered her purse and sweater. Did he imagine things, or did she look relieved to leave?

"We'll meet you by the elevator," Beau said. He and Lia left the room.

Jorie kissed Shann goodbye and turned to go.

He grabbed her hand. "Do you like my kids?"

She looked at him, but her eyes didn't quite find his. "Don't be silly."

"Why don't you stay?"

"I'm tired. I'll be in the way. Call me tomorrow." She walked away.

He tucked the blankets around his son in the darkened room. Then he saw the truth. He'd been stringing Jorie along because of Kiara's rules.

Give her a chance.

Shann had. The truth of the matter though, he didn't love her.

Knowing all along he'd never love her, why was he annoyed she didn't love his kids?

Regardless of Kiara's stipulations, even if he never had a chance with her—and he didn't because she was heading north and didn't love God—he needed to end his relationship with Jorie.

He sank into a chair. Deep dark had settled outdoors. The nurses bustled around the nurses' station. Dixon's soft breathing became a rhythmic prayer.

Shann lived his life all wrong.

He'd correct it.

Chapter Thirty-One

The sun set and darkness overran Stinking Creek. Kiara dumped dish soap into the sink.

Macie stood on a stool. She splashed a washrag in the sudsy water and ran it over the encrusted pans. "I like washing pots."

Kiara smiled at the imp. The homey activity felt natural. Their bodies bumped into each other as they stood side by side and washed and rinsed the pots and pans.

"What time do you go to bed?" Kiara asked.

"I stay up as late as I want on Saturdays."

"I don't think so. It's dark now. Why don't you change into your pajamas?"

Macie skipped into the bathroom. Water ran. Kiara assumed she washed.

While the child readied herself for bed, Kiara rewashed the pots Macie had helped clean and tucked them back into the drainer. She added soap to the dishwasher and started it.

Macie bounced into the living room. "Read me a story?" She'd buttoned her pajama top cockeyed and toothpaste lined her lips.

"I see you brushed your teeth."

"Daddy says I gots to."

"Come here." Kiara took the damp towel and wiped Macie's mouth.

The child wormed away. "Oww. I'll do it." She grabbed the moist cloth and rubbed her entire face.

"I don't have any books for kids here." Kiara's latest romance novel wouldn't be appropriate for tykes.

"I've got a zillun of them at Aunt Lia's house."

"How many's a zillun books?"

"It's a whole bunch. More'n the libery's got."

Kiara nodded her head. "More than the library?"

"Yep." Macie tugged Kiara's hand toward the front door.

"Well then, let's go pick some out."

With light from her cell phone, they wandered to the McGuffreys'.

Kiara twisted the doorknob. "I think your cousins locked us out."

"I kin fix it." Macie dug through a planter sitting beside the porch. "Here's the key."

Inside, Macie ran into the back room.

Kiara filled Youtee's water bowl and opened the door for him to go out and do his business. The hound stared at her with huge eyes.

"Hungry?" She called to Macie. "Where's Youtee's food?"

The child stumbled back to the kitchen armed with more material than the two could read in a month. She plopped the books on the table. In a room off the kitchen, Macie fumbled with a bin of dog food and dumped kibble into his bowl.

Youtee inhaled the dog food and begged to go out.

She opened the door, and he ran around the yard barking at shadows.

Then Kiara couldn't coax him back in.

Twenty minutes later, after they'd lured the pooch back into the house, they scooped up books and headed home.

Halfway across the road, Macie dropped her books. The two stooped together and piled them into Kiara's arms. With her free hand she gripped Macie's palm and glanced up. "Look at the stars." She jutted her chin heavenward. "I've never seen so many."

Macie stared at the sky. "Daddy said there's a candy bar up there. I think he's joking me."

"A candy bar?"

"The Milky Way."

Kiara grinned. "Not a candy bar." She tightened her grip on Macie's hand. "We better not lollygag in the road."

"Lollipop?"

"Lollygag. It means stand around. A car might come along and zap us." She led Macie across the bridge, then looked up again. "Millions of stars crowd close together in our galaxy. The ancient Greeks said a cow kicked over a milk bucket, so astronomers called it the Milky Way."

"There're cows up there?"

Kiara shook her head. *Kids.*

"Can you show me it?"

"Cow?"

"No, silly, the Milky Way."

"I'd love to."

In her cabin, Kiara found an old blanket and the laser pointer she'd used for presentations when she was called to teach or lecture on art. "Come with me."

"Where're we going?"

"On an adventure."

"In the dark?" Macie clapped her hands. "Too bad Dixon can't come. He loves 'ventures."

Kiara led Macie to the meadow behind her house. At a spot clear of trees and padded by dying weeds and wildflowers, she shook out the blanket, and the two lay down side by side.

Macie wiggled close.

Kiara stretched out her arm, and the munchkin burrowed into her. "See the swirl." Kiara aimed the laser toward the Milky Way. "Those stars make up your candy bar."

"Wow." The child's mouth gaped. "There's a gobullion of them."

"Gobullion?"

"That's more than a zillun."

"Quite a few." She pointed the laser again. "See the big pot?" She connected the ends of the constellation. "We call this one the Big Dipper."

"I see it." Macie wiggled closer.

The child's warmth seeped through Kiara's fleece. It comforted and made Kiara want to cuddle all night. "One side looks like the sky's pouring out the dipper's liquid." Again, she waved the laser back and forth between the two stars on the constellation's side.

"I see it." Macie grabbed at the laser. "Let me point."

"Not now. We call those two stars Merak and Dubhe."

"Wow. You know *everything*."

"That's what I told my folks." Kiara took Macie's hand in hers and folded the child's fingers into a fist. "Count four fists away." She moved her clenched hand. "There. See the faint star? That's Polaris or what most people call the North Star."

"Daddy says sailors use that one to figure out where to go. How can they? It's almost invisible."

"I know. I always expected it to be as bright as a street light. Even though it's faint, Polaris helps sailors because it never changes its position. Also, the North Star never disappears from the night sky, so everyone knows which way is north."

"Daddy says the North Star's like God. He never changes and always points the way."

"You like stars."

"Yep. Daddy took us camping this summer. He taught me everything there is to know about them." Macie wiggled against Kiara.

"If you think we have a gobullion stars, look there." She moved the laser. "We call this clump of stars Andromeda. That galaxy has more of them than ours."

"No way." Macie shrieked the words.

They lay a few minutes, then Macie sang "Twinkle, Twinkle Little Star." Soon her voice quieted. Her breaths came slow and still.

Several minutes later, Kiara propped herself on her elbow and studied the sleeping beauty. She should take her inside and put her to bed. The cool breezes blew over them and lulled her.

She lay back down and stared upward. Stars shown with a brilliance she'd never seen. All her life she'd lived in big cities— Singapore, Portland, and Manhattan. Their clamor blotted out the galaxies. To see the night sky in the city, she had to visit a planetarium. Still, man's counterfeit universe paled compared to the real thing.

The dome of this universe dwarfed her. Each of those dots of light twinkling above her could be a sun warming other worlds. Scientists said Andromeda was so big because it swallowed other galaxies.

Who was she compared to the cosmos? It had been there for—as Macie called it—a gobullion-zillun years. Needing light years to reach earth's atmosphere, perhaps those stars had burnt out.

How long would she live? Bryce made it to forty-five. How many years had the world been around? Four billion give or take a day? What did any of us matter?

She wiggled and pulled Macie closer. A chill breeze blew over her, but the sky and the dozing child rooted her to the pasture.

Her gaze danced across the universe.

How'd those stars get there? She believed in the big bang theory. However, the beginning bang had to have something to throw out into the galaxies. Where'd all the materials for the big burst come from?

A meteor zipped by.

She gasped and hoped for more but only twinkling lights, more glorious than the ones at Christmas, winked back at her.

Asteroids—splendid but fleeting.

The air cooled more, and Kiara shivered. The night promised the first frost of the season. She shook Macie, but the girl wouldn't wake. Kiara picked her up and carried the dead weight into the living room.

Macie flopped like a rag doll onto the couch. Kiara pressed the blanket around her and smoothed the stray curls off the waif's forehead.

Kiara stood over the child. Her heart melted as she studied Macie's perfect skin and golden hair. Long lashes fluttered against her rosy complexion.

The child shifted and broke the spell holding Kiara close to her side.

I never left a note for Chris or Paul. Do they know about Dixon?

She dialed the McGuffreys, and Paul answered. She explained about Dixon, then climbed the stairs to bed.

Pitch filled the room when she shifted on the mattress a while later. She stretched and turned, then bumped into Bryce. Kiara threw her arm over him and nuzzled his head. He smelled different. Not like his Acqua di Parma.

She opened her eyes. Nestled next to her, Macie lay fast asleep. Kiara ran her hand over the child's curls. "Didn't want to be alone, did you?" she whispered. "I don't blame you."

She propped herself up on her left arm. Stray beams from the nightlight in the bathroom at the foot of the stairs filtered into the room.

Macie's lips parted, and her shoulders rose and fell in a regular rhythm.

She twirled Macie's curls with her fingers. So soft. Beautiful.

In Kiara's stillness, her baby bumped inside her womb. She lay back down and let the thumps rock her back to sleep.

Chapter Thirty-Two

A soft tap at her front door woke Kiara. She flung on her robe and scurried downstairs. After flipping on the porch light, she opened the door.

Delia Mae stood in the lamp's warm glow. "I'm here for Macie."

"Come in." Kiara touched her shoulder and guided her into the living room. "She's sound asleep. If you'd like, she can stay."

Delia Mae scanned the room. "Where is she?"

"She snuck into bed with me."

"I'm sorry. You should've made her—"

"It was comforting. How's Dixon?"

Tears sprang to Delia Mae's eyes.

"No." Kiara took her friend's arm and led her to the couch.

"These are tears of relief." Delia Mae sank on the sofa and clasped her hands between her legs. "He's good. Now."

"I need details." Kiara stepped to the stove. "I'll brew us a cup of tea."

"I should let you go back to bed."

"You know I say and do what I like." She glanced at Delia Mae. "Like my mirror twin."

"It's nearing midnight."

Kiara filled the kettle. "It's well after. My stove clock says 12:02. The microwave disagrees. At 12:05, you're right. It is way too late." She threw Delia Mae a smile to let her know she teased and turned on the burner. "You're my prisoner until I hear every detail." Kiara faced Delia Mae and leaned against the counter. "What's Dixon's prognosis? Did Shann get to the hospital?"

"One question at a time." Delia Mae smiled.

Kiara poured two cups, then settled next to Delia Mae as she spewed the night's activities. With the slant of the couch, the two shifted closer together. Within a half hour, the two of them curled on the sofa like mama and daughter.

It felt so right.

~~

More than an hour later, Lia left Kiara and sleeping Macie.

Across the road, her home looked lonely. Lights glowed from somewhere in the depths of her residence. *How can light be so cold?*

One nice thing about being friends with a non-church member was that Kiara liked her because she was Lia McGuffrey and not Pastor Beau's wife or the mission director or a food pantry worker.

Kiara, even though she was twenty years younger, felt like a mother to Lia. As ornery as her own Ma. As mouthy as Lia was. So similar, they could be related.

Lia crossed Sheep Loop Road and returned home.

Beau's study light shone.

She headed there. "Will you be much longer?"

He looked up with eyes weighted with fatigue. His shoulders slumped. "I don't think so." He glanced at the computer. "The congregation will have to settle for what I have."

"Why don't you extemporize? You know what you want to say."

"Never comfortable speaking from an unscripted sermon. It has to be right."

"God doesn't expect perfection. Only He can give it."

"You're talking about not being perfect?" Beau reached out his arms. "Come here and kiss me."

She stepped over and kissed his head.

He pulled her into his lap. "I'm sorry."

"For what?" She brushed his hair off his forehead. Seeing as God made all things work for good, maybe Dixon's accident would help their marriage.

"I should've watched better."

"We all lose track of things—especially those little whirlwinds." She kissed him good night. "See you upstairs."

While Lia poured a glass of water in the kitchen, Chris tiptoed in from the yard.

"I thought you were in bed." Lia scowled. This wouldn't sit well with Beau. "Curfew's midnight."

"Sorry, Ma." He fiddled with the lock.

"Where were you? The van and four-wheelers were in the driveway. I thought you got home in time."

"I didn't drive." Chris headed toward the hallway.

"Who drove?"

He didn't stop walking toward the stairs. "Friends."

"Get back here." Lia stepped toward him. "Look at me."

Chris's shoulders stiffened, then sagged.

"Where were you?" She stepped back as hints of yeast and hops filtered between them. "Have you been drinking?"

"A couple of beers."

"Two beers? You're eighteen. It's illegal—not to mention immoral."

"Ma, a beer or two never hurt anyone." Still, he kept his eyes averted.

She glanced down the hall. Beau would hear about this, but not tonight. She looked at her son. "By the smell of your breath, you drank more than two."

"Ma."

She grabbed his shoulder. "Look at me."

His eyes met hers.

"While you were out being a hooligan—"

"I'm not a hooligan. Just because Paul's a Goody Two-shoes don't mean I'm an outlaw."

Lia dropped her arm. "Your behavior has nothing to do with Paul. The drinking age is twenty-one, so you broke the law. Not only were your actions illegal, but you broke our trust. Who were you with?"

He studied his sneakers.

"No need to tell me. Bobby and Leo." She inhaled and examined the ceiling, then studied her son. "Bobby, I can understand. You've known him forever. Something about Leo bothers me though."

"You always lecture about judging people. Leo's cool."

"While you were partying with the *cool* guys, Dixon fell. He's in the hospital with a broken leg and a concussion. For now, you're lucky tomorrow's service is preoccupying Daddy. We won't have to deal with this until after church. Go to bed."

"Yes, ma'am." Chris headed up the stairway.

Lia watched him as he left, then she flipped on the light beneath the microwave for Beau and went upstairs. Once dressed for bed, she sank her into the mattress and stared at the ceiling. Her body ached with exhaustion, but when Beau found out about Chris's drinking ... She twisted onto her right side.

Why couldn't Chris be more like Paul?

She flipped onto her back.

Chris never followed rules. He always pushed the limits making life unpredictable.

Again she turned.

Rules made life safe.

She liked it that way.

Eons later, Beau stood beside the bed and undressed in the dark.

She flipped over.

"Still awake?" He slipped into bed beside her.

She murmured.

"I won't be for long." Beau kissed her. Minutes later he snored.

She lay in bed and tried not to move. She dozed. Barely asleep, she'd startle. At some point she must've slept as the clocked jumped an hour or so every time she checked.

The sun rose.

She climbed out of bed.

Today would not be pleasant.

Chapter Thirty-Three

Macie skipped down Kiara's steps early the next morning. "Will you go to church with me?"

Kiara glanced up from the counter where she mixed pancake batter. "No, sweetie. I don't go to church."

Macie looked as though someone told her the Easter Bunny stole all the candy he was supposed to leave in order to elope with The Elf on the Shelf. "Why not?"

'There is no god' seemed too harsh for the innocent. Delia Mae would more than likely object. She picked up a bag of chocolate chips. "I heard you like these in your pancakes."

The child's face lit up, and Macie dragged a chair next to Kiara. She stood on it and watched as Kiara made funny faces in the pancakes with the chips. "You can come to Uncle Beau's church with Aunt Lia and me. I like Daddy's church better, but it's far, far away." She waved her arm behind her as though pointing out the direction. "I don't know how to get there."

Kiara flipped the pancakes over to brown the uncooked side. "Do you want milk?"

"Yes, ma'am. Thank you."

Ma'am? Am I old enough to be a ma'am? Kiara lifted the imp off the chair, poured two glasses, and placed them on the coffee table.

"Let's surprise Aunt Lia and sneak in late."

"Sneak in where?"

"Church at Uncle Beau's." Macie shook her head like a mama instructing an unenlightened child.

Kiara slipped a plate of pancakes at each of their spots. "You say grace." She bowed her head and clasped her hands. With a little luck, Macie wouldn't start out with 'Dear, Jesus. We love you, blah, blah.'

Before the prayer would end, a week would pass and the pancakes would mold.

~~

After church, Lia helped Macie out of the van. The child hadn't stopped pouting since Kiara brought her home.

"Chris," Beau grumbled. "Help your ma." He picked up his notes and *Bible*. His eyes looked as though they carried the entire Samsonite line of bags under them.

"Paul, take these." He handed off his pile of papers and started for the house.

Instead of heading indoors, he walked to the MINI Cooper, bent over and lifted a dangling license plate. "Lia, remind me to fix this after lunch. We lost a bolt." He straightened, and although he tried to square his shoulders, still they slumped. Beau regarded her with eyes heavier than Rip Van Winkle's before he snoozed.

Lia could let Chris's drinking slide and not tell her husband. She could mete out a punishment and let Beau rest. He'd be in a better frame of mind.

Inside the house, Youtee jumped on her husband.

"Down, boy." Beau dusted off his trousers while his jaw worked as though he ground his choppers into bonemeal. His breaths were audible. Without a word, he held the kitchen door open, and the dog bounded out. "You latched the gate, dint you?" He gave Lia a fleeting glance.

"I always do," Lia answered. "Why don't you lie down after lunch?"

He yawned while he nodded and pulled out his chair at the table. After easing himself into his usual spot, Beau picked up the sports section of the Sunday paper.

"Dad." Chris's voice cracked.

Beau looked at his son.

Chris stared at the floor. His arms hung at his sides.

Lia gasped. She read his body language as if he spoke his mind. Could she telepathize her thoughts to him?

Bad timing. Chris, shut up. Lia widened her eyes and leaned toward her son. She forced her thoughts toward him. Her stomach squeezed so tight it would make Arnold Schwarzenegger envious of her abdominal crunching ability.

"Last night, me, Bobby, Leo, and a few other guys had us a bonfire."

Beau nodded.

"Leo brought beer. I had ... ." He cleared his throat. "I drank a few cans." He inhaled but made no other movement.

Beau said nothing for a hundred hours, or so.

"Define a few," Beau sounded neutral.

"Two." Chris's eyes studied the floor.

Beau raised his brow but said nothing.

"Three. Ain't gonna lie." Chris's voice lowered more than before. Still, he did not meet his father's gaze.

Lia closed her eyes. *Now you decide to be truthful? You know your father's temper*. She peeked at Beau from beneath her lashes.

He still sat at the table, the paper before him. Chris hadn't moved.

Appliances whirred.

The floor creaked beneath Chris's feet as he shifted.

Lia's heart stopped beating.

"I'm sorry. It was wrong." He lifted his chin and held his father's gaze. "I don't want Ma to have to tell you."

Beau glared at her. "You knew?"

She pinched her lips together.

He glared at Chris. With one arm propped on the table, he jabbed the other finger toward his son. If his eyes were coals, they all would've burned to death. "I have two things to say." His voice smoldered. His pause lasted an eternity.

Lia swallowed hard.

"First, you are grounded for a week."

Chris nodded.

Lia breathed.

Beau sat back. "Then, never will you see Bobby James and his friends again. Especially, Leo Marsh. I heard bad things about him. Remember, I don't chew my cabbage twice."

"You'll never have to tell me again." Chris left the room.

Beau glanced at Lia. "Why did you hide this from me?"

"I didn't."

"Don't lie. Seeing as the first I heard of it came from Chris, you hid it."

"It was late when he came home. I was going to tell you this afternoon."

Beau's lips worked. His head nodded.

Lia knew what this silence meant. She held her breath and waited.

"Never did I think lies would fill my house." He picked up the paper. He rattled it.

Lia exhaled. *What's worse? A tongue lashing or silence?* She pulled hamburger out of the fridge to start lunch.

The paper crinkled behind her. She stiffened her shoulder.

"Your son has had his last chance."

She nodded.

"Look at me, Lia."

She faced him but studied the spot on the table in front of Beau.

"This is Chris's last chance. Do you understand?"

She nodded.

"Now get our meal going."

~~

Never had happiness overtaken Shann like this, except when Abby married him.

His little boy chattered away. He made race car noises as he rolled his wheelchair in circles in the parking lot next to Shann's truck.

"Daddy, I wished I went to school."

"You *do* go to school."

"Not at home. No one can see me at home."

Shann lifted the booster seats from the back of the truck and laid them on the front floor.

"Hey. How'm I gonna get home?"

"What do you mean? I'm driving us." Shann looked for his son, but Dixon now wheeled himself in the traffic lane of the lot. "Wheel yourself back here. A car will hit you."

Dixon rolled back to the truck. "I need to be safe. I have to ride in my driver's seat." He pointed to the boosters.

"You have to keep your leg up." Shann lifted his son. He winced as he manipulated Dixon's leg to lay it on the back seat without mangling it more.

His son's limb was swollen and red. Thick pins poked through Dixon's skin and had been drilled into a bone deep beneath the surface.

Shann wished the doctors had used an old-fashioned, bright blue swath of plaster—something everyone could sign, and Macie would draw on. A wrapping would hide the mess Dixon made of his leg.

Several minutes later with Dixon settled, Shann fitted the seat belt around him. "We'll be careful driving home. I promise."

Lia would have difficulty maneuvering his son.

He couldn't leave him in Stinking Creek and finish his Tennessee tour. Vern Murphy would have to continue to fill in for him. This tour paid him well. Now? Bills had a habit of showing up every month. Also, his kids liked to eat.

"I'm hungry," Dixon said.

"We'll go to McDonald's, okay?"

"Yippee. I should break my leg every day. We *never* eat at McDonald's."

Shann winced. What was he going to do?

Maybe this year's Christmas craft shows would make up for his lost gigs? Advertising his sales to Arvol Hogg and Bridget Bedmeister might help. He sighed. Not going work. Country greats like those two wouldn't sell enough high-end guitars to help him feed his family.

Abby's salary would've helped. He did have her life insurance monies stashed away.

Why'd he have to love an artist who made as little money as he?

Then he thought about Jorie. He'd have to do something. Soon.

Fifteen minutes later they sat in McDonald's parking lot chowing down on Big Macs and Happy Meals. It was easier to let Dixon eat in the truck than hauling the wheelchair and a little boy held together with nuts and bolts and steel rigging into the restaurant.

Dixon chatted to his new Happy Meal toy—a mutant nuclear worm from the latest animated cartoon. This creature was neon green and gooey to the touch. A lot like a booger. Considering the nutritional value and the caloric count of the food, the toy was appropriate.

While Dixon slurped, Shann dialed Jorie. "Hey."

"Hello, Shann. You're not home, yet?"

"Nope. We're sitting in the lot at McDonald's clogging our arteries."

"You've got to be tired."

"Not bad." *She didn't ask about Dixon.* "The excitement about bringing my son home is keeping me awake."

"Be careful driving. It's been a long haul for you."

He'd made the right decision.

"I went back to Sheep Loop Church this morning. Beau's eyes looked so tired."

No questions about my son, but she worries about my brother? Who does she love—him or me?

"Jorie." He inhaled. Breaking up was harder than making the kids eat Brussels sprouts. He'd never make a career as an *homme fatale*. "You like Sheep Loop Church, don't you?"

"I do."

"I don't." He glanced over his shoulder at his son who grinned as he inched the worm up the seat back, making it growl and snuffle. "Also, I think we're opposites as far as our faith."

"I—"

"Listen to me. I can't lead you on any longer. I'm not in love, and you need to find someone who will treasure you the way you deserve."

"Is this about Kiara?"

Yes. "No." He understood the truth. He loved Kiara, but if she didn't love Jesus, he'd have to give up on her. If she moved back to Manhattan, he wouldn't follow. Plus, Beau accepting her was as likely as Dixon's mutant worm snuffling in the back seat speaking for itself. "This deals with faith. I'll never be happy following Beau's brand."

"It's not a brand."

"Yes. It is. I like Grace Church. Can we be friends?"

"Of course. I'll miss our time together."

They hung up.

He leaned back. *That's it? I'll miss our time?*

Dixon roared, and Shann jumped. He twisted around. "What are you doing?"

"My worm likes my bolts."

"I like them too." Shann's appetite fled. He crumpled his bag and tossed it on the floor on the passenger's side. He didn't have Kiara or Jorie or the blessing of his brother. Still, he had everything he needed. His kids. His integrity. Best of all—his path back to faith.

Chapter Thirty-Four

Darkness settled over the cabin when Kiara's phone rang. Little happened during the past two weeks. Even phone calls became rare.

"Key. It's me, with good news."

"Imani! It's been too long."

"Guess what?"

"You're pregnant, too?"

"Too?"

Kiara shuddered. *Oops. I let the pussycat out of his satchel.*

"Key? Are you still there?"

Kiara refocused. "Sorry. I got distracted. You were saying?"

"Did you say *too*?" Imani didn't drop the subject. "Too means one thing. You're gonna be a mama." She squealed. Imani would be jumping and clapping her hands about now.

Kiara grimaced and chewed her nail. "Guess I forgot to mention it last time we talked." She glanced at her countertop where the envelope addressed to New Beginnings lay. If she didn't mail it soon, the baby would be born, and it would have no home. "So are you and Lance—?"

"Not at all. Her voice took on a dreaming tone. "We're still on our honeymoon. We'll chat about *your* baby in a minute. My news can't wait." She paused.

Seconds ticked away. "Well?"

"I never thought you'd ask." As though to make up for the few seconds of silence, Imani's words spilled out like an auctioneer's. "A spacious loft is coming on the market for two grand a month in a great neighborhood near us having everything you want."

"Slow down," Kiara said. "I've lived in the South too long and can't understand fast-talking Yankee."

"The loft I found is a steal. The landlord's going to advertise it at the end of the week after he paints and does minor repairs. I should say, he'll advertise it *if* it remains vacant."

"Two grand? It *is* a good deal." Kiara calculated the savings she had left. It didn't take long as she kept tabs on her dwindling finances nanosecond by zeptosecond. "At that price, I can cover rent for six months and still eat." *Food?* She faced the fridge. "Lately, eating is costing big bucks. I need to buy shares in a grocery market. Tell me more." She pulled out a bowl of grapes and popped one into her mouth.

"It's in Brooklyn. The loft's a walk-up and has a thousand square feet. The subway is around the block, and it's three miles from us."

"I'll take it," she said around a mouthful of fruit.

"The apartment's in a neighborhood that's a little dicey. I'd have you wire me the money, but you need to check it out to be sure. The owners want a year lease. If the apartment's not workable, it's a long wait for the contract to end or an expensive deal to break the lease."

"You said it's not on the market yet?"

"Right. Friends of ours from church told us about it. Their cousin rented it, but he got transferred to Philly, so he needs to move."

"I'll be there tomorrow. As soon as we hang up, I'll call the airlines. I'll text you my flight info. When I'm home, I'll fill you in on the baby."

The dial tone barely stopped reverberating when Kiara fired up her computer and logged on for flights. She found one for six o'clock the next morning. She punched in her credit card numbers and chose her seat. A screen popped up asking if she wanted flight insurance.

She'd been stuck here for two full months. If she didn't leave Hicksville now, her life would be over. Good weather was promised for the morning, so the plane wouldn't cancel its plans because it might get wet. She felt her forehead for a fever. No sign of a cold or celiac disease or werewolf syndrome. No need to waste money on flight insurance. Nothing under heaven would have her miss this chance.

Five hundred dollars later, Kiara booked her flight to JFK. She emailed Imani the details and added five happy face emojis. She'd head home sober this time and in a plane via the sky, not in her truck along the riverbed.

After grabbing a bag of chips, she climbed to her loft and dug her suitcase from under the pile of dirty clothes. She searched for clean garments to pack. She owned few items her Tweedledee frame fit into. If she used the suitcase the size of Grant's Tomb, the clothes would get lost. At least she wouldn't have to worry about it being overweight and paying more for luggage.

She could get away with a carry-on. She plopped a fistful of chips into her mouth. *Will I ever be full again?*

She'd keep this oversized bag and fill it up with food. Except the airline would stow it in the belly of the plane and wouldn't allow her belly access to it. She'd fill her carry on with treats.

She ran her hands over her stomach, then stopped with them frozen over her belly.

Four months to go with this pregnancy.

Her information for the adoption agency sat on the kitchen counter.

Still.

Every day she meant to toss it in the mailbox. Every day she forgot.

She had to move this process along, or she'd become a mother and end up changing diapers while filling out applications for the kid's preschools. In New York, you had to gain admission *before* you conceived.

She jogged down the steps and picked up the envelope holding the forms. Across the street, Kiara plopped them into the mailbox.

Back inside, she danced as she finished packing.

Home. I'm going home!

~~

Lia stepped onto the porch. *Where are you, Chris? It's almost midnight.* She rubbed her arms in the cool night air and studied the road for car lights. The phone jangled, and she jumped. She hurried inside to pick it up before it woke Beau.

"Ma." Chris's voice choked. He said nothing more. In the background metal clanged, voices shouted.

"Did you forget curfew?"

"Please, don't yell."

The silence filling the receiver shot a shiver down her back. "Where are you?"

"In jail."

"Not funny."

"I'm not joking. I've been arrested."

She opened her mouth. Breath caught in her throat and choked her. Lia sucked air like her pa when his black lung flared.

"Ma? Are you there?"

She nodded. Lia clutched her chest as though holding it would quiet her pounding heart.

"Ma? My time's almost up."

"What happened?"

"I didn't do anything. Honest. They arrested me for possession of stolen opioids. I can't talk. Too many cops around. I'm in Jacksboro. Can you call a lawyer? Get me out of here. I'm innocent."

"Who were you with?" She didn't need to hear his answer. She knew.

A gruff voice called in the distance. "Time's up."

The line went dead.

The dial tone droned as the phone clattered to the countertop. She exhaled. Her heart pounded, but her lungs wouldn't inhale. Her wobbly legs buckled her knees.

"Lia?" Beau called from the bedroom. "You coming to bed?"

She opened her mouth to answer. The action sucked all air out of her muscles, and Lia slid down against the cupboards. On the floor, she pulled her knees to her chest and tilted her head against the smooth surface of the cabinets. She stared into the distance.

"Lia?" Beau called again.

What would she tell Beau? *No need to guess his reaction.*

The trembling stopped. Still, no tears came. She breathed in. Exhaled. Tried to suck in air once more. No way, no how could she handle this.

Did she have any choice but to face it?

Slow, steady footsteps clicked in quiet, sure footfalls down the stairs as though the moon hadn't fallen from the sky. "Lia! What on earth?"

Heavy steps pounded as they approached. He stooped beside her. "Take my hand." Reaching down, he tugged her to her feet. "Sweetheart, what's wrong?" His strong arms held her and pulled her tight. "Is it your pa? Have Emmett's lungs sent him to the ER again?"

"Chris."

"Our son?" Fear etched Beau's voice. "Is he okay?" He ran his fingers through her hair. His kiss, warm and sweet on her head, folded her into him. Tension ebbed in his arms, and her muscles melded into him.

"He's been arrested."

He stiffened against her.

She pulled back.

His face hardened. His eyes became agates, and his arms dropped to his sides. "Arrested for what?"

The tone of his voice—clipped and angry—froze her bones.

The hardness of his jaw and the jumping of the muscle along his jawline told her Beau would turn meaner than a striped snake.

"Chris had his liberty for a whole week. Seven full days and he goes out and gets himself tossed in the clink? Did he say what for?"

"Stolen drugs." She barely heard herself say the words.

Beau's head jolted as though he choked. He opened his mouth. Shook his head and shut his mouth again. "Did you say drugs? *Stolen* drugs?"

She nodded. "Can you call the church lawyer?"

His face reddened. His eyes bulged. "No!"

Lia shrunk from him.

"Chris has had his chances. Last summer he took the car without permission, creased the fender, and got a ticket. The deductible cost a thousand dollars we didn't have. Two months ago, he went hunting on the atheist's property after being told not to. He hangs out with reprobates and heathens when forbidden. He drinks. Misses curfew. Now drugs?

"He's had his chances. It's time for tough love. He can have the courts assign him a lawyer. Let him learn sin has consequences."

"He's our *son*." Surely Beau spoke from frustration. He'd see reason once he calmed down. "You know he's a good boy."

"How many chances do we give him? Our leniency will teach him evil. Let him hang out with the criminals in the lockup. Maybe he'll lose his fascination with sin."

"But college? His chance for scholarships?"

"You know this is God's way of correcting his path. The Lawd's keeping him from going to a college where they teach liberal propaganda and turn our children's mind from everything just and holy." Beau straightened. He towered over Lia. "We're done."

"You can't be serious."

"This has to play out on its own. Christopher has to learn his lesson." He marched down the hall.

Lia ran after him.

At his study, Beau slammed the door. The lock clicked.

Lia hammered on the door with the palm of her hands. "Beau, how can you believe Chris would do drugs? Don't you know anything about our boy?"

Her hand reddened with banging. Beau heard as few of her pleas as the wood she thumped. She dropped her hand.

Enough was enough.

For too many years, she'd catered to this man who lorded everything over her. She allowed rules to shackle her desires. Too many times she denied herself, like putting her face in a fan. Everything blew back on her.

Never again.

She hated Beau. Despised this merciless man.

Breathing the same air as him, looking at his pharisaical face, catering to his every whim poisoned her as much as the coal dust had poisoned her pa. She wouldn't stay here any longer.

She stormed out of the house and slammed the door behind her. Lia hoped it splintered in her wrath. If God were just, it would be pulverized.

It was one a.m. Her folks would be asleep—each in their own room. She couldn't run there, especially with Pa feeling so poorly these last few weeks. It was too late to call Junior or Cornie. Besides, Cornie married Jimmy, Beau's brother.

A car rumbled past her house. Its lights glinted off Kiara's window.

Lia hurried across the road like a sailor drawn by the North Star. She knocked.

No one came.

She twisted the knob. Kiara had locked it tight against her. She pounded again.

223

Feet padded to the door. The porch light flicked on. Locks clicked. Kiara stood in the doorway, her eyes swollen with sleep, panic etching them. "What's going on, Delia Mae?"

No words formed. Lia clenched and unclenched her hands dangling at her side.

Kiara took Lia's shoulders. "Come inside."

Lia stepped into the living room.

"Look at me." Kiara's eyes peered at Lia.

She focused on them, swam in the compassion and love glinting in the warm, golden-brown.

Her neighbor led her to the couch. They slid down, both perched on the sofa's edge. Kiara's warm hand held her shoulder.

"I'm sorry. I needed someone. I thought ... "

"What's wrong?"

"I'm leaving Beau."

Kiara blinked rapidly.

Did I give her a stroke?

"Why?" Kiara stuttered.

The story spewed in a low hiss that gained volume. Lia leaned against the sofa's back. The emotion drained from her muscles leaving her limp.

"Delia Mae."

"Please call me Lia." She shook her head in long slow sweeps. "I've been so mean to you. Forcing you to use a name I hate."

"Calling you Delia Mae wasn't hateful. You told me to."

"I made you use it out of spite. I'm awful."

"If you're awful, I'm appalling. In everything you've done for me, you've shown kindness and love and honesty. You've been more of a mother to me than anyone in my life." Kiara's firm voice told Lia she needed to believe her. "If Christians behaved like you I'd convert to agnosticism. Without the rules."

Lia chuckled, a sad little sound wiping away fragments of pain.

Silence ticked for five minutes—or an hour. Kiara's eyes gazed into the distance. She chewed her bottom lip. With a loud inhale, Kiara turned to Lia. "I've got a piece of good karma for you."

Lia held her breath.

"I know almost no one. However, one of my art students, Annie Joy Grizzle, is a lawyer. I'll call her. If she can't take Chris's case, she'll know someone." She stepped to the phone, flipped through a directory and dialed.

Protests rose in Lia's chest, but all self-direction vanished. Like a baby, having someone care for her chased away the tension steeling her back muscles.

Kiara turned from Lia and spoke into the phone. "Sorry for calling so late ... My friend's son's been arrested ... What time ... ? Do you think my friend will be able to see her son ...?"

Fragments of the conversation floated over Lia. A few points settled on her. Bit by bit, tension and sorrow disappeared.

"Annie Joy wants to see us at eleven. She believes she'll be able to see Chris before then. However, if she can't confer with him before our meeting, she'll change the time."

"I can't afford a lawyer." Lia couldn't inhale. "We've got a second mortgage. Beau's so mad his nether regions'll sip coffee."

Kiara laughed hard. She snorted and choked on her chortles.

"What's so funny?" Lia sniggered in spite of herself.

"Your expressions are as bad as your mother's. What's coffee got to do with his hind end?"

"Ma uses a more off-color version."

"It does make your point." Kiara's laughs subsided. She laid both hands on Lia's shoulder. She frowned and her eyes became distant as though searching for something she lost. Kiara tilted her chin. Her voice became crisp and businesslike. "I'll be by you every step of the way. I have money for a retainer. Depending on the charges and bail and fines, I have property I own free and clear. We can use it for bail." Her lips trembled.

Lia shivered. The quivering intensified as though an arctic blast froze her bones. She didn't want Kiara's money. Without it? Chris would rot in jail.

Kiara folded Lia in her arms until the tremors subsided.

Lia pulled away. "Courts cost a lot. At least I think they do. Never been in one. "

"Me neither, thank heaven. I don't know how much it costs, but we'll work it out."

Lia rose halfway then plopped down on the couch. "I should let you go back to bed."

"You're not acting like you want to leave." Kiara's gaze locked on Lia.

As though Kiara's eyes hypnotized her, Lia remained motionless.

"You said you were leaving Beau. Do you want to go home?"

Tears threatened, and Lia's nose ran. "I can't breathe around him any longer. I can't." She turned her head as though she found the wall fascinating.

"If you can't go there, why are you acting like you're going to leave my house?"

Lia's tongue thickened and her mouth became cotton.

"Sleep here." Kiara patted the couch. "I'll fetch the extra blankets. The sofa's surprisingly uncomfortable."

"I don't think I should."

Kiara stood and walked to the bathroom. She came back with a bundle of linens. "My finest. The stains are antiques. The frayed edges," she held up a blanket edge, "are trendy. They give the blanket a distressed appearance." After tossing them onto the side chair, she held out her palm. In it lay two white capsules. "I'll pour you a glass of water."

Lia clutched her hands to her chest. Her lips pressed in a thin line.

"It's melatonin," Kiara said. "A hormone—one our body makes all the time. The doctor said it was safe for me. It'll be okay for you. It'll help you sleep."

Lia swallowed the pills. Her heart stilled knowing someone would help her.

Kiara spread out the sheets. "Sleep here for now. Tomorrow we'll figure out what to do with Chris, and with Beau. And with you."

Lia lay down. Whether from the hormones she took or Kiara's comfort, sleep came quickly.

~~

Kiara climbed her stairs. Her luggage sat by the dresser ready for an early morning flight. Her chin trembled as she packed up her dreams while unpacking the cases.

She would not cry.

Her eyes watered. She blinked.

Home. All Kiara wanted since she landed in Stinking Creek, like Dorothy in Oz, was to go home.

She sank on her bed. Annie Joy Grizzle didn't need her to go *with* Lia, did she? If she handed over a few checks ... ?

No. Her chest heaved. Lia needs someone.

If I give her my money, I can't pay for an apartment.

Brooklyn had a gobullion apartments.

None I can afford.

She had to call Imani. How without letting Lia know?

Dragging herself off the bed, Kiara flipped up the top to her computer. Minutes passed while the machine came to life. Two minutes later, she fired off an e-mail to Imani. Hopefully, she'd read it before she ran to the airport tomorrow.

She crawled under her covers and studied the dark ceiling. So dark, unlike New York. Too quiet.

Why was she doing this?

She curled on her side and hugged her pillow to her chest. This would be the last time she didn't take out flight insurance. The airlines would refund her nothing with this cancellation.

More than life itself, she'd wanted out of here. Why did something more important than life come up?

Chapter Thirty-Five

Shann climbed out of the loft designed for a munchkin. *Why couldn't Dixon climb this in a wheelchair? And why won't Lia teach the kids on Saturday?* The twins complained when he suggested it to them.

He nuked oatmeal for Dixon and Macie and started his coffee. With Dixon's accident, Shann's work ground to a stop. Maybe Lia could help out today?

He picked up the phone and dialed.

The phone rang.

Rang some more.

He composed his voice mail message in his head. Then Beau picked up. "Is Lia there?"

"No."

"When will she be back?"

"Don't know. I'll tell her you called." He hung up.

Kiara?

She "hated" kids in the same manner Jorie had said she "loved" them. Women didn't know how they felt.

"Dad!" Dixon called from his room.

"What?"

"Macie's watching me."

"So." He stepped over to his former room.

Dixon jiggled on the wheelchair. Nature called.

"Let's go, Macie." Shann would have to haul the kids to the workshop and hope they didn't climb on the roof and pretend they were Elijah ascending to heaven in a chariot of fire.

That would do one of two things—cause one or both to leap from the roof. Worse than trying to fly, they'd set the whole shebang on fire.

~~

Lia studied Kiara as her neighbor drove her to Jacksboro and the office of Faircloth, Enfinger, and Grizzle. How she had misjudged this woman from the day she met her. Had she actually called Kiara, a Yankee she couldn't be friends with?

A shudder rippled through her. *How rude I was.* Who'd have figured how much she needed this sweet woman?

Inside a modest brick building on Main Street, a middle-aged woman smoothed her tailored navy blue skirt suit as she ushered them into her office. Her rich, brown hair, in a French braid, fell in a thick rope down her back. Sweet watercolors resembling Sheep Loop Road hung on the walls.

"I'm Annie Joy Grizzle." She shook Lia's hand. "Have a seat." The woman motioned to a leather chair facing a lovely desk of dark-red wood.

Lia sat. Despite the comfortable chair, she sat as though rebar splinted her back.

"I'm glad you framed them." Kiara stood with hands behind her back studying the watercolors.

"There're the first ones worth framing."

"Someone taught you well."

"She better have at sixty-five bucks an hour." Ms. Grizzle smiled.

Kiara faced her. Her eyes didn't reflect joy in the compliment. She sighed. "I'm sure your fees will be higher."

"Two-fifty an hour."

Lia gasped and half rose. "I can't—"

"Two dollars and fifty cents?" Kiara laughed and the vapor of sorrow Lia imagined a minute ago evaporated. "I've got it covered." She pressed her hand on Lia's shoulder. "Hear Annie Joy out, and we'll decide from there."

Lia sat, but perched stiffly on the chair's edge. "What's Chris charged with, Ms. Grizzle?"

"Call me Annie Joy, please. Grizzle is an awful name. I should divorce my husband and marry someone named Christian or Prince. Annie Joy Prince sounds good to me."

"Why didn't you keep your maiden name?" Kiara asked.

"Zaborowoski wasn't much of a keeper, either." She flipped open a folder. "Can you imagine the tongue twister if I hyphenated it?"

"Zaborowoski-Grizzle?" Kiara said. "I think you'd win every case pronto, so no one had to say it."

Lia laughed. The funny name chased her fears about Chris away. She leaned back in the chair, and the rebar running up her back melted. *Chris!* She stiffened again. Feeling lighthearted at this moment proved she was a bad mother.

"If you'll excuse us, Kiara, and step into the waiting room. Most of what I have to say is public record, but in case we drift into confidential issues, we need privacy."

Kiara turned to Lia. "I'm here for everything you need."

When the door clicked, Annie Joy spoke. "Chris and I met this morning. He signed a waiver allowing us to talk. Without it, I'd only reveal what's in the public record."

Lia nodded.

"I warned him against signing the waiver."

Lia leaned forward. "Why?"

"Things said with another person present lose the protection of confidentiality. However, he's so adamant he did nothing warranting an arrest, he didn't care."

Words caught in Lia's heart. She nodded.

"He's been charged with simple possession and casual exchange. That's a misdemeanor. They've impounded your car. It'll cost a hundred dollars a day while in impound. It won't be released until after his arraignment—if then. His fees should cost twenty-five and bail will be about five thousand."

Lia gulped. Her breathing came heavy.

"If found guilty, it'll be a misdemeanor. The penalty carries a year in jail. However, seeing as he has no record, he'll probably get probation, do community service and his record expunged in a year."

"Chris would *never* consider doing drugs."

Annie Joy's face showed no emotion, as though she didn't believe Lia.

"He's a good boy." Lia widened her eyes. "Honestly. He's good."

"They stopped him for a missing plate on the car. When the officer checked for his license, he found an open container of beer in the console's cup holder. A search followed. They found OxyContin under the passenger seat."

"OxyContin?" Lia didn't think her heart could shatter more.

"Allegedly, Chris stole it from ..." she rifled through papers, "a Hilda Humphrey. She reported a break-in on Wednesday, October tenth, sometime between seven and nine when she was out of the house."

"On Wednesday, every *single* Wednesday, Chris is in church with us from five until ten. We have prayer meeting and his father —"

"That may be. His alibi will prove he wasn't the thief, not that he didn't buy the pills from someone else."

Lia's heart would split into each individual atom. By now, the shards looked like fragments of the Milky Way. "You said he'd be arraigned on Monday?"

Annie Joy nodded.

"Will he be able to come home?"

She shook her head.

"Why?"

"Chris demanded a drug screen. He said if it came back clean, it would prove he hadn't been using drugs or drinking."

"That's good, isn't it?"

"It'll give the judge a reason to believe him. However—"

"Howevers are never good," Lia said.

"He'll have to be remanded until the results come in. That will take a couple of weeks."

"That's crazy." Lia stood and rubbed her hands. "The courts would let him out on bail without a drug screen, but they keep him in if he has one?"

"Yes it's crazy. Yet, it's the way it works." Annie Joy said. "We're also waiting on fingerprints. They weren't going to dust for prints on the beer can and pills. Again, the lack of prints won't prove his innocence. It will add time to his incarceration while we wait, but Chris insists he knew nothing of the Oxy. He never touched the beer can. In the long run, it could help dismiss all charges."

"Can I go see him?" Lia asked.

Annie Joy scribbled something on a sheet of paper. "Call this number and make an appointment."

"I have to make an appointment?"

Annie Joy nodded. "I'll call when we have more information." She called through the door. "You can come back in, Kiara."

Kiara stepped into the room. She handed Annie Joy a check. "Here's your ransom payment."

Annie Joy stood and took the check. "I'll let you know when I need to extort more." She sat back down, pulled out a receipt book and wrote.

Half of Lia yearned to reach over and tear up the check. She didn't want Kiara to spend all this money. The courts would return the bail to her, but not the lawyer's fees. Then there'd be money for fines. How much would the impound cost once everything's settled? She needed her car. What if Kiara insisted on paying for those?

No. Beau would pay when they exonerated Chris.

He'd pay in every way imaginable.

She knew her boy. Crazy. Social. But good.

Kiara and Annie Joy chatted about something Lia didn't catch.

Was Chris good? She'd so misjudged her artist friend. Did she know good character?

~~

Back at the cabin, Lia hovered near Kiara who rummaged in her freezer. "You sure you don't mind? My folks sleep in separate rooms because of Pa's wheezing. They don't need my burdens. If I go to Cornie's, the gossip would fly all over Campbell County."

Kiara eyed Lia. "I think I only have frozen pizza."

231

Panic fluttered like hummingbird wings. "Don't tell anyone about this, please!"

Kiara pulled out a box of supreme pizza and swiveled toward the oven. "Uh, duh? You met the sum total of everyone I know in Tennessee. Who am I going to tell?" She punched buttons on the stove.

"Junior lives up in Jellico, but I need to be able to teach the kids. I can go home during the day and keep up their schooling."

"Shut up, Lia. If you can handle the couch, I can live with you. I think I have cucumbers and tomatoes to go with the pizza."

"I'm not hungry."

The preheated oven dinged. "I am. Humor me and have dinner. I'm tired of eating alone."

~~

"Daddy, I'm hungry," Macie whined.

"Me, too."

Since he started work, the mighty duo hadn't quit complaining. At least they changed their melody from "I'm bored" to "Feed me."

The last coat of varnish had to dry over the inlay on the neck of the guitar Barfly and Scole ordered. Currently, the duo topped the country charts. When they brandished his instrument onstage, business would hit the charts, too.

"What d'you say we go eat?" Shann asked.

Macie leaped. Dixon tried to, but his erector set drilled into his tibia or fibula, or both, kept him nailed in his wheelchair. Shann pushed it up the hill to the cabin while Macie frolicked across the lawn.

Inside, Shann hunted for dinner. They had fish, lima beans, taters and Popsicles. He pulled the fish out of the freezer.

"Yuck. I *hate* fish," Dixon said.

"You caught these."

"I don't care. I'm hungry," Dixon whined. "Ain't we got macaroni and cheese?"

"It's 'do we have—'"

"You say ain't."

"I hate macaroni and cheese." Macie crossed her arms and scowled. His daughter must be the only human in creation who despised boxed mac and cheese.

"Why don't y'all watch TV?" He dialed Lia's number. Maybe she had leftovers. "Beau, is Lia there?"

"Nope."

"Do you have any leftovers? Meals on Wheels or HOPE International is going to hear about us and send relief packages."

"We've got stuff in the freezer if you want to come by."

He sounded curter than usual.

"Maybe I'll take the kids to We Knead Pizza up in Jellico."

"Eat a supreme for me." Beau hung up.

Shann eyed the dead phone in his hand. *Why does Lia stay with my brother?* He dropped it back onto the receiver.

The kids had been so good, according to the twin definition of good, all day. They deserved food they loved. Shann loaded them into the truck. With the gyrations needed to maneuver Dixon into his vehicle without breaking something else, Shann was going to become the world's greatest contortionist.

He headed down his usual route, the one taking him past Sheep Loop Church. Barely out of his driveway, he made a U-turn.

Lia hadn't been around all day. He should check on her.

Or maybe Kiara was gardening in a bikini in her front yard. Either way, he'd take the long way to Lowes Branch Road and drive by their homes. Perhaps he'd get a clue.

Light shone in both houses. Besides the lights, he saw no sign of life.

Chapter Thirty-Six

Another doctor's appointment. It'd been four days since Kiara lost her chance to ditch hill country. Now, the sun, sitting low in the sky, blinded her as she drove along Lowes Branch Road. She blinked, then discovered a truck barreling down on her. Her eyes widened. She swerved and stomped her brakes. Her pickup veered toward the shoulder as the oblivious truck continued on its merry way.

Her pulse thudded. Kiara shifted into park and allowed it to settle.

She threw her head against the headrest and breathed. Ten minutes ago, she'd left her five-month checkup. Dr. Hussey said she and the baby were healthy. Little did she expect to nearly terminate both lives so soon after.

The sudden stop emptied her purse onto the floor. She bent and gathered the contents, among them new sonogram pictures. She fingered the printouts and studied them, trying to guess her baby's gender. Dr. Hussey offered to tell her but knowing the child's sex would make the adoption more difficult. She was getting used to this tubby creature in her gut without fantasizing names for it.

A few feet ahead, a grassy lane led into the woods.

One of her art students had said someone wanted to develop land up here. Did this unpaved road lead to the development? She inched the car to the opening of the path and peered down the well-worn trail. Deep, rutted tire tracks, about a car-width apart, ran on either side of the weedy-mossy middle. She was about to pull away when a patch of orange caught her attention. She squinted.

A box turtle.

Dixon would love the critter.

Given their hard shells and slow motion and lack of body secretions, she didn't mind picking them up. She pulled the truck into the one-lane grassy roadway and waddled to the turtle.

He didn't put up much of a race. She picked him up, and leathery legs and head and tail tucked themselves into the shell which closed upon itself.

Back at the truck, she plopped the turtle on the passenger seat. No need to worry about Mr. Donatello, her ninja turtle, running away. All she'd have to do was tap its shell, and he'd retract. He couldn't sprint away if he sealed himself in his house. She slammed the truck door.

From the overgrown lane, a vehicle sounding like an ATV approached. She needed to move out of the way to let it pass. Before she rounded the front of the truck, she recognized the driver and quit walking.

The ATV stopped. "Howdy, Miss Kiara." Bobby James said.

"You should be wearing a helmet. It's dangerous driving without one."

He twisted his lips. "Ain't skeered."

"How about laws in Tennessee? In New York—"

"Laws don't worry me. Ain't no cops along here."

"I'll get out of your way." She took a couple of steps toward the driver's side. She turned back to Bobby. "I know laws don't bother you."

Keep your mouth shut, Key. "Your good buddy is sitting in jail because of you."

So much for listening to myself.

"I heared he got busted. Never took him for no druggie."

She shook her head. "He's not."

"Jew know when he's gettin' out?"

"Perhaps when you confess." She crossed her arms and pinned her gaze on him.

His eyes shifted. "Don't know what jew talkin' 'bout." He nodded toward the truck. "If'n you don't mind. I need to go."

"Remember, Chris McGuffrey's been a good friend. He believed in you. He's facing a misdemeanor—for most people, not too big a deal. For a man of his character, it's major. If you go to the cops, you can make it right." She climbed into her truck and backed it out of the dirt road.

Bobby James roared onto the main road then drove down the pavement several yards. He turned onto another trail across the way.

Long shadows crossed the road with Wednesday's late afternoon sun. Kiara climbed into her truck. She tapped Donatello whose head and legs had reemerged. Faster than she could've predicted, he drew them back into his shell.

What was Bobby doing back there?

She glanced at Lowes Branch Road, then the path Bobby came down. Kiara turned her truck into the darkening woods. Keeping the tires on the center median and the edge of road, well out of the ruts so she wouldn't bottom out, she drove into the woods. A quarter mile down the lane, it branched off. The path straight ahead was overgrown. The one to the right was well worn. She turned.

The road to nowhere narrowed. Trees crowded the edges.

How am I going to turn around?

A little way down, a trail branched off. She turned into it to make a U-turn. Beyond the trees, now almost empty of leaves, a clearing opened and revealed a trailer with a dilapidated porch. She inched the truck forward. The trees gave way to a field overrun with weeds and new growth trees. She stopped. Leaving the truck running, she strode to the mobile home.

This place made hers look palatial. It had signs of activity though. Paths entered the woods, no cobwebs clung to the porch, and ample beer cans littered the yard.

A padlock held the door fast. Weird for an abandoned dump.

She peered in the grimy window at a living room. The walls needed a coat of paint. Old furniture cluttered the space. The place was run-down, but maybe someone lived here. Perhaps she was trespassing.

Instinct said something else.

She walked to the windows on the other end of the deck. They opened into a kitchen. Inside, bleach and drain cleaners sat on a counter. Pots were stacked on the stove. Used blister packs littered the floors.

She didn't know a bundle about drugs, but from what she knew, this place was a meth lab.

She stumbled back and clasped her stomach. Meth labs meant toxic waste. Not good for her, and definitely not healthy for her kid.

The windows continued to draw her, and she took one last peek. As the sky darkened, she saw nothing more.

If Annie Joy hears about this, could it help Chris? As far as she was concerned, Bobby James was connected to the opioids in the car.

Then she remembered the party and catching him and Leo smoking in the McGuffreys' yard. She never told Lia. Had she helped create Chris's mess? What if he was connected to this, too?

No. No McGuffrey would ever be lawless. McGuffreys followed the rules.

Aside from their toxic properties, Kiara knew one other thing about meth. Pushers had no scruples. She had to leave before the dealers came back and shot her and buried her in the woods where her body wouldn't be found. Ever again. Except by paleontologists excavating the ruins in the next millennium.

Besides, her baby demanded food. Again.

She climbed into her truck to discover Donatello had fallen on the floor. He lay on his back, his little legs waving. She lifted him and laughed. "You know, Donny, I resemble you." She puffed out her stomach. "I need help rolling off my back these days, as well."

With the turtle sitting beside her, Kiara headed home.

~~

A truck pulled up to Shann's as he slipped plates of fish and lima beans in front of his sulking kids.

A knock at the door made him turn.

He opened the door. Grinned like an idiot. "Kiara. You're in time for dinner."

"Miss Muffet!" Macie scooted out of her seat and threw her arms around Kiara's legs.

"Get back to the table." Shann jostled Macie's shoulder propelling her to her seat and turned to his pretty neighbor once more. "Don't get too high an opinion of yourself. They're hoping you'll eat the food they're stuck with. Since Saturday, I've been threatening them with this meal. Come in."

"I can't." She held a box turtle high. "I found Donny here."

"Donny?"

"Donatello, one of the mutant teenagers. I thought Dixon would like it."

"Cool." Dixon held out his hand.

"Sorry, Dixon. We have to let him go." Shann took the turtle and put him in the sink for safekeeping.

"Daddy!" Dixon pouted and crossed his arms.

"Why?" Kiara asked.

"Owning a turtle's illegal in Tennessee."

From her dropped jaw and widened eyes, Shann saw she didn't know much about Tennessee laws.

"I'm sorry. I hoped to look generous and give you a gift I found. Don't want to bet busted, though."

"No one's going to arrest you. They won't even fine you." He took her shoulder. "Come in at least long enough to let us know how you found Donny."

"I can stop a second. Lia's waiting—"

"Lia's with you?"

Kiara stepped back as though someone pushed her. "I need to go."

"Y'all finish your dinner. Remember," he ruffled the back of his head, "these eyes will see you." He ushered Kiara onto the porch.

"What's going on with Lia?"

"What do you mean? Nothing's wrong."

"I didn't mention anything wrong, so don't tell me nothing's happening with my brother's family. She's never home when I call. Of course, I see her during school hours."

"She's busy. Homeschooling stops for no one."

"And she'd never let her kitchen become the mess it is. You saw it during Queenie's party. Spotless. The Board of Health takes lessons from her."

"You know her schedule. She must be busy." Kiara glanced toward her truck.

He crossed his arms. "Sure."

"Shann, I can't tell you anything. I promised her I'd say nothing."

"Is she living at your place?"

"What a crazy idea."

"Daddy, my fish fell on the floor," Dixon called.

"I've got to go before my kids throw lima beans at each other."

He stepped inside but edged the curtain aside and studied Kiara as she drove off. He'd find out on his own.

~~

Lia peered out Kiara's kitchen window and frowned. What did she hope to see? Beau'd left for church with Paul an hour ago. He'd stopped demanding she return, but ordered she tell no one about their separation. Like Sheep Loop Church wouldn't figure it out soon enough.

Dinner simmered in the slow cooker she hauled from home because Kiara's kitchen lacked everything.

With no threat of running into Beau, Lia stepped out and crossed the street. At the mailboxes, she grabbed Kiara's mail. Before she crossed the road again, Shann's truck pulled out of his driveway. She raced to Kiara's. *Please don't come this way, Shann.*

The truck pulled in behind her. A white truck—Kiara, not Shann. "I got your mail." Lia held up the fistful of circulars.

Kiara slammed the truck door.

"I was afraid you were my brother-in-law."

"Nope. I'm me."

Inside, Lia tossed the mail on the counter.

"Dinner smells good," Kiara said.

"You'd think roasted coon smelled good the way your baby's been eating. So what're you having? Boy or girl?"

Kiara shook her head. "Don't want to know. Not keeping it." She sat on the chair by the coffee table. "It's nice coming home to someone else cooking. Your stuff's better than Sugar Creek Diner." Kiara fished through her purse. "Speaking of the diner, I went there for lunch and the new waitress gave me Joey's number."

"I thought you looked it up."

"I tried. There were a couple of Shellnuts but no Joey or Leslie and no one on Stinking Creek."

"She held up a slip of paper. "I'll call him tonight."

"Is he home from Nashville now?" Lia scooped chicken and dumplings into a bowl. She placed it on the counter near the mail. Lia eyed the top letter and raised her eyebrows.

238

Kiara shrugged. "If Joey's not there, I'll leave a message."

Lia scooped a second bowl. "Talking about messages, you got several calls from people wanting lessons. I left their names and numbers by the phone. Seems if Annie Joy wants to quit being a lawyer, she's got a job in promotion. They all found out about you from her." Lia brought the bowls and the mail to the coffee table. She handed Kiara a serving of steaming dumplings.

Kiara bent and inhaled. "If this is what they dish out in heaven, you will convert me."

Lia bowed her head and said a quick grace. Kiara would wait until she uttered her amen.

Kiara nearly moaned when she ate. "Your cooking is ambrosia. I'm never letting you move out."

"So why don't you want to know if you're having a boy or girl?"

"I've told you. I'm not keeping it."

"Seems your subconscious is telling you otherwise." Lia picked up a letter. "I don't know about you Yanks, but down here, the post office don't deliver without stamps." She handed off the envelope. "You ain't adopting out your child if the agency doesn't receive the information."

Kiara groaned for real. "I'm losing my mind."

"So why were you at Shann's?"

The question churned Kiara's stomach. Fifteen minutes ago, it growled and snarled at her—demanded food. Now it soured.

"Found a box turtle Dixon would like."

Lia exhaled. "Does he know I'm here?"

Kiara shrugged. "I've got news that might help Chris." She related her news about Bobby James and the potential meth lab.

Lia sat straighter. "Can we call now? I'll drive you to the sheriff's."

"In what? The MINI Cooper's still in impound. Beau's got the van. All you have left are ATVs."

"You have a truck."

"I'll call the sheriff after dinner while you do the dishes."

Cleanup never sounded better to Lia.

Chapter Thirty-Seven

"Can't we stay home?" "I want to do art with Miss Muffet." "We wanna stay with you."

Shann's kids complained more than Oscar the Grouch or Oscar Madison.

In the Mule, Macie kicked the back of Shann's seat as he hauled them to Lia's for school. The minute ride seemed like an hour.

Dixon became a dead weight as Shann lifted him out of the vehicle. How could a kid make himself heavier without moving a muscle?

His daughter didn't get out.

"Let's go, Macie. Now." He pushed Dixon in his wheelchair into Lia's kitchen.

Lia studied the pile of books before her and never glanced his way.

"You're a hard one to find these days," Shann said.

"It's been crazy." Lia handed a sheet with basic addition problems to the kids. She opened a box of LEGOS. "Count the blocks if you forget your sums.

"The kids were asking about trunk or treat for Halloween," Shann said. "What time is Sheep Loop Church doing it?"

She shrugged.

"How can you not know? The church secretary calls you for event dates and times."

"You'll have to ask your brother." Lia's voice held a bitter edge.

"Don't snap at me," Shann said. "Just asking."

"Ma." Paul stepped into the kitchen with his iPad. "Can you help me with the subjunctive case? I thought Spanish was the easy language."

"Sure." She slapped down the pencil she'd been holding. "If you'll excuse me, I've got to teach."

"Where's Chris? I haven't seen him all week."

"He's out." Lia still didn't meet his eyes.

"During the school day?" He glanced at Paul.

Paul's eyes widened and shifted away.

"Will you excuse us?" Shann asked Paul.

He nodded and scurried to the den as though being chased by a polecat.

Shann faced Lia. "Is everything okay?"

She looked at him for the first time. Her eyes narrowed and sliced through him. The line of her lips tightened. "Shann, I've got to work. This may be homeschool, but it's more rigorous than anything the public schools dish out."

He studied her a few seconds and stroked his beard. "You know I'll find out sooner or later."

"Leave, please." She shoved her chair away from the table and stood. "We won't meet our requirements if we don't do the assignments."

Shann kissed his surly kids goodbye, then returned to his cabin. At his mailbox, he grabbed his copy of the *LaFollette Press*. It only came out on Thursdays but filled him in on Campbell County's issues and upcoming events. Mostly, he enjoyed his two guilty pleasures—the obits, a pleasure when his name didn't appear and the arrest reports—also nice to not have himself listed. As he no longer heard firsthand reports about arrests from Abby, he resorted to reading the public records. Something about seeing other people's faults made him feel more upright.

He poured a cup of coffee, took it to his recliner and laid it on the end table. He pulled the foot lever and raised his feet and rattled the paper just as the old coots like Emmett did. Or like his brother. He needed to change his habit. No way would he ever be like Beau.

He got to the arrests, at last. *Don't know him. That one? No one's surprised.* The third notice sounded familiar. Then—

He snapped upright. Blinked to clear his eyes. Reread the notice. He recognized the fourth arrest. Emmett Christopher McGuffrey of Sheep Loop Road. Drug possession. Casual exchange.

His nephew arrested and his brother didn't tell him? Lia mum? How could they not let him know? This was his nephew, his self-righteous brother's son, and Lia's oldest. Shann could've helped—offered support, whatever.

Stomach acids rose and churned. They burned his throat. He coughed as heat rose up his neck and warmed his face.

Betrayal—all of them betrayed him. He'd asked Lia not even an hour ago about Chris, and she gave an evasive answer. Didn't they trust him?

With the paper in hand and folded on the public records page, he bounded to his truck. Shann gunned the engine, and a minute later, swerved into his brother's yard.

The kitchen door banged behind him. He slammed the paper on the table where Lia sat with his kids reading a primer.

"You need to step outside," he hissed.

She gave him the slightest of nods.

The twins flinched and looked at their father with terror. Or hope.

He marched onto the porch.

Seconds later, Lia stood next to him.

"What is going on?" While gripping the paper, he crossed his arms and glowered.

Her lips worked, and she studied the porch floor.

He grabbed her shoulders and forced her to look at him.

She sighed. As though the exhale broke the dam holding back her worries, the story spilled. "Beau's in a rage. Chris got into trouble, and Beau won't help."

"Of course not."

Lia held out her hand. "Please."

"Why didn't you tell me?"

She hiked a shoulder.

"You're not living here?"

"In order to cool off, I'm staying ..." She jutted her chin indicating Kiara's home.

"So this ..." He inhaled. No need to yell at Lia. His brother did enough bellowing for all of Campbell County. He exhaled hoping to blow away his anger. "All of this," he waved his hand, "coming here every day to teach is a lie? You wanted to deceive me?" He shook his head. His mouth gaped. "How could you?" He stopped. Quieted his voice again. "Lia, how could you not trust me?"

Her eyes looked as mournful as Youtee's.

Shann raked his hand through his hair, then paced to the end of the porch. He stared into the distance and stroked his beard. *Not her fault.* He pivoted and stood before Lia. "I'm sorry."

"For what?"

"Comin' upside your head with a tuba for." He grinned at his standard joke. "You've got a world of trouble of your own. I won't add to it. As for my brother? I'll kill him and swear he died."

"Shann." Lia reached out.

He shook it off. "Beau's a pompous, abusive man." His anger, like trying to squeeze water, wouldn't be compressed. His voice rose, again. "He's a hypocrite." Shann stomped off the porch.

"Shann?"

He didn't turn toward Lia's plea. Back in his truck, Shann peeled out of the driveway burning rubber. Gravel and dirt spewed in its wake. He rocketed past his cabin. A mile down the road, he roared into the parking lot at Sheep Loop Church. Beau's white van sat in the lot next to Jimmy's Ford and the church secretary's Toyota.

With long strides, and with the rolled-up paper in his hand, he pounded across the lot. Inside, he gave the secretary a curt nod and barged into Beau's office.

242

"Shann?" Beau half rose behind the desk. Across from him sat their brother, Jimmy. "I'm in a meeting."

"I don't care. Jimmy should know about your lies and cover-ups."

Jimmy stood. "Shann—"

"Let me handle this privately, Jimmy," Beau said.

Their brother glanced from Beau to Shann. "If you think it's wise."

"I can handle myself," Beau said.

"If you need me, I'll be down the hall." Jimmy walked out of the office, glancing back before shutting the door halfway.

Beau's glare bored into Shann. "You've got some nerve barging in on my meeting." His jaw worked like he chewed barbed wire and would spit out nails. "We were discussing sensitive issues."

Shann leaned across the desk, grateful for the barrier between him and his brother, or else his threat uttered to Lia could become more than hyperbole. He leaned on both arms, his hands planted firmly on the desk with the paper wedged under his right hand. If he didn't weight them down, they'd tear off Beau's legs, and he'd beat him with them. "I don't care about your church matters. For years, you lectured me on my reprobate status."

"You lived—"

"You, you, you." The words became a curse. "Who rebuked your wife in front of everyone for any little thing you thought she did wrong? No one else tallied our sins like a football score. *You*," Shann jabbed his finger in Beau's face, "found us all wanting, then you don't understand why we can't latch on to God's grace."

"Shann, what's this about?"

"You damn your son to jail." He shoved the paper, opened to the arrest notices, across the desk. "Your attitude has your wife hiding at Kiara's, too afraid to tell anyone about Chris."

"This is a family matter."

"I'm not family?"

"It's between Lia and me."

Shann stabbed his finger on the notices. "Not anymore."

Beau eyed the newspaper. When his gaze returned to Shann, no remorse shown in his eyes. "Sin has consequences."

"That it does. Yours caught up with you."

"Mine?"

"Yours."

"You're a fine one to talk. As a reprobate, you let your children run wild. You dump a lovely, godly woman and lust after a heathen."

Shann straightened. All his anger fled. Why should he cast his pearls before swine?

He leveled his eyes back at his brother. "I pray you wake up before you lose everything for good." He grabbed the door handle. "One last thing. I can't stop what you do to your family. I can protect mine. The twins will never be near you or your influences. They won't grow up believing they've fallen short of anyone's love."

He slammed the door behind him.

At the sound, the secretary and Jimmy jerked to attention.

"Bet you got an earful." Shann stomped back to his vehicle.

He drove to Wynn Habersham Elementary. Tomorrow his twins would attend public school. Better they associate with the unsaved than the pharisees.

~~

This had to be how it was when every disciple deserted Jesus. Lia watched Shann haul his kids out of her house. Out of Beau's house.

He snapped at her when she tried to strap Dixon into the truck.

She watched as he drove them home. Long after dust and quiet settled once more over their corner of hell, she stood staring down the road.

Tomorrow the kids headed for public school.

No sooner had she stepped back into her kitchen than her phone rang. The church's number showed in the caller ID. She clicked it on, then disconnected.

Gripping the quiet receiver, Lia stared at nothing. Time hung heavy. Chris had been in jail nearly six full days, and she heard nothing from Annie Joy about him being released.

Trunk or treat was coming up in less than a week. Someone had to organize it. She always loved doing it. Yet, working for the church meant seeing Beau. She wasn't sure she ever wanted to again. She dropped the phone to the counter. Her head throbbed.

"Paul?"

He popped into the kitchen.

"I've got a headache."

He grinned. "I'm working on my theology now. Don't need help. I'll do it in my room." He left.

She stepped outside. A black Mercury parked in Kiara's driveway. A magnetic realty sign clung to its door. That's right. Kiara had a showing this morning.

What could she do with her time? Who could offer any comfort?

Her parents always gave good advice. She could sit with them until the realtor left.

"Howdy, Lia." Pa kissed her cheek. "Dint 'spect you so airly."

"Thursday's my slow day. Do y'all have time for a visit?"

"I thank it's 'bout time." Pa pulled out a chair. "Set."

Ma joined them at the kitchen table. She crossed her arms in her usual attempt to look stern. "When was you goin' ta tell us 'bout Chris?"

"You read the paper." It was a statement, not a question.

"We did." Pa wheezed as though the words took the last of his breath. "Called that tush hog you'd married airly this mornin'. He told us to mind air own business."

"Honey," Ma said. "Why dint you trust to tell yer own folks?"

Lia squinted against the pain in her temples. Light drilled a hole through them. She wanted to go home, but potential buyers roamed Kiara's house.

Pa held Ma's hand. Married since they were eighteen—more than sixty years. Lia'd never heard her pa speak harshly to Ma.

"Do you have any Advil?" She asked.

Ma tottered to the bathroom and came back with two pills and water. All the while Pa drummed his fingers on the table keeping his gaze on her.

Lia took the medicine, and Ma put the kettle on.

Pa shoved a pie carrier toward Lia. "Yer favorite. Coconut cream. Et some. It always makes abiddy happy."

Ma poured tea, then served a slice of pie to Pa and Lia. She settled in her chair. "It's time ta talk."

"I don't think I can stay married to Beau." She cringed, not from her pounding head, but from the tongue lashing her folks would let loose.

"Is hit what jew want?" Ma asked.

Lia closed her eyes. *Do I?* She opened her eyes and studied the pie. To buy more time to figure her answer, she picked up a fork and poked at the creamy custard. At last, she looked at her mother, then her pa. "How'd y'all make it so long?"

"Almost dint," Ma said.

For the first time since the headache began, Lia's eyes widened, and the light didn't seem so harsh. She leaned in toward her mother "Almost didn't? How come I never knew?"

Pa coughed. They waited until the wheezing subsided. "'Cause children need protecting. We weren't gone hurt jew iffn we dint have to."

"What made you stay?"

"Almost dint," Ma said. "I had packed my bags and was goin' to tek you and Junior and Cornie to Mamaw's. She was all set fer us. Pa was working a second shift at the mine when they had an explosion."

"I remember. I was five, I think. You took us to Mamaw's and left us there a couple of days."

She nodded. "Ma tekked you in so's I could keep vigil at the mine. All the time I waited, I knowed one thing, and one thing only. My

245

Emmett had to be alive 'cause I couldn't live without him. The little things he did makin' me want to leave dint matter no more."

Pa leaned forward and patted Lia's hand. "They wasn't too little. Yer ma's still pertectin' air lil' girl."

"Nothing Emmett done mattered. He always were a good'un, and I loved him. When he come out alive, and not everybody did, I vowed to the Lawd I'd work on air marriage."

"It wernt easy," Pa said. "The both of us decided we would make it work."

"A one-legged duck ain't goin' nowhere," Ma said.

Lia understood. If Beau didn't want their marriage, even God Himself wouldn't intervene. Sometimes free will proved to be a problem.

Chapter Thirty-Eight

After helping Ma with chores, Lia came home, or rather, returned to Kiara's, with the rest of the pie. After her mother's tale of her near divorce, Lia's slice of coconut custard pie had tasted much better. If Beau would change, she could save her marriage.

The two-letter word—I-F—presented a problem of biblical proportions. For the past dozen years, only one person became what the other needed.

Beau had to want his marriage to succeed. Dancing the tango alone didn't work.

When she stepped into the cabin, Kiara held up a wonderful smelling meatloaf. Lia's stomach grumbled as though she hadn't eaten two behemoth slices of pie and drunk a hefty glass of milk. "You cooked?"

"We're celebrating."

"Did you get an offer?" A part of Lia's heart hoped not, but for Kiara's sake, she prayed the house sold.

"Don't know. I baked this, as you would say, 'in faith.' Maggie looked optimistic when she pulled out."

"What does optimistic look like?"

"She smiled at me."

"Oh, so very hopeful."

Kiara laid the meatloaf on a potholder. "Did you make us a pie?" She nodded at the pie carrier Lia held.

"Nope. Ma did."

"Well, I baked. Sugar Creek Diner created the meatloaf, and I stuck it in the oven. After the disgusting pizza I forced on you the other day, I shopped for home-cooked meals at the best diner in town."

"The only one in town."

Kiara grinned. "I'll rephrase. Sugar Creek Diner, the best restaurant in this hamlet, created the dinner I cooked tonight. The table's all set, and if Maggie McLemon doesn't come up with a buyer soon, I'm going to have to invest in a grown-up table. My baby's killing my back and leaning over a slab of laminated wood makes it worse. Thumbelina would have to bend over this thing."

Although Kira doted on her today, Lia yearned to pamper the young woman like she was her own child.

"Everyone knows about Chris," Lia said.

"You told all of Stinking Creek?"

She shook her head. "*LaFollette Press* did."

"It's a good thing our town doesn't have a billboard like the one in Times Square," Kiara said.

"How so?" Lia asked.

"In the busiest part of town, Times Square scrolls headlines in ten-foot letters." Kiara waved her hand as though a headline rolled through the air. "Emmett Christopher McGuffrey—thrown in the hoosegow." She winked. "How're you doing now the whole of Campbell County knows?"

"I discovered the *Bible* should've coined the proverb, 'A problem shared is a problem halved.'"

"The press notice made things easier?"

Lia lifted a piece of meatloaf, paused with it near her lips. "Yes." She popped the forkful into her mouth. The room turned quiet as she chewed. "Oddly, a dump truck full of stress slid off my back. Unfortunately, Shann will never speak to me again."

"That angry?"

Lia nodded.

"Don't underestimate Beau's brother."

"Everyone sympathizes with me and Chris."

"Why wouldn't they?"

"Shame's a funny thing. You want to hide it, but exposing it heals you."

"You have nothing to be ashamed of. Chris is a good, young man. Even if he did buy the drugs, it wasn't because you did anything wrong."

They stacked their dishes for clean-up. Someone knocked as they filled the dishwasher. Without an invitation, Cornie, in a wave of Chantilly perfume, strode into the house. "What's this Jimmy's telling me? It's in the paper before you say anything? I'm your sister."

"I'll head up to my studio," Kiara said. "Macie's helping me with a 'good' portrait of the twins. I need to correct her help."

Lia yearned to grab Kiara, make her stay. Instead, she turned to her sister. "Sit. I'll tell you what I can." They sat across from each other in the living room. "How d'you know I was here?"

"Before Jimmy left for work tonight, he told me you left Beau."

Lia played with her fingers clasped in her lap.

"Of course, he shoots this mortar round of gossip at me when he's late for his shift at Thermador, so I can't drill him," Cornie said. "I have no choice but to track you down on my own. Give me the dirt."

"You know as much as I can tell you. Beau ain't going to help Chris. I can't abide the self-righteous ...." She couldn't bring herself to use the word circulating her brain. Matthew 5:22 scared the bejeebers out of her. She heaped enough guilt into her cranium without subjecting herself to the dangers of hellfire by using the four-letter word—fool.

"I ain't agoing to blame you—although Jimmy, being a McGuffrey, has a word or two about the matter." She plopped her oversized purse on the coffee table.

Cornie crossed her legs and grinned at her sister. "Do you want your marriage to work?"

"Yes." Lia didn't need to pause and think. "No solutions to our problems exist. I've prayed for years and put my faith to work. Hard work. The more effort I put into controlling things and pleasing Beau, the more out of whack our marriage had gotten."

Cornie opened her behemoth pink purse.

"If I carried a pack like yours, I'd need a dolly to pull it."

"It's why I go to the gym three times a week." Cornie retrieved a business card holder.

"I don't see how you organize your junk. I'd need a filing cabinet."

"Given all you do, you'd have to pack a four-draw cabinet. Here." She handed Lia a card.

"Dr. Ian McPherson: Family Counselor?" Lia looked at her sister.

Cornie nodded.

"Why are you carrying around a business card for a therapist?"

"Do you think Jimmy—a bona fide McGuffrey—is any easier to live with than Beau?"

"How is Shann related to those men?" Lia asked.

"He took after their Ma."

"Without her facial hair."

"I don't know." Cornie laughed. "You've seen pictures of her."

Lia gave a playful slap to Cornie's arm.

"Jimmy didn't accept my style of dress and hair without a fight." She struck a pose and giggled. "He'd point to you and lecture about what an exemplary wife you were. He quit when I told him if you were the paragon, to go and marry you."

"Hey."

"Seriously, if you want the marriage to work, see Ian, with or without Beau." She stood. "Now before you want me to help with them pots, I gotta go." She wiggled her fingers in front of Lia. "Can't ruin my manicure."

"You got a manicure? Jewelry, colored hair, now a manicure? What's next?"

"Sex therapy." Cornie laughed and flounced out of the house while Lia stood staring at the door with her mouth agape.

249

She is kidding, isn't she?

Chapter Thirty-Nine

"Sorry. I won't take the offer," Kiara told Maggie McLemon when she phoned two weeks later with the final proposal for her cabin.

"I'd hoped they'd come up in price. When you didn't call, I assumed they had no interest."

"One fifty is weak, I know, but I have to bring every genuine bid to your attention," she said. "I'm afraid this will be a tough sell."

"If it's meant to sell, it will. It's only been on the market for two months." Kiara hung up. She couldn't believe the buyers would insult her with an offer so low. *Dumb hicks.* Even though the potential buyers lived in Cincinnati, they had to be a Buckeye version of a Tennessee hillbilly with no concept of real estate.

Like Bryce.

One solution to her realtor woes existed. Painting.

Kiara had to prep examples of watercolor techniques for her first extended workshop. She'd never advertised for art classes or seminars, but somehow, everyone in East Tennessee called about them.

Too bad her lessons didn't even cover her food bills.

At least, for the next three Saturdays from nine a.m. until five, she'd be hosting a retreat. The best part of the extended seminars, Sugar Creek Diner would cater lunch.

Instead of leaving this backwater, it sucked her in. She should take the pitiful offer McLemon proposed. Get out with whatever she could before this place devoured her like the timber rattler who digested the rabbit.

Three weeks for the seminars. After they finished, nothing held her here. Over Thanksgiving, regardless of the sale of the house, of Chris's court dates, of Shann—where'd thoughts of him come from?—she'd skedaddle. She'd call Imani and arrange for a visit during the holiday.

Lia dragged herself into the studio at two o'clock with a fistful of mail. Her shoulders slumped so much Kiara thought they'd touch the floor.

"What's wrong?" Kiara asked. "It's the weekend. You don't have to work. Like teaching Paul is hard labor. Both your boys are one degree shy of being as smart as me."

251

Lia studied the twins' abstract portrait.

"Do you like it?"

"No."

"You're blunt."

"Did you spill paint?" She pointed to a blotch. "I like this area."

Kiara harrumphed. "Macie painted it. I'm fixing it now."

"I prefer the portrait you did for me."

"Macie likes this style."

"What about Dixon?" Lia asked.

"He wants a dressed-out deer right there in the middle of the canvas. He says it needs guts hanging. I vetoed his idea."

Lia grinned. "I thought these squiggles were entrails."

"Enough insults," Kiara said. "Now tell me, why do you look like Eeyore on benzos?"

"Last night's trunk or treat went well."

"Success makes you sad?"

"They don't need me at Sheep Loop Church." Lia handed Kiara a collection of circulars. "I meant to leave these in the house."

Kiara grabbed the mail, but Lia didn't let go.

"I'm sorry." Lia pulled them back. "I'll take them to the cabin. My brain's on backward today. You don't need your mail here."

"Because a church function worked right, doesn't mean people don't need you. You don't have to control everything. Take it easy. Enjoy life. Try sitting back and snorting the roses."

"They're out of season right now." Lia smiled and shuffled the circulars. She stopped at one letter. "Who's Grace Rafferty?" She held up the letter addressed to Grace. "It's from Singapore."

Kiara rolled her eyes. "If you continue to live with me, you're going to know all my dirty little secrets."

"It's you?"

Kiara nodded. "It's the name my parents gave me. I hate it, so I changed it when I turned eighteen. My mother refuses to call me Kiara."

"Grace is lovely."

"I like it better now that I'm older."

"Like twenty-five's old."

"At least I'm not a fossilized forty-five."

Lia grinned and light shone in her eyes. She pulled up a stool and tossed the mail on a nearby table.

"I guess you're making yourself at home."

"Until you tell me the full double-scoop with a cherry on top as to why you picked Kiara for a new name. It's weird."

"Like Delia Mae." Kiara pulled another stool across from her. "It's as weird as everyone down here being called by their middle names. If parents preferred the middle ones why not move them to the front?"

"We love tradition," Lia said. "Now, why did you pick Kiara?"

"It picked me." She laughed. "Seriously, I wanted something to play up my art, seeing as it already defined me by the time I left high school. Chiaroscuro is the play of light and dark."

"Thank goodness you didn't name yourself chiaroscuro. No one would be able to spell it."

"Nor pronounce it. Kiara played on the word chiaroscuro," she said. "I especially hated Grace because Jillian called me Spacey-Gracey."

Lia made a face. "She's a doting stepmom."

Kiara picked up the letter from her mother. "If you examine my mail, you'll notice none ever comes from Portland. Jillian makes Cinderella's stepmother look like Mother Teresa."

"Grace means the free, unmerited favor of God. It's the bestowal of blessings," Lia said. "It fits you."

"Remember," she held up a finger. "I'm an atheist."

"Atheism is the veneer of your faith— "

Lack of faith."

"No. You've got it," Lia said. "It's in nothingness. Your faith rests on science. On nihilism."

"I am, indeed, the great skeptic."

"Nothing is as it seems, Kiara. Not our perceptions of each other or, as you would claim, of the cosmos. I won't dog you with my religion. Just let me love you. Be my friend, and we'll let the universe play out its plan."

Kiara stood. "Let me finish my setup. Tomorrow, a bunch of Andrew Wyeth and Georgia O'Keeffe wannabes will descend—or, given the hill up to the studio—will ascend on me and expect to master the genre.

~~

Lia made an appointment with Ian McPherson who promised to work her in late Monday. She picked up her knitting and sat in the living room. Only Kiara's kitchen light shed any brilliance in the empty cabin.

A soft tapping sounded somewhere.

She tilted her head and was about to assume she was hearing things, when a louder rap hit the front door. She laid the shawl aside and opened the door.

Her heart pert near stopped. "Chris!" Lia threw her arms around her son and rocked him to her. "When'd you get out?"

He pulled away and peered down at his mother.

Lia wouldn't let go. She ran her hands along his arms. Her eyes drank in his presence.

"Yesterday."

"So long ago?" She became aware of the cabin once more. "Come in. Let me look at you."

"Like you haven't stopped gawking since I got here?" Chris stepped inside and shut the door. "They released me yesterday, midafternoon. It was late, so I went to the high school and registered."

She swallowed his news as though she'd gulped a dead crappie. "School?"

"I need some papers to finalize the registration."

Lia led him to the sofa. With her back to him, she used the time to compose her features. Judging from her heart and the heaviness weighting her, her face had to show her despair. He wouldn't allow her to teach him. His last months before college would be without her. "I'll get whatever you need in a moment." She gazed at him once more. "Sit. Tell me when you're coming home."

"I'm not."

Her heart stopped. Tears refused to come. No words formed.

"My father's unbearable."

"But—"

He threw up his hand. "I love you, Ma. Why you stay with that man—"

"That man's your father." Would her heart ever start beating again?

"By the time I registered, and settled in at Aunt Cornie's, it was late. I didn't have this number, and I didn't want to call. I needed to see you face to face."

"Do you have a trial date?"

He shook his head. A small grin played along his lips.

"You're happy with no trial date?"

"The tox screens came back negative for everything—probably even caffeine. Like I told them. No fingerprints of mine showed up on anything. Although they did say one set of prints matched someone's in the system. Wouldn't say who, but I'd bet my ATV they was Bobby's." He leaned against the sofa's armrest. "With all this, Ms. Grizzle thinks she has a good chance of getting the charges dropped. At the most, I'd get probation, community service, and the record expunged. We'll find something out next week."

"How long are you going to stay at Aunt Cornie's?"

"As long as I can tolerate Uncle Jimmy. I'd go to Uncle Junior's house, but then I'd have to enroll at Jellico."

"You could come home."

He stood.

Lia closed her eyes.

"Like you still live with my father?"

She nodded in understanding.

"I'll never forgive your husband for abandoning me."

254

"My husband? He's your father."

He gave a long slow shake of his head. His face hardened.

"Chris, unforgiveness will eat you like Herod's worms."

"I love you, Ma, but them worms're devouring you, too." Chris hugged her. "Let's get the papers while your husband's out."

~~

Ian McPherson looked like the stereotypical therapist. He wore a sports jacket, bow tie, and dark rimmed glasses. They glinted in the late afternoon sunlight slanting through his windows. After the preliminary chitchat, he asked, "What do you want from your marriage, Mrs. McGuffrey?" he asked.

"Please call me Lia."

"Lia, what do you need in your marriage."

"For it to work."

"I figured as much or you wouldn't be here," he said. "At what cost?"

At one time, she would have said at any cost. Not anymore. Chris and Paul mattered more than being Beau's wife.

She loved Betina and Rosalyn. She missed working with them, missed her fellowship at Sheep Loop. For the most part, she wanted her church family. Some days, the longing for them ate her more than Kiara's former termites gnawed her house.

If Beau would change, if he'd be the man she married, the husband she'd seen glimpses of these past months, she'd reconcile. She looked at McPherson and a heavy burden shifted inside. "I'd prefer to work it out, but I can't sacrifice myself anymore."

"What do you mean by not sacrificing yourself?" He steepled his hands in front of him. It made him appear so shrink-like she almost laughed.

"Marriage is a two-legged duck," she said.

He arched his brows. "A duck?"

With two fingers she mimed a duck paddling. "Ain't gonna work without two laboring together. Beau'd been demanding everything from me and gave back little. He dictated my tastes and my theology. His control and my misunderstanding of God's grace, made me try to be as holy as God."

McPherson laughed outright.

"Yeah. My attitude would make an otter grimace."

"Lia," McPherson leaned forward and rested his elbows on his knees, "for a first session, you've shown a lot of insight. If you convince your husband to come to counseling, you can rescue your marriage."

"I'd imagine I'd need a full-fledged miracle or it ain't gonna be saved."

"We're Christian-based. I've seen those miracles happen." He became somber. "A word of caution, though. I've also seen them fail."

They shook hands. She strolled toward her car feeling—what? Relieved? Assured?

No. For the first time in years, confidence and acceptance of God's will chased self-doubts away.

As she drove back to Stinking Creek, she prayed for Beau while the local radio station played mellow rock. If Beau heard this music, he'd lecture her longer than when the Apostle Paul made the young man Eutychus fall asleep and tumble from a window.

The song ended, and they introduced the news. She passed the railroad trestle and rounded a curve, lost in McPherson's counsel.

"The big headline," the radio announcer said, "the Campbell County sheriff's department busted a meth lab off Lowes Branch Road in Stinking Creek. They arrested Bobby James of Duff and Patrick Hill of Tazewell. More arrests are pending."

They blathered on. Lia heard nothing. She swerved into a clearing on the side of the road. Driving while drunk with this news would have her in a ditch like Kiara.

Bobby James busted? What did it mean for Chris? Maybe nothing. More than zilch. Zippo. Still, the Lord was the God of mercy and pardon.

Lord, make Bobby admit to being the owner of the pills.

Her heart thrummed with hope, and she sang along with Celine Dion and Whitney Houston the rest of the way home.

~~

Thursday's lessons ended by noon. Paul took the ATV out to finish up his biology experiment. Lia packed her school supplies to head back to Kiara's. Half-way across the road, Cornie's car approached. Lia stepped into Kiara's driveway. The car pulled in behind her.

"Cornie, what brings you here? No one wants a perm."

The driver stepped out.

"Chris? Those tinted windows disguised you." She kissed her son. "What're you doing here? School shouldn't be out yet."

"Court today." He grinned so broadly his cheeks nudged his eyes, made them into slits.

"Has to be good news. Your smile's exposing your wisdom teeth." The November wind blew. "Let's go inside. It's rather airish."

Barely had the door closed when Chris spoke. "Every charge against me has been dropped."

Lia's feet refused to move. Her back faced Chris, and she couldn't turn. *Dropped?*

Chris's hands took her shoulders and turned her to him. "Ma, Bobby James 'fessed up."

The words jumbled in her brain. People didn't confess to things, especially if it got them into trouble.

Chris's eyes sparkled like they used to on Christmas and birthdays and Easter. "He's taking a plea deal so they can nab the kingpins in this drug ring. Ms. Grizzle said he'd take the deal *if* he pled to owning the ones in my vehicle. We were all shocked when the DA agreed. I've still got probation for six months, but no record. More than that, I have the proof of innocence your husband needs."

"Are you coming home?"

"No." The word came sharp and hard. "Don't lecture me about it."

"I won't. You can make your own choices." Lia hugged Chris once more. "I made banana pudding last night. Kiara said it was disgusting so we have a big bowl left over."

"She said it was *disgusting*?"

"We're frank with each other."

"Anyone with half an ear has heard the honesty between you two," Chris said. "How can *anyone* not like banana pudding? Besides, I saw her devour the squirrel I caught for Mamaw's birthday. She'll eat anything."

"She's a Yankee." Lia pulled the bowl out of the fridge. "They've got weird ways."

"I'd say. There's no need for banana pudding to go to waste."

For the next hour, the two sat at the table, each with a spoon and the large bowl of pudding between them. They talked until they scraped the bowl clean.

~~

Thoughts of church woke Lia earlier than usual on Sunday. She lay on the couch and ached, not from the couch's stupid spring threatening to give her a spinal tap, but with the need for church.

She could go to Grace with Shann. She shifted upright.

She'd rather go to Sheep Loop Church.

Stupid idea. She lay back down. She'd spoken with Beau no more than fifteen minutes since she left him. Most of the conversation condemned her for walking out on the marriage. How could she crawl into his church without warning? She closed her eyes.

Sleep wouldn't come. Neither would the dawn. Time tiptoed by in its own broken-clock manner. It was senseless to lie here and misalign her back. She rose, slipped on her dress and shoes and wrapped herself in her coat. She stepped onto the porch.

Frost flowers bloomed in the yard. Columns of frost popped up in random places like Styrofoam sculptures or like God squeezed the frozen water through a piping bag like when she decorated cakes. They cropped up like wildflowers in the Arctic.

She needed to move and work the kinks out of her back.

More than her body, Lia had to work the strain from her soul.

She walked past her parents' and rounded the bend. Soon the heat of activity warmed her, and she unbuttoned her coat.

She crested a hill where the landscape overlooked the meadows. The sunrise painted the countryside. Prayers puffed from her mouth with the breath frozen in the early morning.

Chris had been exonerated. Kiara's chance encounter with a ninja turtle freed her son. Kiara called it providence. Little did she know the divinity of it.

The sunrise faded and without movement, it grew cold once more. Lia walked back down the hill. Her spirit weighed heavily upon her.

Because of Bobby's confession, Chris had been freed from the law of the land. He hated his father, still, and so defied the law of Christ and love. Although she claimed she wanted her marriage to survive, she hadn't forgiven Beau, either. She needed to. Not for Beau or Chris's sake. For her own.

How much was Beau to blame for her misery?

Plenty, for sure.

She came abreast of her parents' yellow trailer once more. The light shown in the chicken coop. The two of them tended early morning chores in a partnership stronger after sixty years together than it was in its prime.

What about her life?

She wasn't blameless. Cornie, five years older than she, was beautiful. Stylish but modest. Had flair without flaunting it. Pious. God-fearing.

But her?

She looked five years older than Cornie. Every command Beau gave, she jumped to fulfill. She denied herself. Allowed Betina and Rosalyn and others to take control of her life. She'd made herself a pastor's wife according to their design. Not according to God's.

When she quit living the life others required of her, what was the result? The world continued to revolve without her.

Back at Kiara's, bacon sizzled, and omelets fried.

"I was hoping I'd get to eat all this myself." Kiara lifted a plate and handed it to Lia.

Lia took the warm plate. In its steam, eggs and bacon scented the air and made Lia salivate.

Kiara carried the carafe of coffee to their coffee table—not saying a word.

The women ate in silence.

Quietly they did the dishes.

"What's eating you?" Kiara asked after she started the dishwasher.

"I want to go to church."

"Why?" Kiara's voice didn't condemn. It sounded neutral. Curious.

"I miss God and worship. I miss my duties and my life there."

"Will you go to Shann's church?"

"No. To Beau's. I want to save my marriage."

"Won't he yell at you from the altar? Have a coronary?"

"Remember, he has an audience."

Kiara smiled. "True, but why are you putting up with his garbage?" Her voice hardened, and she crossed her arms.

"I believe marriage is for life."

"A life of misery?"

"If you knew the man I'd married, you'd know what my life with him had once been. What it could become again."

"He's abusive. Does your God want you to live as though you're litter to be trampled underfoot?"

"No. He doesn't," Lia said. "From this point on, I won't let Beau mistreat me. If I need to live alone for the rest of my days, I will. I believe the *Bible*. God hates divorce."

Kiara opened her mouth to speak.

Lia touched Kiara's lips. "I know the core of the man I married. I want him. If he doesn't want me, it will be his choice." She stood a minute more. "Regardless of the fate of my marriage, I need to forgive him."

"Why do *you* have to forgive?"

"To heal myself."

"You Christians are weird."

"We are."

"It's after ten. Shouldn't you be heading there?"

Lia nodded. "I'm scared."

Kiara leaned against the counter. "Why?"

"The woman who left her husband two weeks ago has vanished. I don't want to be her anymore. I want grace."

Kiara grinned and flung her arms wide. "Here I am."

Lia swatted her.

"Besides the obvious joke, I'm here for you. I'll go with you."

"You hate church."

"I hate the dentist, too, but I go. You love me." She quirked a brow. "I love you, as well. What's an hour on Sunday for a cherished friend?

One church service isn't going to affect me. Let me put on something presentable. If you need moral support, I'm the Grace you begged for."

Chapter Forty

Lia wrung her hands as they pulled into the church lot. She saw nothing but the building. Although a small church, it loomed as large as a gothic cathedral whose gargoyles would devour her. "This a bad idea."

"We can leave. Drive down to Knoxville and go to IHOP. I love their holiday specials."

"You just ate."

"It'll take an hour to get there. I'll be hungry again."

"You eat more than a catfish."

"Not me. This kid." Kiara rubbed her stomach as she bumbled out of her jalopy. "Trucks weren't made for whales." She waddled toward the church. Stopped and turned. "Are you coming? I'm not going in alone."

Lia climbed out, her eyes still trained on the church. What would people think of her? What would Beau's reaction be? "We should call and warn Beau."

"Think he'll pick up his phone in the middle of church?"

"No, silly. Later tonight. Make an appointment. He doesn't like surprises."

"Too bad." Kiara beeped the lock with her key remote. "You're not getting back in. Let's go."

The warmth in the foyer flooded Lia and thawed her bones, frozen with terror. She gulped. No way could she step through the doors of the sanctuary.

"Which way do we go?" Kiara pointed to double doors. "There?"

Lia nodded. She couldn't swallow or move. Fear glued her feet to the foyer's tile floor.

Kiara looped her arm in Lia's and half dragged her in.

The sanctuary was fuller than usual. No one had left the congregation because of her absence. Perhaps more came. *Was she needed? Did anyone miss her?* She looked to Kiara and pled with her eyes, tried to make her friend understand her panic.

Kiara's eyes stayed focused on the altar.

To Lia's right sat Jorie. With the noise of their entry, Jorie glanced their way. Her face lit up when their eyes met. She gave a shy little wave reminding Lia of an innocent child.

Lia's heart warmed.

Next to Jorie sat an attractive man who was new to the congregation. He appeared to be in his twenties. Adoration shown in his eyes when he looked at Jorie.

Good for you. Lia's joy for the young woman chased more of her stress from the pit of her stomach. Lia waved and smiled back.

To her left, Betina turned as well. She sat with Rosalyn in the middle of a row near the front. Several open seats surrounded them. Betina patted a chair and wiggled a finger asking Lia to come.

No way would she climb over all those legs to join her friend. She shook her head, then searched for Cornie. She sat with Jimmy in the center of the front.

Beau studied his notes on the pulpit. The projector displayed the sermon's Scripture on the front wall. "Cursed be he that confirmeth not all the words of this law to do them. And all the people shall say, Amen, Deut. 27:26."

"Today we continue our series," Beau looked to Lia's left, "on the giving of the law." He glanced down at his notes. When he resumed speaking, he faced Lia's right. "The Israelites didn't realize at the foundation of the law stood grace. We need to see what God requires of us ... ."

His eyes met hers.

Lia clutched the neckline of her dress and pulled it a little higher. Her heart thumped against her breastbone.

Beau didn't look back at his notes. "The Lawd requires ..." His lips trembled. He loosened his tie.

For a moment, Lia thought he'd collapse.

Lia leaned against the doorjamb. She tilted her head toward Kiara and whispered, "I can't do this."

Beau straightened and scanned his papers. "The law was given ..." Again he stopped. He sounded breathy as though he'd sprinted a hundred meters. He lifted his head toward the men in the sound room. "Turn off the slides, please."

The words vanished from the walls.

Beau flipped over his papers. "The Lawd, just now, has spoken to me." He sighed and studied the pulpit as though his unscripted words were carved into the wood. "Jesus, the God of grace, has shown me what He requires of us—all of us. This morning He's telling me. 'Pastor Beau, you must do justly. You must love mercy and walk humbly with Me.'" His voice caught, and at last, he looked up—first at the ceiling, then at the congregation.

Lia thought tears glinted in his eyes.

"I confess to you, I have defied the Deity." His voice lost its preacherly quality, one he had honed throughout the years. He sounded like Beau, the husband and father. Like Beau, the humbled man.

Murmurs rippled across the sanctuary.

Heads turned. Some stared at Lia, others at nearby friends and family.

Cornie's eyes lit up. Her gaze caught Lia's. She bit back a grin and held up crossed fingers.

He held up his hands to quiet the crowd. "I've sinned against God and my wife. By extension, I've wronged y'all." His eyes found Lia's and he focused on her.

No one else existed in the church. Lia couldn't break her gaze.

"Can you forgive me, Lia?" His voice was soft and tender. It quavered.

Lia stepped back. Her fingers twisted the fabric of her shirt.

Her husband eyed the congregation. "In being so very righteous, I've become all that Jesus hated." His blue eyes widened as he frowned. "We see what I have become in a passage we love. Even the unsaved know it." He took a deep breath and stared at the ceiling once more before he began again. "A man, a Jew, had been attacked by robbers and lay on the roadside. Along came a priest. He was a godly man who strove with all his being to fulfill every jot and tittle of the law. Fearing to stain his hands because he hurried to offer sacrifices to the Lawd, he avoided the dying man. He averted his eyes. He plugged his ears to the pain of the beaten stranger."

Lia trembled. Tears brimmed her eyes.

"Along came a Samaritan," he continued.

"According to the priest, this nonbeliever had it all wrong. He only saw her errors, never her virtue." His eyes focused on Kiara. "The priest judged her without knowing her, yet this Samaritan fulfilled all the law of God in her life. At her own expense, she bound up the wounds—the messy, pus-filled gashes. She tended the victim's broken spirit and sacrificed her own life. She behaved more Christ-like than the man who supposedly served God." Beau stepped away from the pulpit and walked down the aisle.

Every head turned to follow his progress.

In the eyes of the congregation, tears shimmered. Some reached for tissues. Others clasped their hands prayer-like before their chests.

Beau unwound Lia's fingers from the cloth she clutched. "Forgive me, I beg. I've not been the husband you needed nor the one you deserved." Tears clung to Beau's lashes and threatened to spill. He blinked hard.

Although he spoke softly, the head mic carried his voice. "I am the self-righteous priest. In my attention to detail and in my zeal to conform my life to 1 Peter 1:16 and be holy as God is holy, I forgot it could only be achieved by grace, by living according to the law of mercy. In this sin, I led my congregation astray." The tears spilled. Beau bit his lips and sniffed.

Sobs and whimpers skittered throughout the congregation.

"In my legalism," Beau's voice steadied. "I lost our son. Christopher is innocent." He kissed the palm of Lia's hand. "You knew it before the judges proclaimed it. You understood Chris's character and believed in him. Me? I had to wait until a judge and lawyer proved it. I was so self-righteous. I'd rather damn my own child as a sinner than to believe him to be the man he is. I lost him." He clicked off the mic. "I love you, Lia. I will do anything to atone for my actions."

"Will you go to Dr. Ian McPherson's for counseling with me?"

Beau paused.

Lia held her breath.

Beau studied the carpet.

Coming here was a mistake. Her husband would never change.

Beau clicked on his mic. "I need healing and guidance as well as repentance. I'd be honored to do whatever you need."

Lia fell into his arms, and he kissed the top of her head.

With his arm looped around Lia, he turned to Kiara who stood against the back wall. "Kiara, the congregation needs to hear my confession. I hope making it public doesn't hurt you. You've been a good woman. A daughter to my wife. A help in trouble. You sacrificed your dreams for us. Please, I beg, forgive my want of charity and my judgments. From this point forward, I will only see you through the lens of Jesus. Can you forgive me?"

Tears filled Kiara's eyes. She nodded. "I'd do anything for Lia."

Chapter Forty-One

Kiara slipped out of the church as people lined the aisles to talk to Beau and Lia. Her visit to Sheep Loop Church changed something inside. Beau's spiel—no, spiel was too glib a word—his declaration before all those people took guts. He showed he had character. If his behavior toward his family changed, she'd have to reevaluate this god stuff.

But then, which god stuff would she follow? Buddha? Allah? Jesus? So many gods.

She passed Shann's little cottage, braked and backed up. He was never going to believe what she witnessed.

"Kiara?" Shann flung open his door. "What're you doing here?"

"Are you going to interrogate me in the freezing cold or invite me in?" She stepped inside.

"Miss Muffet!" Macie raced from her room in nothing but her underwear and clung to Kiara's legs.

"Go put your clothes on." Shann gave his daughter a playful shove into her room.

"Miss Kiara," Dixon called from behind closed doors. "Come here."

"Dixon, finish dressing. Then you come into the living room and talk to Miss Kiara like a gentleman." Shann picked up the coffeepot and wiggled it. "Decaf."

"I'd love a cup."

"It's crazy after church, especially when I don't let them suck up all the treats at the fellowship table. They think I'm a dictator." He handed her a mug of java. "Why am I blessed with a Sunday morning visit?"

"Afternoon." She pointed to the stove clock. Then before Shann could ask another question, the morning's events spilled out.

"Are you sure you went to Beau's church?"

"Maybe not." She winked and sipped her brew. "Somewhere in his monologue, he said he took control of God's church. I don't think he ever called Sheep Loop his." She sat up as proudly as she could. "The best part, he said he liked me."

Shann held up two fingers.

"What does that mean?"

"If I heard you right, two of your four stipulations have been met."

Kiara raised her brows. "My stipulations?"

"From our evening at the Bijou in Knoxville. You said four things had to be met before we can be together. Using his right hand, Shann folded down his middle finger on his left. "Jorie doesn't love me." He pushed down the pointer finger. "Beau likes you."

"I'm still a thinking non-believer."

"We're moving toward faith. You're not defining yourself as an atheist. You liked the Samaritan stuff in the sermon. Samaritans had the kernel of the true faith."

"I'm still moving to New York."

"I don't see people lining up to buy your house."

She needed to change the subject. "Lia says you go on a Christmas tour. When do you leave?"

"Not this year."

"Why not?"

"Lia may have forgiven my brother, but I've known him longer than her. He hasn't convinced me the zebra has changed his stripes."

"What do zoo animals have to do with your tour?"

"I don't want my kids around him until I know his ideology changed."

Macie skipped back into the room with her shirt on backward and her jeans unzipped. "What's eye-doggoly, Daddy?" She climbed on Kiara's lap. "When're you gonna give me another painting lesson? We have to finish our portrait."

Dixon wheeled his wheelchair into the living room. "I'm hungry."

Shann walked into the kitchen.

Kiara wiggled Macie off her lap. "Let me fix you." She twisted her shirt so the front faced the correct direction. She watched Shann who slathered peanut butter on white bread. "What does his philosophy have to do with you not touring?"

"Cut the crusts off," Dixon called.

"This one," Shann nodded to the imp who Kiara lifted from the floor as she wrestled the stubborn zipper. "And the hungry one. I can't send them you know where because of eye-doggoly. I have no way of watching them."

Kiara raised her hand.

"You're allowed to speak without waving your hand in the air."

"They're in school until three, right?"

"The bus drops them off at four."

"That gives me a whole day to work. When I have lessons, they can play on the ground floor of the barn."

"That's too much."

"Maybe you know someone who could insulate an area and create a cozy playroom for them."

"What happens if you sell the farm?"

"I'll celebrate."

"Don't you hate kids?"

"I do, but these two have grown on me."

~~

Back at her cabin, Kiara climbed her stairs. Beau's apology and tears humbled her. She rubbed her sternum, a sign she needed to inhale a bottle of TUMS, but today something else burned her heart.

In her closet, she found the 8x10 picture of her and Bryce. After she learned about him and Gina, she'd hidden it, but never had the heart to throw it out. She brushed dust from the glass. "You were good to me. I can't hold your affair with Gina against you any longer."

She set the frame on the dresser, stepped back and stared at it. "I did to your wife what Gina did to me. Even though we made excuses for our behavior, you were still married. Amanda and your kids got hurt." She adjusted the picture. "We were wrong."

As the baby kicked, Kiara rubbed her stomach. "Little Birch, don't ever hold a grudge. It'll poison your life." She rubbed her sternum once more. "Or give you heartburn."

Her front door rattled.

"Kiara?" Lia called.

She hurried down the stairs. "From the glow on your face, I'd say you were happy with the service today."

Lia nodded.

Kiara frowned. "Please, whatever you do, don't go jumping full force back into your world."

"We'll take it slow. Beau's going to live in Chris's room until we heal our marriage."

She clasped her hands, and her smile, so innocent and full, warmed Kiara. "I'm glad. You deserve respect and love."

Lia pulled her slow cooker off the baker's rack and added utensils into it. When the pot could hold nothing more, she faced Kiara. "I'm not so naïve as to think old habits won't resurrect."

"No. Our old ways always come back and haunt us."

"We're going to change. I will not be abused again."

"I hope so." She hitched a thumb to her sofa. "If he *ever* treats you bad again, I've got a wretched couch for you."

Lia crossed the road loaded down with kitchen supplies. With her shoulders straight and her step quick, happiness radiated out of her.

Even as Kiara watched her back, the years fell away from her friend's posture.

I hope he loves you the way you deserve.

Chapter Forty-Two

Kiara watched Shann drive off toward Memphis. She promised him she'd keep the kids away from his brother.

The dust from the road settled and coated her with longing. He didn't kiss her, but his eyes hungered like he would. If only he had. She missed her bearded friend.

"Miss Muffet, what's for dinner? I'm hungry." Macie tugged her hand.

Inside, Kiara diced potatoes.

Macie pulled up a chair and stood next to her as she poured them into the stew. "I hate stew," Macie whined. "Can we have chicken fingers?"

"I ain't eating no stew," Dixon yelled from his bedroom. He hobbled out on the crutches he'd started using two days ago.

"The way you run with those things, you should join the circus," Kiara said. "You're quite the acrobat."

"I want sketti."

Kiara ignored him. She strained to see up the road through the kitchen window. She could glimpse the edge of her property, nothing more. This evening, Maggie McLemon would show the farm to two potential buyers. Of course, she'd show up after Shann had framed in a window and French doors in the attempt to make the bottom of the barn as inviting for his kids as her studio was to her.

If McLemon had shown up earlier in the week, Kiara could've saved a bundle of bucks on the materials. When she'd told Maggie about the improvements, she reiterated her refrain, "Barns won't sell the property."

Kiara set the table, and the kids sat. Both shoved their bowls of stew away.

"If you don't eat those, there's more for me." Kiara chucked a forkful into her mouth.

Dixon's jaw dropped. "You dint pray."

"'Member what we do?" Macie folded her hands and bowed her head.

Dixon followed suit.

No one said a word, but Kiara studied the imps. Their cherubic faces made her want to believe. How could these urchins be descended from chimps?

Before her heart grew too maudlin, Dixon passed gas.

Macie screeched and bolted from the table while holding her nose.

When they settled down again, both demanded she say the prayers.

A couple of hours as a mother. She didn't think she'd survive.

~~

The next morning, the kids climbed onto the bus, and for nine blissful hours, the school would care for them.

She went straight to her barn and worked all afternoon.

Around three-thirty, she remembered two monkeys would return soon and want something for dinner. Maybe she had 'sketti' in her house.

She rummaged for food and found an envelope she'd tucked behind her toaster for safe keeping. A letter she forgot about. She ripped it open. New Beginnings wanted to set up an appointment.

She picked up her phone and discovered she had several messages. Before dialing the adoption agency, she rang her voice mail.

"You'll never believe this," Maggie McLemon sounded breathless. "You have two offers. One for one-ninety. The other for full asking. I think we can get a bidding war going."

Full price? Maybe more? She dialed Maggie, told her to work out a deal. She gave the realtor Shann's number and said to call her there.

Then she trotted—or rather—waddled off to collect her charges before the bus driver returned them to the school and stored them in their cubbies overnight.

She arrived at Shann's as the bus rumbled up the road.

Macie bounced off and threw her arms around Kiara's legs.

She rubbed Macie's head as she waited for Dixon.

He climbed down the bus steps without help. Dixon maneuvered the crutches as though they were a natural extension of his legs. He hobbled to Kiara, a paper crumpled in the hand clutching the crutch's handgrip. "Lookit what I made for you." He balanced on his good leg and handed the crushed drawing to her.

The crude picture showed a geometric collection of boxes.

"What's this?" She studied the paper while still playing with Macie's curls.

"I designed the barn so we can play." He dropped his backpack. "Let's go inside."

"I'll read to you tonight, Miss Muffet. I knowed how now."

The trio settled on the sofa. Dixon pointed to a box on his paper. "This is Macie's doll room." He jabbed another box. "My trucks and LEGOS go here." He prattled on.

Macie nudged in closer.

Three hours later, Shann Skyped with the kids. The duo glowed with excitement.

"Look what I drawed." Dixon waved the crushed paper he'd shown Kiara early. "I was going to let Macie use this room for her dolls."

"You're not any longer?" Shann tilted his head.

"No. Miss Kiara says I should be in a circus. So wild animals will live here."

Kiara bit back her grin at Shann's expression. He raised his brows so high, he wiggled his trademark flat top cap. She thought it would fall off.

"Let me read now." Macie held up a book. "Fluffy the cat plays with Silky the mouse." She held up the book and pointed to each character.

Shann nodded. "They're good friends."

Kiara studied his face in the computer screen. His eyes dazzled her as he focused on his children. His eyes danced as if the information his kids shared enchanted him. He never stopped grinning even when Macie forced him to comment on each picture of her book. His cheeks tightened against his smile. Love looked beautiful.

An hour later, she plopped the kids into bed.

Maggie McLemon called Shann's line. "I've got an offer you can't refuse. Ten thousand over asking!"

"Wow." Breathing came hard, still Kiara managed to make an appointment to sign papers for ten the next morning.

Later, as she lay on the sofa, sleep wouldn't come. She'd sold her house. She hugged herself, then closed her eyes and dreamed. *How long did it take for a real estate closing in Tennessee?* Maybe she wouldn't have to come back after her Thanksgiving visit with Imani?

Breathing became difficult with the baby pressing on her diaphragm as she lay on her back. The baby grew so much. How big was it? Four pounds? Putting on layers of fat? The way she ate, lots and lots of fat.

She sat upright and slapped her head. With Maggie's news and the kids' arrival home, she'd never called New Beginnings. This would be her first order of business as soon as the kids boarded the bus in the morning.

Kiara shifted to her side and sighed. New York. Until now it held all her hopes, but it didn't hold the McGuffreys. Life would be empty without them.

They joked about Lia adopting her. She'd always wanted a mother like Lia. Kiara flipped onto her back once more. More than the baby weighted her. Why wasn't she happy?

Maybe it was because this sofa was not made for a roly-poly-prego. Hoisting herself off the couch, Kiara tiptoed to Macie's room.

The child sprawled and took up all the bed.

She slipped in next to Dixon who still slept on Shann's bed.

The little boy hugged a stuffed monkey to his chest. His index finger plugged his belly button. Such a baby—not the big tough he claimed to be.

How could she say goodbye to them?

She closed her eyes. As sleep fell, Shann's arms hugged her. She got lost in his beard and panicked. The hair tangled around her and drew her closer to his chest. She tried to scream and couldn't. She bolted upright.

No. This is not what I want. Her panicked breathing quieted after the dream cleared.

Morning dragged itself to Stinking Creek. She packed lunches, helped Dixon climb onto the bus then went home.

Remembering the phone call she needed to make, Kiara dialed a number she now knew by heart. The office number, not the cell phone. No one would be at the office at seven a.m.

"Maggie, you're going to hate me. I'm taking my property off the market. I can't leave Stinking Creek."

~~

A week later came Kiara's bills. Electric and water and Internet. The day of reckoning had arrived. Blue Cross sent her their new rates. Increased. *Do I buy food or pay bills?*

She put on tea water. *Why'd I decide to stay? I can't pay these bills.* Once more, Kiara messed up her life.

Lia breezed into the cabin. "Can't stay long, sweetheart." She kissed Kiara on the cheek. "You feeling okay?"

Kiara tossed the bills onto the counter. "Why do you ask?"

"You look like I did not so long ago." She reached into her pocket. "Here's the first payment for the retainer fee."

"You don't have to."

"Beau insists.

The kettle boiled, and Kiara poured two cups.

Lia took one, doctored it and sat on the couch. She patted the sofa, and Kiara hunkered down next to her. "My husband guarantees he'll pay every last cent. Your forgiveness and Chris's must be earned."

"No one needs to do a thing for me. I misjudged you hillbillies as bad as you did me." Kiara peered at the check. It'd cover her takeout from Sugar Creek Diner for a week. "However, this will help. I sold a painting in Gatlinburg, and the lessons add to my coffers, but I've gotten an unexpected cost I'd love to pay in full."

"I'll pray, sweetie."

For the next fifteen minutes, the women sipped tea and chatted. Lia left to supervise Paul's lessons.

Kiara puttered.

A jeep pulled into her driveway, and a lady with close-cropped hair dyed Kelly green climbed down. She wore multicolored poncho and a pair of leggings matching her hair. A long hand-painted silk scarf fluttered at her neck.

Another student would keep the lights on for a week. She opened the door before the woman knocked. "Can I help you?"

"Are you *the* Kiara?"

"Yes. Do you want art lessons?" Kiara's heart skipped in hope.

"No. You've left several messages. I'm sorry I haven't gotten back to you sooner. It's been crazy with my mother."

"Who are you?"

"Joey Shellnut."

Kiara's jaw dropped.

"Is something wrong?"

"It seems since I came here, I've made the wrong assumptions about everything. Please come in." She stepped aside and ushered Joey in. "Forgive me. I thought you were a man since all the art dealers I know are male."

"Nope. Jolene by birth—Joey by preference."

"I assumed Leslie was the female half of the Shellnut family?"

"Why?"

"Isn't the name Leslie female?"

"My husband puts on a pretty good imitation of a man. Also, the only female Leslie I know is Leslie Stahl. Can I see your work?"

"It's in my studio. Come."

The two chatted as they walked the hill, which seemed a mite easier these days. "I couldn't find your address. It took forever to get your number. I'm glad you found me."

"We use a post office box. Too many crazies hunting me down. Artists are weird."

Kiara looked at her hair and smiled.

They stepped into the loft. "Here's my latest."

Joey's eyes widened. "That *is* a genuine Kiara. Such luminosity." She cocked her head, walked in close and studied the abstract portrait. "So much joy in these faces. Three of them?" Her finger, hovering inches above the canvas, outlined the faces rollicking in scrolls of paint

Kiara shivered in delight and grinned. Joey *got* her work. She saw what Kiara saw. Felt the emotion." We just finished the painting. It's one of my favorites."

"We?"

Kiara nodded. "It's also a self-portrait. One little girl had to get in on it."

"I can tell it's a joint effort." She pointed to a section in the lower right. "Not your style."

"Macie McGuffrey helped."

"I'm so sorry I've been out of town so long. Mom's moving back here, so I can tend to her. She broke her hip. Chemo made her bones brittle. This came a month after Dad died."

"I'm sorry."

Joey waved away her condolences. "Kiara, I know plenty of places to get you shown. Do you give lessons?"

Hope skittered Kiara's heart. It skipped like Dixon racing after toads. "I do give them. They don't pay much."

"They won't in the Creek, but I've got connections in Asheville and Branson. And further west in Oklahoma City and even Phoenix."

Kiara struggled to keep from clapping like Macie and jumping like they had on the trampoline.

"With your talents, we are golden. I have places begging for named artists to teach. The one in Asheville needs filling." Joey eyed Kiara. "It's in February."

"I'll be busy." Kiara rubbed her belly.

"I assumed so. The Branson, Missouri co-op is booking for June." She smiled at Kiara. "I'm willing to sign you if you're interested."

Oh, Lia, you've been praying. She inhaled to calm her pounding heart. "Give me a pen. I'll sign."

Joey handed her a business card, and Kiara saw her out. In the distance, the rumble of a school bus approached. She didn't think another ounce of joy could fill her heart, but the kids were coming home. Tonight they'd Skype with Shann.

Who'd have thought a mundane world would be so heavenly.

Chapter Forty-Three

Kiara held the warm, tiny bundle in her arms.

She had a son.

On Valentine's Day, Lia had helped Kiara coax her baby boy into this world. Her Stinking Creek Mama labored all night with Kiara.

The baby lay warm and sleepy against her breast. Kiara peeled her attention from her child and glanced at Lia. "You're crying?"

Lia swiped her eyes. "Joy."

"I'm glad you convinced me to keep my baby."

"It seems to me, you wanted him. I found the New Beginnings letter asking you to call in the pile of mail on your counter. You know you can throw stuff away?"

Kiara shook her head. "No. Not from adoption. The way I was before the McGuffreys got their claws into me, adoption would've been the best option." She ran her finger over her son's face, then smiled at Lia. "From killing him. How could I have ever considered abortion?" Kiara shifted and pain radiated as the involuntary contraction hit. "No more babies for me." She rubbed her belly.

"I never heard a woman eager for childbirth right after giving birth."

Kiara cradled the little — well not so little — boy. "Nine pounds three ounces."

"The way you ate, I'm surprised he's not twenty pounds."

Kiara swatted Lia.

"Seeing as you're beating me up, I'm going to go home and clean up. The crew wants to see the child."

"They wanted to be in the delivery room."

Lia kissed the top of Kiara's head and left.

Kiara turned her attention back to her son. He was the hairiest infant she'd ever seen. He had a shock of red hair begging for dreadlocks. Fine newborn down still covered his skin. She slid her fingers over his teeny ones. Every digit had a pale, pink fingernail. So perfect. And long. They needed cutting seeing as he'd already scratched his chubby cheeks.

275

Her heart swelled like it did when she and Macie studied the night sky in back of her cabin. Or at the one service she attended at Beau's.

What a miracle. No way could this being be an accident of the cosmos or even a product of intelligent design. What harm would there be in believing a doting God created him?

No evolution from monkeys.

Well, he was a hairy, little boy. If he belonged to anyone else, she'd say it proved evolution.

My baby.

The door rattled. On a draft of cool air from the hallway, Shann breezed in. "Lia says you have a son."

Kiara lifted her baby, and Shann cradled him in his arms. He looked so natural as the infant cuddled against his chest. Shann bent his head and gazed at the child. Love sparkled in his crystalline eyes. He murmured something and rocked the baby. "Lia says you won't tell anyone his name until I know."

"That's correct." She shifted more upright in the bed.

Silence settled for a beat or two.

"Are you going to say anything, or do I have to guess?"

"Oh, you want me to tell you?"

They laughed together.

"Bryce Birch Rafferty."

Shann rocked baby Bryce a few minutes. Finally, he gazed back at Kiara. "You know, down here, everyone uses middle names. He's going to be called Birch."

"I like it. Birch."

"So do I. Sounds like a good wood for my guitars."

While Shann studied Birch once more, she held up four fingers.

He turned toward the motion of her hands and grinned. "Jorie's in love."

She folded down a finger.

"Beau likes you, and you're staying on the Creek." He turned down the next two of her fingers. "You believe?"

"This child proves God."

"Whether you love me or not, Kiara, knowing Jesus is most important."

"I do love you. Not sure about what you call salvation—although I do know God exists, and I want Him in my life."

"Your love for Him will come."

"Just don't make me roll down church aisles."

Shann's face glowed like hers probably had when Joey gave her the contract. *We're a perfect match. Two grinning fools.* She ran her fingers through his beard. "I think from the moment I looked into your eyes, something inside of me knew, despite this monkey-beard," she tugged it, "we belonged together."

"You've been the only woman who could take Abby's place."

"I don't want to take her place. You can't replace Bryce. We can share our love with them."

With baby Birch snuggled against his chest, Shann leaned over and kissed her.

More than the first time they kissed, Shann's lips carried her away to love and faith.

The door crashed open. "Eww." Dixon ran in. "Kissing's gross."

Lia and Beau followed the twins in.

Macie leaped onto the bed and Kiara groaned.

"Careful, Macie," Kiara said. "You clean up good, Lia."

Lia wiggled her fingers. "Give me my grandson."

Shann handed Birch off. "He resembles you," Lia said. A strand of hair fell into her face.

Beau tucked it behind her ear.

She glared at him—her scowl freezing his movement. Lia pulled the lock forward.

"Sorry," Beau said with hands raised. "Old habits die hard." He held out his arms. "Let me hold our grandson."

Lia whispered to Kiara. "My hair's annoying me, but no way will Beau touch it." Lia handed him over. "His name?"

"Birch," Kiara said.

"Weird," Lia retorted.

"No worse than Delia Mae or Grace."

"Or Cletus Emmett." Lia ran fingers over the baby's skin as Beau rocked him. "Birch makes me think of you, Shann."

Shann slipped his hand into Kiara's and stroked his beard. "Birch has enough hair to be my child."

Kiara gazed back into Shann's magnificent eyes. "Enough love to be yours, as well."

Shann lifted Macie from the bed and sat next to Kiara. His eyes told her everything she ever wanted to hear.

Something good did come from Stinking Creek.

If *A New York Yankee on Stinking Creek* pleased you, please consider leaving a review on Amazon, Barnes and Noble, Goodreads, or wherever you purchased your book.

Also from Carol McClain

Yesterday's Poison

After her boyfriend betrays her, Torie Sullivan careens into a ditch in a drunken fury. Paramedic Adam Benedict rescues the unconscious woman, then realizes she's one of the middle school bullies who tormented him twelve years ago. The encounter rips open scars he thought had healed.

While kayaking one morning, Adam discovers Torie bathing in the frigid waters of Hookskill Preserve. He then learns she's living in a lean-to in the forested preserve. Despite his hatred for her, Adam's innate compassion won't allow him to leave Torie in the wilds of Albany County. He offers her a secure, private room in his minuscule cabin.

When tragedy strikes Adam's family, his girlfriend Maya Vitale gives Torie a room in her apartment. Torie envies Maya's idyllic life, unaware she, too, hides a dark and shameful past.

Each character drinks yesterday's poison. Their friendships intertwine their lives and expose their toxic pasts. They must learn to forgive the unpardonable.

www.ingramcontent.com/pod-product-compliance
Lightning Source LLC
Chambersburg PA
CBHW072350110726
47909CB00003B/660